THE DARK HOURS

MICHAEL CONNELLY

GRAND CENTRAL
PUBLISHING

NEW YORK   BOSTON

Grand Central Publishing
Hachette Book Group
1290 Avenue of the Americas, New York, NY 10104
grandcentralpublishing.com
twitter.com/grandcentralpub

Originally published in hardcover and ebook by Little, Brown & Company in November 2021
First trade paperback edition: April 2022

Grand Central Publishing is a division of Hachette Book Group, Inc. The Grand Central Publishing name and logo is a trademark of Hachette Book Group, Inc.

The publisher is not responsible for websites (or their content) that are not owned by the publisher.

The Hachette Speakers Bureau provides a wide range of authors for speaking events. To find out more, go to hachettespeakersbureau.com or call (866) 376-6591.

Library of Congress Control Number: 2021939727

ISBNs: 9781538708477 (trade paperback), 9780316256568 (ebook)

Printed in the United States of America

LSC-C

Printing 1, 2022

This is for Robert Pepin,
translator, editor, friend since the start.
Merci beaucoup, mon ami.

PART ONE

MIDNIGHT MEN

1

It was supposed to rain for real and that would have put a damper on the annual rain of lead. But the forecast was wrong. The sky was blue-black and clear. And Renée Ballard braced for the onslaught, positioning herself on the north side of the division under the shelter of the Cahuenga overpass. She would have preferred being alone but was riding with a partner, and a reluctant partner at that. Detective Lisa Moore of the Hollywood Division Sexual Assault Unit was a day-shift veteran who just wanted to be home with her boyfriend. But it was always all hands on deck on New Year's Eve. Tactical alert: everyone in the department in uniform and working twelves. Ballard and Moore had been working since 6 p.m. and it had been quiet. But it was now about to strike midnight on the last day of the year and the trouble would begin. Added to that, the Midnight Men were out there somewhere. Ballard and her reluctant partner needed to be ready to move quickly when the call came in.

"Do we have to stay here?" Moore asked. "I mean, look at these people. How can they live like this?"

Ballard surveyed the makeshift shelters made of discarded tarps and construction debris that lined both sides of the underpass. She saw a couple of Sterno cook fires and people milling about at their meager encampments. It was so crowded that some shanties were even pressed up against the mobile toilets the city had put on the sidewalks to preserve some semblance of dignity and sanitation in the area. North of the overpass was a residential zone of apartments fronting the hillside area known as the Dell. After multiple reports of people defecating in the streets and yards of the neighborhood, the city came through with the portable toilets. A *humanitarian effort,* it was called.

"You ask that like you think they all want to be living under an overpass," Ballard said. "Like they have a lot of choices. Where are they going to go? The government gives them toilets. It takes their shit away but not much else."

"Whatever," Moore said. "It's such a blight—every overpass in the fucking city. It's so third world. People are going to start leaving the city because of this."

"They already have," Ballard said. "Anyway, we're staying here. I've spent the last four New Year's Eves under here and it's the safest place to be when the shooting starts."

They were quiet for a few moments after that. Ballard had thought about leaving herself, maybe going back to Hawaii. It wasn't because of the intractable problem of homelessness that gripped Los Angeles. It was everything. The city, the job, the life. It had been a bad year with the pandemic and social unrest and violence. The police department had been vilified, and she along with it. She'd been spat on, figuratively and literally, by the people she thought she stood for and protected. It was a hard lesson, and a sense of futility had set upon her and was deep in the marrow now. She needed some kind of a break. Maybe to go track down her mother in the mountains of Maui and try to reconnect after so many years.

She took one of her hands off the wheel and held her sleeve to her nose. It was her first time back in uniform since the protests. She could make out the smell of tear gas. She had dry-cleaned the uniform twice but the odor was baked in, permanent. It was a strong reminder of the year that had been.

The pandemic and protests had changed everything. The department went from being proactive to reactive. And the change had somehow cast Ballard adrift. She had found herself more than once thinking about quitting. That is, until the Midnight Men came along. They had given her purpose.

Moore checked her watch. Ballard noticed and glanced at the dashboard clock. It was off by an hour, but doing the math told her it was two minutes till midnight.

"Oh, here we go," Moore said. "Look at this guy."

She was looking out her window at a man approaching the car. It was below 60 degrees but he wore no shirt, and he was holding his dirt-caked pants up with his hand. He wore no mask either. Moore had her window cracked but now hit the button and closed and sealed the car.

The homeless man knocked on her window. They could hear him through the glass.

"Hey, officers, I got a problem here."

They were in Ballard's unmarked car but she had engaged the flashing grille lights when they parked in the median under the overpass. Plus they were in full uniform.

"Sir, I can't talk to you without a mask," Moore said loudly. "Go get a mask."

"But I been ripped off," the man said. "That sumbitch o'er there took my shit when I was sleepin'."

"Sir, I can't help you until you get a mask," Moore said.

"I don't have no fucking mask," he said.

"Then I'm sorry, sir," she said. "No mask, no ask."

The man punched the window, his fist hitting the glass in front of Moore's face. She jerked back even though it had not been a punch intended to break the glass.

"Sir, step back from the car," Moore commanded.

"Fuck you," he said.

"Sir, if I have to get out, you're going to County," Moore said. "If you don't have corona now, you'll get it there. You want that?"

The man started to walk away.

"Fuck you," he said again. "Fuck the police."

"Like I never heard that before," Moore said.

She checked her watch again, and Ballard looked back at the dash clock. It was now the final minute of 2020, and for Moore and most people in the city and the world, the year couldn't end soon enough.

"Jesus Christ, can we move to another spot?" Moore complained.

"Too late," Ballard said. "I told you, we're safe under here."

"Not from these people," Moore said.

2

It was like a bag of popcorn cooking in a microwave. A few pops during the final countdown of the year and then the barrage as the frequency of gunfire made it impossible to separate it into individual discharges. A gunshot symphony. For a solid five minutes, there was an unbroken onslaught as revelers of the new year fired their weapons into the sky following a Los Angeles tradition of decades.

It didn't matter that what goes up must come down. Every new year in the City of Angels began with risk.

The gunfire of course was joined by legitimate fireworks and firecrackers, creating a sound unique to the city and as reliable through the years as the changing of the calendar. The over/under at roll call was eighteen in terms of calls related to the rain of lead. Windshields mostly would be the victims, though the year before, Ballard had caught a callout on a case in which a bullet fell through a skylight and hit a stripper on the shoulder as she was dancing on a stage below. The falling bullet didn't even break the skin. But a jagged piece of falling skylight glass did give a customer sitting close to the stage a new part in his hair. He chose not to make a police report, because it would reveal that where he was didn't match where he had told his family he would be.

Whatever the number of calls, patrol would handle most of them unless a detective was warranted. Ballard and Moore were mostly waiting for one call. The Midnight Men. It was a painful reality that sometimes you needed predators to strike again in hopes of a mistake or a new piece of evidence that could lead to a solve.

The Midnight Men was the unofficial moniker Ballard had bestowed on the tag team rapists who had assaulted two women in a five-week span. Both assaults had occurred on holiday nights—Thanksgiving and Christmas Eve. The cases were linked by modus operandi, not DNA, because the Midnight Men were careful not to leave DNA behind. Each attack started shortly after midnight and lasted as long as four hours while the predators took turns assaulting women in their own beds, ending the torture by cutting off a large hank of each victim's hair with the knife that had been held to her throat during the terrifying ordeal. Other humiliations were included in the attacks and helped link the cases beyond the rarity of a two-man rape team.

Ballard, as the third-watch detective, had been the responding detective on both cases. She then handed the cases over to the day-watch detectives from the Hollywood Division Sexual Assault Unit. Lisa Moore was a member of that three-detective unit. Since Ballard worked the shift when the attacks had occurred, she was informally added to the team.

In past years, a pair of serial rapists would have immediately drawn the attention of the Sex Crimes Unit that worked out of the Police Administration Building downtown as part of the elite Robbery-Homicide Division. But City Hall cutbacks in police funding had seen the unit disbanded, and sex assault cases were now handled by the divisional detective squads. It was an example of how protesters demanding the defunding of the police department had achieved their goal in an indirect way. The move to defund was turned away by the city's politicians, but the police department had burned through its budget in dealing with the protests that followed the death of George Floyd at the hands of police in Minneapolis. After weeks of tactical alert and associated costs, the department was out of money and the result was freezes on hiring, the disbanding of units, and the end of several programs. In effect, the department had been defunded in several key areas.

Lisa Moore was a perfect example of how all of this led to a downgrade in service to the community. Rather than the Midnight Men investigation going to a specialized unit with many resources as well as detectives who had extra training and experience in serial investigations, it had gone to the overworked and understaffed Hollywood Division Sexual Assault team, which was responsible for investigating every rape, attempted rape, assault, groping, indecent exposure, and claim of pedophilia in a vast geographic and population-dense area. And Moore was like many in the department since the protests, looking to do as little as possible between now and retirement, no matter how far away it was. She was looking at the Midnight Men case as a time suck taking her away from her normal eight-to-four existence, where she dutifully filed paperwork the first half of the day and conducted minimal investigative work after that, leaving the station only if there was no way the work could be done by phone and computer. She had greeted her assignment to work the midnight shift with Ballard over the New Year's holiday as a major insult and inconvenience. Ballard, on the other side of that coin, had seen it as a chance to get closer to taking down two predators who were out there hurting women.

"What do you hear about the vax?" Moore asked.

Ballard shook her head.

"Probably the same as you hear," she said. "Next month—maybe."

Now Moore shook her head.

"Assholes," she said. "We're first-fucking-responders and should get it with the fire department. Instead we're with the grocery workers."

"The fire guys are considered health-care providers," Ballard said. "We're not."

"I know, but it's the principle of it. Our union is shit."

"It's not the union. It's the governor, the health department, a lot of things."

"Fuckin' politicians…"

Ballard let it go. It was a complaint heard often at roll calls and in police cars across the city. Like many in the department, Ballard had already contracted Covid-19. She had been knocked down for three weeks in November and now just hoped she had enough antibodies to see her through to the vaccine's arrival.

During the brooding silence that followed, a patrol car pulled up next to them on Moore's side in one of the two southbound lanes.

"You know these guys?" Moore asked as she reached for the window button.

"Unfortunately," Ballard said. "Pull your mask up."

It was a team of P2s named Smallwood and Vitello, who always had too much testosterone running in their blood. They also thought they were "too healthy" to contract the virus and eschewed the department-mandated mask requirement.

Moore lowered the window after pulling her mask up.

"How's things in the tuna boat?" Smallwood said, a wide smile on his face.

Ballard pulled up her department-issued mask. It was navy blue with LAPD embossed in silver along the jawline.

"You're blocking traffic there, Smallwood," Ballard said.

Moore looked back at Ballard.

"Really?" she whispered. "Small wood?"

Ballard nodded.

Vitello hit the switch for the light bar on the patrol car's roof. Flashing blue lit up the graffiti on the concrete walls above the tents and shanties on both sides of the overpass. Various versions of "Fuck the Police" and "Fuck Trump" had been whitewashed by city crews but the messages came through under the penetrating blue light.

"How's that?" Vitello asked.

"Hey, there's a guy over there wants to report a theft of property," Ballard responded. "Why don't you two go take a report?"

"Fuck that," Smallwood said.

"Sounds like detective work to me," Vitello added.

The conversation, if it could be called that, was interrupted by the voice of a com center dispatcher coming up on the radio in both cars, asking for any 6-William unit, "6" being the designation for Hollywood, and "William" for detective.

"That's you, Ballard," Smallwood said.

Ballard pulled the radio out of its charger in the center console and responded.

"Six-William-twenty-six. Go ahead."

The dispatcher asked her to respond to a shooting with injury on Gower.

"The Gulch," Vitello called over. "Need backup down there, ladies?"

Hollywood Division was broken into seven different patrol zones called Basic Car Areas. Smallwood and Vitello were assigned to the area that included the Hollywood Hills, where crime was low and most of the residents they encountered were white. This was a move designed to keep them out of trouble and away from confrontational enforcement with minorities. However, it had not always worked. Ballard had heard about them roughing up teenagers in cars parked illegally on Mulholland Drive, where there were spectacular views of the city at night.

"I think we can handle it," Ballard called across. "You boys can go back up to Mulholland and watch for kids throwing their condoms out the window. Make it safe up there, guys."

She dropped the car into drive and hit the gas before either Smallwood or Vitello could manage a comeback.

"Poor guy," Moore said without sympathy in her voice. "Officer Smallwood."

"Yeah," Ballard said. "And he tries to make up for it every night on patrol."

Moore laughed as they sped south on Cahuenga.

3

The Gower Gulch was the name affixed by Hollywood lore to the intersection of Sunset Boulevard and Gower Street, where almost a hundred years ago it was a pickup spot for day laborers. These laborers waited at the corner for work as extras in the westerns the movie studios were turning out by the week. Many of the Hollywood cowboys waited at the intersection in full costume—dusty boots, chaps, vests, ten-gallon hats—so it became known as the Gower Gulch. It was said that a young actor named Marion Morrison picked up work here. He was better known as John Wayne.

The Gulch was now a shopping plaza with the fading facade of an Old West town and portraits of the Hollywood cowboys—from Wayne to Gene Autry—hanging on the outside wall of the Rite Aid drugstore. Going south from the Gulch, a stretch of studio stages as big as gymnasiums lined the east side all the way down to the crown jewel of Hollywood, Paramount Studios. The storied studio was surrounded by twelve-foot-high walls and iron gates, like a prison. But these barriers were constructed to keep people out, not in.

The west side of Gower was a contradiction. It was lined with a stretch of car repair shops sharing space with aging apartment buildings where burglar bars guarded all windows and doors. The west side was marked heavily by the graffiti of a local gang called Las Palmas 13, but the east-side walls of the studios were left unmarred, as if those with the spray paint knew by some intuition not to mess with the industry that built the city.

The shooting call took Ballard and Moore to a street party in the tow yard of an auto body shop. Several people were milling about in the street, most without masks. Most were watching officers from two patrol cars who were taping off a crime scene inside the gated and asphalt-paved yard, which was lined with vehicles in different stages of repair and restoration.

"So, we have to do this, huh?" Moore said.

"I do," Ballard said.

She opened the door and got out of the car. She knew her answer would shame Moore into following. Ballard was pretty sure she was going to need Moore to help with this.

Ballard ducked under yellow tape stretched across the entrance to the business and quickly ascertained that the victim of the shooting was not on scene and had been transported. She saw Sergeant Dave Byron and another officer trying to corral a group of potential witnesses in one of the business's open garages. Two other uniforms were stringing an inner boundary around the actual crime scene, which was marked by a pool of blood and debris left behind by the paramedics. Ballard walked directly over to Byron.

"Dave, what do you have for me?" she asked.

Byron looked over his shoulder at her. He was masked but she could tell by his eyes that he was smiling.

"Ballard, I have a shit sandwich for you," he said.

She signaled him away from the citizens so they could talk privately.

"Folks, you all stay right here," Byron said, holding his hands up in a stay-put motion to the witnesses, which Ballard took to mean that they might not understand English.

He joined Ballard by the front of the rusting body of an old VW bus. He looked at what he had jotted down in a small notebook.

"Your victim is supposedly Javier Raffa, owner of the business," he said. "Lives about a block from here."

He pointed a thumb over his shoulder, indicating the neighborhood west of the body shop.

"For what it's worth, he has a known affiliation with Las Palmas," Byron added.

"Okay," Ballard said. "Where'd they transport him?"

"Hollywood Pres. He was circling."

"What did the wits tell you?"

"Not much. Left them for you. Raffa apparently has the gates open and puts out a keg every New Year's Eve. It's for the neighborhood but a lot of Las Palmas shows up. After the countdown, there was some shooting of firearms into the sky, and then suddenly Raffa was on the ground. So far nobody is saying they actually saw him get hit. And you've got shell casings all over the place. Good luck with that."

Ballard shot her chin toward a camera mounted on the roof eave over the corner of the garage.

"What about cameras?" she asked.

"The cameras outside are dummies," Byron said. "Cameras inside are legit but I haven't checked them. I'm told they are not in a position to be of much help."

"Okay. You get here before the EMTs?"

"I didn't, but a seventy-nine did. Finley and Watts. They said it was a head wound. They're over there and you can go talk to them."

"I will if I need to."

Ballard checked to see if either of the uniforms who were marking the boundary was a Spanish speaker. Ballard knew basic Spanish but was not skilled enough to conduct witness interviews. She saw that one of the officers tying the crime scene tape to the sideview mirror of an old pickup was Victor Rodriguez.

"You mind if I keep V-Rod to translate?" she asked.

Ballard thought she saw the lines of a frown form on Byron's mask.

"How long?" he asked.

"Preliminary with the witnesses and then maybe the family," Ballard said. "I'll get somebody from another unit if we transport anybody back to the station."

"All right, but anything else comes up, I'm going to need to pull him back out."

"Roger that. I'll move fast."

Ballard walked over to Rodriguez, who had been with the division for about a year after transferring from Rampart.

"Victor, you're with me," Ballard said.

"I am?" he said.

"Let's go talk to witnesses."

"Cool."

Moore caught up to Ballard in step toward the group of witnesses.

"I thought you were staying in the car," Ballard said.

"What do you need?" Moore said.

"I could use someone at Hollywood Pres to check on the victim. You want to take the car and head over?"

"Shit."

"Or you can interview witnesses and family while I go."

"Give me the keys."

"I thought so. Keys are still in the car. Let me know what you find out."

Ballard briefed Rodriguez in a whisper as they approached the witnesses.

"Don't lead them," she said. "We just want to know what they saw, what they heard, anything they remember before they saw Mr. Raffa on the ground."

"Got it."

They spent the next forty minutes doing quick interviews with the collected witnesses, none of whom saw the victim get shot. In separate interviews, each described a crowded, chaotic scene in the lot, during which most people were looking up at the stroke of midnight as fireworks and bullets cut through the sky. Though no one admitted doing it themselves, they acknowledged that there were those in the neighborhood crowd who had fired guns into the air. None of these witnesses revealed anything that made them important enough to transport to the station for another round of questioning. Ballard copied their addresses and phone numbers into her notebook and told them to expect follow-up contact from Homicide investigators.

Ballard then signaled Finley and Watts into a huddle to ask them about first impressions of the crime. They told her the victim was nonresponsive upon arrival and appeared to have been hit by a falling bullet. The wound was at the top of the head. They said they were mostly occupied with crowd control, keeping people away from the victim and creating space for the paramedics.

As she was wrapping up with them, Ballard got a call from Moore, who was at Hollywood Presbyterian Medical Center.

"The victim's family is all here, and they're about to get the word that he didn't make it," she said. "What do you want me to do?"

I want you to act like a trained detective, Ballard thought but didn't say.

"Keep the family there," she said instead. "I'm on my way."

"I'll try," Moore said.

"Don't try, do it," Ballard said. "I'll be there in ten. Do you know if they speak English?"

"I'm not sure."

"Okay, find out and text me. I'll bring somebody in case."

"What's it looking like over there?"

"Too early to tell. If it was an accident, the shooter didn't stick around. And if it wasn't, I've got no camera and no witnesses."

Ballard disconnected and walked over to Rodriguez.

"Victor, you need to drive me to Hollywood Pres," she said.

"No problem."

Ballard informed Byron of where she was going and asked him to keep the crime scene secured until she got back.

As she crossed the lot, following Rodriguez to his car, she saw the first drops of rain hitting the asphalt amid the bullet casings.

4

Rodriguez used the lights but not the siren to speed their drive to the hospital. Ballard used the minutes to call her lieutenant at home to update him. Derek Robinson-Reynolds, the OIC of Hollywood detectives, picked up immediately, having texted Ballard his request for the update.

"Ballard, I was expecting to hear from you sooner than this."

"Sorry, L-T. We had several witnesses to talk to before we could get a handle on this. I also just heard that our victim is DOA."

"Then I'll have to get West Bureau out. I know they're already running full squad on a two-bagger from yesterday."

Homicides were handled out of West Bureau. Robinson-Reynolds was ready to pass the investigation off but knew it would not be well received by his counterpart at West Bureau Homicide.

"Sir, you can do that, of course, but I haven't determined what this is yet. There were a lot of people shooting guns at midnight. Not sure if this was accidental or intentional. I'm heading to the hospital now to get a look at him."

"Well, didn't any of the witnesses see it?"

"Not the witnesses who stuck around. They just saw the victim on the ground. Anybody who saw it happen scrammed out of there before the unis got on scene."

There was a pause as the lieutenant considered his next move. They were a block from the hospital. Ballard spoke before Robinson-Reynolds responded.

"Let me run with it, L-T."

Robinson-Reynolds remained silent. Ballard made her case.

"West Bureau is running on the two-bagger. We don't even know what this is yet. Let me stay with it and we'll see where it stands in the morning. I'll call you then."

The lieutenant finally spoke.

"I don't know, Ballard. Not sure I want you capering out there on your own."

"I'm not alone. I'm with Lisa Moore, remember?"

"Right, right. Nothing on that tonight?"

He was asking about the Midnight Men.

"Not so far. We're pulling into Hollywood Pres now. The family of the victim is here."

It pushed Robinson-Reynolds to make a decision.

"Okay, I'll hold off on West Bureau. For now. Keep me informed. No matter the hour, Ballard."

"Roger that."

"Okay, then."

Robinson-Reynolds disconnected. Ballard's phone buzzed with a text as Rodriguez was pulling to a stop behind Ballard's car, which had been left by Moore in an ambulance bay.

"Was that Dash?" Rodriguez asked. "What did he say?"

He was using the short name ascribed to Robinson-Reynolds by most in the division when not addressing the lieutenant personally. Ballard checked the text. It had come from Moore: No English spoken here.

"He gave us the green light," Ballard said.

"Us?" Rodriguez said.

"I'm probably going to need you in here too."

"Sergeant Byron told me to double-time back."

"Sergeant Byron's not in charge of the investigation. I am, and you're with me until I say otherwise."

"Roger that—as long as you tell him."

"I will."

Ballard found Moore in the ER waiting room, surrounded by a group of crying women and one teenage boy. Raffa's family had just gotten the bad news about their husband and father. A wife, three adult daughters, and the son were all exhibiting various degrees of shock, grief, and anger.

"Oh, boy," Rodriguez said as they approached.

Nobody liked intruding on the kind of trauma unexpected death brings.

"I heard you want to be a detective someday, V-Rod," Ballard asked.

"Fuck, yeah," Rodriguez responded.

"Okay, I want you to help Detective Moore interview the family. Do more than translate. Ask the questions. Any known enemies, his association with Las Palmas, who else was at the shop tonight. Get names."

"Okay, what about you? Where are—"

"I need to check the body. Then I'll be joining you."

"Got it."

"Good. Let Detective Moore know."

Ballard split off from him and went to the check-in counter. Soon she was led back to the nursing station that was in the middle of the ER. It was surrounded by multiple examination and treatment spaces separated by curtain walls. She asked a nurse if the body of the gunshot victim had been moved yet from a treatment space and was told that the hospital was waiting for a coroner's team to pick it up. The nurse pointed her to a closed curtain.

Ballard pulled back the pastel-green curtain, entered the single-bed examination space, and then closed the curtain behind her. Javier Raffa's body was faceup on the bed. There had been no attempt to cover him. His shirt—a blue work shirt with his name on an oval patch—was open and his chest still showed conduit ointment, likely from paddles that had been used in an attempt to revive him. There were also whitish discolorations on the brown skin of his chest and neck. His eyes were open, and there was a rubber device extending from the mouth. Ballard knew it had been placed in his mouth before the paddles were used.

Ballard pulled a pair of black latex gloves out of a compartment on her equipment belt and stretched them on. Using both hands, she gently turned the dead man's head to look for the entry wound. His hair was long and curly, but she found the entry at the upper rear of his head under hair matted by blood. Judging from its location, she doubted there was an exit wound. The bullet was still inside, which in terms of forensics was a break.

She leaned farther over the bed to look closely at the wound. She guessed that it had been made by a small-caliber bullet and noticed that some of the hair around it was singed. It meant that the weapon had been held less than a foot away when discharged. She saw specks of burnt gunpowder in Javier Raffa's hair.

In that moment, Ballard knew this had been no accident. Raffa had been murdered. A killer had used the moment when all eyes were cast upward to the midnight sky and there was gunfire all around to hold a gun close to Raffa's head and pull the trigger. And in that moment, Ballard knew she wanted the case, that she would find a way to keep this conclusion to herself until she was too deeply embedded to be removed.

She knew this could be the solve she needed to save herself.

5

Ballard pulled the curtain closed after stepping out of the treatment bay and walked over to the nursing station so she would not block traffic in the busy ER. She took out her phone and called the number for the Hollywood Division Gang Enforcement Detail. No one picked up. She then called the inside line in the watch office. Sergeant Kyle Dallas answered and Ballard asked him who was working second twelves from GED.

"That would be Janzen and Cordero," Dallas said. "And I think Sergeant Davenport is around too."

"Out or in?" Ballard asked.

"I just saw Cordero in the break room, so I guess they might have all come in now that the witching hour is passed."

"Okay, if you see them, tell them to stay put. I need to talk to them. I'll be in soon."

"You got it."

Ballard went through the automatic doors to the waiting room and saw Moore and Rodriguez sitting in the corner with the Raffa family in a group interview. Renée was annoyed that Moore had not conducted individual interviews but then she reminded herself that Moore was used to investigating sexual assaults, which usually involved solo interviews of victims. Moore was out of her league here and Rodriguez just didn't know any better.

Ballard saw that the son was sitting outside the huddle and looking over the shoulders of two of his sisters at Moore. He was young enough to still be in school, which meant he might speak English. Moore should have known this.

She walked up and tapped him on the shoulder.

"Do you speak English?" she whispered.

The boy nodded.

"Come with me, please," Ballard said.

She led him over to another corner. The waiting room was surprisingly uncrowded. Surprising for any night of the week but particularly for post-midnight on New Year's Eve. She pointed to a chair for the boy to take and then pulled a second chair away from the wall and positioned it so they could talk face-to-face.

They both sat down.

"What's your name?" Ballard asked.

"Gabriel," the boy said.

"You are Javier's son?"

"Yes."

"I'm sorry for your loss. We are going to find out what happened and who did it. I'm Detective Ballard. You can call me Renée."

Gabriel eyed her uniform.

"Detective?" he asked.

"We had to be in uniform for New Year's Eve," Ballard said. "Everybody out on the street, that sort of thing. How old are you?"

"Fifteen."

"What school do you go to?"

"Hollywood."

"And you were at the shop's tow yard tonight at midnight?"

"Yes."

"Were you with your father?"

"Uh, no, I was…over by the Caddy."

While at the crime scene, Ballard had seen a rusting old Cadillac parked in the lot. Its trunk was open and there was a beer keg sitting in a bed of ice inside it.

"Were you with anyone by the Caddy?" Ballard asked.

"My girlfriend," Gabriel said.

"What's her name?"

"I don't want to get her in trouble or nothing."

"She's not in trouble. We're just trying to figure out who was there tonight, that's all."

Ballard waited.

"Lara Rosas," Gabriel finally said.

"Thank you, Gabriel," Ballard said. "Do you know Lara from school or the neighborhood?"

"Uh, both."

"And she went home?"

"Yeah, she left when we came here."

"Did you see what happened to your father?"

"No, I just saw after. Him lying there."

Gabriel was exhibiting no emotion and Ballard saw no tear lines on his face. She knew this meant nothing. People process and express shock and grief in different ways. Unusual behavior or a lack of obvious emotion should not be considered suspicious.

"Did you see anybody at the party that you thought was strange or didn't belong?" Ballard asked.

"Not really," Gabriel said. "There was a guy there at the keg who didn't look like he belonged. But it was a street party. Who knows."

"Was he asked to leave?"

"No, he was just there. He got his beer and then I guess he left. I didn't see him no more."

"Was he from the neighborhood?"

"I doubt it. I never saw him before."

"What makes you say that he didn't look like he belonged?"

"Well, he was a white guy, plus he seemed kind of dirty, you know. His clothes and stuff."

"You think he was homeless?"

"I don't know, maybe. That's what I thought."

"And this was before the shooting that you saw him?"

"Yeah, before. Definitely. It was before everyone started looking up."

"You said his clothes were dirty. What was he wearing?"

"A gray hoodie and blue jeans. His pants were dirty."

"Was it dirt or grease?"

"Like dirt, I think."

"Was the hoodie up or down? Could you see his hair?"

"It was up. But it kind of looked like he had a shaved head."

"Okay. What about his shoes, do you remember them?"

"Nah, I don't know about his shoes."

Ballard paused and tried to commit the details of the stranger to memory. She was not writing anything down. She thought it would be better to maintain eye contact with Gabriel and not possibly spook him by taking out a notebook and pen.

"Who else did you notice who wasn't right?" she asked.

"Nobody else," Gabriel said.

"And you're not sure if the guy in the hoodie hung around after getting his beer?"

"I didn't see him again."

"So, when you last saw him, how long was that before midnight and all the shooting started?"

"I don't know, a half hour."

"Did you see anybody like your dad ask him what he was doing there or ask him to leave?"

"No, because it was like a block party. Everybody welcome."

"Did you see any other white people at the party?"

"A few, yeah."

"But they weren't suspicious."

"No."

"But this other guy was."

"Well, it was like a party and he was dirty. And he had the hoodie up, you know?"

"Your father had a work shirt on. Was that usual?"

"'Cause it had his name on it. He wanted all the neighbors to know who he was. He always did that."

Ballard nodded. It was now time to ask more difficult questions and hold this kid to her side as long as she could.

"Did you fire any weapons tonight, Gabriel?" she asked.

"No, no way," Gabriel said.

"Okay, good. Are you associated with Las Palmas Thirteen?"

"What are you asking me? I'm no gangster. My dad said no way."

"Don't get upset. I'm just trying to figure out what's what. You're not associated, that's good. But your father was, right?"

"He quit that shit a long time ago. He was totally legit."

"Okay, that's good to know. But I heard there were guys from Las Palmas in the shop yard for the party. Is that true?"

"I don't know, maybe. My father grew up with these people. He didn't just throw them in the trash. But he was legit, his business was legit, he even had a white man as his partner. So don't go starting no shit about 'gang related.' That's bullshit."

Ballard nodded.

"Good to know, Gabriel. Can you tell me, was his partner there?"

"I didn't see him. Are we done here?"

"Not yet, Gabriel. What is the partner's name?"

"I don't know. He's a doctor up in Malibu or some shit. I only seen him once when he came in with a bent frame."

"A bent frame?"

"His Mercedes. He backed into something and bent the frame."

"Got it. Okay, I need two more things from you, Gabriel."

"What?"

"I need your girlfriend's phone number and I need you to step outside to my car for a minute."

"Why should I go with you? I want to see my father."

"They're not going to let you see your father, Gabriel. Not till later. I want to help you. I want this to be the last time you have to talk to the police about this. But to do that, I need to wipe your hands to make sure you're telling the truth."

"What?"

"You said you didn't fire a gun tonight. I wipe your hands with something I have in my car and we'll know for sure. After that, you'll only hear from me when I come by to tell you we caught the person who did this to your father."

Ballard waited while Gabriel considered the options.

"If you won't do it, I have to assume you lied to me. You don't want that, do you?"

"All right, whatever, let's do it."

Ballard walked over to the group first to ask Moore for the car keys. Moore said they were in the car. She then led Gabriel out to the ambulance bays. Here she pulled a notebook out of her back pocket. After writing down the cell number for Gabriel's girl, she jotted down his description of the man in the hoodie. She then opened her car's trunk. She took out a packet of wipe pads for gunshot-residue testing, used separate pads to wipe both Gabriel's hands, then sealed them in plastic bags to be submitted to the lab.

"See, no gunpowder, right?" Gabriel said.

"The lab will confirm that," Ballard said. "But I already believe you, Gabriel."

"So, what do I do now?"

"You go in and be with your mother and your sisters. They're going to need you to be strong for them."

Gabriel nodded and his face contorted. It was as though telling him to be strong had kicked his strength out from beneath him.

"You okay?" Ballard asked.

She touched his shoulder.

"You're going to catch this guy, right?" he said.

"Yeah," Ballard said. "We're going to catch him."

6

Ballard didn't get back to the station until almost 3 a.m. She went up the stairs off the back hallway and into the room shared by the Gang and Vice units. It was long and rectangular and usually empty because both units worked the streets. But now the room was crowded. Officers from both squads, in uniform like Ballard, sat behind desks and at worktables going down the length of the room. Most of them were not wearing masks. The large crowd could be explained in a number of ways. First, it was difficult to work vice and gangs in full uniform, as dictated by the department's tactical alert. This meant the alert, which was supposed to put as many officers on the street as possible during the New Year's celebration, was having the opposite effect. It could also mean that, because it was beyond the witching hours of midnight to 2 a.m., everyone had returned to the house on break. But Ballard knew that it could also be that this was the new LAPD—officers stripped of the mandate of proactive enforcement and waiting to be reactive, to hit the streets only when it was requested and required, and only then doing the minimum so as not to engender a complaint or controversy.

To Ballard, much of the department had fallen into the pose of a citizen caught in the middle of a bank robbery. Head down, eyes averted, adhering to the warning: nobody move, and nobody gets hurt.

She spotted Sergeant Rick Davenport at the end of one of the worktables and headed toward him. He looked up from a cell phone to see her coming, and a maskless smile of recognition creased his face. He was mid-forties and had been working gangs in the division for over a decade.

"Ballard," he said. "I hear El Chopo got it tonight."

Ballard stopped at the table.

"El Chopo?" she asked.

"That's what we called Javier back in the day," Davenport said. "When he was a gangster and using his padre's place as a chop shop."

"But not anymore?"

"He supposedly went straight after his wife started dropping kids."

"I was surprised I didn't see you out at the scene tonight. That why?"

"That and other things. Just doin' what the people want."

"Which is staying off the street?"

"It's pretty clear if they can't defund us, they want to de-see us, right, Cordo?"

Davenport looked for affirmation to a gang cop named Cordero.

"Right, Sergeant," Cordero said.

Ballard pulled out the empty chair on Davenport's right side and sat down. She decided to get to the point.

"So, what can you tell me about Javier?" she asked. "Do you believe he went straight? Would Las Palmas even allow that?"

"The word is that twelve or fifteen years ago, he bought his way out," Davenport said. "And as far as we know, he's been clean and legit ever since."

"Or too smart for you?"

Davenport laughed.

"There's always that possibility."

"Well, do you still have a file on the guy? Shake cards, anything?"

"Oh, we've got a file. It's probably a little dusty. Cordo, pull the file on Javier Raffa and bring it to Detective Ballard."

Cordero got up and walked to the line of four-drawer file cabinets that ran the length of one side of the room.

"That's how far this guy goes back," Davenport said. "He's in the paper files."

"So definitely not active?" Ballard pressed.

"Nope. And we would have known if he was. We follow some of the OGs. If they were meeting, we would have seen it."

"How far up was Raffa before he dropped out?"

"Not far. He was a soldier. We never made a case on the guy but we knew he was chopping stolen cars for the team."

"How did you hear he bought his way out?"

Davenport shook his head like he couldn't remember.

"Just the grapevine," he said. "I can't name you the snitch off-hand—it was a long time ago. But that was what was said, and as far as we could tell, it was accurate."

"How much does something like that cost?" Ballard asked.

"Can't remember. It might be in the file."

Cordero returned from the cabinets and handed a file to Davenport instead of Ballard. He in turned handed it to Ballard.

"Knock yourself out," he said.

"Can I take this?" Ballard asked.

"As long as you bring it back."

"Roger that."

Ballard took the file, got up, and walked out. She had the feeling that several of the men were watching as she left the room.

She was not popular in the office after a year of cajoling and then demanding intel and help in her investigations from people bent on doing as little as possible.

She went down the stairs and into the detective bureau, where she saw Lisa Moore at her desk. She was typing on her computer.

"You're back," Ballard said.

"No thanks to you," Moore said. "You left me with those people and that kid cop."

"Rodriguez? He probably has five years on the job. He worked Rampart before coming here."

"Doesn't matter. He looks like a kid."

"Did you get anything good from the wife and daughters?"

"No, but I'm writing it up. Where is this going anyway?"

"I'm going to keep it for a bit. Send whatever you've got to me."

"Not to West Bureau?"

"They're running all teams on a double murder. So I'll work this until they're ready to take it."

"And Dash is okay with that?"

"I talked to him. It's not a problem."

"What do you have there?"

She pointed to the file Ballard was carrying.

"And old Gang file on Raffa," Ballard said. "Davenport said he hasn't been active in years, that he bought his way out when he started a family."

"Aw, isn't that sweet," Moore said.

The sarcasm was clear in her voice. Ballard had long realized that Moore had lost her empathy. Working sex cases full-time probably did that. Losing empathy for victims was a self-protective measure, but Ballard hoped it never happened to her. Police work could easily hollow you out. But she believed that losing one's empathy was losing one's soul.

"Send me your reports when you're ready to file," Ballard said.

"Will do," Moore said.

"And nothing on the Midnight Men, right?"

"Not yet. Maybe they're lying low tonight."

"It's still early. On Thanksgiving we didn't get the callout till dawn."

"Wonderful. Can't wait till dawn."

The sarcasm again. Ballard ignored it and grabbed an empty desk nearby. Because she worked the late show, she didn't have an assigned spot. She was expected to borrow a desk in the room whenever she needed one. She looked at a few of the knick-knacks on the one shelf in the cubicle where she sat and quickly realized it was the workstation of a dayside Crimes Against Persons detective named Tom Newsome. He loved baseball, and there were several souvenir balls on little pedestals on the shelf. They had been signed by Dodgers players past and present. The gem of the collection was in a small plastic cube to protect it. It wasn't signed by a player. Instead the signature was from the man who had called Dodgers games on radio and TV for more than fifty years. Vin Scully was revered as the voice of the city because he transcended baseball. Even Ballard knew who he was, and she thought that Newsome was risking the ball getting stolen, even in a police station.

Opening the file in front of her, Ballard was greeted by a booking photo of Javier Raffa as a young man. He had died at age thirty-eight, and the photo was from a 2003 arrest for receiving stolen property. She read the details on the arrest report the photo was clipped to. It said Raffa had been pulled over in a 1977 Ford pickup truck with several used auto parts in the bed. One of these parts—a trans-axle—still had the manufacturing serial number embossed on it, and it was traced to a Mercedes G-wagon reported stolen in the San Fernando Valley the month before.

According to the records in the file, Raffa's lawyer, listed as Roger Mills, negotiated a disposition that got the twenty-one-year-old Javier probation and community service in exchange for a guilty plea. The case was then expunged from Raffa's record when he completed probation and 120 hours of community service without issue. The file noted that his community service included painting over gang graffiti on freeway overpasses throughout the city.

It was the one and only arrest record in the file, although there were several field interview cards paper-clipped together there. These were all dated before the arrest and went back to when Raffa was sixteen years old. Most of these came out of basic gang rousts—patrol breaking up parties or Hollywood Boulevard cruise lines. Officers taking down names and associates, tattoos, and other descriptors to be fed into Gang Intel files and data-bases. As the son of a body shop owner, Raffa was always driving classic and restored cars or low riders that were also described on the shake cards.

From early on in the cards Raffa had the nickname El Chopo ascribed to him. It was an obvious riff on the moniker of one of the biggest cartel kingpins, known as El Chapo, which meant *Shorty* in Spanish. One note that caught Ballard's eye and was repeated on the four cards written and filed between 2000 and 2003 was the description of a tattoo on the right side of Raffa's neck. It depicted a white billiard ball with an orange stripe and the number 13—a reference to Las Palmas 13 and its association with and deference to la eMe, the prison gang also known as the Mexican Mafia. The 13 was a reference to M, the thirteenth letter of the alphabet.

Ballard thought about the discoloration she had seen on Raffa's neck. She realized it was laser scarring from when he'd had the tattoo removed.

There was a photocopy of an intel report in the file dated October 25, 2006, that was a bullet-point recounting of multiple nuggets of unsubstantiated bits of gossip and information from a confidential informant identified as LP3. Ballard assumed that the informant was a Las Palmas insider. She scanned through the separate entries and found the one about Raffa.

- Javier Raffa (El Chopo) DOB 02/14/82 — said to have paid Humberto Viera $25K cash tribute for no-strings separation from the gang.

Ballard had never heard of someone buying their way out of a gang. She had always known of the *blood in, blood out, till death do us part* rule of gang law. She picked up the desk phone. Newsome had taped a station phone directory to it. She called the extension next to GED and asked for Sergeant Davenport. While she waited for him to come on the line, she picked one of the baseballs off its pedestal and tried to make out the signature scribbled on it. She knew little about baseball or Dodgers players past and present. To her, the first name of the signature looked like Mookie but she thought she had to have that wrong.

Davenport came on the line.

"It's Ballard. Got a question."

"Go ahead."

"Humberto Viera of Las Palmas, is he still around?"

Davenport chuckled.

"Depends on what you mean by 'around,'" he said. "He's been up in Pelican Bay for at least eight, ten years. And he isn't coming back."

"Your case?" Ballard asked.

"I was part of it, yeah. Got him on a couple of one-eight-sevens of White Fence guys. We flipped the getaway driver, and that was it for Humberto. Bye-bye on him."

"Okay. Anyone else I could talk to about Javier Raffa buying his way out of the gang?"

"Hmm. I don't think so. That goes pretty far back, as far as I remember. I mean, there are always OGs around, but they're original gangsters because they toe the line. But for the most part, these gangs turn over membership every eight or ten years. Nobody's going to talk to you about Raffa."

"What about LP-three?"

There was a pause before Davenport answered. And it was clear that earlier, when he had claimed not to remember the snitch, he was lying.

"What do you think you'll get out of her?"

"So it's a woman?"

"I didn't say that. What do you think you'll get out of him?"

"I don't know. I'm looking for a reason somebody put a bullet in Javier Raffa's head."

"Well, LP-three is long gone. That's a dead end."

"You're sure now?"

"I'm sure."

"Thanks, Sergeant. I'll catch you later."

Ballard put the phone in its cradle. It was clear to her from Davenport's gaffe that LP3 was a woman and possibly still active as an informant. Otherwise he would not have been so clumsy in trying to cover up his slip of the tongue. Ballard didn't know what it meant in terms of her case, considering that Raffa had apparently separated from the gang fourteen years earlier. But it was good to know that if the case turned toward the gang, the GED had an insider who could provide insight and information.

"What was that about?" Moore asked.

She was sitting across the aisle from Ballard.

"Gang Enforcement," Ballard said. "They don't want me talking to their Las Palmas CI."

"Figures," Moore said.

Ballard wasn't sure what that meant but didn't respond. She knew Moore was one and done on the late show. Her involvement in the case would end when the sun came up and her shift was over, the tactical alert was ended, and all officers returned to their normal schedules. Moore would be back on dayside, but Ballard would be left alone to work in the dark hours.

It was exactly the way she wanted it.

7

Ballard began putting together the murder book on the Raffa case. This effort started with the tedious job of writing out the incident report, which described the killing and identified the victim but also included many mundane details such as time of the initial call, names of responding patrol officers, ambient temperature, next-of-kin notification, and other details that were important in documenting but not solving the case. She then wrote summaries of the witness interviews she had conducted and collected from Lisa Moore, though Moore's reports were short and perfunctory. A summary of the interview with Raffa's youngest daughter had only one line: "This girl knows nothing and can contribute nothing to the investigation."

All of this was put into a three-ring binder. Lastly, Ballard started a case chrono that recorded her movements by time and included mention of her discussion with Davenport. She then made copies of the documents in the GED file and put them in the binder as well. She got all of this done by 5 a.m. and then got up and approached Moore, who was looking at email on her phone. Their shift ended in an hour but that didn't matter to Ballard.

"I'm going to go downtown to see what Forensics collected," Ballard said. "You want to stay or go?"

"I think I'll stay," Moore said. "There's no way you'll be back by six."

"Right. Then do you mind taking the GED file back up to Davenport?"

"Sure, I'll take it. But why are you doing this?"

"Doing what?"

"Running with the case. It's a homicide. You're just going to turn it over to West Bureau as soon as everybody wakes up over there."

"Maybe. But maybe they'll let me work it."

"You're giving the rest of us a bad name, Renée."

"What are you talking about?"

"Just stay in your lane. Nobody moves, nobody gets hurt, right?"

Ballard shrugged.

"You didn't say that about me jumping on the Midnight Men case," she said.

"That's rape," Moore said. "You're talking about a homicide case."

"I don't see the difference. There's a victim and there's a case."

"Well, put it this way: West Bureau will see a difference. They're not going to be nice about you trying to take away one of theirs."

"We'll see. I'm going. Let me know if our two assholes hit again."

"Oh, I will. And you do the same."

Ballard went back to her borrowed desk, closed her laptop, and collected her things. She pulled up her mask for the walk down the back hallway to the exit. There was a prisoner lock-down bench there and she wanted the extra protection. There was no telling what the arrested bring into the station.

After leaving the station, she took the 101 toward downtown, driving through the pre-dawn grays toward the towers that always seemed lit at any hour of darkness. Traffic had generally been cut in half during the pandemic, but the city at this hour was dead, and Ballard made it to the 10 east interchange in less than fifteen minutes. From there it was only another five minutes before the exit to the Cal State L.A. campus. The Forensic Science Center, the five-story lab shared by the LAPD and the L.A. County Sheriff's Department, was at the south end of the vast campus.

The building seemed just as quiet as the streets. Ballard took the elevator up to the third floor, where the crime scene techs worked. She buzzed her way in and was met by a criminalist named Anthony Manzano, who had been out at the Javier Raffa crime scene.

"Ballard," he said. "I was wondering who I was going to hear from."

"It's me for now," Ballard said. "West Bureau is running with a double and it's all hands on deck there."

"You don't have to tell me. Everybody but me is working it. Come on back."

"Must be a hairy case."

"More like a TV case and they don't want to look bad."

Ballard had been curious about why no media had turned up at the Gower Gulch case. She had thought that the initial theory, that someone was killed by a falling bullet, would be catnip to the media, but so far, there had been no inquiries that she was aware of.

Manzano led her through the lab to his workstation. She saw three other criminalists at work in other pods and assumed they were on the West Bureau case.

"What's the case out there?" she asked casually.

"Elderly couple robbed and murdered," Manzano said.

After a pause he delivered the kicker.

"They were set on fire," he said. "While alive."

"Jesus Christ," Ballard said.

She shook her head but immediately thought, yes, the media would be all over that case, and the department would throw several bodies on it to give the appearance of leaving no stone unturned. That meant she stood a good chance of being able to keep the Raffa case if she could get the approval of Lieutenant Robinson-Reynolds.

There was a light table in Manzano's pod, and spread across it was a wide piece of graph paper on which he had been in the process of sketching the crime scene.

"This is your scene right here and I've been plotting the locations of the casings we collected," Manzano said. "It looked like the shootout at the O.K. Corral out there."

"You mean the firing into the sky, right?" Ballard said.

"I do, and it's interesting. We have thirty-one shells recovered and I think it adds up to only three guns in play—including the murder weapon."

"Show me."

Beside the graph paper was a clipboard with Manzano's notes and drawings from the scene. There was also an open cardboard box containing the thirty-one bullet casings in individual plastic evidence bags.

"Okay, so thirty-one shots produced thirty-one shells on the ground," Manzano said. "We have three separate calibers and ammunition brands, so this becomes pretty easy to figure out."

He reached into the box, rooted around in it, and came out with one of the bagged bullet casings.

"We have identified seventeen casings as nine-millimeter PDX1 rounds produced by Winchester," Manzano said. "You will have to get confirmation from FU, but to me, as a nonexpert, the firing-pin marks on these look alike, and that would suggest they all came from a nine-millimeter weapon that would hold sixteen rounds in the clip and one in the chamber if fully loaded."

Manzano had referenced the Firearms Unit, which was no longer called that because of the other meaning associated with the acronym. It had been updated to Firearms Analysis Unit.

"I think you are probably looking at a Glock seventeen or similar weapon there," Manzano said. "Then we have thirteen casings that were forty-caliber and manufactured by Federal. I looked at our ammo catalog, and these likely were jacketed hollow points, but FU would have an opinion on that. And of course these could have been fired by any number of firearms. Twelve in the clip, one in the chamber."

"Okay," Ballard said. "That leaves one."

Manzano reached into the box and found the bag containing the last casing.

"Yes," he said. "And this is a Remington twenty-two."

Ballard took the evidence bag and looked at the brass casing. She was sure it was from the bullet that killed Javier Raffa.

"This is good, Anthony," she said. "Show me where you found it."

Manzano pointed to an *X* on the crime scene schematic that had the marker number 1 next to it and was inside the rectangular outline of a car. To the right of the car was a stick figure that Ballard took to be Javier Raffa.

"Of course, the victim was transported before we got there, but the blood pool and EMT debris marked that spot," he said. "The casing was nine feet, two inches from the blood and located under one of the wrecks in the tow yard. The Chevy Impala, I believe."

Ballard realized that they had caught a break. The ejected

shell had gone under the car and that made it difficult for the gunman to retrieve it before people started to notice that Raffa was down.

She held up the evidence bag.

"Can I take this to Firearms?" she asked.

"I'll write a COC," Manzano said.

He was talking about a chain-of-custody receipt.

"Do you know if anyone is over there?" Ballard asked.

"Should be somebody," Manzano said. "They're on max deployed like everybody else."

Ballard pulled her phone and checked the time. Tactical alert would end in fifteen minutes. It was Friday and the January 1 holiday. The Firearms Analysis Unit might possibly go dark.

"Okay, let me sign the COC and get over there before they leave," she said.

The FAU was just down the hall and Ballard entered with ten minutes to spare. At first she thought she was too late—she didn't see anyone. And then she heard someone sneeze.

"Hello?"

"Sorry," someone said. "Coming out."

A man in a black polo shirt with the FAU logo stepped out from one of the gun storage racks that lined one wall of the unit. The unit had collected so many varieties of firearms over the years that they were displayed in rows of racks that could be closed together like an accordion.

The man was carrying a feather duster.

"Just doing a little housekeeping," he said. "We wouldn't want Sirhan's gun to get dusty. It's part of history."

Ballard just stared for a moment.

"Mitch Elder," the man said. "What can I do for you?"

Ballard identified herself.

"Are you about to leave at the end of the tac alert?" she asked.

"Supposed to," Elder said. "But...whaddaya got?"

It had been Ballard's experience that gun nuts always liked a challenge.

"We had a homicide this morning. Gunshot. I have a casing and was looking for a make on the weapon used, maybe a NIBIN run."

The National Integrated Ballistic Information Network was a database that stored characteristics of bullets and casings used in crimes. Each carried markings that could be matched to specific weapons and compared crime to crime. Casings were a better bet than bullets because bullets often fragmented or mushroomed on impact, making comparisons more difficult.

Ballard held up the clear evidence bag with the casing in it as bait. Elder's eyes fixed on it. He didn't take long.

"Well, let's see what you got," he said.

Ballard handed him the bag and then followed him to a workstation. He put on gloves, removed the casing, and studied it under a lighted magnifying glass. He turned it in his fingers, studying the rim for marks left by the weapon that had fired it.

"Good extractor marking," he finally said. "I think you're looking for a Walther...but we'll see. This will take a little time for me to encode. If you want to go get breakfast, I'll be here when you get back."

"No, I'm good," Ballard said. "I have to make a call."

"Then maybe we can get breakfast after we're done."

"Uh...I think I'll probably need to keep moving with the case. But thanks."

"Suit yourself."

"I'm going to find an empty desk."

She walked away, almost shaking her head. She was annoyed with herself for adding the thanks at the end of the rejection.

She found a workspace that was completely bare except for

a phone on the desk. She pulled her own phone and called Robinson-Reynolds, clearly waking him up.

"Ballard, what is it?"

He seemed annoyed.

"You told me to update you no matter the time."

"I did. Whaddaya got?"

"I think our shooting was a homicide—a murder—and I want to stick with it."

"Ballard, you know it needs to go to—"

"I know the protocol but West Bureau is running with a big media case and I think they would welcome me taking it off their hands—at least until they come up for air on the double they've got."

"You're not a homicide detective."

"I know, but I was. I can handle this, L-T. We've already conducted witness interviews and I've been to Forensics and now I'm at Firearms running NIBIN on the shell we found."

"You shouldn't have done any of that. You should have turned it over as soon as you knew it wasn't an accidental."

"West Bureau was busy; I ran with it. We can turn it over now but they won't jump on it, and hours and maybe days will go by before they do."

"It's not my call, Ballard. It's their call. Lieutenant Fuentes over there."

"Can you call him and grease this for me, L-T? He'll probably be happy we want to take it off his hands."

"There is no 'we' on this, Ballard. Besides, you are supposed to be off duty starting ten minutes ago. I got no overtime for you."

"I'm not doing this for OT. No greenies on this."

"Greenies" was a reference to the color of the 3 x 5 cards that had to be filled out and signed by a supervisor authorizing overtime work.

"No greenies?" Robinson-Reynolds asked.

"Nope," Ballard promised.

"What about the Midnight Men, and where is Moore in all of this? You're supposed to be working together."

"She stayed at the station to start putting together the murder book and writing up witness statements. Nothing came up on the Midnight Men but I'll still be working that. I'm not dropping it."

"Then that's a lot on your plate."

"I wouldn't ask for this if I couldn't handle my plate."

There was a pause before Robinson-Reynolds made a decision.

"Okay, I'll make the call to Fuentes. I'll let you know."

"Thanks, L-T."

The lieutenant disconnected first and Ballard walked back over to Elder's workstation. He was gone. She looked around and saw him sitting at a computer terminal by the window that looked out on the 10 freeway. It meant he was on the NIBIN database. She walked over.

"Ballard, you've got something here," Elder said.

"Really?" Ballard said. "What?"

"Another case. The bullet is linked to another murder. Almost ten years ago up in the Valley. A guy got shot in a robbery. The shells match. Same gun was used. A Walther P-twenty-two."

"Wow."

Ballard felt a cold finger go down her spine.

"What's the case number?" she asked.

Elder dictated a number off the computer screen. Ballard grabbed a pen out of a cup next to the computer terminal and wrote the number in her notebook.

"What's the vic's name?" she asked.

"Lee, Albert, DOD two-two-eleven."

She wrote it all down.

"It's an open case?" she asked.

"Open-unsolved," Elder said. "An RHD case."

Robbery-Homicide Division, Ballard's old unit before she was unceremoniously shipped out to work the late show in Hollywood. But 2011 was before her time there.

"Does it say who the I/O is?" she asked.

"It does but it's out of date," Elder said. "Says here the investigating officer is Harry Bosch. But I knew him and he's been retired awhile."

Ballard froze for just a moment before managing to speak.

"I know," she then said.

8

Ballard pulled to a stop in front of the house on Woodrow Wilson. She yawned and realized that going home first had probably been a mistake. Changing out of the stiff uniform was a good thing, but then dozing on the couch for an hour had somehow only served to underline her exhaustion, not knock it down.

She could hear music coming from the house as soon as she opened the car door. Something high velocity but more bluesy than she was used to hearing from Harry Bosch. And there were vocals. It made her think that maybe someone else was inside listening.

She knocked loudly on the door to be heard over the music. It was immediately cut off and then the door opened. It was Bosch.

"Well," he said. "The prodigal detective."

"What?" Ballard said. "What's that supposed to mean?"

"Well, I just haven't heard from you in a long time. Thought you forgot about me."

"Hey, you were the one who went off to the dark side, working for that defense lawyer. I thought there was no time for me."

"Really?"

"Really. So, you get the vaccine yet? How do you feel about having visitors inside? I've got antibodies and can keep my mask on."

Bosch stepped back for her to enter.

"You can come in and you can lose the mask. I haven't got the vax yet but I'll risk it. And for the record, I didn't work *for* Mickey Haller. I work for myself."

Ballard crossed the threshold, ignoring the comment about Haller and keeping her mask on.

"It sounded like you were having a party in here."

"I mighta had the volume up a bit."

The house was unchanged. The galley kitchen was to the right of the entry area and she stepped forward toward the view, passing by the dining area into the living room. The sliders were open to the deck and the view of the Cahuenga Pass. She pointed to the open doors.

"Letting everybody in the canyon hear your beats," she said. "Nice."

"Is that what this is?" Bosch asked. "A noise complaint?"

She turned and looked at him.

"Actually, it's a complaint but about something else."

"Great way to start off the new year—with the LAPD mad at me. Might as well hit me with it."

"Not the LAPD. So far. Just me. This morning I drove all the way out to Westchester to the new homicide library they opened out there. You know, where they keep all the murder books from open cases. They finally put them all in one central place. And I asked for a book from one of your old cases and they told me it was gone, last checked out by you."

Bosch frowned and shook his head.

"I read about that place in the paper," he said. "Sponsored by the Ahmanson family. But the grand opening was long after I was out the door at LAPD. I've never set foot in that place, let alone checked out a book."

Ballard nodded like she anticipated his response, and had an answer.

"They moved the archives from the divisions over one at a time," she said. "If a book was checked out, they moved the checkout card over so there would be a space on the shelf at Ahmanson. The card on your case was from 2014—three years after the murder and before you pulled the pin."

Bosch didn't respond at first, like he was checking facts in his head.

"The case was 2011?" he finally asked. "What was the name?"

"Albert Lee. Killed with a Walther P-twenty-two. You recovered the casing, apparently. But that's about all I know, because you took the damn murder book. I need it back, Harry."

Bosch held up his hand like he was trying to stop the accusation.

"I didn't take the book, okay?" he said. "When I left, I copied the chronos of every case I still had open. On some I copied everything. But I never took a book. And with the archives in the divisions, anybody could have taken that book and put my name on the checkout card. There was no security around the books. We supposedly didn't need it, because they were considered safe—they were in police stations, after all."

Ballard folded her arms across her chest, not ready to give in on the point just yet.

"So, you're saying you might have the chrono but you don't have the book?"

"Exactly. I kept the chronos in case they ever got cleared and I got pulled into court to testify about the initial investigation. I wanted to be able to refresh my memory, that sort of thing. I remember the Albert Lee case. It wasn't the kind of case where I'd even want to steal the book."

Ballard shifted her stance and looked back at the dining room table. She saw a six-inch stack of documents she had not noticed when she had entered. The top page was clearly the front page of an autopsy report. She pointed to it.

"And what's that?" she asked. "That looks like a whole book at least."

"It's parts of about six books," Bosch said. "But it isn't Lee. Look for yourself if you don't believe me. Why would I lie to you about this, Renée?"

"I don't know. But stealing books is not cool."

"I agree. That's why I never did it."

She walked over to the table and used a hand to spread the stack out over the table so she could see some of the documents. One of the documents had what looked like a surveillance photo attached to it. It showed a man getting into a car in what was clearly the parking lot of an In-N-Out restaurant. There was no time-and-date stamp, so it wasn't an official stakeout shot.

"Who's this?" she asked.

"It's not the Lee case," Bosch insisted. "It's something else entirely, okay?"

"I'm just asking. Who is it?"

"Finbar McShane."

Ballard nodded. It explained the stack. Some cases spawn many murder books. Especially the unsolved cases.

"I thought so," she said. "Can't let it go, can you?"

"And what, you think I should?" Bosch asked. "He killed a whole family and got away with it. I should let it go?"

"I'm not saying that. I know it's your white whale, Harry. We've talked about it."

"Okay, then you know."

Ballard wanted to switch the conversation back to her case.

"You said Lee wasn't the kind of case you'd copy a whole book for," she said. "What do you mean by that?"

"It didn't get its hooks into me," Bosch said.

"Why not?"

"Well, as you know, or as I guess you will come to know, some people are sort of the architects of their own demise. And others, they get hit by the bus. They're just in the wrong place at the wrong time and they did nothing to bring on their fate. They're innocent."

Bosch gestured to the pile of documents spread out on his table.

"And they're the ones who get their hooks in you," he said.

Ballard nodded and was silent for a moment, as if giving all those who were innocent her respect.

"Hooks or no hooks, can you tell me what you remember about Lee?" she asked. "I've made a ballistic connection to the killing of a man in Hollywood last night."

Bosch raised his eyebrows. He was finally intrigued.

"Last murder of the year, huh?" he said.

"Actually, the first," Ballard said. "When the shooting started at midnight, somebody put one in my victim's head."

"Audio camouflage. Clever. Who's the vic?"

"Harry, you're not the one asking questions here. Tell me about Lee first, then we can talk about my case. Maybe."

"Got it. You want to sit?"

He gestured toward the table instead of the more comfortable living room. He moved behind it, where his back would be to a wall of unkempt stacks of books, files, CDs, and LPs, and sat down. Ballard sat across from him.

As Bosch spoke, he pushed the files Ballard had spread out back into a squared-off pile.

"Albert Lee, black male, I think he was thirty-four when he died. Maybe thirty-three. He had a good idea. Rappers were

becoming stars overnight, making their own tapes, coming right
out of the ghetto and all of that. He borrowed money and opened
a recording studio up in North Hollywood. It was nice, it was
out of the gang territories of South Central, and people could
come in, rent time in the studio, and lay down their raps. It was
a great idea."

"Until it wasn't."

"Right, until it wasn't. I mentioned he borrowed the money.
He had a monthly nut he had to pay, plus rent and other
expenses. Plus some of these people who came up to his place to
record—"

"Were gangsters."

"No. I mean, yeah, they were, but what I was going to say
was they had no money for studio time, and Albert—he had a
soft side—he'd let them record if they signed over a piece of
whatever they made off the beats, you know?"

"Got it. Just try to collect on that down the line."

"Exactly, and a few of these people hit it sort of big, but even
then collecting was slow. He sued a couple of those guys and it
got all tied up in the courts."

"He was going out of business?"

"That would have been the case but he took on an investor.
Do you know what factoring is?"

"Nope."

"It's a high-interest business loan that is sort of a bridge loan.
It's secured by your accounts receivable. Make sense?"

"Not really, no."

"Say your company is owed a hundred dollars but it's not
going to come in for a couple months. A factor loan would
give you the hundred so you can keep the business rolling, but
it's not secured by property or equipment, because none of that
stuff is owned by the company. It's all rented. The only value

the company has for securing a loan is what it's owed—accounts receivable."

"Okay, I got it."

"So that's what Albert Lee did. Only these are high-interest loans—it gets right up to the edge of loan-sharking but doesn't cross the line. It's legal and that's the road Albert went down. He took out three different loans totaling a hundred thousand, got upside down, and couldn't pay them because his lawsuits were delayed and delayed. So, soon his loan guy takes over the business. He leaves Albert in charge and running the place, he pays him a salary, and—and this is the thing—he makes him take out a key person insurance policy in case something happens to him."

"Oh, shit. How much?"

"A million."

"So Albert gets whacked and the loan guy gets paid."

"Exactly."

"But you couldn't make a case."

"Couldn't get it there."

Bosch gestured to the stack of documents on the table.

"Like this one. I have a pretty good idea who did it, but I can't get it there. But unlike this family, Albert went down the road with his killer. For some people, the wolf breaks into the house. With people like Albert, they invite the wolf in."

"So no sympathy for the guy who invites the wolf in. How does that fit with 'everybody counts or nobody counts'?"

"The guy who opens the door still counts. But the innocents come first. When I get all of those solved, we can talk about the next wave. Everybody still counts. There are only so many hours in the day and days in the year."

"And this is why a guy who kills an entire family is on the top of your pile."

"You got it."

Ballard nodded as she digested Bosch's view of what it took to either get hooked by a case or be able to put it at the end of the line.

"So," she finally said. "On the Albert Lee case, who was the factor?"

"It was a doctor," Bosch said. "A dentist, actually. His name was John William James. His offices were down in the Marina and I guess he made so much money capping teeth that he started factoring."

"You said 'was.' His name 'was' John William James."

"Yeah, that's going to be a problem with your case. John William James is dead. A couple years after Albert Lee got murdered, James got himself whacked as well. He was sitting in his Mercedes in the parking lot outside his office when somebody put a twenty-two in his head too."

"Shit."

"There goes your lead, huh?"

"Maybe. But I'd still like to see if you can find the chrono on the case, and whatever else you've got."

"Sure. It's either in the carport closet or under the house."

"Under?"

"Yeah, I built a storage room under there after I retired. It's pretty nice. I even have a bench for when I go down and look through cases."

"Which I'm sure you do often."

Bosch didn't respond, which she took as confirmation.

"By the way," Ballard said. "How are you doing with everything…from the radiation case?"

She hesitated saying the word *leukemia*.

"I'm still kicking, obviously," Bosch said. "I take my pills and that seems to keep it in check. It could come back but for now I've got no complaints."

"Good to hear," Ballard said. "So do you mind looking for that chrono now?"

"Sure, I'll be right back. It might take me a few. You want me to put the music back on?"

"That's okay, but I was going to ask, what was that you were playing when I pulled up? It had a groove."

"'Compared to What.' Some people say it was the first jazz protest song: 'Nobody gives us rhyme or reason. Have one doubt, they call it treason.'"

"Okay, put it back on. Who is it?"

Bosch got up and went to the stereo to hit the play button. Then he adjusted the volume down.

"Originally Eddie Harris and Les McCann, but this version is John Legend and The Roots."

Ballard started to laugh. Bosch hit the button again.

"What?" he asked.

"You surprise me, Harry, that's all," Ballard said. "I didn't think you listened to anything recorded this century."

"That hurts, Ballard."

"Sorry."

"I'll be right back."

9

Ballard was in the garage of her condominium complex, grabbing her kit bag out of the back, the printouts from Bosch under her arm, when a man approached her. She tensed as she scanned the garage and saw no one else around. Her gun was in the kit bag.

"Hello, neighbor," the man said. "I just wanted to introduce myself. You're twenty-three, right?"

She knew he meant her apartment number. She'd been in the building just a few months, and though there were only twenty-five units, she had not yet met all of her neighbors.

"Uh, yeah, hi," she said. "Renée."

They bumped elbows.

"I'm Nate in thirteen, right below you," he said. "Happy New Year!"

"Happy New Year to you," Ballard said.

"My partner is Robert. He said he met you when you were moving stuff in."

"Oh, right, yeah, I met Robert. He helped me get a table into the elevator."

"And he said you're a cop."

"Yes, that's me."

"I guess it's not a great time to be a cop these days."

"It has its moments. Not all good, not all bad."

"Just so you know, I did join the Black Lives Matter protest. Don't hold it against me."

"I won't. And I agree, Black lives matter."

Ballard noticed he was carrying a helmet and wearing cycling gear, including the tight biking shorts with padding in the butt that look awkward whenever you're off the bike. She wanted to change the subject without being rude to a neighbor.

"You ride?" she asked.

It was a dumb question but the best she could manage.

"Every chance I can," Nate said. "But I sure see that you have a different hobby."

He pointed to the boards Ballard had propped against the garage wall in front of her Defender. One was her paddleboard for flat days, the other her Rusty Mini Tanker for surfing the Sunset break. The rest of her boards were in the condo's storage room, but her closet was full and she knew leaving her most used boards in the garage risked theft. She hoped the cameras on the exits were a deterrent.

"Yeah, I guess I like the beach," she said, immediately not liking her answer.

"Well, good to meet you and welcome," Nate said. "I should also tell you I'm current president of the homeowners association. I know you rent from the corporate owners—we approved that—but if you need anything HOA-related, knock on my door on the first floor."

"Oh, okay. I will."

"And I hope to see you at one of the mixers down in the courtyard."

"I haven't heard about that."

"First Friday of every month, not including today, of course. Happy hour. It's BYOB but people share."

"Okay, good. Maybe I'll see you there. And nice to meet you."

"Happy New Year!"

"Same."

Ballard was still getting used to having neighbors and felt awkward during the meet and greets—especially when it came out that she was a cop. She had spent most of the last four years alternating between a tent on Venice Beach and using her grandmother's house in Ventura for sleeping. But Covid-19 shut the beaches, while the growing homeless population in Venice made it a place she didn't want to be. She had rented the apartment, which was only ten minutes from the station. But it meant having neighbors above and below and to the left and right.

Nate headed toward the elevator, while she decided on the stairs so she wouldn't have to ride with him and make more small talk. Her phone started to buzz and she struggled to pull it from her pocket without dropping the paperwork from Bosch. She saw on the screen that it was Lisa Moore calling.

"Fuck me," Lisa said by way of hello.

"What's wrong, Lisa?" Ballard asked.

"We got a case and I'm five minutes from the Miramar with Kevin."

Ballard interpreted that to mean the Midnight Men had claimed another victim and Moore was almost to the resort in Santa Barbara with her boyfriend, a sergeant at Olympic Division.

"What's the case?" she asked.

"The victim didn't call it in till an hour ago," Moore said. "I thought we were clear."

"You mean she was raped last night but just reported it now?"

"Exactly. She sat in a bathtub for hours. Look, they took her to the RTC....Is there any chance you can handle it, Renée? I mean, it will probably take me two-plus hours to get back from here with the traffic and shit."

"Lisa, we were on call the whole weekend."

"I know, I know, I just thought that after we talked, I was clear, you know? We'll turn around. It's uncool to ask you."

Ballard turned around and headed back to her car. It was a big ask from Moore, not just because this was technically her case. Ballard knew that any trip to the rape treatment center would leave a mark on her. There weren't any uplifting stories to come out of the RTC. She opened the door of her Defender and put the kit bag back in.

"I'll handle it," she said. "But at some point Dash is going to check in and he might call you. You're the one from Sex. Not me."

"I know, I know," Moore said. "I was thinking I would call him now and say we got the call and one of us will update him after we talk to the victim. If you call him later, that should cover me. And if you need me tomorrow, I'll come back."

"Whatever. I just don't want my ass in a sling for covering for you."

"It won't be. You're the best. I'll call you later to check in."

"Right."

They disconnected. Ballard was annoyed. It wasn't because of Moore's lack of work ethic. After a year of pandemic and anti-police sentiment, commitment to the job was sometimes hard to find. The why-should-we-care disease had infected the whole department. What annoyed her was the disruption of her plan to spend the evening at home, ordering in from Little Dom's, digging into the chronological record on the Albert Lee killing, and looking for connections to the Javier Raffa killing. Now that she had pulled a fresh Midnight Men case, Lieutenant Robinson-Reynolds would be sure to turn the Raffa investigation over to West Bureau Homicide first thing in the morning.

"Shit," she said as she started the Defender.

The RTC was an adjunct to the UCLA Medical Center in Santa Monica. Ballard had been there many times on cases, including the time she herself was examined for evidence of rape. She knew most of the women—it was all women who worked there—on a first-name basis. She entered the unmarked door and found two dayside uniforms she recognized as McGee and Black—both males—standing in the waiting room.

"Hey, guys, I can take it from here," she said. "How'd the call come in?"

"She called it in," Black said. "The victim."

"She thought about it all day and then decided she'd been raped," McGee said. "Whatever evidence there was went down the bathtub drain."

Ballard stared at him for a moment, trying to read the sentiment behind such an asshole statement.

"Well, we'll see about that," she finally said. "Just so you know, I'm guessing she had no doubt about whether she was raped, okay, McGee? Her hesitation was most likely about making a report to a department and officers who don't give a shit and don't view rape as much of a crime."

McGee's cheeks started to blotch red with either anger or embarrassment or both.

"Don't get upset, McGee," Ballard said. "I didn't say I was talking about you, did I?"

"Yeah, bullshit," McGee said.

"Whatever," Ballard said. "She told you it was two suspects?"

"She did," Black said. "One got in, then let the other one in."

"What time was this?" Ballard asked.

"Right about midnight," Black said. "She said she didn't stay up to see in the new year. Got home from work around nine-thirty, made some dinner, then took a shower and went to bed."

"What was the address?" Ballard asked.

"She lives up in the Dell," Black said.

He pulled a field interview card out of a back pocket and handed it to Ballard.

"Shit," Ballard said.

"What?" McGee asked.

"I was sitting under the Cahuenga overpass at midnight," Ballard said. "Right when these guys were up there behind me."

The Dell was a hillside neighborhood a few blocks north of the overpass where Ballard and Moore had waited out the New Year's fusillade. Looking at the field information card, she saw that the victim, Cynthia Carpenter, lived up on Deep Dell Terrace. It was almost all the way up the hill to the Mulholland Dam.

Ballard held the card up as if to ask, is this all you've got?

"You'll do the IR today, right?" she asked.

"As soon as we get out of here," Black said.

Ballard nodded. She needed the incident report as the starting point of the investigation.

"Well, I've got it from here," she said. "You can go back to the six and write it up."

"And you can go to hell, Ballard," McGee said.

He didn't move. Black grabbed him by the arm and pulled him toward the door.

"Let's just go, dude," he said. "Let it go."

Ballard waited to see how McGee wanted to play it. There was a tense moment of silence and then he turned and followed his partner out to the parking lot.

Ballard took a breath and turned toward the admittance desk.

The receiving nurse, Sandra, smiled at her, having heard the exchange.

"You tell 'em, Renée," she said. "Your victim's in room three with Martha. I'll let her know you'll be in the hallway."

"Thanks," Ballard said.

Ballard went behind the desk and down the short hallway, which had doors to four examination rooms. Ballard had been there at times when all four contained victims of sexual assault.

The hallway was pastel blue and a mural of flowers had been added, growing from the baseboard, in an attempt to make things seem more pleasant in a place where horrors were documented. On the wall between rooms 1 and 3 was a billboard with various posted offerings of post-traumatic stress therapy and self-defense classes. Ballard was studying a business card tacked to the board that offered firearms instruction from a retired LAPD officer named Henrik Bastin. She found herself hoping that he got a lot of business out of this place.

The door to room 3 opened and Dr. Martha Fallon stepped out, pulling the door closed behind her. She smiled despite the circumstances.

"Hey, Renée," she said.

"Martha," Ballard said. "No holiday for you, huh?"

"I guess when rape takes a holiday, we'll get one, too. Sorry, that sounded trite and I didn't mean it that way."

"How is Cynthia?"

"She prefers Cindy. She's, uh, well, she's on the dark side of the moon."

Ballard had heard Fallon use the phrase before. The dark side of the moon was where people lived who had been through what Cindy Carpenter had just been through. Where a few dark hours changed everything about every hour that would come after. The place that only the people who had been through it understood.

Life was never the same.

"You may have heard—she bathed," Fallon said. "We didn't get anything, not that it really matters."

Ballard took that last part to be a reference to the backlog of rape kits waiting to be opened at the Forensics Unit for DNA typing and other evidentiary analysis. That fact alone seemed to stand for where the department and half of society, let alone Officer McGee, located sexual assault on the spectrum of serious crime. Every few years, there was a political outcry and money was found to process the backlog of rape cases. But then the furor subsided and the cases started backing up again. It was a cycle that never ended.

Fallon's report was no surprise to Ballard. There had been no DNA recovered in the other two Midnight Men cases either. The unknown perpetrators planned and executed their crimes carefully. The cases were connected simply by modus operandi and the rarity of a tag team pair of rapists. It was in fact so rare that it had its own acronym, MOSA—multiple offender sexual assault.

"Are you finished?" Ballard asked. "Can I talk to her?"

"Yes, I told her you were here," Fallon said.

"How is she?"

Ballard knew the victim wasn't doing well. Her question referred to the level of psychological trauma within the range known to Fallon from treating thousands of rape survivors over the years, with stranger rapes being the most difficult to deal with.

"She's not good," Fallon said. "But you're in luck, because right now she's angry, and that's a good time to talk. Once she has more time to think, it will be more difficult. She'll pull into her shell."

"Right," Ballard said. "I'll go in."

"I'll get her some take-home clothes," Fallon said. "I assumed you would take her walk-in clothes and bagged them."

The women went in opposite directions. Ballard moved to the door to room 3 but stood outside for a moment and read what Officer Black had put down on the FI card he had filled out while transporting Cindy Carpenter to the RTC.

Carpenter was twenty-nine years old, divorced, and the manager of the Native Bean coffee shop on Hillhurst Avenue. Ballard suddenly realized she might recognize this victim because the coffee shop was in her neighborhood in Los Feliz, and while Ballard had only moved in a few months prior, Native Bean had become her go-to spot to pick up coffee and an occasional blueberry muffin in the mornings after work, especially if she wanted to stave off sleep and head to the ocean.

Ballard knocked lightly on the door and entered. Cindy Carpenter was sitting up on an examination table and still in a gown. Her clothes, even though she had dressed after bathing, had been collected as evidence and were in a brown paper bag on the examination room counter. It was protocol and the bag had been sealed by Dr. Fallon. There was a second evidence bag in which Black and McGee had had the presence of mind to place the nightgown Carpenter had on when attacked as well as the sheets, blanket, and pillowcases from her bed. That was standard procedure but it was often overlooked by patrol officers. Ballard had to grudgingly give McGee and Black high marks for that. Also on the counter was a prescription written by Fallon for the morning-after pill as well as a card with instructions for how to access the results of HIV and STD testing that would follow the RTC examination.

Ballard did indeed recognize Carpenter. She was tall and thin and had shoulder-length blond hair. Ballard had seen her through the take-out window many times at Native Bean. She had ordered from her on some of those occasions, though it was clear Carpenter was more than a barista and was in charge of the business. Ballard had been looking forward to the day when the interior of the shop would reopen post-pandemic and she could go in and sit at a table. She always did good work in coffee shops. It had been one of the things she missed most in the last year.

Nothing on the FI card or from what Fallon had said in the hallway had prepped Ballard for Carpenter's physical condition. She had hemorrhagic bruising around both eyes from being choked and lacerations on her lower lip and left ear from being bitten. There was also an abrasion on one eyebrow that Ballard knew from the prior cases had likely occurred when a mask that had been taped over her eyes had been roughly pulled off. And lastly, her layered blond hair was imbalanced by a purposely haphazard cut by her attackers, an indignity that Ballard knew Carpenter would tell her came at the end, and was a creepy coup de grâce of the assault. The rapists would have taken the hair with them.

"Cindy, my name is Renée," Ballard said, trying to be informal. "I'm a detective with the Hollywood Division of the LAPD. I'm going to be investigating this case and I need to ask you some questions, if you don't mind."

Left alone in the room, Carpenter had been crying. She was holding a tissue in one hand, her cell phone in the other. Ballard wanted to know who she had been calling or texting, but that could come later.

"I almost didn't call you people," Carpenter said. "But then I thought, what if they come back? I wanted someone to know."

Ballard nodded that she understood.

"Well, I'm glad you did call," Ballard said. "Because I'm going to need your help catching these men."

"But I can't help you," Carpenter said. "I didn't even see their faces. They were wearing masks."

"Well, let's start right there. Did you see their hands? Other parts of their bodies? Were they white, black, brown?"

"Both were white. I could see their wrists and other parts of their bodies."

"Okay, good. Tell me about the masks."

"Like ski masks. One was green and one was blue."

This was consistent with the other two attacks. The connection between the three cases was now more than theory. It was confirmed.

"Okay, that is helpful," Ballard said. "When did you see the ski masks?"

"At the end," Carpenter said. "When they ripped the mask off my eyes."

This was an unusual part of all three attacks. The Midnight Men brought premade tape masks they put on their victims, only to remove them at the end of the assaults. It indicated that they didn't want to leave the masks behind as evidence. But more important, it was an indication that they weren't masking the women to prevent them from seeing them. Their own ski masks protected their identity. It meant they wanted to hide something else from their victims.

"Did you see anything else about them? Or just the ski masks?"

"One of them was pulling on his shirt. I saw a bandage on his arm."

"Which guy, green or blue?"

"Green."

"What kind of bandage? What did it look like?"

"It was like one of the biggest ones you can get? It was square. Right here."

She pointed to the inside of her upper arm.

"Do you think it was to cover up a tattoo?"

"I don't know. I only saw it for, like, half a second."

"Okay, Cindy, I know this is difficult, but I want to go through what they did to you, and I also need to take my own photos of your injuries. But first I want to ask, Did they say anything to you, anything at all, that might mean that they knew who you were before last night?"

"You mean, like, that it wasn't random? No, I didn't know these guys. At all."

"No, what I mean is, do you think they saw you somewhere, like the coffee shop or where you shop or anywhere else, and decided to target you? Or was it the opposite? They targeted your neighborhood and picked you that way."

Carpenter shook her head.

"I have no idea," she said. "They didn't say stuff like that, they just threatened me and said shit. Like, you think you're so cool and so high-and-mighty. They—"

She stopped to bring the tissue up as a wave of tears came. Ballard reached out and touched her arm.

"I'm sorry to put you through this," Ballard said.

"It's like I'm having to relive it," Carpenter said.

"I know. But it will help us catch these two…men. And stop them from possibly hurting other women."

Ballard waited a few moments for Carpenter to compose herself. Then started again.

"Let's talk about last night before anything happened," she said. "Did you go out or stay in for New Year's?"

"Well, I worked till nine, when we closed the shop," Carpenter said.

"You're talking about Native Bean?"

"Yes, we call it the Bean. One of my girls has Covid and the schedule is all messed up. I had to work the last shift of the year."

"I like your shop. I moved over to Finley a few months ago and I've been getting my coffee there. Your blueberry muffins are fantastic. Anyway, so you closed up at nine and then you went home? Or did you stop somewhere?"

Ballard guessed she would say she stopped at the Gelson's supermarket on Franklin. It would be on her way home, and one of the other victims had shopped there the night of her attack.

"I went right home," Carpenter said. "I made dinner— leftover takeout."

"And you live alone?" Ballard asked.

"Yes, since I got divorced."

"What did you do after dinner?"

"I just took a shower and went to bed. I was supposed to open this morning."

"You open most mornings, right? That's when I've seen you."

"That's me. We open at seven."

"Do you usually take your shower in the morning, before going to work?"

"Actually, no, I'd rather sleep later, so I— Why is this important?"

"Because at this point we really don't know what's important."

Ballard's disappointment in not getting the Gelson's connection had disappeared when Carpenter mentioned taking a shower. The two previous victims had said they showered before going to bed on the nights they were assaulted. With only two victims saying this, it could be coincidence. But three out of three became a pattern. Ballard felt her instincts stirring. She believed she might have something to work with.

10

Cindy Carpenter refused further medical attention to her physical injuries. She told Ballard she just wanted to go home. It was a long ride back from the RTC to the Dell, and Ballard used it to go through the story again. By now Carpenter was wrung out and tired but she cooperated, telling the story again in all its humiliating detail, telling what the rapists made her do, what she had heard, and what she had managed to see when the mask taped over her eyes began to come loose. From the first telling at the RTC to the second in the car, Carpenter told the same story, adding or subtracting a few details here and there, but not contradicting herself at any point in the narrative. This was good, Ballard knew. It meant she would be a good witness in terms of the investigation and at trial, should a case ever be made.

Ballard complimented her and told her why. It was important to keep Carpenter cooperating. Often victims grew reluctant when they started to weigh their psychic recovery against trusting the system.

Ballard had purposely not recorded either session. A recording taken in the hours after the assault could be gold in a defense lawyer's hands. She—yes, smart rapists often employed female attorneys for jury optics—could take any inconsistency between court testimony and a first recounting to tear a hole in the case wide enough for a bus called reasonable doubt to carry the jury through. Ballard always had to think about the moves ahead while trying to solve the present case.

Carpenter had supplied numerous details that incontrovertibly connected her assault to the two previous cases. Chief among these were the time of the attacks, the specific acts of sexual assault the women endured, and the measures taken by the rapists to avoid leaving evidence behind. These efforts included wearing gloves and condoms and, notably, bringing with them a Dustbuster, which was swept over the victim and locations in the house before the suspects exited.

A couple new details did come up in Cindy's telling of her story in the car. One was that Mr. Green, as they had taken to calling the suspect with the green ski mask, had red pubic hair, while Mr. Blue had dark, near-black pubic hair. Assuming their body hair matched their scalp hair, Ballard now had partial descriptions of both perpetrators. The previous two victims had never seen anything, because the tape placed across their eyes had never come loose. While all three of the victims had said that they could tell by the touch of the rapists that they wore gloves, Carpenter revealed during the drive that she had seen their hands when the tape had come loose, and the gloves they wore were disposable black latex. Ballard knew such gloves were widely available. It wouldn't be strong evidence of guilt, but it was one of the many details that could be important if suspects were ever identified.

There was another piece of evidence connecting the three cases as part of the MO. During the car-ride questioning, Ballard had focused on how the men spoke and the instructions they gave Carpenter. Ballard did not prompt Carpenter with specific examples because that might lead to a false confirmation of connection. She had to ask Carpenter more generally to try to remember what had been said to her, but the young woman came through with a key connection.

"At the end, before they left, one of them—I think it was Mr. Blue—said, 'You're going to be all right, doll. You'll look back on this one day and smile.' Then he laughed and they were gone."

Ballard had been waiting for this. The half apology at the end. The other two victims had reported the same thing, right down to the throwback vernacular of calling the victim "doll."

"You're sure he said that? He called you 'doll'?"

"I'm sure. Nobody's ever called me that before. It's like 1980s or something."

Ballard felt the same way, but that played against Carpenter's estimate, based on what she had seen of her attackers' bodies through the loose tape, that they were in their late twenties or early thirties.

There was still an hour or so of light by the time they pulled to a stop in front of the small bungalow where Carpenter lived on Deep Dell Terrace. Ballard wanted to check the house to see if she could find a point of entry and determine if it would be worth calling for a full forensic examination of the premises. She also wanted to walk the neighborhood in daylight and then return after midnight so she could judge the lighting conditions and vigilance of other residents of the hillside neighborhood.

Once inside, Ballard asked Carpenter to sit on the couch in the living room while she conducted a quick sweep of the house.

"You think they'll come back?" Carpenter asked.

There was the tightness of fear in her voice.

"It's not that," Ballard said quickly. "I want to look for

anything the patrol guys may have overlooked. And I want to figure out how the bad guys got in. You're sure nothing was left open or unlocked?"

"Nothing. I'm OCD about locking the doors. I check them every night, even when I know I haven't gone out through them."

"Okay, just give me a few minutes."

Ballard started moving around the house alone, pulling on a pair of latex gloves from her pocket. There was a door in the kitchen that she assumed led directly to the attached single-car garage. It had a simple push-button lock on the knob and no dead bolt. The door was currently unlocked.

"Does this door in the kitchen go to the garage?" she called out.

"Yes," Carpenter called back. "Why?"

"It's unlocked. Is that the way you had it?"

"I don't think so. But I may have missed it because the trash cans are in the garage and the garage is always locked anyway."

"You mean closed? Or closed and locked?"

"Well, closed and locked. From the outside you can't open it without the remote."

"Is there also an outside door into the garage? Besides the overhead door?"

"No. Just the overhead."

Ballard decided not to open the door to the garage, even with gloves on, until Forensics checked it. It could have been the means of entry. She also had to consider that either McGee or Black had opened the door while checking the house during the initial callout. She could ask them but she knew that neither would admit to such a gaffe. She would only know for sure whether they had opened the door if one of them had left fingerprints on the knob.

Ballard decided she would view the garage last, coming in

from the outside. She moved into a hallway that led to two
bedrooms and a bathroom. She checked the bathroom first and
saw no evidence of intrusion through the small window over
the bathtub.

She moved into the master bedroom, where the assault had
occurred. There she found a window that had been sealed shut
by several coats of paint applied over many years. She looked at
the bed. Carpenter had said she had not known of the intrusion
until she woke up with one of the men on top of her and putting
tape over her eyes and mouth. He then tied her hands to a railing
of the bed's brass headboard. He told her not to move or make a
sound and then she heard him leave the room and open the front
door for his partner.

Ballard got down on her knees and looked under the bed. It
was clear except for a few books. She slid them out and saw that
they were all written by female authors: Alafair Burke, Steph
Cha, Ivy Pochoda. She slid them back under and got up. She
swept her eyes across the room again but nothing stood out to
her. She stepped back into the hallway and checked the second
bedroom. This was neat and spare, obviously a guest room. The
closet door was four inches ajar.

Ballard opened the closet all the way without touching the
knob. Half the space was crowded with stacked cardboard boxes
marked as Native Bean supplies. The other half was empty,
apparently for the use of guests. She got down on her knees
again to study the carpeted floor. She saw nothing on the carpet
but there was a distinct pattern in the weave that was indicative
of recent vacuuming. Still on her knees, she leaned back on her
heels and called for Cindy to come to the room.

She came right away.

"What is it?"

"You said you have no Dustbuster, no vacuum at all, right?"

"No, why?"

"This closet was vacuumed. I think this is where he hid."

Cindy stared down at the carefully manicured carpet.

"We put that in because the previous owner had stored paint cans there and some had spilled on the floor. It looks awful underneath."

"'We'?"

"My husband and I. We bought the place and then after the divorce, I kept it."

"The door—do you leave it open? Like, to keep air circulating in there or something?"

"No, I keep it closed."

"You're sure you closed it after the last time you got stuff out for the coffee shop?"

"I'm sure."

"Okay. Listen, I'm sorry, I know you probably just want to be left alone but I want Forensics to come here and process the closet and maybe the rest of the house."

Carpenter was crestfallen.

"When?" she asked.

"I'll call them right now," Ballard said. "I'll get it done as fast as possible. I know it's an intrusion but we want to get these guys and I don't want to leave any stone unturned. I don't think you do either."

"Okay, I guess. Will you be here?"

"If they can come now, I'll stay. But in a few hours I start another shift. I'll have to go check in at the station."

"Try to get them to come now, please."

"I will. Uh, you mentioned your husband. Is he still in L.A.? What is your relationship with him?"

"He's here and we're fine because we don't see each other. He lives in Venice."

But there was a clear tension underlying the way she said it.

"What's he do?" Ballard asked.

"He's in the tech industry," Carpenter said. "Works for start-ups and stuff. He finds investors."

Ballard stood up. She had to take a step to hold her balance. She realized that sleep deprivation was manifesting.

"You all right?" Carpenter asked.

"I'm fine—not enough sleep," Ballard said. "How was your ex with you getting the house?"

"He was fine. Why? I mean he didn't like it, but…What is this about?"

"I just have to ask a lot of questions, Cindy, that's all. It's not a big deal. Is he the one you were texting?"

"What?"

"When I came into the examination room today, you looked like you were texting or making a call."

"No, I was texting Lacey at the shop, telling her she had to hold things together till I got back."

"You told her what happened?"

"No, I lied. I said I was in an accident."

She gestured to the injuries to her face.

"I have to figure out how to explain this," she said.

This gave Ballard pause because she knew that what Carpenter told people now could come back around to haunt the case if it ever went to trial. As crazy as it seemed, a defense that the sex was consensual might gain support in a juror's mind if there was testimony from the alleged victim's friend that she had never mentioned being assaulted. It was a far-fetched possibility but Ballard knew she would need at some point to school Carpenter on this. But now was not the time.

"So, will you tell your ex about this?" she asked. "About what happened?"

"I don't know, probably not. It's not his business. Anyway, I don't want to think about that right now."

"I understand. I'm going to call Forensics now, see if I can get them out. You're going to have to stay in the living room, if you don't mind. I want them to do your bedroom."

"Can I go get my book to read? It's under the bed."

"Yes, that's fine. Just try not to touch anything else."

Carpenter left the room and Ballard pulled her phone. Before calling for a forensics team, she squatted down and took a photo of the closet carpet, hoping the vacuum pattern would be discernible in the shot. She then called Forensics and got an ETA of one hour.

In the living room Ballard told Carpenter that the forensics tech would be at the house soon. She then asked if there was a remote in the house that opened the overhead garage door. She explained that she didn't want to touch the knob on the door from the kitchen. Even a gloved hand might destroy fingerprint evidence.

"I use the garage for storage and just park out front or in the driveway," Carpenter said. "So I have a clicker in my car that opens it, and there's a button on the wall just inside the garage next to the kitchen door."

"Okay," Ballard said. "Can we go out to the car and use the clicker?"

They stepped out and Carpenter used a remote key to unlock her car. The parking lights blinked but Ballard did not hear a distinctive snap of the locks.

"Was your car locked?" she asked. "I didn't—"

"Yes, I locked it last night," Carpenter said.

"I didn't hear the locks click."

"Well, I always lock it."

Ballard was annoyed with herself for not first checking to see whether the car had been locked. Now she would never know for sure.

"I'm going to enter from the passenger side," she said. "I don't want to touch the driver's door handle. Where is the garage clicker?"

"On the visor," Carpenter said. "On the driver's side."

Ballard opened the door and leaned into the car. She had pulled her own set of keys from her pocket and used the end of her apartment key to depress the button on the garage remote. She then exited the car and watched the garage door open with a loud screeching of its springs.

"Does it always make that sound?" she asked.

"Yeah, I have to get it oiled or something," Carpenter said. "My husband used to take care of things like that."

"Can you hear it from inside when it opens?"

"I could when my ex still lived here."

"Do you think it would wake you up in the bedroom?"

"Yes. It shook the whole house like an earthquake. You think that's how they—"

"I don't know yet, Cindy."

They stood on the threshold of the open garage. Carpenter had been right. There was no room for a car. The single bay was crowded with boxes, bikes, and other property, including three containers for trash, recycling, and yard waste. It looked like Carpenter stored more supplies from Native Bean in the garage as well. There were stacks of cups and snap-on covers in clear plastic sleeves as well as large boxes of various sweeteners. Ballard went to the door leading to the kitchen. She noted the button that operated the garage door on the wall to the left of the doorjamb.

She bent down to look at the keyhole in the knob but could not see any sign that it had been tampered with.

"So, we don't know for sure that this door was locked," she said.

"No, but it is most of the time," Carpenter said. "And like I said, the garage was definitely closed."

Ballard just nodded. She did not tell Carpenter her current theory, that one of the rapists got into the house before she even came home from work and hid in the guest room closet until she had showered and gone to sleep. He then made his move, incapacitated her, taped her mouth and eyes, and let the other rapist in.

A workbench to the right of the kitchen door was crowded with equipment that Ballard guessed had come from the coffee shop. There was an open toolbox with tools haphazardly piled on a top tray. She saw a screwdriver sitting on the bench by itself, as if it had been taken out of the toolbox and left there. She wondered if the rapists brought their own tools to break in or relied on finding something in the garage of a home lived in by a single woman.

"Is this screwdriver yours?" she asked.

Carpenter stepped over to look at it. She reached a hand out to pick it up.

"No, don't touch it," Ballard said.

"Sorry," Carpenter said. "It might be. I can't really tell. All of this stuff, the tools, were left by Reggie."

"Your ex."

"Yes. Do you think they used it to get in? Then how did they get in the garage?"

There was a shrill note in her voice.

"I don't know the answer to either question," Ballard said. "Let's see what Forensics finds."

Ballard checked her phone and said Forensics was now due in forty-five minutes. While she was looking at her screen, a call came in. It was Harry Bosch.

"I need to take this," she said to Cindy. "Why don't you go back to the living room for now."

Ballard headed out of the garage to the street and answered the phone. But then she turned quickly to stop Carpenter from touching the knob of the kitchen door.

"Cindy, no," she called. "I'm sorry, can you come out this way and go in through the front door?"

Carpenter did as instructed and Ballard returned to the call.

"Harry, hi."

"Renée, sounds like you're in the middle of something. I was just checking in. You get anything out of the chrono that helps?"

It took Ballard a moment to remember what case and what chrono he was talking about.

"Uh, no," she said. "I got sidetracked, called out on a case."

"Another murder?"

"No, serial rapists we've been looking for."

"Plural? MOSA?"

"Yeah, weird," she said. "It's a tag team. Last night we got a third victim but she didn't call it in till after I'd been by your place."

There was a silence.

"Harry, you there?"

"Yeah, I was just thinking. A tag team. That's pretty rare. MOSAs are usually gang rapes. Not two guys with the same psychopathy."

"Yeah. So, I've been running with that all afternoon. We're calling them the Midnight Men."

"When you get two guys like that…you know, who think the same way…"

He went silent.

"Yeah, what about it?" Ballard asked.

"It's just that one and one doesn't make two, you know?" Bosch said. "They feed off each other. One and one makes three...they escalate, get more violent. Eventually the rape is not enough. They kill. You have to get them now, Renée."

"I know. Don't you think I know that?"

"I'm sorry. I know you're on top of it. Anyway, I've got a book here somewhere that you should read."

"What book?"

"It's about the Hillside Strangler case way back. Bob Grogan—he was a legend in RHD. But on that one, it turned out it was two stranglers, not one. Grogan caught them and there's a book about it. I have it here somewhere. It's called *Two of a Kind*."

"Well, if you find it, let me know. I could come up and get it. Maybe it will help me understand these two creeps."

"So then, if you're going to be running with the rape case, how about I do a little work on the other thing? The shooting last night."

"I have a feeling that it's going to be taken off my plate. We now have three connected rape cases. They'll keep me on this and kick the homicide to West Bureau."

"Well, until then I could be working. I'd need to see what you've got, though."

Ballard paused for a moment to think. Bringing in an outsider on a live case—even if it was someone with the experience of Harry Bosch—could put her into the shit. Especially after Bosch had worked with the defense lawyer Mickey Haller the year before on a highly publicized murder. No one in command staff would approve of that. No one in the whole department would.

It would have to be extracurricular.

"What do you think?" Bosch prompted.

"I think, if you find that book, we might be able to trade," Ballard said. "But this is dangerous—department-wise—for me."

"I know. Think about it. If I see you, I see you."

11

While waiting for Forensics to show up, Ballard took a walk around the neighborhood and started thinking in terms of what made this assault different from the first two. She had no doubt that it was the same perpetrators. There were too many similarities. But there were also things about this latest occurrence that were unique.

Ballard started listing these in her head as she walked. The primary difference was geographic location. The first two cases occurred down in the flats in gridded neighborhoods that afforded the rapists multiple escape routes should something go wrong. Not so with Deep Dell Terrace. It was a road that led to a dead end. It was also a winding, narrow mountain road in a neighborhood that ultimately had only two or three ways up and back down. There was no route in this neighborhood that led over the mountains. This was an important distinction. It was riskier to pick a victim in this neighborhood. If things had gone wrong for the rapists and a help call had gone out, the escape routes could easily have been covered by a police response. At the same time that she mentally marked this difference in pattern she also acknowledged that patterns evolved. The success of the first two rapes could have emboldened the rapists, leading them to new, riskier hunting grounds.

The second aspect that was notably different from the first two cases was topography. Ballard, as well as Lisa Moore, had been operating according to the theory that the assaults were carefully planned. Once a victim was targeted, the rapists watched her routines and prepped for the break-in and assault. This most likely meant walking into the neighborhood from outside. Each of the prior victims lived a few blocks from main east-west thoroughfares—Melrose Avenue in the first case and Sunset Boulevard in the second. It was theorized that the rapists walked in and then stealthily moved about, casing the victim, her home, and the routines of the area. Therefore, a gridded, flat neighborhood allowed better access to the prey and escape after the crime. But as Ballard walked down Deep Dell Terrace, it was immediately clear that this sort of prep and exit strategy would be difficult here, if not impossible. Access to the back of Cindy Carpenter's house was severely restricted by the steep mountainside. The houses backing it on the next street up the hill were cantilevered out over an almost sheer rock facing. There was no moving between and behind houses here. These homes didn't even need fences and gates; the natural topography provided security.

All of this told Ballard that they had been looking in the wrong direction. They had been looking for a pair of wanderers, voyeurs, who came into the neighborhood off a busy commercial street, moved between and behind houses, and discovered their prey while looking through windows, possibly to strike then or to come back later. This was backed up when interviews of the victims and the limited cross-matching of their habits and movements in the prior days found no nexus that linked the two women. They moved in different circles with no overlap.

By all indications, the third case changed all that. The third case indicated that the victim had been targeted as prey somewhere else and followed to her home. This changed things about the investigation and Ballard silently scolded herself for time wasted looking the other way.

Ballard got an email alert on her phone and opened the app to see that Officer Black had sent her a copy of the incident report. She opened it and scanned through the two pages on her small screen. Nothing stood out in the details as new information. She was closing down the app when she was startled by a silent vehicle whooshing by her. She turned and recognized it as one of the BMW electrics that were used by the forensics teams.

The department had bought a fleet of them for use by detectives, but the sixty-mile range per battery charge limited their usefulness when detectives needed to go farther while riding the momentum of a case. The advertised range also dropped considerably in freeway driving, and it was a rare thing to conduct an investigation in L.A. without driving on a freeway. Stories of detectives being marooned with dead batteries abounded, and the cars were withdrawn and parked on the roof of a city garage for more than a year before being distributed again, this time to units like Forensics and Audio/Visual, which conducted single-destination trips to crime scenes and then back to the mother ship.

Ballard started walking back toward Cindy Carpenter's house and met the forensics tech as he was getting out of the BMW. He popped the rear hatch.

"Ballard, Hollywood Division," she said. "I called."

"I'm Reno," the man said. "Sorry if I scared you back there. These things are so quiet. I've had people literally walk in front of me without looking."

"Well, maybe if you slowed down some, that wouldn't happen."

"Do you know the speed on these things? You barely touch the pedal and you're at forty. Anyway, what do you need here?"

He closed the rear hatch and stood ready, holding the handle of a large equipment case in one hand, its weight tilting his shoulders. He was a slightly built man in dark blue coveralls. SID was stitched in white letters over a breast pocket.

"We had a hot prowl rape with two suspects last night," Ballard said. "I cannot find point of entry but I think it was the garage. I want you to start in there. There's a screwdriver on a workbench—maybe we get lucky with that. After that, there's a closet in the guest room I want you to take a look at."

"Okay," Reno said. "Victim in the hospital?"

"No, she refused further medical. She's inside."

"Oh."

"She knows you're coming and I'll stay with you. But I want you to do the car, too."

She pointed to the Toyota parked on the street behind Reno's car.

"Was it in the garage?" Reno asked.

"No, but she left the remote in the car, and I'm thinking they got in the car, then got in the garage, then got in the house. Just a knob lock on the door into the kitchen."

"Wasn't the car locked?"

"Not sure. Possibly. The remote's on the visor."

"Got it."

"Be quick, okay? She's had a very bad day."

"Sounds like it. I'll be quick."

"And I'll go get the key to open the car."

While Reno was organizing his equipment, Ballard stepped back into the house and asked Cindy for her car key. She explained why and Cindy seemed to take it as another level of violation—her house, her body, and now even her car had been invaded by these evil men. She started crying.

Ballard recognized that Cindy was moving into a very fragile state. She asked if there was a friend or family member she could call to see if they could stay with her. Carpenter said no.

"I saw on the incident report that you listed your ex-husband as closest relative," Ballard said. "Would he come?"

"Oh my god, no," Carpenter exclaimed. "And please don't call him. I only put him down because I couldn't think straight. And he's the only one in L.A. My entire family is down in La Jolla."

"Okay, I'm sorry I asked. It's just that you seem kind of fragile."

"Wouldn't you be?"

Ballard realized she had walked right into that one.

"I'm sorry," she said. "That was stupid. What about Lacey from the shop?"

"You don't seem to understand. I don't want people to know about this. Why do you think I thought about it for so long before calling you people? I'm fine, okay? Just do what you have to do and then leave me alone."

There was no comeback to that. Ballard excused herself and took the key out to Reno. He was already using silver powder on the driver's-side door handle, looking for fingerprints.

"Anything?" she asked.

"Just smears," Reno said.

"Like it was wiped?"

"Maybe, maybe not."

That was useless. Ballard put the car key on the roof of the car.

"I'm going to knock on a few doors. I should be back before you're finished. If not, have coms call me. I don't have a rover."

"And she knows I'm coming in?"

"Yes, but knock first."

"Got it."

"Her name is Cindy."

"Got that too."

Ballard stuck with the houses on the east side of Carpenter's house, her thinking being that there was a better chance of the residents on that side seeing something unusual, because the west side led to the dead end. Anyone leaving Carpenter's house by foot or car would have to go east.

Canvassing a neighborhood after a rape was a delicate thing. The last thing a victim needed was for everyone on the street to know what had happened. Some victims steadfastly refused to be stigmatized but others ended up feeling ashamed and losing confidence after such an attack. On the other hand, if there was a danger in the neighborhood, residents needed to know about it.

In addition, Ballard was handcuffed by the law. Under California statutes, victims of sexual assault are granted full confidentiality unless they choose to waive that right. Ballard had not even broached the subject with Cindy Carpenter and was for the moment bound by law not to reveal her as a rape victim to anyone outside of law enforcement.

Ballard pulled her mask all the way up and was holding her badge up when the door of the house next door to Carpenter's was opened by a woman in her sixties showing one of the signs of being locked down for nine months. She had a thick band of gray at the base of her brunette hair, marking the last time she had been to a salon for a dye job.

"LAPD, ma'am. I'm Detective Ballard and I'm sorry to bother you, but I'm talking to all the neighbors in the area. We had a crime on this street last night after midnight and I am just asking if you saw or heard anything at all unusual during the night."

"What kind of crime?"

"It was a break-in."

"Oh my gosh, which house?"

Her asking which house instead of whose house indicated to Ballard that this woman might not know her neighbors personally. That wouldn't matter if she had heard or seen some-thing. But it did mean she might not start a gossip line with neighbors after Ballard left. This was good. Ballard didn't want neighbors already knowing she was coming when she knocked on their doors.

"Next door," Ballard said. "Did you hear or notice anything unusual last night?"

"No," the woman said. "Not that I remember. Was anyone hurt?"

"Ma'am, I can't really discuss the details with you. I'm sure you understand. Do you live alone here?"

"No, it's my husband and I. Our kids are grown. Was it the girl next door? The one who lives alone?"

She pointed in the direction of Cindy Carpenter's house. But calling her "the girl" instead of using her name was another indication that this woman did not know her neighbors well, if at all.

"Is your husband home?" Ballard asked, ignoring the ques-tions. "Could I speak to him?"

"No, he went golfing," the woman said. "At Wilshire Country Club. He'll be home soon."

Ballard pulled a business card and gave it to the woman, in-structing her to have her husband call if he remembered hearing or seeing anything unusual the previous night. She then took the woman's name for her records.

"Are we safe?" the woman asked.

"I don't think they'll be back," Ballard said.

"They? It was more than one?"

"We think it was two men."

"Oh my gosh."

"Did you happen to see two men on the street last night?"

"No, I didn't see anything. But now I'm scared."

"I think you're safe, ma'am. Like I said, we don't expect them to come back."

"Was she raped?"

"Ma'am, I can't talk about the case."

"Oh my god, she was raped."

"Ma'am, listen to me. I said it was a break-in. If you start spreading rumors, you are going to cause a lot of pain for your next-door neighbor. Do you want that?"

"Of course not."

"Good. Then please don't. Tell your husband to call me if he heard or saw anything unusual last night."

"I'll call him right now. He should be driving home."

"Thank you for your time."

Ballard walked back to the street and went to the next house. And so it went. In the next hour she knocked on seven more doors and had conversations with residents at five of them. Nobody had any useful information. Two of the homes had a Ring camera on their door but a review of video from the night before provided nothing useful.

Ballard got back to Cindy Carpenter's house just as Reno was packing the back of his electric ride.

"So, what'd you get?" Ballard asked.

"A big fat nothing," Reno said. "These guys were good."

"Shit."

"Sorry."

"What about the screwdriver in the garage?"

"Wiped clean. Which means you were probably right. They used it to pop the door, then wiped it. Thing is, that garage door is loud. The springs creak, the motor grinds. If they got in that way, how come it didn't wake her up?"

Ballard was about to explain to Reno that she thought at least one of the intruders was already in the house when Carpenter got home from work. But she suddenly realized the fallacy of that theory. If they opened the garage with the remote from the car, then the car had to have been back at the house, meaning Carpenter was home from work. This changed her thinking on what connected the three victims.

"Good question," Ballard said.

She wanted to get rid of him so she could work these new thoughts.

"Thanks for coming out, Reno," she said. "I'm going to go back in."

"Anytime," Reno said.

Ballard went back up to the front door, knocked, and then entered. Carpenter was sitting on the couch.

"He's leaving and I'll get out of your hair as well," Ballard said. "Are you sure there's no one I can call for you?"

"I'm sure," Carpenter said. "I'll be fine. I'm getting a second wind now."

Ballard wasn't sure what a 'second wind' could be considering the trauma that had occurred. Carpenter seemed to read her.

"I'm thinking about my father," she said. "I don't remember who said it but he always quoted some philosopher when I would skin my knee or have something bad happen. He'd say, if it doesn't kill you, it makes you stronger. Something like that. And that's what I'm feeling now. I'm alive, I survived, I'll get stronger."

Ballard didn't respond for a moment. She took out another business card and put it down on a small table near the door.

"Good," she said. "There are my numbers if you need me or think of anything else."

"Okay," Carpenter said.

"We're going to get these guys. I'm sure of it."

"I hope so."

"Can you do something for me and then maybe we talk tomorrow?"

"I guess."

"I'm going to send you a questionnaire. It's called a Lambkin survey. It's basically questions about your recent history of movements and interactions—both in person and on social media. There is a calendar to track your whereabouts that you will be asked to fill out as best as you can. I think it goes back sixty days but what you really want to focus on are the last two to three weeks. Every place that you can remember. These guys saw you at some point and some place. Maybe it was the coffee shop but maybe it was somewhere else."

"God, I hope it wasn't the shop. That's awful."

"I'm not saying it was. But we have to consider everything. Do you have a printer here?"

"Yes. It's in a closet."

"Well, if you could print out the survey and fill it in by hand, that would be best."

"Why is it called a lamb-whatever-you-said?"

"It's the name of the guy who put it together. He was the LAPD's sex crime expert until he retired. It's been updated with the social media aspects. Okay?"

"Send it to me."

"As soon as I can. And I can come by tomorrow and go over it with you if you want. Or just pick it up once you're finished."

"I have to open tomorrow and probably will be there all day. But I'll take it with me and fill it out when I can."

"Are you sure you want to go in tomorrow?"

"Yes. It will help take my mind off things."

"Okay. And I'm going to be in the neighborhood a little while longer. Just so you know, my car will be out front."

"Are you telling the neighbors what happened to me?"

"No, I'm not. Actually, under California law I can't anyway. I'm just saying there was a break-in in the neighborhood. That's it."

"They'll probably know. They'll figure it out."

"Maybe not. But we want to catch these monsters, Cindy. I have to do my job, and maybe one of your neighbors saw something that can help."

"I know, I know. Did anybody tell you they saw something?"

"So far, no. But I still have this end of the street to go."

She pointed west.

"Good luck," Carpenter said.

Ballard thanked her and left. She walked to the house next door. An old man answered, who proved to be no help, even revealing that he took out his hearing aids at night to sleep better. Ballard then crossed the street and talked to another man, who said he saw nothing but provided a helpful piece of information when asked what he heard.

"You being directly across from the garage across the street, do you ever hear when that goes up or down?" Ballard asked.

"All the F-ing time," the man said. "I wish she'd oil those springs. They squawk like a parrot every time the door goes up."

"And do you remember whether you heard it last night?"

"Yeah, I heard it."

"Do you remember what time, by any chance?"

"Uh, not exactly, but it was sort of late."

"Were you in bed?"

"No, not yet. But about to hit the sack. I never watch any of that New Year's stuff. It's not my thing. I just go to bed and it's one year and then I wake up and it's the next. That's how I do it."

"So, before midnight. Do you remember what you were doing or watching on TV? I'm trying to narrow in on a time."

"Hold on, I got it for you."

He pulled a cell phone out of his pocket and opened up the text app. He started scrolling through messages.

"I got an ex-wife in Phoenix," he said. "We couldn't live together but now we're friends because we don't. Funny how that works. Anyway, she watches the ball drop in New York so she can go to bed early. So I texted her happy new year on New York time. That was when I heard the garage."

He held the phone's screen out to Ballard.

"There you go."

Ballard leaned in to look. She saw a "Happy New Year" text sent to someone named Gladys that went out at 8:55 the night before.

"And this is the same time you heard the garage?"

"Yep."

"Did you hear it open and close, or just open?"

"Open and close. Not as loud going down as it is going up, but I hear it."

Ballard asked the neighbor his name for her records and thanked him. She didn't tell him that he had just helped her drop a piece of the puzzle into place. She was sure that he had heard the Midnight Men entering Cindy Carpenter's house. Cindy had worked till 9 p.m. and didn't park in the garage anyway.

Ballard could think of no other explanation. One of the rapists had entered the garage, used the screwdriver to easily open the kitchen door, and then waited in the guest room closet for Cindy to come home.

But adding a piece of the puzzle pushed another one out. If Cindy Carpenter was still at work and her car was with her, then how did the Midnight Men open the garage?

12

Harry Bosch's house was in a neighborhood just across the freeway from the Dell. She called him once she started heading his way.

"I'm nearby," she said. "Did you find that book?"

"I did," he said. "You're coming now?"

"I'll be there in five. I need to borrow your Wi-Fi too."

"Okay."

She hung up. She knew that she should be going to Hollywood Division to sit in on the roll call for the start of her watch, but she wanted to keep moving. She instead called the watch office to see which sergeant would be handling roll call and then asked to speak to him. It was Rodney Spellman.

"Whaddaya got, Ballard?" he said by way of a greeting.

"We had a third hit by the Midnight Men last night," she said. "Up in the Dell."

"Heard about it."

"I'm out running with it and won't make roll call. But can you bring it up and ask about last night? Especially, the fifteen and thirty-one cars? I want to know if they saw anything, jammed anybody, anything at all."

"I can do that, yes."

"Thanks, Sarge, I'll check back later."

"That's a roger."

She disconnected. She crossed the 101 on the Pilgrimage Bridge and soon was on Woodrow Wilson, heading up to Bosch's place. Before she got there, she got a call from Lisa Moore.

"What's happening, sister Ballard?" she asked.

Ballard guessed she was already hitting the wine, and her salutation rang false and annoying. Still, Ballard needed to talk to somebody about her findings.

"I'm still working it," Ballard said. "But I think we need to rethink this. The third case is different from the first two and we might be looking the wrong way."

"Whoa," Moore said. "I was hoping to hear I'm okay to stay up here till Sunday."

Ballard's patience with Moore ran out.

"Jesus, Lisa, do you even care about this?" she said. "I mean, these two guys are out there and—"

"Of course I care," Moore shot back. "It's my job. But right now it's fucking up my life. Fine, I'm coming back. I'll be in tomorrow at nine. I'll meet you at the station."

Ballard immediately felt bad about her outburst. She was now sitting in the car outside Bosch's house.

"No, don't bother," she said. "I'll cover it tomorrow."

"You sure?" Moore said.

She said it a little too quickly and hopefully for Ballard.

"Yes, whatever," Ballard said. "But you're taking my shift, no questions asked, next time I need it."

"Deal."

"Let me ask you something. How did you do the cross-referencing of the first two victims? Interview, or did you have them fill out a Lambkin survey?"

"That thing's eight pages long now with the updates. I wasn't going to ask them to do that. I interviewed them and so did Ronin."

Ronin Clarke was a detective with the Sexual Assault Unit. He and Moore weren't partners in the traditional sense. They each carried their own caseload but backed each other up when needed.

"I think we should give them the survey," Ballard said. "Things are different now. I think we had the victim acquisition wrong."

There was silence from Moore. Ballard took this as disagreement, but Moore probably felt she could not voice an objection after having split town, leaving Ballard working the new case solo.

"Anyway, I'll handle it," Ballard said. "And I should go now. Got a lot to do and I have my shift tonight."

"I'll check in tomorrow," Moore said helpfully. "And thank you so much, Renée. I will pay you back. You name the day, I'll take your shift."

Ballard disconnected and put on her mask. She got out with her briefcase. Bosch's front door opened before she got to it.

"Saw you sitting out there," Bosch said.

He stood back against the door so she could enter.

"I was just being a fool," Ballard said.

"About what?" Bosch asked.

"My partner on the rapes. Allowing her to run off for the weekend with her boyfriend while I'm working two cases. I'm being stupid."

"Where'd she go?"

"Santa Barbara."

"Are places open up there?"

"I don't think they plan on leaving the room much."

"Oh. Well, like I said, I'm here and I can help. Wherever you need me."

"I know. I appreciate it, Harry. It's just the principle of it. She's totally burned out. No empathy left. She should ask for a transfer from sex crimes."

Bosch gestured toward the table in the dining room, where he already had his laptop open. They sat down facing each other. There was no music playing. Also on the table was a hardcover book with yellowed pages. It was *Two of a Kind,* by Darcy O'Brien.

"It does hollow you out, sex crimes," Bosch said. "What's happening since we talked?"

"It's going upside down," Ballard said. "Like I told you, three cases definitely linked, but this third one—it's different from the first two. It changes things."

Ballard put her briefcase on the floor next to her chair and slid out her laptop.

"You want to run it by me, since your partner is gone?" Bosch asked.

"What, are you like my favorite uncle that I never had?" Ballard asked. "Are you going to give me a dollar bill for candy when I leave?"

"Uh…"

"I'm sorry, Harry. I don't mean—I'm just out of sorts with Lisa. I'm mad at myself for letting her skate like that."

"That's okay. I get it."

"Can I still use your Wi-Fi?"

She opened her laptop and Bosch walked her through connecting to the Internet. His password to the Wi-Fi account was his old badge number, 2997. Ballard pulled up a blank copy of the Lambkin survey and sent it to Cindy Carpenter, getting her email off the report Black had sent her. She hoped Carpenter wouldn't ignore it.

"You know what will teach your partner a lesson?" Bosch said. "Bagging these assholes before she gets back."

"That's highly unlikely. These guys…they're good. And they just changed the game."

"Tell me how."

Ballard spent the next twenty minutes updating Bosch on the case, all the while thinking she should be updating Lisa Moore in such detail. When she was finished, Bosch had the same conclusion and opinion as Ballard. The investigation needed to shift. They had been wrong about the Midnight Men and how they acquired their victims. It was not the neighborhood that was chosen first. It was the victims. They were picked and then followed to their neighborhoods and homes. All three women had crossed the perpetrators' radar somewhere else.

Ballard now had to find that crossing point.

"I just sent the latest victim a Lambkin questionnaire," Ballard said. "I hope to get it back tomorrow or Sunday. I have to talk the first two victims into doing it, because Lisa thought it was too much to ask of them at the time. The first rape was back at Thanksgiving and I doubt the victim will have as good a memory now as she would've if she'd been asked to do it in the first place."

"Now I'm getting annoyed with this Lisa," Bosch said. "That was lazy. Are you going to send it to the other two now?"

"No, I want to call and talk to them first. I'll do that after I leave here. Did you know Lambkin when he was in the department?"

"Yeah, we worked some cases. He knew what he was doing when it came to assaults like this."

"Is he still in town?"

"No, I heard he retired out of state and has never come back. Somewhere up north."

"Well, we still use the cross-referencing survey with his name on it. I guess that's some kind of legacy. You want what I've got on Javier Raffa?"

"If you're willing to share."

"You have a printer?"

"Down here."

Bosch reached down to one of the bottom shelves of the bookcase behind his chair. He brought up a boxlike printer that looked like it might have been put into service in the previous century.

"You've got to be kidding," Ballard said.

"What—this?" Bosch responded. "I don't do a lot of printing. But it works."

"Yeah, probably five pages a minute. Luckily I don't have much to share. Give me the connector thing and plug it in. You have paper?"

"Yes, I have paper."

He handed her the connector to her laptop. While he plugged the printer in and loaded paper, she pulled up the case file on her screen and started sending the documents she had put together on her last shift into the print queue. She wasn't wrong. The printer was slow.

"See, I told you it works," Bosch said. "Why do I need a fancy-ass printer?"

He seemed proud of his techno-stubbornness.

"Maybe because I'd like to get to work sometime tonight," Ballard said. "I still haven't even looked at the stuff from your case."

Bosch ignored her and took the first two pages—the only two pages so far—out of the printer's tray. Ballard had sent him the two-page incident report first, followed by the Investigative Chronology, witness statements, and the crime scene map. She wasn't sure what he could do with it all but the chrono was most important because it contained step-by-step summaries of the moves Ballard had made through the night. Though she didn't hold out any hope of being able to keep the case much longer, she knew that if Bosch could come up with a line of investigation that led from the Raffa case back to his old case, the killing of Albert Lee, then she might have something to bargain with when the powers that be came to take Raffa from her.

She waited patiently for the pages to print but she was feeling anxious about not getting to the station and showing her face, let alone tackling the work that was waiting for her on the Midnight Men cases.

"You want something to drink? I could brew some coffee," Bosch said. "This could take a while."

"Will the coffee be faster than this printer?" Ballard asked.

"Probably."

"Sure. I could use some caffeine."

Bosch got up from the table and went into the kitchen. Ballard stared at the decrepit printer and shook her head.

"After you came by here this morning, you didn't get any sleep, did you?" Bosch called from the kitchen.

The printer was not only old, it was loud.

"Nope," Ballard called back.

"Then I'll use the heavy-duty stuff," Bosch said.

Ballard got up and went to the slider leading to the deck.

"Can I go on the deck?"

"Sure."

She opened the door and stepped out. She removed her mask so she could breathe freely. At the railing she saw sparse traffic down on the 101, and it was clear that the multilevel parking garage at Universal City was empty. The amusement park was closed due to the pandemic.

She heard the printer stop. Putting her mask back on, she went inside again. After making sure everything had printed, she disconnected her laptop and shut it down. She stood up and was about to tell Bosch never mind the coffee, when he came out of the kitchen with a steaming cup for her.

"Black, right?" he asked.

"Thanks," Ballard said, accepting the cup.

She pulled her mask down and turned away from Bosch to sip the hot liquid. It was scorching and strong. She imagined she could already feel the caffeine coursing through her body while it was still going down.

"That's good," she said. "Thanks."

"It'll keep you going," Bosch said.

Ballard's phone started to buzz. She unclipped it and checked the screen. It was a 323 number but no name came up.

"I think I should take this," she said.

"Sure," Bosch said.

She connected.

"This is Detective Ballard."

"Detective, it's Cindy Carpenter. I got the survey thing you sent and I'll work on it. But I just remembered something."

Ballard knew that often a crime victim had details of the event emerge hours and sometimes days after the experience. This was a natural part of processing the trauma, even though in court defense lawyers often had a field day accusing victims of conveniently manufacturing memories to fit the evidence against the defendant.

"What did you remember?" Ballard asked.

"I must've blocked this out at first," Carpenter said. "But I think they took my picture."

"Which picture are we talking about?"

"No, I mean a photo. They took my photo...you know, when they were raping me."

"Why do you think this, Cindy?"

"Because when, you know, they were making me do oral, one of them grabbed my hair and tilted my head back for a few seconds and sort of held it. It was like he was posing me. Like some kind of a sick selfie."

Ballard shook her head, though Carpenter could not see this. She felt it was likely that Carpenter had accurately guessed what the rapists were doing. She thought maybe this was the reason behind the masking of the victims as well as the ski masks. They didn't want the victims to know the attacks were photographed or possibly recorded. This opened a new set of questions as to why the rapists were doing this but it still advanced Ballard's thinking on their MO.

And it renewed her resolve to catch these two men, no matter what help she got or did not get from Lisa Moore.

"Are you there, Renée?" Carpenter said. "Can I call you Renée?"

"Sorry, I'm here—and yes, please call me Renée," Ballard said. "I was just writing that down. I think you're right and it's a good detail to know. It helps us a lot. We find that photo on their phone or computer, then they go away. It's ironclad evidence, Cindy."

"Well, then good, I guess."

"I know it's another painful thing but I'm glad you remembered it. I'll be writing up a crime summary that I'll want you to review and I'll put it in."

"Okay."

"Now, on the survey I just sent you. There's a section where it asks you to make a list of anybody you know who might want to hurt you for whatever reason. That's very important, Cindy.

Think hard about that. Both people you know and people you don't really know. An angry customer at the coffee shop, someone who thinks you offended them in some way. That list is important."

"You mean, I should do that first?"

"Not necessarily. But I want you to be thinking about it. There is something vindictive about this. With the photo and the cutting of your hair. All of that."

"Okay."

"Good. Then I'll talk to you tomorrow to see how you're doing with your homework."

Carpenter was silent and Ballard felt that her attempt to inject humor with the homework angle had fallen flat. There was no humor to be found in this situation.

"Uh, anyway, I know you have to work early tomorrow," Ballard continued clumsily. "But see what you can get done and I'll check in with you in the afternoon."

"Okay, Renée," Carpenter said.

"Good," Ballard said. "And Cindy? You can call me anytime you want. Goodbye now."

Ballard disconnected and looked at Bosch.

"That was the victim. She thinks they took a photo during the oral cop."

Bosch's eyes went off her as he registered this and filed it in his knowledge of the evil things men do.

"That changes things some," he said.

"Yes," Ballard said. "It does."

13

After dropping her briefcase off at a desk in the detective squad room, Ballard headed to the watch office to make an appearance and see if there was anything working in the division that might call for a detective. The watch lieutenant was a lifer named Dante Rivera who was closing in on his golden ticket. Thirty-three years in meant a maximum pension of 90 percent of his final salary. Rivera was just five months out, and there was a countdown calendar on the wall of the watch office. He tore off a page every day, not only to keep the count but to remove the profane comments written on the date by a dayside wiseass.

Rivera had spent most of his years working various assignments at Hollywood Division. He was considered an old-timer by department standards, but as he had joined early, he was still not even close to sixty years old. He'd take his 90 percent, supplement it with a part-time security job or a PI ticket and do nicely the rest of his days. But his years on the job had also wrapped him in a tight cocoon of inertia. He wanted each midnight shift to go by as smooth as glass. He wanted no waves, no complications, and no issues.

"L-T," Ballard said. "What do we have happening tonight in the big bad city?"

"Nada," Rivera said. "All quiet on the western front."

Rivera always used that phrase, as if Hollywood were at the edge of the city. Perhaps at night that was valid, as the wealthy neighborhoods out west usually grew quiet and safe. Hollywood was the western front. Most nights, Ballard hated hearing him say all was quiet, because she was looking for a case or something to join in on. But not this night. She had work to do.

"I'll be in the D-bureau and on my rover," she said. "I have follow-ups on last night's capers. Have you seen Spellman around?"

"Sergeant Spellman?" Rivera asked. "He's next door."

Ballard noted the correction as she left the watch office, and walked into the central hallway. She went down to the next office, which was informally called the sergeant's office because it was a spot where the supervisors could separate themselves from the troops to make calls, write reports, or decide whether to write up officers for breaking procedure. Spellman was alone in the room and sitting at a long counter, looking at a video on his laptop. He immediately closed the laptop when Ballard walked in.

"Ballard, what's up?"

"I don't know. Came in to ask you what's going on and to see if anything came up in roll call about my case up in the Dell."

It looked like he had been watching body cam footage of an approach to a parked car. That was part of his job, so his quickly closing the laptop made Ballard think that what was on camera was one of the two Fs: use of force or people fucking—both of which could happen on any traffic or stationary car stop.

"Oh, yeah, forgot to get back to you," Spellman said. "Things got hectic in roll call because we had Vice come in for an intel session, and then I had to get people out on the streets. But I grabbed Vitello and Smallwood at the kit room before they went out. They had nothing remarkable last night. Plus they got pulled out of their zone on a couple backups."

"Okay," Ballard said. "Thanks for asking."

She turned and headed out of the room. It was small and stuffy and smelled like whatever cologne Spellman was wearing.

Ballard took the long way back to the D-bureau so she would not have to walk through the watch office again. She figured out of sight meant out of mind with Rivera. Back at the desk she had borrowed, she got out a notebook, opened her laptop, and called up her files on the Midnight Men cases. She found the cell number for the first victim, Roberta Klein, and called it. She checked the clock on the wall over the TV screens as she waited for an answer. She wrote 9:05 p.m. on a page in the notebook so she would have it when she updated the chrono. Roberta Klein picked up on the sixth ring.

"Hi, Bobbi, it's Detective Ballard at Hollywood Division."

"Did you catch them?"

"No, not yet, but we're working the case—even on the holiday. I'm sorry to call so late."

"It scared me. I thought, 'Who's calling me now?'"

"I'm sorry. How are you doing?"

"Not good. I don't hear from you people. I don't know what's going on. I'm scared. I keep thinking they might come back, because the LAPD can't catch them."

Once more Ballard found herself annoyed with Lisa Moore. Sex assault cases required a lot of hand-holding of victims. They needed to be kept informed, because the more they knew what the police were doing, the safer they felt. The safer they felt, the more likely they were to cooperate. In a rape case, cooperating could mean staring down your attacker in a lineup or in court. That took guts and it took support. Here was just another situation where Lisa had dropped the ball. This was her case. Ballard was only the nightside detective—she wasn't lead. Until now, apparently.

"Well, I promise we're on this case full-time, and that's why I'm calling," Ballard said.

"I left my job," Klein said.

"What do you mean?"

"I quit. I don't want to leave my house until they're caught. I'm too scared."

"Have you seen any of the therapists we told you about?"

"I hate Zooming. I stopped. It's so impersonal."

"Well, I think you should maybe reconsider that, Bobbi. It could help you get through this time. I know it's diff—"

"If you didn't catch them, why are you calling me?"

It was clear that Klein wasn't interested in hearing how a therapist on a computer screen could help her through the dark hours.

"Bobbi, I'm going to level with you because I know you are a strong individual," Ballard said. "We need to refocus the investigation and we need your help with it."

"How?" Klein asked. "Why?"

"Because we were looking at this case from a neighborhood angle. We thought that these men chose the neighborhood first and then looked for a victim in it—because there was easy and quick access in and out."

"And that's not what happened?"

"Well, we think maybe it was victim-specific targeting."

"What does that mean?"

Her voice became a bit shrill as she began to understand.

"They may have crossed paths with you in a different way, Bobbi. And we need to—"

"You mean they picked me specifically?"

There was a sharp scream, reminding Ballard of times when she had inadvertently stepped on her dog's paw.

"Bobbi, listen to me," Ballard said quickly. "There is nothing to be afraid of. We really don't think they will come back. They have moved on, Bobbi."

"What does that mean?" Klein asked. "Is there another victim? Is that what you're saying?"

Ballard realized that the whole conversation had gotten away from her. She had to steer it back on course or end it and move to the next victim, using everything she had learned from mishandling this call on the next one.

"Bobbi, I need you to calm down so I can talk to you and tell you what's going on," Ballard said. "Can you do that for me?"

There was a long silence before the woman on the other end responded.

"Okay," she said in an even tone. "I'm calm. Tell me what the fuck is going on."

"There was another victim, Bobbi," Ballard said. "It happened early this morning. I can't tell you the details but it has changed our thinking on this. And that's why I need your help."

"What do you want me to do?"

"First of all, I need you to tell me if you ever go to the Native Bean coffee shop in Los Feliz."

There was a pause while Klein considered the question.

"No," Klein said. "I've never been there."

"It's on Hillhurst," Ballard said. "Are you sure?"

"I'm sure. Is that—"

"Do you know anyone who works there?"

"No, I never even go over that way."

"Thank you, Bobbi. Now I want—"

"Was someone there attacked?"

"I can't really discuss that with you, Bobbi. Just as you have protections against being identified, so do other victims. Now, I have your email. I'm going to send you a document. It's a questionnaire about your life and your movements and it will help us figure out where you might have initially crossed paths with these men."

"Oh my God, oh my God."

"There is nothing to panic about, Bobbi. It will—"

"Nothing to panic about? Are you kidding me? Those men could easily come back here and hurt me again. Any fucking time."

"Bobbi, that is not going to happen. It's very unlikely. But I'll go to the watch office as soon as we're finished here and ask the lieutenant to increase patrols on your street. I'll make sure they do it. Okay?"

"Whatever. That's not going to stop them."

"Which brings us to the survey I want you to fill out. This *will* help us stop them. Can you take some time tonight and tomorrow and do it for me? You can email it back to me or if you want to print it out and work on it, I'll come by and get it as soon you're finished. Just call me."

"What about Detective Moore? Where is she?"

Good question, Ballard thought.

"We're working this together," she said. "I'm handling the survey."

Ballard proceeded to give the same instructions she'd given earlier to Cindy Carpenter. Being given a task that would distract her from her fears at least temporarily seemed to calm Klein and she finally agreed to fill out the questionnaire. Ballard, in turn, promised to come by to pick it up and to do a security survey of the house. By the time the call ended, Bobbi Klein was talking calmly and seemed ready to go to work.

Ballard was wrung out after the call, and she was feeling exhaustion creeping into her muscles. She decided to put off phoning the second victim. She got up and went to the station break room, where she brewed a cup of coffee on the Keurig machine. It was not as good as Bosch's blend nor as strong. She then went to the watch office and asked Rivera to have the car assigned to the RA encompassing Bobbi Klein's neighborhood do a few extra drive-bys on her street. Rivera said that he would.

When Ballard got back to the desk, she decided to follow through on an idea that had been gestating since she had received Cindy Carpenter's call about her rapists possibly taking a photo of her.

She went on the desk computer, signed in, and pulled up the original crime report and victim addendum. She found the listing for Reggie Carpenter, Cindy's ex-husband, and ran his name through the DMV database. There were several hits, but only one of them carried an address in Venice, where Cindy had said her ex lived. She then ran the name and birth date through the crime database and learned that Reginald Carpenter had both a DUI arrest and an assault on his record from seven years earlier. He got probation for both and had apparently kept a clean record ever since.

Ballard called the number on the victim information sheet that Cindy had provided for her ex-husband. When it was answered, Ballard heard multiple voices—men and women—in the background before one said hello.

"Mr. Carpenter, this is Detective Ballard with the LAPD. Am I catching you at a bad time?"

"Wait— Shut the fuck up! Hello? Who is this?"

"I said, this is Detective Ballard with the LAPD. Do you have a few minutes?"

"Uh, well, what's this about?"

Ballard decided to use a play to see if it would elicit information.

"I'm investigating a crime in your neighborhood—a break-in."

"Really? When?"

"Last night. Shortly after midnight—which I guess would

technically make it today. I'm calling to see if you were home at that time and whether you happened to see any suspicious activity on your street."

"Uh, no. I wasn't here. I didn't get home till pretty late."

"Were you nearby? Maybe you saw something from wherever—"

"No, I wasn't nearby. I was in Palm Springs for New Year's and just got back a couple hours ago. Which place got hit?"

"One-fifteen Deep Dell Terrace. We do think that the perpetrators watched the place before choosing when to—"

"Let me stop you right there. I don't live on Deep Dell anymore. Your information is bad."

"Really. My mistake. So, you have not been in that neighborhood?"

"No, my ex-wife lives there, so I make it a practice to stay away."

There was laughter in the background. It emboldened Carpenter.

"What did you say your name was?"

"Ballard. Detective Ballard."

"Well, I can't help you, Detective Ballard. What happens there is really not my concern anymore."

He said it in an officious way that drew more laughter from the people he was with. Ballard maintained a flat tone, thanked him for his time, and disconnected. She was unsure why she had even made the call. She was riffing off something she had picked up in Cindy Carpenter's voice when she spoke of her ex-husband. It had been a note of apprehension, maybe even fear.

Back on the computer, Ballard opened the county courts system's database and went through the portal to the family courts division. She looked up the Carpenter's divorce, but as she expected, the records were sealed, other than the front page of the original petition to dissolve the marriage. This was not unusual. Ballard knew that most divorce cases were sealed because the parties usually hurled negative accusations at each other, and public dissemination of these could damage reputations, especially without offers of proof.

Ballard was able to glean two facts from the limited information. One was that the divorce action had been initiated by Cindy, and the other was the name, address, and phone number of her attorney. Ballard googled the attorney's name—Evelyn Edwards—which led her to a website for a law firm called Edwards & Edwards specializing in family law. According to the website, the law firm offered its services twenty-four hours a day, seven days a week. Ballard pulled up the bio on Edwards and saw a smiling photo of an African-American woman in her late thirties. Ballard decided to test the firm's claim of being there for you 24/7.

She called the number from the divorce filing and reached a robot answering service that asked her to leave a message and assured her that Ms. Edwards would call back as soon as possible. Ballard left a message.

"My name is Renée Ballard, I'm a detective with the LAPD and I need Evelyn Edwards to call me back tonight. I am investigating a violent crime involving one of her clients. Please call me back."

Ballard disconnected the call and sat unmoving for a long moment, half expecting Edwards to call back immediately. Yet she knew that was unlikely. She started thinking about next moves and the need to start a cross-referencing file into which she would put the data she would receive from the three victims of the Midnight Men.

She opened a new file folder on her laptop, but before she could even name it, her phone buzzed. It was Evelyn Edwards.

"Sorry to interrupt your Friday night."

"Detective, I must say, that was not the kind of message one would like to receive on any night. Which of my clients has been victimized?"

"Cindy Carpenter. You handled her divorce two years ago."

"Yes, she's my client. What happened?"

"She was the victim of a home invasion. Because we have an open investigation, I'm not going to go into details. I hope you understand that."

There was a moment during which Edwards read between the lines.

"Is Cynthia okay?" she asked.

"She's safe and doing better," Ballard said.

"Was it Reginald?"

"Why would you ask that?"

"Because I don't understand why you would call me if this didn't have anything to do with her divorce and her ex-husband."

"I can tell you that her ex-husband is not a suspect at this time. But any thorough investigation includes looking at all possibilities, so that's what we're doing. I looked up the divorce records and saw that they were sealed. This is what brings me to call you."

"Yes, the records are sealed for a good reason. I would be in violation of a court order as well as my obligations to attorney-client privilege and confidentiality if I were to discuss such matters with you."

"I thought maybe there was a work-around on that, that you could tell me about the relationship without breaking the seal, so to speak."

"Did you not ask Cynthia?"

"I did and she was reluctant to talk about it today. I didn't want to press it. She's had a difficult day."

"What are you not telling me, Detective?"

It was always the lawyer who wanted to ask questions instead of answer them. Ballard ignored this.

"Can you tell me this…" Ballard said. "Who asked the judge to seal the records?"

There was a long pause while Edwards apparently reviewed the rules of law to determine if she could answer.

"I can tell you that I asked that the judge seal the record," she finally said. "And that request would have been in open court."

Ballard got the hint.

"You know I am not going to be able to find a transcript of that hearing on a Friday night," Ballard said. "Maybe not even on Monday. Would it break the rules for you to summarize why you asked the judge in open court to seal the record?"

"Without first consulting my client, I will only tell you this," Edwards said. "The cause of action in the divorce contained allegations of things Mr. Carpenter did to my client to humiliate her. Terrible things. She didn't want those allegations contained in any public record. The judge agreed, the file was sealed—and that's all I can tell you."

"Reggie's a bad guy, isn't he?"

It was a shot in the dark. Ballard thought maybe she'd get a response, but Edwards didn't bite.

"What else can I do for you, Detective Ballard?" she asked instead.

"I appreciate your time, Ms. Edwards. Thank you for calling me back."

"Not at all. I hope you get whoever it was who committed this crime."

"I intend to."

Ballard disconnected. She leaned back in her chair to consider what she had learned from Edwards and the call to Reginald

Carpenter. She had just pulled on a string without much reason other than her gut feeling about the way Cindy Carpenter talked about her ex. But this case was about two serial rapists who had attacked three different women. That this would connect to Reginald Carpenter, whether he was an abusive husband or not, seemed far-fetched. Plus, he claimed he had been in Palm Springs. She doubted he would have mentioned that to a detective if it could not be backed up.

Still, the information gleaned from the two calls stuck with Ballard and she decided that at some point she needed to talk to Cindy Carpenter about her ex, despite it obviously being a subject she wanted left alone. She decided in the meantime to go back to the new focus of the case: finding the nexus that connected the three known victims.

She called the second victim, Angela Ashburn, and talked her into filling out the questionnaire that would be emailed to her. Ashburn did not exhibit the same fear and upset that Bobbi Klein had. Though expressing reluctance to reopen thoughts about the assault, she ultimately agreed to work on the Lambkin survey the next day, since she would be off from work. Ballard thanked her and said she would check in with her Saturday afternoon.

Ballard went back to work on her laptop, setting up a file in which she would collate the information that would come in from the victims. She had just begun the task when she heard her call sign come up on the rover she had placed on the desk. She could tell it was Lieutenant Rivera by the slight accent in his voice.

"Go for six-William-twenty-six."

She waited thirty seconds for Rivera to come back up on the radio.

"Code six, Adam-fifteen, Cahuenga and Odin."

This meant patrol officers needed help with an investigation and were requesting a detective. It didn't indicate what the investigation or crime was about. Ballard was often called to a scene where she did not know the details ahead of time. Nine out of ten times a detective was actually not needed and the call was an attempt by patrol officers to lay off some of their responsibilities and work on her. In this case she knew the Adam-15 car was Vitello and Smallwood, and she expected this to be one of those times. But she responded in the affirmative to Rivera without asking for additional information.

"Roger, six-William-twenty-six."

She closed her laptop, put it in her briefcase, and grabbed the rover. Then she went down the back hallway to the station house door.

14

Coming out of the station's parking lot, Ballard went east one block, passing the fire station, and took a left onto Cahuenga. It was a straight shot up to the Cahuenga Pass, where she saw the blue flashers up ahead at the intersection with Odin. She pulled in behind the patrol car, which was behind a dark coupe. Vitello and Smallwood stood between the two cars with a man who had his wrists cuffed behind his back.

Ballard got out with her rover in hand.

"Fellas," she said. "What's up?"

Smallwood signaled her to follow him to the front of the coupe so they could talk out of earshot of the man in cuffs.

"Hey, Mallard, we got one of the dirtbags you're looking for," Smallwood said.

Ballard ignored the play on her name from the officer whose own name provided so much more comedy in the division.

"What dirtbags?" Ballard asked.

"You know, the tag team," Smallwood said. "The rapists that hit last night. This guy's one of them."

Ballard looked over Smallwood's shoulder at the man in handcuffs. He stood with his head down in shame.

"And how do you know that?" she asked. "Why'd you stop him?"

"We stopped him on a deuce," Smallwood said. "But check out the floor of the back seat. We didn't search in case you need a warrant or something. We didn't want to fuck anything up, you know?"

"Let me see your light. Did you talk to this guy at all?"

"Not at all. Didn't want to fuck up."

"Yeah, you said that."

Smallwood gave her his flashlight and she walked down the side of the coupe and pointed the beam through the windows into the car. She scanned the front seats and center console before moving to the back. In the footwell on the passenger side she saw an open cardboard box, and in it she could see rolls of duct tape and blue tape and a box cutter. She felt the beginning of an adrenaline rush.

She stepped behind the car and put the light on the man in handcuffs, blinding him and forcing him to turn away. He had dark, curly hair, was mid-thirties, and had acne scars on his cheeks.

"Sir, where were you coming from when the officers stopped you?"

"I was up on Mulholland."

"You were drinking?"

"I had a couple beers after I finished my work. When I was parked at the overlook."

Ballard picked up what sounded like a slight English accent. None of the victims of the Midnight Men had reported that either of the rapists had an accent. Still, she knew it could be a ploy.

"Where were you going just now when you got stopped?"

"Um, just home."

"Where's that?"

Vitello handed her a driver's license. She put the light on it and read it as the man gave the matching address. He was Mitchell

Carr, thirty-four years old and living on Commonwealth in Los Feliz. Ballard realized he could be her neighbor. She handed the license back to Vitello.

"You run him?" she asked.

"He's clean except for motor vehicle violations," Vitello said.

"I only had two beers," Carr added helpfully.

Ballard looked at him. She noticed something clipped to his belt and put the light on it. It was a retractable tape measure. The adrenaline buzz started to ebb. This didn't feel right.

"Where are you from?" she asked. "Originally."

"New South Wales," Carr said. "A long time ago."

Vitello leaned toward her confidentially.

"Australia," he whispered.

Ballard raised her hand and gestured him back without touching him.

"What do you do for a living, sir?" she asked.

"Interior design work," Carr said.

"You're a designer?"

"Well, no, I work for an interior designer."

"Doing what?"

"Delivering and installing furniture, hanging pictures, taking measurements, that sort of thing."

Ballard looked at Smallwood, who had joined them between the cars. She handed him back his flashlight and turned back to Carr.

"What's with the box cutter and the tape in your car?" she asked.

"I was taping out furniture dimensions in a house," Carr said. "So the owner could see where everything was going to go. How it would fit."

"This was up on Mulholland?"

"Actually, it was on a street up there called Outpost. Right by Mulholland."

"Do you carry a hand vacuum on your job?"

"What do you mean?"

"Like a battery-operated vacuum—a Dustbuster type of thing."

"Oh. No, not really. I supervise furniture installations and those guys usually do the cleanup after."

"Do you mind if we look in your trunk, Mr. Carr?"

"Go ahead. What do you think I did?"

Ballard ignored the question and nodded to Smallwood. He went to the open driver's door, took a few seconds to locate the trunk release, and finally popped it open. Ballard stepped over to look, Vitello following.

"Stay with him," Ballard instructed.

"Right," Vitello said.

Ballard checked the trunk. There were more open boxes containing equipment for Carr's stated profession—rolls of tape, more box cutters, small cans of paint and industrial cleaners. No hand vacuum, coveralls, ski masks, or premade eye masks.

"Thank you, Mr. Carr," she said.

Ballard turned to Smallwood and Vitello.

"And thank you two for wasting my time."

She pushed past them and started back toward her car, bringing the rover up to her mouth and radioing the com center that she was clearing the scene. Smallwood followed her.

"Mallard," he said. "Are you sure?"

Returning to her car, Ballard said nothing. As she opened the door, she stared back at Smallwood, who was still waiting for a response.

"Did you check the height on his DL?" she asked.

"Uh, no," Smallwood said.

"Five eleven. We're looking for guys about five six, five eight max."

She got in the car, checked her side mirror, and then pulled out, leaving Smallwood standing there.

Since she was already out and about, she decided to follow through with her plan to drive up into the Dell to check things out in the dark hours. She slowly cruised down the street, passing Cindy Carpenter's house. The living room lights were on behind drawn curtains. Ballard also saw down the side of the house a light in what would be the guest bedroom. She thought Cindy had probably moved to that room to sleep, leaving behind the room where she had been attacked. She wondered if Cindy would sleep with the lights on from now on.

Deciding to walk up and down the street, she drove down to the cul-de-sac and pulled to the curb. The chill of the night might reinvigorate her and she would see all the shadows and dark places.

The first thing she noted as she walked was that, while the street seemed quiet, the background sound from the nearby 101 freeway was noticeable. Earlier she had been on Harry Bosch's back deck that overlooked the same freeway from the other side, but the traffic noise had not been as intrusive as it was up here. She also imagined that the neighborhood would hear the faint sounds of the Hollywood Bowl, which was positioned directly across the freeway. That was probably a good sound to hear, and would have been missed for almost a year now with the pandemic closure.

The streetlights were positioned too far apart to provide continuous lighting on the street. There were pockets of darkness, and the Carpenter house was in one of these, shaded deeper because the nearest streetlight — at the east end of the property — was out. Ballard pulled out the small light she always carried in the pocket of her Van Heusen jacket and put it up toward the opaque glass globe at the top of the post. It was an antique streetlamp, the kind favored by the residents of the wealthy hillside neighborhoods, where they were more concerned with design and aesthetics than the need for light as a deterrent to crime. Many of the neighborhoods in the hills and wealthy communities were still lit by the dim glow of these lamps. In L.A., decisions about style, intensity, and number of streetlights were left to neighborhood homeowner groups to decide. Consequently, there were dozens of different designs all through the city and most homeowner associations fought any effort to modernize the streetlamps.

The fogged glass top of the light appeared to be intact. Ballard could not determine whether it had been damaged or tampered with. She tracked her flashlight beam down the precast stone post to the base, where there was a steel plate through which the light's internal wiring could be accessed. She was about to stoop down to look for signs of tampering on the plate, when she was startled by a man's voice from behind her.

"That's an acorn."

Ballard whipped around and put her light into the eyes of an old man carrying a small dog in both arms. The dog looked like a Chihuahua and appeared just as old and decrepit as its owner. The man tried to raise a hand to block the light but could not reach high enough without possibly dropping his dog. Ballard lowered the light and pulled her mask up over her mouth and nose.

"I'm sorry," she said. "You startled me."

"Oh, I didn't mean to," the man said. "I see you're admiring our acorn."

"You mean the light?"

"Yes, we call them acorns because of the shape of the globe, you see. We are very protective of them."

"Well, this one isn't doing too well."

"It's been reported to the BSL. I called personally."

"You live on this street?"

"Oh, yes. More than fifty years. I even knew Peter the Hermit back in the day."

Ballard had no idea whom or what he was referencing.

"I'm a police officer," she said. "A detective. Do you walk this street often at night?"

"Every night. Frederic here has gotten too old to walk, so I carry him. I know he likes it."

"When did you report that this...acorn...was out?"

"Yesterday morning. I wanted it fixed before the holiday but they didn't get it done. But I told them, you people screwed it up, get back out here and fix it. I didn't want it put to the back of the line. I know how the BSL works."

"And what is the BSL? And who screwed what up?"

"The Bureau of Street Lighting. But I say it means Bull Shit Lies. They're supposed to preserve but they don't care about history. Or beauty. They want the whole city to look the same. The ugly orange glow from their big steel poles. Sodium vapor. That's why they're out here sabotaging us, if you ask me."

At that moment, Ballard became very interested in the old man.

"What is your name, sir?"

"Jack. Jack Kersey. Chairman of the street-lighting committee, Hollywood Dell Association."

"When did you notice that this one was out?"

"Wednesday night on our walk—day before yesterday."

"And you think it was sabotaged?"

"I know it was. I saw them up here with their van. How many BSL guys does it take to unscrew a streetlight? I guess the answer's two. They were here and then that night it never came on."

Ballard had been pointing her light at the ground. She now pointed the beam back at the access plate at the base of the streetlight.

"They were working on it here?" she asked.

"That's right," Kersey said. "By the time I grabbed Frederic and got up here, they were turning around to leave. I waved at them but they just drove on by me."

"Did you get a look at either one of them?"

"Not really. The guy driving was white. He had red hair, I remember that."

"What about the other guy?"

He shook his head.

"I was just looking at the driver, I guess."

"Tell me about their van. What color was it?"

"It was white. Just a van."

"Were there markings on it—like Bureau of Street Lighting or a city seal or anything?"

"Uh…yeah, I saw it. BSL—right on the door when they blew by me."

"You mean you saw the letters—*BSL*?"

"Yeah, right on the door."

"And could you tell what kind of van it was?"

"Not really. One of their work vans."

"For example, did it have a flat front like the old-style vans with the engines between the front seats? Or more like a sloping front—like the newer vans have?"

"Yes, sloping front. It looked new."

"What about windows? Did it have windows running down the sides, or was it what they call a panel van?"

"Panel. You really know your vans, Detective."

"It's come up before."

She didn't bother mentioning that she had owned several

vans in her life when she was carrying multiple surfboards around.

Ballard put her light on the plate at the bottom of the post again. She could see that two screws held it in place. She had a basic set of tools in her kit bag in the car.

"Mr. Kersey, where do you live?" she asked.

"Just down at the end," he said. "At the intersection."

He gave a specific address and pointed four houses down to the residence at the next streetlight. Ballard realized it was one of the houses where no one had answered her knock earlier in the day.

"Were you out earlier today?" she asked. "I knocked on your door."

"I was at the store, yes," he said. "Otherwise, I was home. Why'd you knock? What's this about?"

"There was a break-in on the street last night. I'm investigating. The light might have been put out by the perpetrators."

"Oh, my. Whose home?"

Ballard pointed to the Carpenter house.

"That one."

"And things had just started to settle down there, too."

"What do you mean by that?"

"Well, there was a guy living there. He was loud, always yelling, throwing stuff around. A hothead is what I'd call him. Then I think she kicked him out, and things got quiet again. Peaceful."

Ballard nodded. She was realizing how lucky she was that Kersey had taken his dog out while she was on the street. His information was important.

"You didn't happen to notice anything unusual in the neighborhood last night, did you?" she asked.

"Last night...I don't think so," Kersey said.

"Nothing at all after eight or so?"

"Nothing comes to mind. Sorry, Detective."

"It's all right, Mr. Kersey. I'm going to go get some tools out of my car, which I parked at the cul-de-sac. I need to open that plate up. I'll be right back."

"I probably should be putting Frederic to bed. He gets tired, you know."

Ballard asked him for his phone number in case she wanted to follow up with any questions or show him photos of vans.

"Thank you, Mr. Kersey," she said. "Have a good night."

"You too, Detective," Kersey said. "Good night and stay safe."

He turned and headed back down the street, murmuring words of comfort to the dog in his arms.

Ballard walked up the street to her car, got in, and drove it down to where the darkened streetlight was. She popped the trunk and opened the plastic mini tool set she kept in the kit bag. After pulling on gloves, she returned to the streetlight with a screwdriver and quickly removed the access plate. The screws were tight but turned easily. It was not what she expected for something that was essentially an antique. She noticed a faded manufacturer tag on the plate that said Pacific Union Metal Division.

Once she had removed the plate, she pointed the beam into the opening and saw a tangle of wires hanging from a metal conduit that she assumed ran up the post to the light assembly. One of the wires had been cut, its copper center still shining brightly in the flashlight beam. The copper was not degraded or oxidized at all, indicating that it had been freshly cut.

Ballard had no doubt. The Midnight Men had cut the wire and killed the light on Wednesday before coming back Thursday night to break into Cindy Carpenter's house to rape her. They had been as unlucky with Jack Kersey as she had been lucky.

He had seen them and he knew something about streetlights. His basic description of the van driver having red hair matched Cindy's description of one of her attackers.

She now felt bad about giving Smallwood and Vitello shit for calling her out on the traffic stop. If they had not done that, she might not have cruised the neighborhood at the right time and run into Jack Kersey. Things felt as though they had aligned for her somehow, and now she was a step closer to the Midnight Men.

She screwed the access plate back into place and then headed back to her car. She wanted to drive south and check the streetlights outside the homes of the first two victims.

15

The streetlights were all now burning brightly on the streets where the first two Midnight Men attacks had occurred. Ballard did, however, get a direct example of the eclectic nature of the city's street-lighting program. The two streets carried different styles of globes and posts, including ornate iron posts and double-globed lights on one street and simple acorns on the other. Ballard was annoyed at herself that she was a detective who worked the midnight shift but had never noticed the difference in streetlights from neighborhood to neighborhood. It served as a reminder to always be observant, to look for the details that made a difference.

She was pulled to the side of the road, looking up an address for the Bureau of Street Lighting, when she got another callout for the night detective. She needed to respond to a death scene under the Gower Street overpass. She noted the address of the nearest BSL office — there were actually many — and started the drive to Gower. She knew she was headed to one of the most crowded, ugliest homeless communities in Hollywood. During the pandemic it had grown from a few tents to a full community of tents, lean-tos, and other ragtag structures — some built with amazing ingenuity — belonging to a homeless community that numbered at least one hundred people. In the past ten months

Ballard had twice been called out to death scenes in Gower Grim, as the homeless zone had been termed by officers in the division. One of these deaths had been attributed to Covid-19, the other to an opioid overdose.

She came up from Hollywood Boulevard, the terrain gently rising toward Beachwood Canyon, the hillside community east of the Dell. She could see the flashers from two patrol cars, which told her a patrol sergeant was on the scene. She parked behind one of the patrol cars and saw the huddle of two P2s and Sergeant Spellman outside a small cubicle with sides made from shipping pallets. On the concrete wall that supported the freeway overpass someone had spray-painted the slogan "No Mask, No Vax, No Problem."

Ballard pulled up her mask, got out, and joined the group of fellow officers.

"Ballard," Spellman said. "Need you to sign off on this one. It's another OD. Looks like fentanyl."

Ballard was there to determine whether to call out the homicide team or write this one off as an accidental death, or "death by misadventure"—the phrase the Medical Examiner's Office liked to use. Her decision would determine whether the whole machinery of homicide investigation would be cranked up, with detectives and forensic units being called out in the middle of the night.

The P2s were La Castro and Vernon, both young men fresh off their probation year and newly assigned to Hollywood from the quiet Devonshire Division in the Valley. They had not yet experienced the open and hostile environment that would return to Hollywood once the pandemic was over.

Ballard snapped on gloves and pulled out her mini-light.

"Let's take a look," she said.

A piece of blue plastic tarp used as a door had been flipped up over the top of the makeshift shack. There was not enough room for anyone other than Ballard to enter. The space was smaller than a cell at the old county jail. There was a dirty mattress on the ground and on it the body of a fully dressed man with unkempt hair and a straggly beard. Ballard estimated that he was in his twenties even though he looked like he was in his thirties, his body aged by drug use and living on the streets. He was on his back, his eyes open in rictus and cast upward. There was no roof. Twenty-five feet above them was the steel underside of the freeway. It rumbled every time a car crossed it, and even at midnight the traffic up there was constant.

Ballard squatted and moved the light in closer to the body. The lips were bluish purple, the mouth slightly open. She could see dried, yellowish vomit on the lips, in the beard, and on the mattress next to the dead man's right ear. She moved the light down the body and noted that the fingers of both hands were curled tightly toward the palms.

A truck rumbled heavily by overhead, causing the pallets to shudder. Ballard moved the light about and saw that the dead man had insulated his home with collapsed cardboard boxes nailed to the pallets. She saw that one box had contained a flat-screen television, the depiction of which was positioned so the man could look at it from his dirty mattress.

There was debris on and around the mattress. Overturned boxes, a dirty backpack pulled inside out, an empty mayonnaise jar that might have contained coins collected at street corners. Whatever else had been there was gone now. The fellow residents of Gower Grim had been sure to pick through the dead man's belongings before alerting the police.

It was difficult with the homeless to determine death by overdose on-site. There were no empty or half-filled pill bottles left behind to help the investigator. The addicted in the homeless camps couldn't afford the luxury of surplus supply, or if they did, it was long gone by the time police were on scene. But more often than not, the threadbare existence determined that the pill that killed them was the last pill they could afford. This man's cause of death would certainly be determined by autopsy and toxicity testing, but she had to make the call now as to whether to crank up the machine. It wasn't a decision taken lightly. The safe thing to do would be always to call out Homicide. But that would often mean crying wolf. That would start a rumble in the ranks that would result in distrust of Ballard. In more than four years on the late shift, she had called out Homicide several times, but she had never been wrong.

She stood up and moved back out to the street. She saw the white coroner's van with the blue stripe down the side pulling in.

"Well?" Spellman asked.

"Purple Haze," Ballard said.

"What's that supposed to mean?"

"Jimi Hendrix asphyxiated on his own vomit after taking too many pills. So did this guy. Did anybody get an ID?"

Spellman started laughing.

"That's good, Ballard," he said. "I gotta remember that."

Ballard immediately regretted using the phrase. It was callous and now this callous patrol sergeant would use it again. It would get passed on and add another layer of callousness to the department.

"ID?" she prompted, to get things back on course.

"No, no ID found," said La Castro. "We asked around—people here just knew him as Jimmy."

"Holy shit!" Spellman said. "Purple Haze is right."

He turned away to jerk his mask down so he could laugh unbound. Ballard saw several of the homeless people watching from the openings in their tents and lean-tos. Ballard felt all their hollow eyes on her as the originator of the joke that had made the sergeant laugh.

Ballard remained at the scene for the next half hour while the coroner's investigator conducted the same overview as she had and came to the same conclusion. The death would not be ruled a homicide. While she waited, she used her rover to call for the unit that carried a mobile thumb reader. If the dead man had ever given a thumbprint while obtaining a California driver's license or being booked into a jail or prison, his identity would come up. The readers were expensive and not distributed to every patrol car or detective.

When the reader arrived, Ballard took it into the dead man's shack and placed his right thumb on the screen. It came back negative. No hits. The man was not in the system. This was unusual—almost unheard of—for a homeless drug user. Ballard took another read off his thumb and again the result was negative. This meant the coroner's office would have to do a deeper dive to identify the man and notify next of kin. If that failed, his body would be kept in refrigeration for a year and then burned, his ashes buried under a number in Evergreen Cemetery in East L.A.

After the body was loaded into the blue-striped van, Ballard drove back to the station to get her paperwork done before end of watch. She first updated the chrono on the Midnight Men investigation, then wrote up the reports on the death of the unidentified man. She learned from the coroner's investigator at the scene that he would be identified in records as John Doe 21-3 until his true identity was determined. Ballard realized that meant that only twenty-four hours or so into the new year, there were already three unidentified bodies in the Big Crypt at the coroner's office. That so many were anonymous and uncounted in this city carried through even in death.

When finished, she printed out her reports and left copies in the mailbox for the detective lieutenant. He would not see them until Monday, when he was scheduled to come back into work. She also emailed the updated chrono to Lisa Moore. This was not necessary but she wanted the sex crimes investigator to see how far she had moved the investigation forward without her help.

The paperwork took Ballard to the end of her shift at six. But she needed to kill another hour because she wanted to swing by Native Bean when it opened at seven. She spent the time checking email and surfing the Web, first putting "Peter the Hermit" into the search engine. She discovered that he had been a legendary denizen of the Dell. He had lived on Ivar Avenue and had long white hair and a beard, which got him work in movies with biblical themes in the 1920s and '30s. He was also credited with being one of the first to work the character impersonator trade on Hollywood Boulevard, posing in his biblical robes for tourists in exchange for tips. He was a mainstay in the Dell into the 1960s, when he passed.

She then found herself going to the Wags and Walks website to check out the latest offering of dogs up for rescue. Ballard was still mourning the loss of her dog Lola, who had succumbed to bone cancer eight months earlier. With increasing frequency she found herself checking out rescue sites, looking at photos and thinking about bringing a dog home. Lola had been a pit bull mix and her look had intimidated more than a few people on Venice Beach. Ballard never had to worry about her belongings when she took her paddleboard out and left Lola at her tent.

But now that she was living in the new apartment, there was a weight limit on acceptable animals and Ballard was looking more for companionship than protection.

She scrolled through the photos and read some of the accompanying stories—all from the dog's point of view. She finally came to Pinto, a Chihuahua mix with golden eyes and a sincere look. He had caught Ballard's eye two weeks ago when he first showed up on the carousel of photos of dogs needing homes. He was still there at the shelter and still available.

Ballard looked up at the clock on the wall. It was time to go catch Cindy Carpenter as she opened the coffee shop for business. She looked back at Pinto. He was brown and white and had a longer snout than a pure-bred Chihuahua—like Frederic, the dog Jack Kersey carried. She clicked on a button under his photo and an email form came up. She typed, "I want to meet Pinto." She hesitated, but only for a second or two, and then added her cell number and clicked the send button.

She was dead tired when she crossed the station parking lot to her Defender. But she was hopeful about Pinto.

She counted the hours since she had slept and it came to almost a solid day. She wanted to take her board out to the Sunset break and let the Pacific restore her, but she knew sleep was imperative. She would go by Native Bean, check on Cindy, then get to her apartment to sleep until at least noon. She drove out of the station lot and up to Sunset. She took a right and it was a straight shot to Hillhurst.

Ballard arrived at Native Bean at seven and saw four people already in line at the window. She parked across the street, pulled up her mask, and got out.

When it was Ballard's turn, she was not waited on by Cindy. Ballard ordered a decaf black and could see Cindy in the background, making the drinks. She called out to her and waved.

"You got a minute?"

"Uh, not right— Let me get these orders out. There's a table on the side."

Because Ballard had not ordered a fancy coffee concoction, she received her cup right away. She took it around the side of the building, where there were four tables spaced properly along the sidewalk of the cross street. She sat at the table next to the side door of the shop and waited. She didn't want the coffee she had just bought, even though it was decaf. She wanted to be able to sleep.

Carpenter came out with her own cup of coffee after about five minutes.

"Sorry, we got busy."

She sat across the table from Ballard. The bruises on her face were spreading and had turned a deep purple. The lacerations were just starting to scab over.

"No problem," Ballard said. "I didn't tell you I was coming. I just wanted to check on you and see how you're doing."

"I'm all right," Carpenter said. "I guess. Considering."

"Yeah, you've been through something nobody should have to experience."

"Is there any news? Did you—"

"No, not really. I mean, no arrests. When we get them, I will let you know right away, day or night."

"Thanks, I guess."

"Did you have time to work on the questionnaire?"

"Yes, but I'm not finished. It's a lot. I brought it with me and I'll work on it after the morning rush."

As if on cue, the screen door of the shop opened and the woman who had taken Ballard's order at the window leaned out.

"We have orders," she said.

"Okay," Carpenter said. "I'll be in."

The employee let the door bang shut.

"I'm sorry," Carpenter said. "I really need to be in there."

"That's okay," Ballard said. "We can talk later when you finish the questionnaire. I just wanted to ask if anything else came to mind. You know, you remembered about the photo, so I wanted to see if more details had come to you."

Carpenter got up from the table.

"No, not really," she said. "Sorry."

"It's okay, nothing to be sorry about," Ballard said. "But one other thing real quick. One of your neighbors saw a white van on the street before the attack on you. Two men, supposedly working on a streetlight, but the light is definitely out. I was up there. So I think it was them and they were disabling the light to make it darker outside your house."

"That's creepy," Carpenter said. "Are you sure?"

"I'll check with the Bureau of Street Lighting to see if they had somebody up there, but I kind of doubt it. One of the wires in that lamppost was cut. Anyway, I just wanted to ask. You don't know anybody who owns a white van, do you?"

"Uh, no."

"Okay, I'll let you get back to work."

After Carpenter went back inside, Ballard got up and dropped her untouched coffee into a trash can. It was time to go to sleep.

16

The buzz from her cell phone infiltrated her sleep, pulling Ballard out of a dream about water. She pushed the sleep mask up onto her forehead and reached for the phone. She saw that it was Bosch calling and it was exactly noon.

"Harry."

"Shit, you were sleeping. Call me back when you're awake."

"I'm awake, I'm awake. What's going on?"

"I think I found the nexus."

His use of the word *nexus* sent Ballard's thoughts toward the victims of the Midnight Men. That was the case she had been running with until exhaustion drove her down into the deep sleep Bosch had just roused her from. She flipped the comforter over, swung her legs to the edge of the bed, and pulled herself up into a sitting position.

"Wait a minute," she said. "What are you saying? You connected the three women? How did—"

"No, not the women," Bosch said. "The murders. Javier Raffa and Albert Lee."

"Oh, yeah, got it. Sorry. I have to wake up."

"When did you go down?"

"About eight."

"That's not enough time. Go back to sleep, call me later."

"No, I won't be able to sleep now. I'll be thinking about the case. Tell you what, you hungry? I never ate anything yesterday. I could bring something up to the house."

"Uh, yeah. If you're sure."

"I am. What do you want?"

"I don't know. Anything."

"I'm going to take a shower and then I'll leave. Text me what you want from Birds. It's on the way. The menu's online."

"I already know what I want. Quarter chicken with baked beans and coleslaw. And I'll take the regular barbecue sauce."

"Text me anyway so I don't forget."

She disconnected, then sat on the bed for a long moment, wondering if she should have taken Bosch's advice and tried to go back to sleep. She turned and looked back at her pillow. After four years on the night shift, working eight to six four nights a week, she had learned that cheating sleep could have bad consequences.

She pushed herself off the bed and headed to the bathroom.

An hour later she pulled to a stop in front of Bosch's house. She carried her laptop and the bag from Birds. The restaurant was only a few minutes from her condo and had become her go-to place during the pandemic for takeout. They also gave anybody with a badge a discount, not that LAPD officers were supposed to take such perks.

Bosch took the bag from her and put it on the dining room table, where he had cleared space amid his laptop, printer, and paperwork. He started to take out the cartons containing their food.

"I got the same as you," Ballard said. "Should be easy. You okay with me taking the mask off to eat? I have the antibodies. Supposedly."

"Yeah, I'm okay. When did you get it?"

"November."

"How bad?"

"I was down a few weeks but obviously I was luckier than others. You think the new president's going to hurry the vaccine along? I don't know anybody in the department who's gotten it so far."

"Hope so."

"What about you? You're eligible."

"I never leave this place. Might be more dangerous for me to go out to get it."

"You should make an appointment, Harry. Don't turn it into a thing."

"You sound like my daughter."

"Well, your daughter's right. How is Maddie?"

"Good. She's doing well in the academy and has a boy-friend now."

He offered nothing else but Ballard guessed that this meant he didn't see her very often. She felt bad about that.

They both ate out of the sectioned cartons the meals came in. Bosch already had real silverware out and waiting, so they left the plastic stuff in the bag.

"In the old days, they used to give cops a discount," Bosch said. "At Birds."

"They still do," Ballard said. "They like having cops as customers."

She gave him some time to savor his first bite of rotisserie chicken slathered in barbecue sauce. It was the kind of food that made you bring a napkin to your mouth after every bite.

"So, tell me about this nexus you found," she said.

"All I have is the public records that you can get online," Bosch said. "Corporate records filed with the state. You're going to have to go deeper with your access to confirm."

"Okay, and what am I confirming?"

"I think it's like the factoring that happened in the Albert Lee case. Ownership of the body shop, including the property it sits on, was transferred from Javier Raffa three years ago to a corporation owned by Raffa and a partner."

"Who's the partner?"

"A dentist named Dennis Hoyle. Office in Sherman Oaks."

"Another dentist. Dennis the dentist. The dentist in the Albert Lee case was down in the Marina, right?"

"Yeah, John William James."

"Any connection between Hoyle and James?"

"That's the nexus."

Ballard could tell Bosch was proud of whatever it was he had found, and of doing so without even leaving his house. She hoped she would still have that mojo if she was around and working cases at his age.

"Tell me," she said.

"All right, you start with Hoyle and James being dentists," Bosch said. "Completely different practices. James, he's down in the Marina with that crowd: celebrities, singles, actors, whatever. Your guy, Hoyle, he's up in the Valley, different clientele, probably more of a family practice. So it looks like never the twain shall meet, right?"

"I guess. Maybe they knew each other from professional associations. You know, Teeth Pullers of Los Angeles, or something like that."

"Close. These guys—dentists—when they put in a crown or an implant or what have you, most of them don't make that stuff in-house. They make a mold of the patient's tooth and send it out to a dental lab that makes crowns and dentures."

"They sent to the same lab."

"They *owned* the same lab. They were partners—until

somebody whacked James. It's all in state corporate records. If somebody wants to spend the time chasing it through a maze of holding companies, it's right there."

"And you spent the time."

"What else am I going to do?"

"Chase your guy Finbar McShane?"

"Finbar's a white whale. You said so yourself. But this? This is real."

Bosch wiped his hands thoroughly on a clot of napkins and then reached over for a sheaf of documents at the side of the table. Ballard could see the state seal of California on the top sheet.

"So you've been printing," she said. "That must have taken all morning."

"Funny," Bosch said. "These are the incorporation filings behind a joint business venture called Crown Labs Incorporated. It's located in Burbank up by the airport. Four other corporations own it, and these I traced to four dentists: James, Hoyle, and two guys named Jason Abbott and Carlos Esquivel."

"How can James still own it if he's been dead for seven years?"

"His company is called JWJ Ventures. Corporate records show the vice president of that company upon its founding was Jennifer James, who—I'm going to take a wild guess—was his wife. Seven months after he gets murdered, the records are amended and Jennifer James is now president. So he's dead but she has his piece of the lab."

"Okay, so James—when he was alive—knew Hoyle and was in business with him."

"And each had an association with a business where the principal owner/operator is murdered."

"With the same gun."

Bosch nodded.

"With the same gun," he repeated. "Very risky. The shells connect the case more solidly than the corporate records. There's got to be a reason."

"Well, twenty-twos are hard to match," Ballard said. "They mushroom, shatter. It was about the shells. And in the Raffa kill, we got a break. The shell went under a car and wasn't readily retrievable."

"Same with Albert Lee—the shell wasn't quickly retrievable. You get into coincidences now, and I don't buy coincidences like that."

"So, maybe we have other kills where there were no shells left behind and we just got lucky with these two."

They both were silent for a moment as they considered this. Ballard thought, but didn't say, that there had to be another reason the killer kept the gun. It belied the planning and precision of the hits. She knew it was something that would need to be answered in the course of the investigation.

"So...," Ballard said, moving on. "Let's suppose that Hoyle's connection to Javier Raffa came out of a factoring deal. These dentists had to have somebody who set these things up. Somebody who knew about these men—Albert Lee and Javier Raffa—needing money."

"Exactly. The factor man."

"And that's who we've got to find."

"You have to go back to the Raffa family and find out when he hit a financial crunch and who he went to about it."

"Well, I know one thing. He had to buy his way out of the gang. Our intel is that he paid Las Palmas twenty-five grand in cash to walk away."

"Where's a guy like that get that kind of cash—without robbing a bank?"

"He could have refinanced the business or the property."

"What, and tell the bank he needed the money to buy his way out of a street gang? Good luck with that."

Ballard didn't respond as she thought it through.

"What about the other two dentists?" she finally said. "Abbott and Esquivel."

Bosch tapped his stack of printouts.

"I got 'em here," he said. "One of them's got a practice in Glendale, the other's in Westwood."

"That's weird," Ballard said. "I just remembered Raffa's son said the other night that his father's partner was a white guy from Malibu."

"Maybe Hoyle lives out there and commutes in to Sherman Oaks. Malibu puts him closer to James in the Marina. You'll have to run all of them through DMV to get home addresses."

"I will. When did Crown Labs first incorporate?"

"In '04."

"So these guys, they've been around."

"Oh, yeah. James was thirty-nine when he got his ticket punched seven years ago."

Ballard finished off the cup of coleslaw that came with her chicken. She then wiped her mouth with a napkin for the final time and closed the to-go carton.

"There is not much I can do to formally run all the connections down with the state till Monday," she said. "And that's only if I'm still on the case."

"There is that," Bosch said.

"Whether I'm on it then or not, what I feel like doing today is skeeing a few of these places. The lab, Hoyle's house, maybe his office. See how high on the hog he's living. I'll run the other two through DMV and put them on the map. But right now there's no real connection to them. That's why I'm going to go skeeing. I want to see what I'm up against. Then I'll go talk to Raffa's family."

Skeeing was pure LAPD jargon—a less formal word for surveilling. It meant doing a drive-by of a person of interest, taking a measure of him. Its origin was debated: One camp thought it derived from the word *schematic,* meaning getting the physical parameters of a suspect's place of business or residence. Others said it was short for *scheming*—taking the first step in a plan to hit a house of criminal activity. Either way, Ballard did not have to translate for Bosch.

"I'll go with you," he said.

"You sure?" Ballard asked.

"I'm sure," Bosch said. "I'll grab a mask."

17

The skee patrol started at the dental lab near the airport. On San Fernando Road in an industrial zone that backed up to the 5 freeway, it was a large single-level building with a gated parking lot on the side. A small sign identifying the business was on the door along with a logo: a cartoon tooth with eyes and a bright smile.

"It's bigger than I thought it would be," Ballard said.

"The four entities own it but it most likely does work for dentists all over the city," Bosch said.

"You'd think a place like this would make them enough money that they didn't need to be involved in factoring and murder schemes."

"Some people can never have enough money. And then again, maybe we're completely wrong and they are completely legit."

"It's not looking that way."

"You want to try to go in?"

"They're closed. No cars in the lot. Besides, we don't want to give them early warning that we're sniffing around."

"Good point. But drive down to the end, see what we can see."

Ballard drove along the fence line until they could see a third side of the building. There was an emergency exit here by a trash dumpster.

"Okay," Ballard said. "What's next?"

Bosch had brought his printouts and had mapped out the order in which they should conduct the skee. Their next stop was nearby Glendale. They drove by a shopping plaza on Brand Boulevard, where Carlos Esquivel had a family dentistry practice. It was on the second level of the plaza and reachable by an outdoor escalator, which had been turned off for the holiday weekend.

"Looks like a nice practice he's got here," Ballard said.

"Let's drive around behind," Bosch said. "See what the parking situation looks like."

Ballard followed his instruction and found an alley that ran behind the plaza and where there was reserved parking for building employees. They saw Esquivel's name on a placard reserving one spot. Right next to it was a spot reserved for a Dr. Mark Pellegrino.

"Looks like he has a partner," Bosch said.

Next stop was Esquivel's home in the hills above Glendale: a multimillion-dollar contemporary with white walls, hard lines, black window frames, and a gated driveway.

"Not bad," Bosch said.

"He's doing all right," Ballard said. "I guess drillin' teeth is drillin' for gold."

"But can you imagine that life? No one's ever happy to see you."

"You're the guy who's going to stick your fingers and metal instruments in my mouth."

"Sucks."

"Not that different from being a cop. These days, people don't want to see us either."

And so it went. They next traversed the Valley, checking out Dennis Hoyle's office and home. DMV records showed that he had previously lived in Malibu, but his current residence was in the hills off Coldwater Canyon. It was a gated property with a view of the whole San Fernando Valley. Next they dropped down through the Sepulveda Pass to the Westwood location, where Jason Abbott practiced dentistry, and then over to the other side of the freeway in Brentwood, where he lived.

They headed south for the final drive-by—the places the late John William James worked, lived, and died. But before they got there, Ballard took an unexpected turn in Venice. Bosch thought she was making a driving mistake.

"This is not it," he said.

"I know," Ballard said. "I just want to make a little detour. One of my Midnight Men victims—the latest one—has an ex that lives down here. And I thought, since we're on skee patrol, that I'd just take a run by and scope it out."

"No problem. You think he's one of the Midnight Men?"

"No, it's not that. But there's something there. They divorced two years ago but she seems afraid of him. I hit him up last night on a pretext call to see what his reaction would be and he sounded like an asshole. He's in the tech-investment field."

"They're all assholes. What address are we looking for?"

"Number five Spinnaker."

They were on a narrow street a block from the beach. The homes were all modern, multilevel, and expensive. Reginald Carpenter was apparently doing better financially than his ex-wife. They found his home two houses off the beach. It was three levels sitting on top of a three-car garage with just enough space between the very similar houses on either side to store trash cans.

"I hope he has an elevator," Bosch said.

There was a door to the right of the garage with a NO SOLICITING sign on it. Ballard leaned toward her window so she could look up the facade of the home. She could see the tip of a surfboard leaning over the railing of a balcony.

"I wonder if I knew this guy from when I used to stay out here," she said.

Bosch didn't answer. Ballard turned the car around and headed back to Pacific Avenue.

Pacific ran alongside the Ballona Lagoon, which separated Venice from Marina del Rey. They took it to Via Marina and then were cruising by homes valued even higher than those in overpriced Venice. They cruised by the condo complex where James had lived and then went out to Lincoln Boulevard, where his dental practice was located in a shopping plaza that backed up to the vast complex of docks and boats that made up the area's namesake marina. Here, the skeeing paid off. The James family dentistry practice was still in business seven years after his unsolved murder. The name listed on the door was Jennifer James, DDS.

"Well, that explains some things," Ballard said.

"She inherited her husband's partnership and his practice," Bosch said. "Unless maybe it was a joint practice all along."

"I wonder what she knew or knows about the factoring."

"And the murders, including her own husband's."

Bosch pointed to an empty parking space in the corner of the parking lot.

"Right there, that's where he was parked," he said. "The gunman supposedly came over from the Marina, crossed the lot, and shot him right through the window. Two head shots, very clean, very fast."

"I take it no brass was left behind?" Ballard asked.

"None."

"That would've been too easy. And the slugs?"

Bosch shook his head.

"It wasn't my case," he said. "But from what I remember, no go on the slugs. They flattened when they hit bone."

Ballard drove out of the parking lot onto Lincoln Boulevard and headed north toward the 10 freeway.

"So, what else do you know about that investigation?" she asked.

Bosch explained that the John William James murder case was handled by Pacific Division Homicide, where it was determined that there were not enough reasons or evidence to connect it to the Albert Lee killing.

"I tried to get it there," Bosch said. "But they wouldn't listen. A guy named Larkin on the table at Pacific worked it. I think he was a short-timer, had, like, three months till he pulled the pin, and wasn't looking for a big conspiracy case. By then I was two years in on Lee and I could not make the connection that would force the issue. Last thing I heard was that they were calling it robbery. James wore a ten-thousand-dollar Rolex his wife had given him. It was gone."

"His wife who inherited his ownership in the lab as well as his practice," Ballard said. "When did she give it to him?"

"That I don't know. But as far as I do know, the case was never cleared. It would now be a cold case and the murder book would be at the Ahmanson Center."

"You want me to make a U-turn?"

"It all depends on what else you've got going today."

"I have my shift tonight and need to call my victims on the Midnight Men thing. They're all working up surveys for me."

"Another nexus to be found."

"Hopefully. I also want to get to Raffa's wife to ask about his twenty-five-thousand-dollar loan."

Ballard saw an opening and made a U-turn on Lincoln. She headed south toward Westchester, the area of the city near LAX.

"What a treat!" she said. "We get to hit airport traffic from two airports in the same day."

"This traffic is a breeze," Bosch said. "Wait till the pandemic is over and people get out and want to travel. Good luck then."

The Ahmanson Training Center was on Manchester Boulevard and was part of the LAPD network of training facilities for new recruits. The department had long outgrown the academy in the hills surrounding Dodger Stadium and had ancillary facilities here and up in the Valley. The citywide homicide archive was also housed here. It had opened only a few years before, when the glut of unsolved cases—six thousand since 1960—had over-burdened filing space in the department's divisions. The murder books were on shelves in a room as big as a regular neighbor-hood library, and there was an ongoing project to digitize cases so there would always be space for more.

"You have your retiree badge or ID card with you?" Ballard asked. "In case they ask."

"I have my card in my wallet," Bosch said. "Didn't think I'd be badging anybody."

"You probably won't need it. On weekends and holidays they just have a couple recruits on shit duty keeping the place open. They'll probably be too intimidated by the likes of you to ask for ID."

"Then I guess it's good to know I can still bring it."

"Why don't you bring your printouts so we can get the date for the book we want to pull."

After parking, they went up the front steps and into a grand hallway with large LAPD do-gooder photographs lining the walls. In a previous incarnation the center had been the corporate headquarters for an oil company. Ballard imagined the walls had then been lined with do-gooder oil-production photos.

The homicide library was on the first floor at the end of the grand hall. Its double doors were unmarked, the thinking likely being that it was not the best thing to advertise that the city had a whole library of murder books from unsolved cases.

There was a lone cadet behind the counter, sitting in a swivel chair and playing a game on his phone. He went on full alert when Ballard and Bosch entered, probably his only visitors of the day. He was the same kid who had been on duty the previous day when Ballard came in for the Albert Lee book. Still, she flipped her badge while Bosch put his printouts down on the counter and started spreading them out.

The recruit was in a training uniform with his name on a patch over the right breast pocket. It was attached by Velcro so it could be easily ripped off should the recruit wash out of the academy. His name was Farley.

"Ballard, Hollywood Division. I was here yesterday. We need to pull another book. This one from a 2013 case."

She looked down at the printout Bosch was focused on. It was his copy of the chrono from the Albert Lee case, and he was running his finger down the page of 2013 entries. He found the one detailing his inquiries to Pacific Division Homicide about the John William James murder. He called out the case number and Farley dutifully wrote it down.

"Okay, let me go look," he said.

He left the counter and disappeared into the warren of shelves lined with plastic binders, each one cataloging a life taken too soon and still with no justice in response.

Farley seemed to be taking a long time to locate the murder book. They were filed chronologically, so it seemed like it would be an easy errand to locate the 2013 shelves and find the John William James binder.

Ballard impatiently drummed her fingers on the counter.

"What the hell happened to him?" Bosch asked.

Ballard stopped drumming as some kind of realization came to her.

"It's not there," she said.

"What do you mean?" Bosch asked.

"I just realized. The Albert Lee book is gone, so why would they leave this one?"

"They? Who's they?"

Before Ballard could come up with an answer, Farley returned from his errand without a murder book in his hands. Instead, he had a lined manila checkout card like the one Ballard had seen when she came for the Albert Lee book.

"It's checked out," Farley said.

"That makes me oh for two," Ballard said. "Who checked it out?"

Farley read a name off the checkout card.

"Ted Larkin, Homicide Unit, Pacific Division. But it says he checked it out five years ago. That was before this place was even here. Like the other one you asked for."

Ballard slapped a hand down on the counter. She could guess that it was probably checked out after Larkin had retired. Somebody had impersonated the lead detectives on the two cases to enter two different police stations and steal the murder books, leaving behind what would be viewed as plausible checkout cards.

"Let's go," Ballard said.

She turned from the counter and headed to the door. Bosch followed.

"Thanks, Farley," she called over her shoulder.

Ballard marched down the wide hallway toward the main entrance, leaving Bosch struggling to keep up.

"Wait a minute, wait a minute," he called after her. "Where are you running? There's nothing you—"

"I want to get out of here," Ballard said. "So we can talk outside."

"Then we can only go as fast as I can go. So slow down."

"Okay. I'm just fucking pissed off."

Ballard slowed her pace and Bosch caught up.

"I mean, this is bullshit," she said. "Somebody's stealing murder books in our own damn department."

The urgency of her voice caught the attention of two cadets walking by in the hall.

"Just wait," Bosch said. "You said let's talk outside."

"Fine," Ballard said.

She held her tongue until they were out the doors, down the steps, and heading across the parking lot to her car.

"They have somebody inside," she said.

"Yeah, we know that." Bosch said. "But who is 'they'? The dentists? Or is there a go-between?"

"That's the question," Ballard replied.

They got in the Defender, and Ballard tore out of the parking lot like she was on a code 3 call. They drove in silence for a long time, until Ballard drove onto the entrance ramp of the 10 freeway.

"So, now what?" Bosch asked.

"We're going to make one last stop," Ballard said. "Then I need to go back to work on my other case. I told the victims I'd be calling."

"That's good. What stop are we making?"

"Dodger Stadium."

"The academy? Why?"

"Not the academy. The stadium. I'm going to get you vaccinated, Harry. You're eligible, and I get the feeling that if I don't help you get it done, it will never happen."

"Look, just take me home. I can get that done on my own time and not waste yours."

"Nah, we're going. Get it done now. Trust the science, Harry."

"I do. But there are a hell of a lot of people who deserve it ahead of me. Besides, you need an appointment."

Ballard pulled the badge off her belt and held it up.

"Here's your appointment," she said.

18

After Ballard cleared roll call without being pulled into anything new, she told the watch commander that she was going up to the Dell for a second interview with the latest victim of the Midnight Men. He told her to make sure she had a rover.

She could have handled Cindy Carpenter by phone, but face-to-face visits with victims were always better. Not only was it reassuring to them to see a detective in person, but there was a better chance of them sharing newly recalled details of the crime. The brain protects itself by switching to essential life support in a time of physical trauma. Only after safety returns do the full details of the trauma start to come back. Carpenter's remembering having the sense that she was filmed or photographed was an example of this. Ballard was hoping that a continuation of the bond between detective and victim would emerge in this visit.

But Carpenter, still wearing her work polo with the Native Bean logo on it, answered the door with "What?"

"Hey, everything all right?" Ballard asked.

"Everything's fine. Why do you keep coming back?"

"Well, you know why. And I was hoping you'd have the questionnaire finished for me."

"I'm not done."

She made a move to shut the door and Ballard put her hand out to stop it.

"Is something wrong, Cindy? Did something happen?"

Ballard quickly reset her goals for the visit. She now just wanted to get inside.

"Well, for one, you called my ex-husband and I asked you not to do that," Carpenter said. "Now I have to deal with him."

"You didn't tell me not to call him," Ballard said. "You told me you didn't want to talk about him, but you also gave the responding officer his name and number as your closest contact. And it—"

"I told you I don't know why I did that. I was confused and terrified. I couldn't think of anybody else."

"I understand all of that, Cindy. I do. But I have an investigation going and I need to follow it wherever it takes me. You put your ex's name down on the incident report, then you don't want to talk about him. That raised a flag for me. So, yes, I called him. I didn't tell him that you were attacked. In fact, I worked my way around it. I take it he called you. What did he say?"

Carpenter shook her head like she was annoyed with how smoothly Ballard was handling this confrontation.

"Can I come in?" Ballard asked.

"Might as well," Carpenter said.

She stepped back from the door. Ballard entered and tried to further diffuse the situation.

"Cindy, I hope you understand that my sole purpose right now is to find the men who attacked you and put them away forever. No matter what moves I make on the investigation, none are intended to cause you further harm or upset. That's the last thing I want to do. So, why don't we sit down and start with what happened after I talked to Reginald."

"Fine."

Carpenter took the spot on the couch where Ballard had last seen her the day before. Renée sat in a stuffed chair across a low-level coffee table.

"He called you?" Ballard prompted.

"Yes, he called me," Carpenter said. "He asked what happened and I ended up telling him."

"And was he sympathetic to you?"

"He acted like he was, but he always made it sound like he cared about me. That was the problem—it was always an act with him. But…"

"But what?"

"This is why I'm pissed off about you calling him. He now has this to hold over me."

Ballard waited for her to say more but she didn't.

"I don't understand, Cindy. What is he holding over you?"

"I left him, okay? I was the one who wanted out."

"Okay."

"And he told me, he said I would regret it. And now, thanks to you, he knows what happened to me and, like I said, he pretended to be sympathetic, but I could tell he wasn't. He was saying I told you so without saying it."

Carpenter turned her face and looked out the window toward the street. Ballard was silent while she thought about the story of the Carpenter marriage. Finally, she landed on a question.

"Cindy, do you remember, when he asked you what happened, did you get any sense that he already knew?"

"Of course he did. You told him."

"I didn't tell him you were sexually assaulted. I said it was a break-in. Did he already know you were attacked?"

"I don't know."

"Try to remember, what exactly did he say?"

"He said, 'I heard that some guys broke in and are you all right.' Things like that."

Ballard paused for a moment. She wanted to get the next question right.

"Cindy, think back to that call. Did he say 'some guys' broke in? He used the plural?"

"I don't know. I can't remember. I might have told him it was two guys, because I told him what happened. The point is, he now knows and I really wish he didn't."

Ballard knew that she had not mentioned that there were multiple suspects when she talked to Reginald on the phone. But now Cindy Carpenter couldn't reliably remember who brought that fact into their conversation. It further advanced Ballard's suspicions, because Cindy's recounting of the conversation revealed more about their marriage. Her description of her ex-husband made him sound petty, selfish, and vengeful.

Again, though, she had to ask herself why she kept coming back to Reginald. He presumably had an alibi. And there was no known connection between Cindy or Reginald Carpenter and the other two victims of the Midnight Men.

"Did Reginald happen to say where he was on New Year's?" she asked.

"He said he'd just gotten back from a golf trip in the desert when you called him," Carpenter said. "He didn't say exactly where that was and I didn't ask. It was the last thing I cared about. Why are you asking that?"

"He just seemed preoccupied when I called him."

"Please stop calling him."

"I already have."

Palm Springs qualified as the desert. As much as Ballard disliked Reginald Carpenter, it seemed unlikely that he was involved in the Midnight Men attacks. She decided to put the ex-husband aside and continue her hunt for a nexus between the three victims.

"How much of the questionnaire did you get through?" she asked.

"I'm almost finished," Carpenter said. "It's right here."

She pulled a folded sheaf of papers off the side table and tried to fling it across the coffee table to Ballard. She missed badly and it ended up on the other end of the couch.

"Oops, sorry," Carpenter said.

Ballard got up and picked up the papers.

"The calendar in there goes back sixty days," Carpenter said. "I can barely remember where I was a week ago. So it's definitely incomplete. But I got the rest of it done."

"Thank you," Ballard said. "I know this was a headache for you to do right now, but it is really valuable to the investigation."

She flipped through the pages and read some of the answers Carpenter had provided in the calendar section. These included restaurants and shopping destinations. The week before Christmas and the day itself were marked with "La Jolla."

"La Jolla?" Ballard asked.

"My parents live down there," Carpenter said. "I always go down at Christmas."

Ballard finished scanning.

"You went the whole month without putting gas in your car?" she asked. "What about gassing up to go down to La Jolla?"

"I didn't know you wanted that kind of stuff," Carpenter said.

"We want everything, Cindy. Anything you can remember."

"I get gas at the Shell at Franklin and Gower. It's on my way to work."

"See, that's exactly what we want. The locations of your routines. When did you last get gas?"

"On my way back from my parents' the day after Christmas. Somewhere in Orange County off the five."

"Okay, we don't care about that, I don't think, since it's a one-off. What about disputes? Anybody at work or elsewhere?"

"Not really. I mean, customers complain all the time—we just give them another coffee and that's it."

"So nothing's ever gotten out of hand? Especially recently?"

"Not that I can think of."

"You have down here Massage Envy—is that the one on Hillhurst?"

"Yes, my employees gave me a gift certificate for Christmas and I used it one day when I got off work early. Nothing happened."

"Male or female masseuse?"

"Female."

"All right. I will probably have more questions after I look through this."

What she did not say was that she might have questions after she cross-referenced Carpenter's answers with those from the other two victims.

"So, did you find out anything about the street-lighting guys?" Cindy asked.

"No, not yet," Ballard said.

"Do you think it was them?"

"It could have been. The questionnaire is important because we need to find out where your attackers crossed paths with you. We want to try to understand who would target you, and why."

Carpenter slapped her hand down on her thigh like she was fed up.

"Why is it my fault?" she said angrily. "Why is it because of something I did?"

"I'm not saying that," Ballard said quickly. "I'm not saying that at all."

Ballard felt her phone buzz. She checked the screen and saw that it was the inside line at Hollywood Station. It was the watch commander and she realized she had left the rover in the charging dock in her city car. She put the phone away without answering the call.

"Well, it sure seems like it," Carpenter said.

"Then I'm sorry," Ballard said. "So let me make it clear: You did nothing to deserve or attract this. What happened to you was not your fault in any way. We're talking about the attackers here. I'm trying to learn where and under what circumstances these sick, twisted individuals decided to choose you. That's all, and I don't want you thinking that I'm looking at it any other way."

Carpenter had her face turned away again. She murmured a response.

"Okay," she said.

"I know that sometimes the investigation is just an ongoing reminder of what you were put through," said Ballard. "But it's a necessary evil, because we want to catch these assholes and put them away."

"I know. And I'm sorry I'm being a bitch."

"You're not, Cindy. And you have nothing to be sorry about. At all."

Ballard stood up and folded the Lambkin questionnaire in half.

"You're going?" Carpenter asked.

After turning her face from her and repeatedly pushing back at her questions, Carpenter now seemed upset that Ballard was leaving.

"It looks like I have another call," Ballard said. "I need to go. But I can check in later if you want me to."

"Okay."

"Are you working tomorrow?"

"No, I'm off."

"Okay, I'll check in with you if I have anything to report."

Ballard left the house and headed to her car, looking at her phone for a message from the watch office. There was none. When she got to her car, she looked back at the streetlight at the front corner of Cindy Carpenter's property. It was still out.

19

Before she got to her city ride Ballard's phone buzzed again. This time it was her detective commander calling. This meant that the watch commander had roused Robinson-Reynolds at home to complain that she was not responding to radio or cell calls.

"L-T," she said. "I'm about to check in with the watch commander."

"What the hell, Ballard?" Robinson-Reynolds said.

"I was with my rape victim. She was very emotional and it wasn't a good time to take the call. Plus I pulled a dead rover when I left the station. It's charging in my car."

"Well, they fucking need you at a scene."

"I'm on my way. What is it? Where is it?"

"I don't know, some kind of an assault in Thai Town. Get the details from the watch commander."

"I'll call him next."

"I don't like getting calls about my people, Ballard. You know that."

"I do, L-T. It won't happen—"

Robinson-Reynolds disconnected.

"—again."

She had hoped to keep him on the line so she could update

him on the cases she was working. Now she would have to wait till Monday. A lot could happen between now and then.

It was a good thing Ballard liked working alone, because the department had a freeze on promotions and hiring until the world cleared the pandemic. But what made solo work difficult was not having a partner to divvy up responsibilities with. Ballard had to cover everything and still fight to keep the cases she wanted to keep. Once in the car, she called the watch lieutenant on the rover. She chose this because the conversation would go out live on the radio. A cell call would have given him carte blanche to harangue her for not answering the initial calls.

Because it was a holiday weekend and people with seniority were taking days, there was yet another watch commander on duty, making it three in three nights. Lieutenant Sandro Puig kept a modulated tone when he told Ballard to respond to an address on Hobart Avenue to investigate a home invasion and assault. She asked if there were any Thai officers on duty and he responded that 6-A 79—the designation for the patrol unit assigned to the Thai Town area—included an officer who could translate.

It took Ballard five minutes to wind her way down and out of the Dell and then another five to get to the address, which was a 1950s two-level apartment building with parking underneath. It looked like the last time anyone had taken a run at painting the place was the previous century. She parked behind a patrol car. She saw no EMT wagon yet, even though the call was billed as an assault.

The entrances to the apartments were along an outside walkway. As she headed up the steps toward apartment 22, a shirtless man with a bloody eye suddenly appeared on the upper landing, saw Ballard coming up, and charged down the stairs toward her.

At the same moment, she heard a woman's shrill voice yell, "Hey! Stop!"

Muscle memory took over. Ballard took a sideways step into the middle of the concrete staircase and brought her arms and hands up to take on the body charging at her from an upper angle. The man hit her with all of his weight. He was small but the impact was solid and she was propelled backward and down. She landed butt-first on the lower landing with the man's weight coming down on top of her. After impact, he immediately started to roll off her. She tried to grab him, but without a shirt, there was no purchase on his sweat-slick body. As fast as the collision had occurred he was up and gone. Ballard could see a female officer coming down the steps toward her. The officer hit the landing, jumped over Ballard's sprawled body, and continued the chase, yelling something that sounded like *"Yood, yood, yood!"*

Ballard realized she had hit her head on the concrete. She wanted to get up and join the chase but the world was beginning to spin. She turned onto her side and then her stomach and then finally raised herself onto her hands and knees.

"Ballard, are you all right?"

She turned her head toward the stairs and saw another officer coming down. Soon she felt a hand on her arm as someone tried to help her up.

"Wait," Ballard said. "Give me a second."

She paused and then looked up at the second officer. It was Victor Rodriguez, her translator from the night of Raffa's killing.

"V-Rod," Ballard said. "Who the fuck was that?"

"That was our goddamn victim," Rodriguez said. "He suddenly jumped up and took off."

"Go after your partner. I'm all right."

"You sure?"

"Go."

Rodriguez hurried off, and Ballard, grabbing the staircase rail, climbed up into a standing position. She was hit with vertigo and held on to the railing for support. Her head finally cleared and she tentatively let go of the railing. After taking a few steps to see if everything was working, she swung her hand up under her jacket to the small of her back to check for blood or other damage but found nothing. She touched the back of her head. There was no blood but she felt a bump swelling at the impact point.

"Shit."

Soon she heard a helicopter cutting across the sky above and knew the officers had called out an airship to help find the running man.

But it was not to be. Rodriguez was soon back with the other officer, Chara Paithoon. Both were huffing from the unsuccessful foot pursuit.

"He got away," Rodriguez said.

"You okay, Renée?" Paithoon asked.

"I hit my head," Ballard said.

Paithoon was one of the few Thai-born officers in the department. She was short and compactly built and wore a short haircut with shaved sidewalls and a waxed front wave. Ballard knew that plenty of female officers adopted utility hairstyles to ward off the unwanted attention of male officers.

"Can I see?" Paithoon said. "Let me check your eyes."

Paithoon snapped on a flashlight. She held the light so the outer edge of its beam touched lightly on Ballard's face. Paithoon was standing in close, looking up at her eyes.

"You've got some dilation," she said. "You should have the EMTs check it."

"Yeah, where are they?" Ballard asked. "I thought this was an assault."

Paithoon stepped back and put away her light.

"We called them but I guess they're tied up," Rodriguez said.

"So what exactly happened here?" Ballard said.

"Neighbor called it in, said there was a fight in twenty-two," Rodriguez said. "We got here, and suspects were gone on arrival. Chara was talking to the guy and then suddenly he pushes her into me and takes off. You know the rest."

"Was he illegal?" Ballard asked.

"Never got to it," Paithoon said. "He wasn't Thai, though. The neighbor who called it in was Thai but this guy was Cambodian. I think this was ABZ business and he was afraid we were going to arrest him, so he hightailed it."

Ballard knew that ABZ meant Asian Boyz, a gang that preyed upon immigrants, legal and otherwise, from Southeast Asia.

Two paramedics entered the apartment building's central courtyard, and Paithoon greeted them.

"Our victim is GOA but you need to take a look at Detective Ballard here," she said. "She took a tumble and hit her head."

The paramedics agreed to check Ballard but wanted to do it at their truck. Paithoon and Rodriguez stayed behind to do mop-up on what was turning out to be an assault call without a victim.

Ballard sat under a light on the fold-down tail of the EMT wagon while a med tech checked her vitals as well as her eyes for dilation and her scalp for bruising and swelling. The name patch on his uniform said SINGLE.

"Is that your name or relationship status?" Ballard asked.

"It's my name but I get asked that a lot," Single said.

"Of course you do."

"So, I think you have a slight concussion. We've got a little bit of dilation of the pupils, some elevated blood pressure."

He used his gloved fingers to press the skin around Ballard's eyes. She could see the concentration in his expression as he worked. He wore a mask but he had sharp brown eyes and full brown hair and was maybe a few years younger than her. One of his pupils had a notch in it slightly off center at five o'clock.

"Coloboma," Single said.

"What?" Ballard asked.

"You're looking at my eye. The notch in my pupil is caused by a birth defect in the iris called coloboma. Some call it a keyhole pupil."

"Oh. Does it…"

"Affect my eyesight? No. But I have to wear sunglasses when the sun is out. So, most of the time."

"Well, that's good. About your eyesight."

"Thanks. And so you're on the other side of the wall, right?"

"What?"

"Hollywood Division?"

"Oh, yeah, Hollywood. You're at the firehouse, then?"

"Yep. Maybe I'll see you in the parking lot someday."

"Sure."

"But what I think you need to do now is punch out and go home and rest."

"I can't do that. I'm the only detective on duty tonight."

"Yeah, well, you're not going to be much of a detective if your brain swells and you go into seizure."

"Seriously?"

"You took a good knock on the head. Coup and contrecoup injuries—bruising of the brain, swelling—can develop over time. I'm not saying you have that, because there is only mild dilation exhibited, but you definitely want to take it easy. You can sleep but you want somebody to wake you and check on you every couple hours or so. Just keep a watch on this. You have somebody at home who can check on you through the night?"

"I live alone."

"Then give me a number, and I'll call you every few hours."

"You're serious?"

"Totally. You don't want to mess around with an injury like this. Call your supervisor and tell him you're going home. If he wants to talk to me, I'll tell him what I just told you."

"Okay, okay, I'll do it."

"Give me a number to call."

Ballard gave him a business card that had her name and cell phone number on it. She remained skeptical that he would call to check on her. But she hoped he would. She liked his look and his manner. She liked the keyhole in his eye.

"So, am I okay to drive?" she asked. "I have a city ride I should turn in and then get my car."

"I can drive your ride back, since we're going back to the station. Where do you live?"

"Los Feliz."

"Well, maybe you can get an Uber or one of the patrol guys can drive you home."

"Sure. I can work on that."

"Good. And I'll call to check on you in a couple hours."

20

It seemed that every time Ballard dropped deeply into a dream, she was pulled out by the buzz of her cell phone, and it was EMT Single making good on his promise to check in on her. This cycle continued through the night into Sunday morning, when he finally said that it was safe for her to sleep uninterrupted.

"You mean now that the sun is up I can get a good night's sleep?" she asked.

"I thought this would be your normal schedule," Single said. "You do work the night shift, right?"

"I'm just giving you a hard time. Thank you for checking on me. It means a lot."

"Anytime. Your next concussion, call me."

She ended the call with a smile on her face despite the headache behind her eyes. She got up, wobbled as she got her footing, and went into the bathroom. After splashing cold water on her face, she looked closely at herself in the mirror. She saw bluish shadows under her eyes but the dilation of her pupils seemed to be back to normal, at least compared to what it had been when she got home the night before. She then thought of EMT Single's keyhole pupil and smiled again.

It was 8 a.m. and she was still tired after the repeatedly

interrupted sleep cycle. She stayed in her sweats and got back into bed, thinking she would doze for a little while longer. She knew there was a lot to do but she needed to be rested and ready for her next shift that night. She closed her eyes and soon all of that was forgotten.

In her dream, Ballard could breathe underwater. There was no need to charge to the surface for air. No burning in her lungs. She looked up through the blue to the sun, its rays penetrating the water with warmth and comfort. She twirled onto her back and moved languidly in the current, looking up and realizing that the sun was shaped like an acorn and was not the sun at all.

The phone's buzz seemed to wake her as soon as she had shut her eyes, but as she reached for it, she saw the time was 3:50 and that she had been asleep for nearly eight hours. The call was from Bosch.

"Have you gotten my messages?"

"No. What? What happened? You called?"

"No, I texted. There's a memorial service for Javier Raffa today."

"Shit, when? Where?"

"It starts in ten minutes at St. Anne's on Occidental."

Ballard knew that wasn't far from her. She put Bosch on speaker so she could scroll through her missed texts and emails. There were three from Bosch and one from her lieutenant. One of the emails that had come in was from Bobbi Klein, the first victim of the Midnight Men. The others were not important.

"I don't know how I slept through all of— I got a concussion last night."

"What happened?"

"I'll tell you later. Are you at the memorial?"

"I'm here but I didn't go in. I think I'd stick out. I've got a good spot and I'm watching people arrive. I think Hoyle is here. At least there's one white guy that I think is him."

"Okay, I'm on my way. Thanks for the wake-up."

"You sure you're all right?"

"I'm fine."

Ballard quickly dressed and headed down to the garage. Her car was there because she had disregarded EMT Single's orders and driven herself home after checking out with the watch lieutenant the night before.

She took Hillhurst all the way to Beverly and then over to Occidental. She found a spot at the curb a half block away and called Bosch.

"I'm here. Are you still in place?"

"I'm here."

"Okay, I'm going to go in. I'll see if we can talk to the widow after."

"Sounds good."

"Anybody else of note arrive?"

"There's a lot of obvious bangers, tattooed to the ears. You want me to go in with you?"

"No, I'll be fine. Do you think it's worth following Hoyle, if it was Hoyle you saw?"

"I don't know. Where's he going to go on a Sunday night? He's probably just here for appearances. There might be suspicions if he didn't show—you know what I mean?"

"Yeah. But wait till the widow Raffa finds out what's going on."

"You're going to tell her in there?"

"No, I'll wait. Okay, I'm going now."

Ballard disconnected and exited her car. She walked up the street and followed a few stragglers arriving late. She hurried to follow them in and use them as cover. The memorial was in a chapel to the side of the main church. That made it too crowded to enter and Ballard stood in the hallway outside with the stragglers. There were speakers in the ceiling, so she heard the testimonials and tearful memories from friends and co-workers as well as a hymn sung by the crowd. The hymn and most of the testimonials were in Spanish. Ballard understood enough to know that many people were lamenting that Javier Raffa had left the violent life to raise a family and run a business, yet in the end, violence still found him and took it all away.

After forty-five minutes, the ceremony ended and the immediate family left the chapel first to form a receiving line outside the door. Ballard hung back and watched from one of the archways that lined the walkway that ran down the side of the church.

She soon saw Javier Raffa's silent partner, Dr. Dennis Hoyle, emerge in the line from the chapel. Ballard recognized him from the studio photos on his family dentistry website. He was all angles: thin, sharp shoulders and elbows. He had graying hair and a salt-and-pepper goatee.

Ballard realized this might be the best time to talk to him, when he least expected to be questioned by the police. She quickly texted Bosch her plan and then watched when it was Hoyle's turn to go down the family line. It was clear he was meeting them for the first time, even the widow. He hugged none of them and gave the widow a two-handed sympathy grasp. He leaned forward to say something to her or possibly identify himself, but Ballard's read on the widow's facial expression and body language was that she had no idea who he was.

Javier Raffa's son, Gabriel, was at the end of the receiving line. Hoyle simply nodded once and gave the young man a hang-in-there clap on the shoulder, then headed away with a look of pure relief on his face. Ballard used her arm to hold her jacket closed over the badge on her belt. She let Hoyle pass by and then turned to follow him.

As Hoyle headed toward the street, Ballard could see Bosch standing out on the sidewalk. He was wearing a suit, just in case he needed to go into the memorial service. But the suit also worked for what they were about to do.

Ballard followed Hoyle out and picked up speed to catch up. Bosch positioned himself in the middle of the sidewalk, slowing Hoyle down as he decided which way to go.

"Dr. Hoyle?" Ballard said.

Hoyle spun around as if shocked that anyone in this part of town would know him by name.

"Uh, yes?" he said.

Ballard pulled her jacket open to show the badge as well as her gun holstered on her hip.

"I'm Detective Ballard with the LAPD. This is my colleague Harry Bosch."

She gestured to Bosch, who was now behind Hoyle. The dentist whipped back to look at Bosch and then forward again at Ballard.

"Yes?" he said.

"I'm investigating the murder of Javier Raffa," Ballard said. "I would like to ask you a few questions, if you have the time."

"Me?" Hoyle said. "Why would you want to ask me questions?"

"Well, for starters, you were his partner, were you not?"

"Well, yes, but I don't know anything about what happened. I mean, I wasn't even there."

"That's okay. We need to be thorough and talk to anybody who knew him. If you were his partner, you must have known him pretty well."

"It was a business investment, that's all."

"Okay, that's good to know. Where are you parked? Maybe we should get away from the church and talk."

"Um, I'm over here but I—"

"Lead the way."

Hoyle drove a four-door Mercedes and by coincidence had parked right behind Bosch's old Jeep. Neither Bosch nor Ballard mentioned this, because it would possibly put cracks in the charade that Bosch was an LAPD detective. When they got to Hoyle's car, he pulled the remote key from his pocket and unlocked the doors. He then turned to Ballard and Bosch.

"You know, right now is not a good time to talk," he said. "I've just been to my friend's memorial and I'm kind of emotional about it. I just want to go home. Can we—"

"How did you know?" Ballard interrupted.

"How did I know he was dead?" Hoyle said. "It was in the paper—online."

Ballard paused for a moment in case Hoyle sputtered out something else. He didn't.

"No, I mean how did you know he was looking for a partner?" she said. "An investor. Somebody to buy him out of the gang."

For a second, Hoyle's eyes widened. He was surprised by her knowledge.

"I...Well, I have advisers for this sort of thing," Hoyle said.

"Really?" Ballard asked. "Who is that? I'd like to speak to them."

"I told you, now is not a good time. Can I go?"

Ballard held her hands wide as if to say she wasn't keeping him from leaving.

"So I can go?" Hoyle said.

"It would be better for you, Dr. Hoyle, if we cleared some of this up now," Ballard said.

"Cleared up what? You just said I could go."

"No, I said it would be better for you to talk to us right now, right here. I don't think you want us coming by your office, do you?"

Hoyle flung the door of his car open and it promptly swung back closed. Exasperated, he opened it again and held it.

"I've done nothing wrong and you are harassing me!"

He jumped in the car and slammed the door. He fired up the engine and took off from the curb, driving by Ballard and Bosch.

"If he thinks that was harassment, he hasn't seen anything yet," Ballard said.

Bosch stood next to her and they watched the Mercedes drive north on Occidental.

"Did I come on too strong?" Ballard asked.

"He thinks so," said Bosch.

"Fuck 'im."

"He's probably calling his partners right now. Did you want that?"

"I wanted them to know I'm here."

21

Ballard and Bosch went back to the church to see if the family was finished with the procession of well-wishers. There was no one at the door of the chapel. Ballard looked inside and saw the widow and the daughters but not the son, Gabriel.

"I need to find Gabriel so he can translate if needed," she said. "Stay here in case they start to leave."

"I'll stall them," Bosch said.

Ballard went back down the hallway and looked through the double doors leading to the larger cathedral. She saw Gabriel sitting in a pew by himself. She entered and quietly walked down the center aisle. Gabriel was using a penknife to scratch something into the wooden bench. It said "GOD S," and she didn't think after the last three days that he was working on the word "SAVES."

"Gabriel," she said. "Stop."

He was so badly startled that he dropped the knife and it clattered to the marble floor. Ballard could see smeared tears on his face.

"Look," she said. "I know what has happened to your family is horrible. If you want to help do something about it, help me talk to your mother. Come."

She stepped back into the aisle. He hesitated, then started to reach down for his knife.

"Give me that," Ballard said. "You don't need it, and it will only get you into trouble. Let's go talk to your mother."

Gabriel came out of the pew and handed her the knife. He walked with his head down all the way to the chapel. Ballard folded the knife closed and put it in her pocket.

"What was done to your father wasn't right," Ballard said. "But he got out of the street life and that's what he wanted for you. Don't let him down, Gabriel."

"I won't," Gabriel said.

"You told me the other night that your father had a partner — a white guy from Malibu. Did he come to the memorial today?"

"I think so. He was the white guy, right?"

"I don't know, Gabriel. I'm asking you. Do you know his name?"

"No, I don't remember it. I only saw him one time when he came to the shop."

Bosch was waiting outside the door of the chapel. He nodded to Ballard, indicating that the rest of the family was still inside.

Ballard and Gabriel entered. Bosch followed but hung back by the door. Ballard reintroduced herself to the family and said she needed to ask some questions. She said Gabriel had volunteered to translate if necessary. The mother was named Josefina and she agreed to talk to Ballard. She looked as if the tears of the last days had left permanent lines on her brown face. She had the look that Ballard had seen a hundred times before on women whose men were taken by violence — the look that asks, How do I live? How do I take care of my family?

"First, I want to assure you that we are doing everything we can to find out who did this to Javier," Ballard began, speaking slowly. "We have some leads that we are following and hopefully they will bring us to an arrest. I can't tell you everything we're doing, so some of my questions might seem strange. I just ask you to be patient and to know the information you provide is important. Do you understand, or would you like Gabriel to translate?"

"I understand, yes," Josefina said.

"Good. Thank you. Let me start with what we asked the other night at the hospital. Do you know of anyone who wanted to harm Javier?"

"No. Who would do this? Javier was good man."

"Did he say anything recently about angry customers or employees?"

"No. Everybody happy. It was a happy place."

"Did Javier have a will?"

Josefina's face showed confusion. Ballard looked at Gabriel, trying to think of how to explain. Bosch called from the back of the chapel.

"Ultimo testamento."

Ballard looked back at him and nodded, realizing he'd had many such conversations in his years as a homicide detective. She looked back at Josefina, who spoke to her son in Spanish.

"She doesn't know," Gabriel said.

"Did he have a lawyer?" Ballard asked. *"Abogado?"*

"Sí, sí, sí," Josefina said. *"Dario Calvente es su abogado."*

Ballard nodded.

"Thank you," she said. "We're going to call on him and he may ask you for permission to talk to us."

Gabriel translated and Josefina nodded.

"Did Mr. Calvente come today?"

Josefina nodded.

"Did you know your husband's business partner?" Ballard asked.

"No," Josefina said.

"Was he here today? Dr. Hoyle?"

"I don't know."

It was clear to Ballard that Josefina knew little about Javier's business dealings and that she needed to talk to the lawyer for clarity on things like the will, insurance, and records pertaining to the partnership.

"Josefina, did you know that Javier had to pay his way out of the Las Palmas gang?" Ballard asked.

Josefina nodded and seemed to take a moment to compose her answer. She spoke in Spanish and Gabriel translated.

"We could not have a family if he was doing these things with the gang," he said.

"How much did he have to pay?" Ballard asked.

"*Veinticinco,*" Josefina said.

"Twenty-five thousand?"

"*Sí.* Yes."

"Okay. Where did he get that money?"

"*El dentista.*"

"His partner."

"*Sí.*"

"How did he know the dentist? Who brought the dentist?"

Gabriel translated the question but there was no answer to translate back. Josefina shook her head. She didn't know.

Ballard said that she would be in touch when she had something more to report on the investigation and asked Gabriel to translate for Josefina to make sure she understood. She and Bosch left then and walked to his car.

"Should we see if we can run down Dario Calvente, the *abogado*?" Ballard asked.

"It's a Sunday," Bosch said. "I doubt he'll be in his office."

"We can find him. Let's take my car. I'll bring you back afterward."

"Perfect."

Ballard googled the lawyer's name on her phone and found his website. Before she got to the car, she was leaving a message on his office line. Like Cindy Carpenter's attorney, Calvente's website promised 24/7 service.

"I'll run his DMV and get his home address if he doesn't call back pretty quick," she told Bosch.

They got into the Defender and almost immediately Ballard got a call with a blocked ID that she assumed was Calvente.

"Detective Ballard."

"Ballard, are you ducking my calls?"

She recognized the voice of Lieutenant Robinson-Reynolds.

"L-T, no. I, uh, was in a church so I had my phone off."

"I know it's Sunday, Ballard, but I didn't think you were the church type."

"It was a memorial for my homicide victim. I needed to speak to the family and, you know, see who showed up."

"Ballard, you should not be working. You should be in the hospital."

"I'm fine, Lieutenant. It was just a knock on the head."

"Look, the overnight report said an EMT told you to go home. I don't want this on an EMT, okay? I want you to go to an ER and get checked out before you do any more work."

"I'm following a lead and I'm telling you, I'm—"

"This is not a suggestion, Detective. This is an order. We are not going to risk anything with a head injury. Go to the ER and get checked out. Then call me back so I know."

"Fine. I'll finish up here and go."

"Tonight, Detective. I want to hear from you tonight."

"You got it, L-T."

She disconnected and told Bosch about the order.

"Sounds like a smart move," he said.

"You too now?" she said. "I'm fine and this will be a big waste of time."

"You're a cop. They'll get you in quick."

"Well, I'm not going to do it until I'm on duty. I'm not wasting my own time. And speaking of time, I'm not going to wait for this *abogado* to call back. Twenty-four-seven, my ass."

She called the com center, identified herself and gave her serial number, then asked for a DMV check on Dario Calvente. She got lucky. There was only one that had a Los Angeles address. She thanked the operator and disconnected.

"Silver Lake," she said. "You still want to go?"

"Let's do it," Bosch said.

It took them fifteen minutes to drive over. Calvente lived in a 1930s Spanish-style house across from the reservoir. They climbed a set of stone stairs to get to the front porch. There was a large picture window with a view of the lake, but it was covered with a sign that said BLACK LIVES MATTER.

Ballard knocked on the door and had her badge off her belt and in her hand. The door was answered by a man of about forty whom Ballard recognized from the receiving line at the memorial. He still had his suit on but the tie was gone. He had a thick mustache and brown eyes as dark as Bosch's.

"Mr. Calvente, LAPD," Ballard said. "Sorry to bother you at home, but we left a message at your office and you didn't return it."

Calvente pointed at her.

"I saw you today," he said. "At the memorial for Javier."

"That's right," Ballard said. "My name is Renée Ballard and this is my colleague Harry Bosch. Josefina Raffa told us you were her husband's attorney and we would like to ask you a few questions."

"I don't know what I can tell you," Calvente said. "I did some work for Javier, yes, but it was in trade for work on my car. I wouldn't call myself his lawyer per se."

"Do you know if he had another lawyer?"

"No, I don't think so. This is why he asked me if I could help."

"And when was this?"

"Oh, a few months ago. My wife, she had an accident and I had the car towed to Javier's. When he found out I was a lawyer, he asked me to do some work."

"What was the work? Can you tell us?"

"There was privilege involved but it was a contract he had signed. He wanted to know how to dissolve a partnership."

"Was this for his business?"

Calvente looked past them and out at the reservoir. He canted his head back and forth as if weighing whether to answer. Then he looked at Ballard and nodded his head once.

"Were you able to help him?" Ballard asked.

"Contract law is not my specialty," Calvente said. "I told him that I saw no place in the contract that I thought he could attack. And I told him he should seek a second opinion from a contract attorney. I asked if he wanted a referral and he said no. And for this he gave me a discount on the repairs of our car. That was it."

"Do you remember, was the partner named Dennis Hoyle?"

"I think that was the name but I can't be sure. It's been a few months."

"Did he tell you anything about why he wanted to break the contract?"

"He just said it was not a good situation, because he had long ago paid off a debt to this man but he had to keep paying him out of the profits. I remember the contract had no termination. It was a full partnership for the life of the business."

"What was Hoyle's stake in the business?"

"I think twenty-five percent."

"If this review was all you did for him, why did you go to the memorial today?"

"Well, I, uh, wanted to express my condolences to the family and say I was available for anything they might need. In a legal capacity, of course."

"How did you know, by the way, that he had been the victim of a homicide?"

"I saw the memorial scheduled at the church when I attended this morning. I did not know it was a homicide until I was there today. It was a terrible thing for the family."

Ballard turned to Bosch to see if he had any questions that she had missed. He shook his head and she looked back at Calvente.

"Thank you, Mr. Calvente," she said. "You've been very helpful."

"You're welcome," Calvente said.

Bosch took the steps down to the street slowly. Ballard had to wait for him. When he reached the sidewalk, he whispered under his breath.

"Ambulance chaser. He barely knows the guy and he goes to his memorial?"

"Yeah. You ever see that Sidney Lumet movie *The Verdict*?"

"I don't think so. I don't go to a lot of movies anymore."

"It's an old one with Paul Newman. I went through a Paul Newman phase. Anyway, he's a lawyer — a drunk, actually — and he tries to drum up business by going to funerals and passing out business cards."

Bosch looked back up at the house.

"This guy must go to a lot of funerals," he said.

"Well, what he gave us was good," Ballard said. "Javier wanted out of the contract. There's a motive in that."

"There is. But Hoyle's going to be protected by the contract. Calvente said it was legit. We still need to find the factor man and hope he leads us to the man with the Walther P-twenty-two."

"Tonight I'll go back to Gang Intel. They had a snitch who told them years ago that Javier bought his way out of Las Palmas. I think it was a woman. They wouldn't give me her name before but I'll make them give it to me now. She might know who set him up with Hoyle."

"That sounds like a plan."

Fifteen minutes later Ballard had just dropped Bosch at his car and was on her way to the ER at Hollywood Presbyterian when she got a call from EMT Single.

"How are you feeling?" he asked.

"Actually, I'm on my way to the ER," she said.

"Oh, no, what's happening?"

"Nothing, I'm fine. My boss won't let me go back to work tonight unless I get a clean bill from the ER. I told him a very good EMT had cleared me today but they're making me go anyway."

"Oh, that's too bad. I was about to invite you to a firehouse dinner."

"Wow, I've never had an invitation like that before. What are you guys having?"

"All kinds of stuff. Grilled cheese, chili. I think somebody dropped off a couple of apple pies. We've got some salad, some corn on the cob."

"Well, I'd take a salad and grilled cheese."

"Ooh, it sounds like we've got a veggie on our hands."

"Just no red meat anymore."

"Not a problem, but I thought you're going to the ER."

"I'd rather come for dinner and go to the ER on company time."

"Well, come on over. Dinner's in thirty-five minutes. Unless we catch a call and go out on a run."

"On my way. But are you allowed to invite a guest?"

"One of us can. One guest allowed a night. I traded with a guy to get tonight 'cause I hoped you'd like firehouse chili. But grilled cheese is just as good."

"All right, cool. See you in a bit. One last question..."

"Sure."

"What's your first name?"

"Oh, it's Garrett."

"Garrett. Cool. I'll see you soon, Garrett."

After disconnecting, Ballard created an entry with Single's full name in her contact list. She hoped it would stay in there for a while. She parked her car behind the police station. Before going over to the firehouse, she ducked into the locker room in the station and put on some light makeup. She was only going to a firehouse for a grilled cheese dinner, but she wanted to make an impression.

22

The dinner was fun, with Single introducing Ballard to his colleagues and her receiving a round of applause. And the grilled cheese was not bad, but the food and fun were cut short when EMT Single and his rescue team were called out on a traffic accident at Highland and Hollywood, one of the busiest intersections in the city. They raced off to the scene, and Ballard carried the second half of her grilled cheese sandwich on a napkin around the wall that separated the firehouse from the police station. She finished eating in the station while sitting in on the mid-watch roll call. Mid-watch rolled out at eight—Ballard's usual start time—and it was small squad, making roll calls less crowded and more informal. No one objected to her finishing her sandwich.

After, she went directly down the second-floor hallway to the GED squad room to look for Sergeant Davenport. He was sitting where she had last seen him three nights earlier. If he wasn't in different clothes, she might have thought he had never moved. She pulled the file he had given her out of her briefcase and dropped it on his desk. She pointed at the file.

"LP-three," she said. "I need to talk to her. For real this time."

Davenport took his legs off the upside-down trash can where they had been propped up and sat up straight.

"Ballard, you know I can't just hand out the name of a CI," he said.

"I do know," Ballard said. "You have to go through the captain. Or you could go see the CI and I could tag along. Either way is fine with me but this is now a premeditated murder case that's connected to another premeditated murder case and I need to find out what she knows. So how do you want to play that?"

"First of all, I told you, I'm not saying it's—"

"A woman, yeah, I know. Let's just say I guessed. Are you going to help or hinder this investigation?"

"If you would stop cutting me off and just listen, you would learn that LP-three is no longer active—hasn't been active in years—and is not going to be interested in talking to reminders of her dirty history."

"Okay, then. I'll call the captain at home."

Ballard turned toward the door.

"Ballard, come on," Davenport said. "Why do you always have to be such a bi—"

Ballard turned back to him.

"What?" she said. "Such a bitch? If you call wanting to solve a homicide being a bitch, then fine, I'm a bitch. But there are still people in this department who want to get off their asses and knock on doors. I'm one of them."

Davenport's temples grew pink with either rage or embarrassment. As a Sergeant II he was one rank above her Detective II, but though he was in street clothes, he was not a detective, and that difference knocked down his rank advantage. Ballard could say what she wanted to say to him without consequence.

"Okay, look," Davenport said. "It's going to take me a while to reach her and talk her into it. I'll do that and let you know."

"I want to meet tonight," Ballard said. "This is a homicide. And by the way, you just revealed again that she's a woman."

"It was pretty much out of the bag, wouldn't you say, Ballard?"

"I have to run over to Hollywood Pres for a few minutes and then I expect to hear from you that we have a meet set up."

"Fine, you do that."

"I'll call you when I'm clear."

Ballard checked out a rover and drove her city car over to the hospital, where she badged her way to the front of the line at the ER. She was checked out and cleared by a doctor and then, back in the car, called Lieutenant Robinson-Reynolds at home and gave him the news.

"That's good, Ballard," he said. "I'm glad you're okay."

"I told you I was," Ballard said.

"Yeah, well, we had to make it official," he said. "Those paramedics are a bunch of yahoos. If my mother was the one thrown down the stairs, I'd want a doctor looking at her, you know what I mean?"

Ballard didn't know which part of that to object to or whether it was even worth it. But the part about her being thrown down the stairs could have later consequences in terms of how Robinson-Reynolds viewed her and her capabilities.

"I don't know what you were told, L-T, but I wasn't thrown down the stairs," she said. "I was going up the stairs when the so-called victim came running at me. I grabbed him and we both went down."

"Semantics, Ballard," Robinson-Reynolds said. "So, you're ready to go back to work?"

"I've been working. I never stopped."

"Okay, okay, my bad. So, why don't you just tell me what you've been doing, since you never stopped working. Where are we on the cases?"

Ballard took a moment to think.

"On the Raffa case—the homicide—I'm setting up a meeting

with a gang snitch that I hope gives us a line on a money man with a motive to kill Raffa."

"What's the motive? He owed him money? That's never a good motive. Why kill the guy who owes you money? Then he can't pay you."

"That's not the motive. Raffa took money—twenty-five thousand—from this money man back in the day to buy his way out of Las Palmas. That got him a silent partner. With Raffa now dead, the silent partner gets the business, the insurance policy, if there is one, and, most important, the land the repair shop sits on. That's where the money and the motive is."

"Got it, Ballard. That's good. Real good. But you know this is probably all going to West Bureau when they come up for air."

"I know, Lieutenant, but do you want me to just babysit it or hand them a case to be made? I mean, this reflects on you, doesn't it?"

Robinson-Reynolds was silent but it didn't take him long to connect those dots.

"No, you're right," he said. "I don't want you sitting on it. I want it worked until we have to hand it off. Did they do an autopsy?"

"Not yet," Ballard said. "Right now I'm lead investigator, so they'll call when they're ready to go. Probably tomorrow sometime."

"Okay. And on this snitch, you going to take backup?"

"Rick Davenport in Gangs is setting it up. He'll be there."

"Okay, what about the Midnight Men and the new case?"

"We have all three victims filling out Lambkin surveys and tomorrow I expect the whole sex crimes team will start cross-referencing and seeing where that gets us. We're now looking at victim acquisition differently, based on the new case."

We. Ballard was annoyed with herself for continuing to cover for Lisa Moore.

"Okay," Robinson-Reynolds said. "I'll get into it with Neumayer tomorrow morning."

Matthew Neumayer was the detective in charge of the division's three-person sex crimes unit and Lisa Moore's immediate supervisor.

"Then I guess I'll get back to it," Ballard said.

"Sure," Robinson-Reynolds said. "I'll be in early tomorrow, maybe catch you before you clock out."

Ballard disconnected and immediately called Davenport.

"Ballard."

"So, are we going to do this tonight or not?"

"Don't get so pissy. We're going to do it. I will get her and bring her to meet you. What time? She doesn't want you anywhere near where she lives."

Ballard felt a charge go through her. She was going to get to LP3.

"How about in an hour?"

"An hour's good."

"Where?"

"The beach lot at the end of Sunset."

Ballard knew it well from her many mornings surfing there after work. But it was a trek to get all the way out there.

"I'm on duty and that pulls me forty minutes out of the division. If I get a call, I'm fucked."

"Do you want to talk to her or not? Her life's over there now and she's not coming back to Hollywood."

Ballard felt she had no choice.

"Okay, one hour. I'll be there."

"And Ballard, no names. Don't even ask her."

"Fine."

She knew she could get the name later if she needed to for court reasons. Then the powers that be would come down on Davenport and make him give her up. Right now, Ballard was only interested in whether LP3 could get her closer to the man with the Walther P-22.

After ending the call with Davenport, she drove back to the station and informed the watch lieutenant that she would be off radar and out of the division for the next two hours. It was Rivera on duty for the last night of the holiday weekend and he didn't seem to care much as long as Ballard had a rover with her, in case, as he said, all hell broke loose.

Afterward, she went to the squad room to print out a photo of Javier Raffa, put fresh batteries in her mini-recorder, and grab a fully charged rover out of the dock before heading back out to the car.

Traffic on Sunset dropped off quickly once she made it through the Strip and into Beverly Hills. Even with all the clubs and restaurants closed down for nearly a year, the crawl of people cruising slowed things down. Ballard felt the temperature drop as she drove west. It was a clear and crisp night. She knew she'd have to put on the down jacket she kept in the trunk for long nights at crime scenes. The wind off the Pacific would chill the parking lot where she was going to meet the informant, and she didn't know if they would talk in the open or be in a car.

It was said that anyone who wanted to know Los Angeles needed to drive Sunset Boulevard from Beginning to Beach. It was the route by which a traveler would come to know everything that is L.A.: its culture and glories as well as its many fissures and failings. Starting in downtown, where several blocks were renamed Cesar E. Chavez Avenue thirty years ago to honor the union and civil rights leader, the route took its travelers through

Chinatown, Echo Park, Silver Lake, and Los Feliz before turning west and traversing Hollywood, Beverly Hills, Brentwood, and the Palisades, then finally hitting the Pacific Ocean. Along the way, its four lanes moved through poor neighborhoods and rich neighborhoods, by homeless camps and mansions, passing iconic institutions of entertainment and education, cult food and cult religion. It was the street of a hundred cities and yet it was all one city.

Thinking about it made Ballard think of Bosch. She pulled her phone and called him, putting it on speaker.

"I'm going to meet LP-three."

"Now? By yourself?"

"No, my GED contact, Davenport, will be there. He set it up. He's getting her and bringing her to the meet."

"Where?"

"Sunset Beach. The parking lot."

"That's kind of weird."

"I wasn't too happy about it myself. She's out of the gang life and lives out there. I had no choice, according to Davenport."

"And this is going down now?"

"In about forty-five minutes. I'm on my way there."

"Okay, look, if something goes wrong, send up a flare or something. You won't see me, but I'll be there."

"What? Harry, nothing's going to go wrong. Davenport will be there. And this CI is a square Jane now. Just stay at home and I'll call you after. Besides, you just got the shot yesterday, so you should lie low till you're sure there are no side effects."

"I'm fine, and you're forgetting something. The only way those murder books could have disappeared out of two different divisions is if somebody inside the department took them. I'm not trying to frag Davenport, but he was at Hollywood when I was there and I didn't like the guy. I'm not saying he's dirty, but he was lazy and he liked to talk. And we don't know who he's been talking to about this."

Ballard didn't respond at first as she thought about Bosch's concerns.

"Well, I can confirm he's lazy but I thought that was more of a recent thing," she said. "His personal answer to defunding. But I don't think there's going to be a problem. I told my lieutenant what I'm doing and the watch L-T, because I'm going so far out of the division. I'm not going to stop you from coming, Harry—we can even meet and talk after. But I think it's going to be fine."

"I hope you're right, but I'll be there. And I should leave now."

They disconnected and Ballard thought about Bosch's words the rest of the way as she followed the curving lanes of Sunset Boulevard.

23

After the last curve, Sunset dropped down to the beach, and Ballard saw a vast parking lot next to a closed tourist restaurant. There was only one car in the lot and it did not have the boxy lines of a city ride. Ballard had forgotten that Davenport likely drove undercover wheels for his gang work. While she waited for the traffic light to change, she called him.

"You there yet?"

"We're here waiting and you're late."

"What car are you driving? I'm about to pull in."

"It will be obvious, Ballard. We're the only car in the lot. Just get in here."

He disconnected. Ballard looked at the glowing red light in the traffic signal. She acknowledged to herself that Bosch had spooked her. She checked the gas station on the corner and the supermarket parking lot beyond it and didn't see Bosch's old Cherokee. There was no way he could have gotten here from his house so quickly.

The light changed to green and she crossed into the parking lot. The arm was up on the ticket dispenser because it was after hours. She drove toward the car parked in the middle of the lot at an angle that put her headlights through the driver's-side window. As she got close, she recognized Davenport behind the wheel. She then made a looping turn and saw his passenger was in the front seat. She pulled her car up alongside so they could speak window to window and dropped the transmission into park. Before she killed the engine she took out her mini-recorder, turned it on, and started recording. She slid it into the side air-conditioning vent, where it would not be seen by the informant but would catch every word. She then held the rover up and called in her location to the com center so there would be a record of her last location should anything go wrong.

She lowered her window and killed the engine.

The woman sitting three feet away in Davenport's undercover ride was Latina and maybe forty years old. She had heavy eye makeup, long brown hair, and a high collar on her blouse that Ballard thought probably hid tattoos or the scars left by their removal.

Davenport leaned forward so he could see around his passenger to Ballard.

"What's with the cloak-and-dagger, Ballard? And you called this in? Are you fucking kidding me?"

"Robinson-Reynolds told me to."

"You shouldn't even have told him about this."

"I had to. You pull me forty minutes out of the division and I had to tell someone. He told me to tell coms when I—"

"Yeah, well, he's a fuckhead. You've got twenty minutes, Ballard. Ask your questions."

Ballard looked at the woman. She seemed put out by the shouting coming from Davenport beside her.

"Okay, what's your name?" Ballard asked.

"No names!" Davenport yelled. "Jesus Christ, Ballard, I told you. No. Names."

"Okay, okay, what do you want me to call you?" Ballard

asked. "I want this to be a conversation and I'd like to have a name for the person I'm talking to."

"How about Jane Doe?" Davenport yelled.

He pronounced the *J* like an *H*.

"Okay, never mind," Ballard said. "Let's start with what your association was with Las Palmas Thirteen."

"My fiancé—at least the man I thought was my fiancé—was a leader at the time I was with him," the woman said. "A shot caller."

"And you were an informant at that time?"

"Yes, I was."

"Why?"

The woman spoke without hesitation or trace of an accent. She spoke matter-of-factly about the potentially deadly double life she had led.

"He started fucking around on me. Stepping out with other girls. Gang whores. And nobody does that to me."

"So you didn't leave him. You became an informant."

"That's right. And I was paid too. My information was good."

She glanced back at Davenport as if to get confirmation. Davenport said nothing. Ballard had to guess that the fiancé she was talking about was Humberto Viera, who Davenport said went away to Pelican Bay and was never coming back. Ballard was talking to the living embodiment of the scorned-woman warning. Hell hath no fury.

"Fifteen minutes," Davenport helpfully called out.

"You told your LAPD handler about fourteen years ago that Javier Raffa bought his way out of Las Palmas," Ballard said. "He paid twenty-five thousand dollars to Humberto Viera. Do you remember that?"

"I do," the woman said.

"How did you come up with that piece of intel at the time?"

"I saw the money. I saw him deliver it."

Her seeing the transaction seemed to further confirm that Viera was her fiancé and that his sentence to Pelican Bay was in part due to her vengeance.

"How did that deal come about?" Ballard asked. "Did Raffa just make the offer?"

"It was negotiated," the informant said. "Raffa wanted out and knew there was only one way—in a box. But my man was greedy. He always thought about himself before the gang. And before me. He told Raffa he could pay his way out. He set the price and helped Raffa get it."

"Chopping cars?"

"No, Raffa was already doing that. That was his job. He was even called El Chopo by them. Like a joke."

"So then, where did he get the money?"

"He had to get a loan."

"Where do you get a loan to get out of a gang?"

"There was a man. People knew him. A *banquero callejero*. He went to him."

"A street banker."

"Yes, he got the money from him. The *banquero* knew people to get it from. People who wanted to make a loan."

"Do you remember his name or who he was?"

"I heard he was a cop."

Davenport flung his door open and came around the front end of the car to Ballard's window.

"What are you doing?" Ballard said.

His arm came at her and she ducked back. He reached in and pulled her key out of her car's ignition.

"That's it," he said. "No more."

"What are you talking about, Davenport?" she said. "This is an investigation."

"And I didn't sign up to drag no cop into this. Not on my fucking watch."

"Give me my key."

Davenport was already moving around his car again, back to his open door.

"I'll bring it back after I get her where you can't fucking find her."

"Davenport, give me the key. I will fucking one-twenty-eight you on this if you—"

"Fuck you, Ballard. I'll one-twenty-eight you right back. We'll see who they believe. You are one beef from the fucking door."

He jumped back in the car and slammed the door. Ballard focused on the woman.

"Who was the cop?" Ballard asked.

"Don't you fucking answer," Davenport yelled.

He looked down at his left, and the passenger window started going up.

"Who was it?" Ballard asked again.

Davenport started the car. The informant just stared at Ballard as her window closed. The car took off, racing across the parking lot to the exit.

"Goddammit!" Ballard yelled. "Shit!"

Then her phone started to buzz and she saw Bosch's name on the screen.

"Harry!"

"What just happened?"

"I'll tell you later. Where are you? Can you see them?"

"You mean the other car? Yeah, he just blew the light and started up the PCH toward Malibu."

"Can you follow him? He grabbed my key and I'm stuck. He's taking her home and I need to know who she is and where she lives."

"I'm on it."

Ballard heard the phone clunk into the center console as Bosch fired up his car and took off. Ballard jumped out of her car and scanned the businesses and parking lots along Pacific Coast Highway. She saw the squared-off Jeep Cherokee coming out of the supermarket lot onto the PCH and heading through the light at Sunset and toward Malibu.

"Get 'im, Harry," she said out loud.

24

Davenport didn't come back for nearly forty minutes. Ballard was leaning against the side of her car with her arms crossed as she watched his car come across the lot to her. He held his arm out the car window, the key to Ballard's car dangling from his hand. He wasn't staying. He kept his eyes cast forward through the windshield as he spoke.

"Had to do it, Ballard."

Ballard grabbed the key out of his hand.

"Why?"

"Because we're sinking, Ballard. All we need is to drag another cop into another scandal. Don't you get that?"

"No, Davenport, I don't get it. Who's the cop you're protecting?"

Now he turned his face to her.

"I don't know and I didn't ask her, because I don't want to know. It's the department I'm protecting, Ballard, not the cop. That's why if you beef me and I beef you, you're going to lose. The department always comes first. The department always wins. Think about that."

He hit the gas and his car took off. Ballard didn't flinch or move. She tracked the wide turn he made to go back to the gate, then pulled her phone and called Bosch.

"Harry, you got her?"

"She's in a house up here on PCH. On the water just past the light at Topanga Canyon. What happened? Did he bring back your key?"

"I have it. Give me the address and I'll come to you."

Fifteen minutes later, Ballard pulled to the side of Pacific Coast Highway behind Bosch's Jeep. She got out, walked up, and got into the passenger seat next to him.

"It's that one with the portholes," Bosch said.

He pointed across the street. The road was lined with houses cantilevered over the rocks, sand, and water. They were jammed next to each other like teeth in a mouth, so close that it was impossible to tell they were on the ocean save for the sound of the waves echoing from behind them. The house Bosch pointed at was a two-story with a single-slot carport. It was gray wood with white trim and two round windows on the second level. Ballard knew the view would be on the other side. There would be big glass looking out over the ocean.

"They pulled up," Bosch said. "He walked her in, stayed two or three minutes, and then left. What's going on, Renée?"

"She was about to name the money man," Ballard said. "She called him the street banker and said he was a cop. Then Davenport jumped in and shut it down. He acted all noble like he was trying to protect the department. But I don't buy it. I think she was about to reveal something he knew about."

"He's dirty?"

"Where's the line on dirty? I think he at least knows something about the department that could damage it. His decision is to cover it up rather than clean it up. If that's dirty, then, yeah, he's dirty. But whatever it is, he didn't know she was going to spill it. Otherwise, he wouldn't have set up the meeting."

"Makes sense. So, what do you want to do?"

"I want the street banker's name."

"Then let's go get it."

It was a Sunday night and Malibu had emptied out at the end of the holiday weekend. There was little traffic and no threat to Ballard and Bosch as they crossed four lanes of PCH in the dark. The front door to the house where the informant apparently lived was off the carport near the driver's side of the Porsche Panamera parked there. Ballard banged hard with the side of her fist so it would be heard over the sound of the waves crashing behind the house.

The door was opened before she had to hit it again. A man stood there. He was in his sixties, white, with the cliché attempts to look younger on full display: earring, bracelets, dyed hair and chin beard, fraying blue jeans, and a gray hoodie. It all went with the Porsche.

"Yes?" he asked.

Ballard badged him.

"We're here to see the woman dropped off a half hour ago," Ballard said. "I believe she may be your wife."

"I don't know what you're talking about," he said. "It's midnight and this is out—"

He was interrupted by the informant walking up behind him to see who was at the door.

"You," she said. "What do you want?"

"You know what I want," Ballard said. "I want the name."

Ballard stepped forward and her intimidating bearing made the man step back, even as he protested.

"Wait a minute here," he said. "You can't just—"

"Is this your wife, sir?" Ballard asked.

"That's right," he said.

"Well, step back unless you want this conversation to take place in a police station," Ballard said.

She then looked directly at the informant.

"You wouldn't want that, would you?" she said. "Going back to the old neighborhood. You never know who from Las Palmas might be on the lockdown bench when we go in the back door at the station."

"Gene," the informant said. "Let them in. The sooner I deal with them, the sooner they leave. Go out on the deck."

"Smart girl," Ballard said.

"It's cold out there," Gene said.

"Just go," the informant commanded. "This won't take long."

"Jesus," Gene protested. "You said this sort of shit was over."

He sauntered toward a set of sliding doors leading to the deck. Beyond the deck, the blue-black waves were beautifully lit by spotlights anchored under the house. The informant waited to speak until Gene was out on the deck and had closed the slider to muffle the sound of the ocean.

"I don't like this," she said. "Davenport told me not to speak to you anymore. And who the fuck are you?"

This last part was directed at Bosch.

"He's with me," Ballard said. "That's all you need to know. And I don't care what Davenport told you or whether you like this. You're going to tell me about the banker or you're going to be in the kind of trouble that Gene's money can't help you with."

"I haven't broken any laws," the informant said.

"There are state laws, and there are gang laws," Ballard said. "You think Humberto Viera up in Pelican Bay thinks you're innocent? You think he doesn't want to know where you've been these last ten years?"

Ballard could see the threat pierce the informant's armor. Ballard had put things together correctly. Viera was the philandering fiancé and he now had the rest of his life in maximum security to consider who had wronged him.

"Sit down over there," Bosch said, pointing to a couch. "Now."

He had read the situation as well. The informant had just gone from tough ex-gang girl to kept woman, scared that her carefully ordered life with a wealthy older man could suddenly change.

She did as she was told and went to the couch. Ballard took a swivel chair across a bamboo coffee table from her, turning it from a view through the sliders to a view of the informant. Bosch walked over to the sliders and stayed standing with his back to Gene, who was trying to watch through the glass.

"What's your name?" Ballard asked.

"I'm not giving my name," the informant said.

Resentment was written all over her face.

"I need something to call you by," Ballard insisted.

"Then call me Darla," the woman said. "I always liked that name."

"Okay, Darla, tell me about the street banker. Who was he?"

"All I know is that he was a cop and his name was Bonner. That's it. I never saw him. I don't know what he looks like. Please leave now."

"What kind of cop?"

"I don't know."

"LAPD? Sheriff's?"

"I said I don't know."

"What was his first name?"

"I don't know that either, or I would have told you."

"How do you know he was a cop? How did you know his last name?"

"From Berto. He talked about the guy."

"He said he was a street banker?"

"He said he was the guy who could get money for Raffa. He told him. I was there."

"Where?"

"We drove to Raffa's father's place. Where they fixed cars up front and chopped 'em up in the back. Raffa came to the car and Berto told him. He gave him a number to call. And he also warned El Chopo that Bonner was a cop. He said he had to be careful about dealing with him because he was a cop and he was serious people."

"What does that mean, 'serious people'?"

"You know, like don't cross him. There are consequences for shit like that."

"Did that mean he was a killer?"

"I don't know. It meant he was serious."

"Okay. Were there other times Bonner was mentioned?"

"Yeah, when Raffa brought the money to Humberto. He said Bonner got it for him from a doctor and he had to sign papers and all of that."

"What kind of doctor?"

"I didn't hear that part or they didn't talk about it. Just a doctor is what I remember."

"How come you never told this to your handler at the LAPD—about the banker being a cop?"

"Because I'm not a fool."

"What's that mean?"

"For one thing, if something happened, Berto would know it came from me because he told me about Bonner in the first place. And the other thing is that you don't rat out cops to cops. That's just stupid. Next thing you know, somebody rats you out to your man. You understand what I'm saying?"

"I do. How do you think Berto met Bonner in the first place?"

"I don't know that. They just got together somehow. They knew each other before I was in the picture."

Ballard knew that was a key connection to make.

"When was that?" she asked. "When you entered the picture?"

"Me and Berto got together when I was seventeen," Darla said. "That was '04. And we were together for six years."

Ballard had some respect for Darla and her path. To come out of East Hollywood and end up on the beach was an unlikely journey. She could see that Darla carried a certain pride in it, despite the choices of men she used to get there.

"Do you know if there were other transactions between Berto and Bonner?" Ballard asked. "I mean besides the deal with Raffa."

"Yeah, they had business," Darla said. "Like when someone needed big money, they would, like, talk and shit. I think there were other deals."

Ballard looked at Bosch to see if he had any questions she had not covered. He nodded.

"How did Berto and Bonner communicate?" he asked.

"By phone mostly," Darla said. "Sometimes they would meet up."

"Where?"

"I don't know."

Darla looked away when she answered. It was the first time in the conversation that Ballard had seen a tell indicating untruthfulness. Ballard glanced at Bosch and he nodded slightly. He had seen it too.

"You sure?" Ballard asked.

"Yeah, I'm sure," Darla said. "You think I asked Berto about his business all the time? That would get me killed."

Darla looked away again while making her protest. Ballard knew she was hiding something. She thought about how to pull it free and considered what Darla would be self-conscious about discussing. Then she hit on what it probably was.

"Come on, Darla, tell us."

"I already told you. I don't know."

"You did see Bonner, didn't you?"

"I told you, no."

"You followed him. Humberto. You followed him because you thought he was going to see a girl, but it was Bonner. You saw them together."

Darla rocked back on the couch as though shocked by Ballard's jump.

"Where'd they meet?" Ballard pressed. "It's important, Darla."

Darla flipped a hand in the air as if to say *Why not? You've gotten everything else.*

"They went up to that place on Franklin where the chicken's so good."

Ballard glanced at Bosch.

"Birds?" she asked.

The place that gave cops a discount.

"Yeah, that's it," Darla said. "I saw them and then I turned around and left."

"What did Bonner look like?" Ballard asked.

"I don't know, white. He was a white guy."

"What color hair?"

"He had a shaved head. Fucker thought he was Vin Diesel."

Ballard thought about the description Gabriel Raffa had given of the man in the hoodie.

"Was Bonner in uniform?" she asked.

Darla laughed.

"Yeah, OG Berto Viera having lunch with a cop in uniform."

"Okay, no uniform. What else do you remember, Darla?"

"That's it. No more."

"You sure. That's the only time you ever saw them?"

"Only time."

Ballard nodded. She had enough for the time being. And she knew where she could find Darla if she needed to. She looked at Bosch and he nodded. He was finished as well. To punctuate the finality of the interview, Gene knocked on the glass from the deck and held his hands wide.

He was cold and wanted to come in.

Ballard waved him in and then looked at Darla.

"Thank you…Darla," she said. "You've been very helpful."

"You going to pay me?" Darla said. "The gang guys always did."

"We do that and we have to open a new snitch jacket on you. I don't think you want that."

Darla looked at Gene as he came through the glass doors, the booming sound of a crashing wave coming in with him.

"No, I guess not," Darla said.

Ballard thanked the happy couple and exited with Bosch. There was no traffic and they crossed PCH at a steady walk.

"That was a nice jump you made with her," Bosch said. "About her following him to check if he was seeing a girl."

"Thanks," Ballard said. "It just suddenly hit me."

They stood between their cars.

"Now what?" Bosch asked.

"I'm going to run down Bonner," Ballard said. "See where it goes from there. Her description matches the one the victim's son gave me of a white guy at the New Year's party. A bald guy in a hoodie."

"There's something that doesn't fit in her story."

"What?"

"If the banker—Bonner—was a cop, why didn't Humberto use that to deal his way out of a life sentence?"

Ballard nodded. It was a good point.

"Maybe he tried to and there were no takers," she said. "Or maybe this Bonner is so 'serious' that he was afraid to. Maybe he thought Bonner being a cop meant he could get to him in County."

"A lot of maybes."

"There always are."

"Let me know what you get. I'll be around if you need me."

"Thanks, Harry. And thanks for being there tonight. We wouldn't be to this point if you hadn't thought Davenport was bent in some way."

"Then I guess we both made good jumps tonight."

"What a team. High five."

Ballard put up her hand.

"We're not supposed to be doing that during Covid," Bosch said.

"Come on, Harry," Ballard urged. "You can do it."

Bosch reached up and half-heartedly slapped her hand.

"We'll have to work on that," Ballard said.

25

After checking in at the watch office with Lieutenant Rivera, Ballard went to the detective bureau to attempt to identify Bonner. The department's active roster was easily accessible through their internal website. There were two Bonners currently on the job but one was a female, Anne-Marie, and the male, Horatio Jr., had not been in the department at the time Javier Raffa bought his way out of the Las Palmas 13. At best, these two could be legacies of the Bonner she was looking for. But asking them was not an option. Their loyalties would be with their father or uncle or whoever it was. They'd alert the Bonner that Ballard was looking for before she could get to him.

Every division had what was called a pension book. It was a binder updated annually with the roster of retired officers receiving pensions—meaning they were still alive. Dead officers were the hardest of all to trace. The listings in the pension book included the ex-officer's contact details as well as badge number, serial number, beginning- and end-of-watch dates, and final division assignment before retirement. The book was used to reach out to former officers in the course of investigations that touched on their activities while on the job. It was particularly handy in cold cases.

Hollywood Division's copy of the pension book was kept

in the detective lieutenant's office, which was locked at the moment because Robinson-Reynolds was off on a Sunday night. Undaunted, Ballard used a set of lockpicks she kept in her file cabinet to work the simple knob lock open. The white binder she was looking for was on a shelf with an assortment of department manuals behind the lieutenant's desk. Knowing she was trespassing, she made it an in-and-out operation. She opened the book on the lieutenant's desk and quickly looked through the alphabetical listings for a Bonner.

She found two: Horatio Bonner, who retired in 2002, so could not be the one Ballard was looking for but presumably was the father of at least one of the Bonners currently employed by the department; and a Christopher Bonner, who had retired seven years earlier after twenty years on the job. His rank and last assignment were listed as detective first grade in Hollywood detectives. This was curious to Ballard. She had never heard of Christopher Bonner. She had arrived in the division two years after he had left but, still, she could not recall ever seeing or hearing about a case that had his name attached to it. What added to the puzzle was that Bosch had not reacted to the name, and it seemed as though their time working in Hollywood might have overlapped, though she was not sure what year Bosch left Hollywood Division for the Open-Unsolved Unit downtown.

After laying the binder open on the desk, she pulled out her phone and took a photo of the entry for Christopher Bonner. As she did so, she noticed a yellow Post-it pad to the side of the desk's center work area. Robinson-Reynolds had written "Ballard" on the top sheet and nothing else. It was obviously a note written to remind him to tell Ballard something or get something from her. Or possibly to talk to someone else about her. Ballard could not think of what that might be, since the last time Robinson-Reynolds was in his office to write the note was during the day shift on New Year's Eve. Nothing she was involved in now had even occurred by then, except for the on-going investigation of the first two Midnight Men assaults.

She pushed the question aside for the moment, put her phone in her pocket, and then returned the pension book to its spot on the shelf. She left the office as she had found it and locked the door behind her.

At her borrowed desk, Ballard transferred the info on Bonner from her photo to her computer screen. Bonner lived in Simi Valley—at least that was where his pension checks were sent—which was a cop haven outside L.A. in Ventura County. It was close enough that he could have lived there while he was with the LAPD. Many cops did. It also put him close to the San Fernando Valley, where the nexus of the four dentists was centered at Crown Labs Incorporated.

Ballard got up and walked back to the watch office, where Lieutenant Rivera was at his desk, holding a cupcake. There was a tray of cupcakes on a counter nearby. As Ballard approached, he pointed at the tray with the cupcake in his hand.

"Citizen appreciation," he said. "Help yourself."

"These days you should have those checked by the lab first," Ballard said. "Senna glycoside, you know?"

"What the hell is that?"

"A laxative. The active ingredient in Ex-Lax."

Rivera stared down at the chocolate-frosted cake in his hand, visions of cupcake eaters lining up at the restroom likely playing in his head. He had already peeled off the paper baking cup. Hesitantly, he put it down on a napkin on his desk.

"Thanks a lot, Ballard," he said.

"Just watching out for you, L-T," she said. "Want me to call the lab?"

"Why are you here, Ballard? It's all quiet on the western front."

"I know. I wanted to ask you about Christopher Bonner."

"Bonner? What about him?"

"You know him?"

"Of course. He worked here."

"He supposedly worked here as a detective."

"Yeah, he had your job."

"What?"

"Worked the late show right up until the day he pulled the pin."

Ballard was shocked by the coincidence but it helped explain why his name was unfamiliar to her. Midnight-shift detectives usually turned their cases over to dayside detectives. As a result, they weren't formally listed as leads on many cases. This could also help explain why Bosch didn't recognize the name.

"So, you must have known him pretty well then," she said.

"Yeah, I guess," Rivera said. "Just like you, he worked for me."

Ballard didn't bother correcting him about who she actually reported to.

"You said 'the day he pulled the pin,'" she said. "Did something happen with him that made him quit?"

"I don't know, Ballard," Rivera said. "He just quit. Maybe he got fed up with all the shit out there. I don't need to tell you what you see out there on the night shift."

"No, you don't."

"Why are you asking about Chris?"

"Oh, his name came up in the homicide from Thursday night. He knew the family from back in the day. I was just curious about him, is all."

Ballard hoped her answer would satisfy Rivera without

suspicion. As a distraction, she bent down over the tray of cup-cakes, holding her hair back so it didn't flop onto the icing.

"You know," she said. "I think these look all right. Mind if I take one?"

"Knock yourself out," Rivera said.

She picked one with vanilla cake and icing.

"Thanks," she said. "Hard to hide something in vanilla."

She headed to the door.

"I'm around if you need me," she said.

"I'll call you," Rivera said.

When she got back to the detective bureau, she dumped the cupcake in the trash can under the desk she was borrowing. She then pulled her phone and called Bosch, hoping he had not already gone to bed.

"You find him?" he asked.

"I think so," she said. "And get this—he had my job here at Hollywood."

"What do you mean? Late-show detective?"

"That's right. He retired two years before I got here, and I think he might have been here when you were."

"I must be losing it. I don't remember that name."

"You probably never came across him. Out of sight, out of mind."

"Is he still local?"

"Simi Valley."

"Well, that puts him in our frame of reference. Looks like he's the money man. Is he also the man with the P-twenty-two?"

"We're not there yet."

"How are you going to work it?"

"Not much I can do with it till tomorrow. But I can go through records, see if there's anything that connects the dots."

"Good idea."

"Yeah, so let me do that, you get some sleep, and I'll let you know if I get anything in the morning after shift. By then I'll also probably know if I still have the case."

"Happy hunting."

This was the homicide detective's sign-off. It was a show of respect, and Ballard thought there was no one in the entire department whose respect she would take over Harry Bosch's.

Before going to work on the department database, she pulled her phone, checked her email, and learned that a woman named Daisy from Wags and Walks had responded to her request to meet the Chihuahua mix named Pinto. The message was that Pinto was still available for adoption and would be happy to meet Ballard.

Ballard, not knowing what the day ahead would bring, responded with a request to see the dog on Tuesday. Since Tuesday was one of Ballard's regular days off, she said in the email that Daisy could name the time of the appointment and she would make it work. She added that she was very excited to meet Pinto.

Ballard put the phone aside and used the desk terminal to enter the department database. She started with the biggest net that she could throw: all cases with Bonner's name and serial number in the reports.

The department was digitized going back to the mid '90s, so Bonner's entire career was covered. The search engine took more than a minute to come back with over 14,000 hits. Ballard thought that was actually low considering that Bonner had put in twenty years. She guessed that by the time she hit her twenty years, she would have more than double that number of engagements in the database.

Checking through that many reports, even those easily dismissed, could take days. Ballard needed to cut it down to hours—at least initially. She pulled up her chrono on her laptop and checked the date of the intel report that Javier Raffa had bought his way out of the Las Palmas gang. It was dated October 25, 2006, meaning that Bonner was already associated in some way with shot caller Humberto Viera at that time. Ballard resubmitted her search for reports with Bonner's name on them, chopping the net down to three years on either side of the date of the report.

This time the search took less time and the computer coughed up 5,403 hits. She then cut this down to 3,544 by searching only two years on either side of the 2006 marker.

Ballard looked up at the clock and saw that it was nearly three. Her shift ended at six but she was going to wait until Robinson-Reynolds came in to work, and that would be between seven and eight, and more likely later than earlier. After that, she planned to meet with Matt Neumayer, head of the Sex Assault team, whether or not Lisa Moore was back from her sojourn in Santa Barbara.

Ballard decided that if she got lucky and there were no callouts, and if she kept herself from going computer blind, she could get through all the reports by the time of her meetings the next morning.

She set to work with a quick protocol for reviewing the reports. She would scan only the front sheet, which contained the name of the victim, suspect—if there was one—and type of crime or callout. This would allow her to quickly move past trivial reports of minor crimes and citizen interactions. If something intrigued her, she would open the full report to read further, looking for connections to Humberto Viera or anyone else whose name had come up so far in the Raffa investigation.

It was Sunday night and calm out on the streets. No calls came in to interrupt Ballard. She got up once an hour for a few minutes to take her eyes off the computer screen and to get coffee or walk up and down the aisles of the detective bureau. At one point a patrol officer came in to find a desk to type up a report, and Ballard sent him to use a terminal on the other side of the room because he wasn't wearing a mask.

Two hours into the search, she had reached the date of October 25, 2006, in the reports and had nothing to show for it. There had been no report with reference to Bonner that involved an arrest, investigation, or interaction with a member of the Las Palmas 13 gang. That in itself was a revelation, because it was hard for Ballard to believe that one could go a solid two years as a midnight-shift detective without a single interaction with a Las Palmas gangster in some form. It told her that Bonner had avoided gang cases, if not overtly looked the other way when it came to gang crimes.

It also told her that she needed to reframe her search. She didn't see going through the next two years of records as the best use of her time. Instead she went back to the search engine and asked for records from 2000 to 2004, producing 3,113 reports with Bonner's name on them.

These reports began with Bonner as a patrol officer in Hollywood Division. He then got a promotion to detective in early 2002 and was assigned to the third watch, which was considered an entry detective position at the time. It still was, but it had not been an entry position for Ballard. Her assignment to the dark hours had come as punishment for pushing back against one of the many ills of the department: sexual harassment. She had lost a departmental skirmish with her boss at the Robbery-Homicide Division and was banished to the night shift in Hollywood.

An hour later, Ballard found the needle in the digital haystack of reports: a report dated October 5, 2004, in which Bonner was listed as the late-show detective who responded to a call about a shooting into an occupied dwelling. The incident occurred at 3:20 a.m. at a home on Lemon Grove Avenue near Western Avenue. The summary stated that the occupants of the home were asleep when a drive-by shooting occurred, a gunman spraying automatic fire from a passing car. No one was hurt and the occupants might not have even called the police, but several neighbors did.

The report listed the occupants of the house as Humberto Viera and his girlfriend, Sofia Navarro. Ballard believed she now knew Darla's real name.

A follow-up report written by Bonner, who at this point had been a detective for less than a year, described Viera and Navarro as uncooperative. The summary described Viera as a high-ranking member of the Las Palmas 13 street gang.

The summary also stated that information from GED indicated that Viera was suspected of having been involved in an abduction attempt of a rival gang member named Julio Sanz. According to the intel, Sanz was a member of the White Fence street gang, which operated out of Boyle Heights but was encroaching on Las Palmas turf. The abduction was an attempt to gain leverage in brokering an agreement between the gangs on the turf border.

Ballard tried one more shot at backgrounding Bonner. The Hollywood Division had always enjoyed the support of a local citizens group called Blue Hollywood. The group supplied equipment, paid for the Christmas party, and staged neighborhood meetings. It also welcomed new transfers and thanked those retiring, often with a story and photo on their website.

Ballard went to bluehollywood.net and put Bonner's name into the search window. She was rewarded with a mention and photo in the monthly "Comings and Goings" column that ran seven years before. It was the formal photo that had been on the division's organization chart outside the captain's office when Bonner had served. Ballard enlarged the photo on her screen and studied it. Bonner had deep-set eyes and a shaved head. His neck was tight against the collar of his uniform. He was not smiling in the photo.

Ballard leaned back and rubbed her eyes. Dawn's light was just beginning to come in through the casement windows that ran along the top of the walls of the detective bureau.

She had directly connected Bonner and Viera, which lent credence and confirmation to what Darla/Sofia had revealed: Viera had put Javier Raffa in touch with Bonner when Raffa needed a big sum of money. She had also found a visual on Bonner that was consistent with the description she had received from both Darla and Gabriel Raffa.

The next connection that had to be made was between Bonner and the dentists and their factoring operation. The money Bonner had arranged and delivered for Raffa came from somewhere, and most likely not from Bonner's own bank account. But Ballard had no idea where the late-show detective and the daytime dentists had crossed paths.

She printed out all the reports on the drive-by shooting incident. And while she waited, she put the name Julio Sanz into the search window and learned that he had been murdered in November 2004, just five weeks after the drive-by shooting of Humberto Viera's house.

Despite her eyes being tired and unable to hold focus on the computer screen, Ballard pulled up the reports on that murder. Sanz had been gunned down in Evergreen Cemetery, where he had gone to visit his father's grave on the anniversary of his death. He was found sprawled across the grave, shot once in the head execution-style.

The case was never solved.

Ballard leaned back from the screen again and considered this latest piece of information. Five weeks after Humberto Viera's home got strafed, and five weeks after Viera met Detective Christopher Bonner on that case, the man thought to be behind the drive-by was murdered in an East L.A. cemetery.

Ballard saw no coincidence in that. She was beginning to see the relationships between elements in her investigation. It was all moving in one orbit, circling the killing of Javier Raffa.

26

Ballard didn't know how early Robinson-Reynolds would be coming in after the holiday weekend. She decided to use the time waiting to switch gears from the Raffa case to the Midnight Men investigation.

She knew that most city services departments began work at seven. She left the station and drove into East Hollywood, where the Bureau of Street Lighting had a service lot at Santa Monica Boulevard and Virgil Avenue. Its location was marked by a procession of the various types of streetlights found in Los Angeles, all planted on the sidewalk in front of the work-and-storage yard. Over at the county museum, there was an art installation of L.A. streetlights that tourists and art aficionados flocked to for selfies. Here was the real thing. Ballard pulled into the yard and parked in front of the office. She knew she needed to be cautious here. It was not outside the bounds of possibility that one or both Midnight Men worked for the BSL. It might explain their familiarity with the various neighborhoods of Hollywood, and their knowing which wire to cut to disable the light outside Cindy Carpenter's house without cutting the line that fed power to all the lights on the street. Ballard had seen a tangle of wires behind the access panel but only one had been cut.

As she got out, she looked around the work yard and into the open bays of a garage. She assumed that most of the BSL trucks were already out in the field by now, but there were two trucks parked in the repair bays. They were white but they were not vans, and each carried a city seal on the driver's-side door with BUREAU OF STREET LIGHTING printed beneath it. Jack Kersey had not mentioned the city seal in his description of the van he had seen up on Deep Dell Terrace.

Ballard stepped into the office, showed her badge, and asked to see a supervisor. She was ushered in to see a man named Carl Schaeffer, who had a cubbyhole office where the time cards and time clock were in his sight and a work schedule dominated the wall behind his desk. His title was yard supervisor. Ballard closed the door and took a good look at Schaeffer. He was in his fifties and far outside the age range the victims had estimated for the Midnight Men.

"I need to confirm some information related to streetlight repairs," Ballard said.

"We cover Alvarado to Westwood and the ten north to Mulholland," Schaeffer said. "If that's where you're looking, then I'm your guy. How can I help?"

"I'm looking for repair records for Deep Dell Terrace for…let's go back the last two months."

"Okay, that one I know without looking because we're sending a truck up there today."

"What's going on up there?"

"Sounds like we have a tampering situation. A homeowner says two of our guys cut power to the post, but we didn't have any guys up there. Sounds like it was vandalism."

"When was this?"

"Happened December thirtieth according to the homeowner."

"Can you cancel the service up there today?"

"Uh, sure I can. How come?"

"I'm going to have the post and access plate processed for fingerprints. There was a crime committed in the area and the suspects may have cut the light ahead of time."

"What kind of crime? Was it a murder?"

"No."

Schaeffer waited for Ballard to say more but she didn't. He got the message.

"But you think somebody cut the light so no one could see them?"

"Possibly. Do you have any records of other work orders for Deep Dell?"

"No. I can go back and look but I would remember anything recent. They got a guy lives up there—whenever they lose a light, we hear from him, and this one on Deep Dell Terrace was the first time I've heard from him in about a year."

"Jack Kersey?"

"Sounds like he calls you folks, too."

"I ran into him up there."

"He's a character. Keeps us on our toes, I'll tell you that."

"I can tell."

"What else can I do for you, Detective?"

"I have two other streets I want to check to see if you've had repair orders there recently."

She did not give him the dates or exact addresses of the first two sexual assaults. She just asked if there had been any repairs to streetlights in the last three months in the 600 block of Lucerne Boulevard or the 1300 block of Vista Street. For these Schaeffer could not answer from memory. He punched the addresses into his computer and then sent two pages to his printer.

"The answer is yes," he said. "I'm printing it out for you.

We got calls on both streets. On Lucerne we got the complaint December second and repaired it the fourth. On Vista it came in on the twenty-eighth and we were shorthanded because everybody wants that week off. Repairs on Vista are going out today as well."

"I want you to stop that repair too," Ballard said.

"Not a problem."

"Thank you. I have a couple more questions. On the Lucerne repair, did you get a report on what the problem was there?"

"Yeah, it's on the printout. That was vandalism—wires cut at the base."

"Multiple wires?"

Schaeffer checked his computer screen.

"We had to replace the whole circuit there," he said. "The feed line and the loop."

That was the street where the first rape occurred. Ballard considered that the Midnight Men had cut two wires there because they didn't know which was the feed. By the time of the Deep Dell attack they had learned.

"So they actually disabled several lights at once?" she asked.

"Exactly," Schaeffer said. "And we got complaints from multiple residents."

By learning to cut just one light—the one nearest the intended victim's house—the Midnight Men were improving their MO and less likely to draw immediate attention to their nefarious efforts.

"Okay," Ballard said. "I noticed that most of your trucks are out in the field, but there are two in the bays. Do you use white vans for service calls?"

"Vans? No. We use flatbeds, so when we have to replace a post or a whole light assembly, we can take what we need on the work truck. You can't put a fourteen-foot streetlight in a van, and that's what we're most often doing—replacing the whole assembly. People like hitting them with their cars."

He smiled at his own attempt at humor.

"Got it," Ballard said. "And your flatbeds are clearly marked as city vehicles? With the city seal and department name?"

"Always," Schaeffer said.

"No vans?"

"Not a one. Do you want to tell me what's going on? Is somebody doing some shit and saying he's with us?"

"I wish I could tell you, Mr. Schaeffer—you've been very helpful. But I can't, and I need you to keep this confidential. Don't talk about it with anyone."

"What am I going to tell? I don't know what's going on."

Ballard reached into her pocket for a business card. It had her cell number on it.

"One last thing," she said. "I need to know about any reported light outages in the Hollywood area for the next two weeks. I don't care if it's a weekend or not, I need you to call me as soon as a report comes in that there's a streetlight out. I don't need to know about car accidents. Just lights that are burned out, malfunctioning, vandalized, whatever. Can you do that?"

"Of course, not a problem," Schaeffer said.

"Thank you, sir. When this is all over, I'll be able to tell you more about it."

"Whatever it is, I hope you catch the bastard. Especially if he's the one out there cutting our wires."

He handed her the printouts with the details of the first two streetlight outages. Ballard thanked him again and left. As she returned to her car, she acknowledged to herself that it was more likely than not that the next report of a vandalized streetlight in Hollywood would come in after it was too late and the next attack had already occurred.

From the work yard, Ballard drove by the exact locations of the streetlights noted on the printouts. In each case, the light where the wiring had been cut was in close proximity to the house where one of the sexual assaults had taken place. It left Ballard with no doubt that the Midnight Men had tampered with the lights before the attacks to further cloak their activities in darkness. She also noticed that in both locations the streetlights were different from the glass acorns in the Dell.

She called SID and requested that a print tech come out and process the access plate at the base of the light on Vista, as well as the light up on Deep Dell Terrace. It was a long shot but Ballard knew that long shots never paid off if you didn't take them. A fingerprint could change the trajectory of the investigation in an instant. She left the Lucerne address off the request because that light had already been repaired and any fingerprint evidence left by the Midnight Men would likely be gone.

She checked her phone and saw that it was almost eight and her lieutenant should be in his office by the time she got back.

Along the way, she took a call from an autopsy coordinator at the County Medical Examiner's Office. With more than a thousand autopsies conducted a week, the coroner needed a coordinator just to set the schedule and make notifications to investigators and families of the dead. She was informed that the autopsy of Javier Raffa was set for 11 a.m. with deputy medical examiner Dr. Steven Zvader.

Ballard said she would be there.

Lieutenant Robinson-Reynolds was behind his desk when Ballard got back to the detective bureau. Ballard knocked on the window next to his open door and he signaled her in.

"Ballard," he said. "I thought maybe you'd already gone home. How's the head?"

"I'm good," Ballard said. "I was just out doing an interview on the Midnight Men thing."

"You need to fill out an IOD."

"I'm okay, L-T."

"Look, you want to get paid for Saturday night when you went home early? Fill out the form."

Ballard knew that filling out an Injured On Duty form would take the better part of an hour and its only purpose was to serve as a record of injuries in case the officer later took action against the department or sought an early retirement due to injury. The city would not cover or accept any financial or retirement request based on injuries not detailed in the IOD form. It didn't matter that some injuries became an issue long after they initially occurred. Bosch was an example. He was exposed to radioactive material on a case. Ten years later, when it manifested as a form of leukemia, the city tried to look the other way because he had never filed an IOD form. Luckily, he had good doctors and a good lawyer and came out okay.

"All right," Ballard said. "I'll get to it before I leave. I have to hang around for the autopsy on Raffa anyway."

"Right," Robinson-Reynolds said. "We should talk about that. Sit down, Ballard."

Ballard sat down in one of the chairs in front of his desk. As she did so, she noticed a small black leather pouch on the corner of the desk. It was blocked from Robinson-Reynolds's view in his seat because of a vertical file in front of it. He must have missed it when he entered the office earlier, probably reading the overnight note as he entered.

The pouch contained Ballard's lockpick set. She had put it down on the desk after entering the office the night before to get to the pension book. She had then forgotten it when she left. If the lieutenant found it, he would not be able to trace it back to

Ballard but he would know that someone had been in his office over the holiday weekend, and she knew suspicion would likely fall on her. She was trying to think of a way to surreptitiously grab it, when Robinson-Reynolds told her she was off the Raffa case.

"Wait, what?" she asked.

"I talked to West Bureau, and they're ready to take it off your hands," Robinson-Reynolds said.

"I don't want it taken off my hands. I was working it all night and have identified a suspect and want to keep rolling with it."

"That's great and I'm sure they will welcome all your good work. But it's not your job. You're not a homicide detective. We have been over this before and I goddamn hate it that every time you don't want to give up a case, you try to make it out as a betrayal. I'm not your enemy, Ballard. There is an established protocol and we must follow it."

"The autopsy's in two hours. Who takes that?"

"I'm assuming you do. But then you call this guy and arrange to hand it all off."

He handed a Post-it Note across the desk to her. It had her name on the top—it was the Post-it she had seen earlier—but now it had another name and a number written under hers: Detective Ross Bettany. Ballard had never heard of him, but he would be the one to take her good work and close the case.

"Tell me about this suspect," Robinson-Reynolds said.

Ballard knew that if she mentioned that she had linked two murders and that the likely hit man was an ex-LAPD cop, she wouldn't even get the autopsy. Robinson-Reynolds would skip over her and West Bureau and go straight to the Robbery-Homicide Division downtown. They would grab it like a hawk snatching a sparrow out of the air. She didn't want that. If she couldn't be lead, she wanted to give it to Bettany in such a way that she still retained a piece of it. That way, Bettany and his partner would need her and her knowledge to close it.

"We think it was about money," she said. "As I told you on the phone yesterday, Raffa's shop was sitting on a valuable piece of land. He had a silent partner and he was trying to break their contract. We think the partner hired a hitter—the go-between who brought them both together in the first place."

Ballard thought she had walked the tightrope without a net. Nothing she had said was false. She just didn't tell the whole story.

"'We'?" Robinson-Reynolds asked.

"What?" Ballard said.

"You said, 'We think it was about money.' Who's 'we'?"

"Oh, sorry, just an expression. I meant 'we' as in the LAPD as a whole. We think."

"You sure?"

"Uh, yeah. Last I checked, the department hasn't filled my partner's slot because of the freeze."

The lieutenant nodded like all of that was true.

"You know a guy named Harry Bosch?" he asked. "Retired LAPD. Worked here at Hollywood for a lot of years, in fact."

Ballard realized that she had just walked into a mantrap. She went in one door and it had locked behind her. The next door had to be opened from the other side. And Robinson-Reynolds was the guy on the other side.

"Uh, yeah, I know him," she said carefully. "We've crossed paths on things before. Why?"

She wanted to get as much from Robinson-Reynolds as she could before she tried walking across the tightrope again.

"Because I got a report here on my desk that came from GED," Robinson-Reynolds said. "They had your victim's memorial service under surveillance so they could see what guys from

Las Palmas showed up. Instead, they got photos of you standing with an old guy identified as Harry Bosch and talking to another guy who didn't look too happy about being talked to."

Ballard's mind was racing as she tried to put together an answer.

"Yeah," she said. "That was Bosch and that was the silent partner I was just talking about. Dennis Hoyle."

She doubted that Robinson-Reynolds would go for the distraction of Hoyle, but it gave Ballard time to think her way through this confrontation. She knew one thing: Davenport was behind this. He had sent the surveillance photos to the lieutenant. Ballard decided she would find a way to deal with him later.

"And Bosch?" Robinson-Reynolds said. "Why was he there? Why was he with you?"

He held up a surveillance photo, and there was Bosch next to Ballard as they confronted Hoyle at his car. Ballard knew that her only way out was to come clean about the first murder. Bosch's case. If she gave that to Robinson-Reynolds, she might survive this.

"Well, you see," she began. "I took—"

"Let me see if I can put it together," the lieutenant said, cutting her off. "You've got a full plate. You catch a murder New Year's Eve and West Bureau's overwhelmed so you have to run with that through the weekend. Then the Midnight Men jump up again and now you've got that. You've got no help because even Lisa Moore's abandoned you for Santa Barbara— yes, I know about that. So you're up against the wall, and you remember Harry Bosch, the retired guy who wishes he wasn't retired. You think, 'I could reach out to him for help and advice, but how do I get to him?' So you pull out your little black bag of lockpicks and you break into my office to get the pension book that has Bosch's number. The only problem besides getting photographed by the GED is that you forgot the little black bag and you put the pension book back in the wrong spot. How am I doing?"

Ballard stared at him in awe. The mantrap door was opening.

"You're a detective, L-T," she said. "That's amazing. But there's another reason I called Bosch."

"And what's that?" Robinson-Reynolds asked.

"Ten years ago he worked a homicide here in Hollywood. I connected the Raffa case to his case through ballistics. His case is still open. I wanted to talk to him about it and we agreed to meet at the Raffa memorial."

Robinson-Reynolds leaned back in his chair as he considered this.

"And when were you going to tell me this?" he asked.

"Today. Now. I was waiting for the chance."

"Ballard..."

He decided not to say what he was going to say.

"Just make sure Ross Bettany gets everything you've got on the case," he said instead.

"Of course," Ballard said.

"And look, I don't mind what you did. But I mind how you did it. You're lucky I think Davenport up there in GED is an empty suit. Why he's mad at you, I don't know. Sounds like professional jealousy. But what I do mind is you breaking into my office. That can't happen again."

"It won't, sir."

"I know it won't. Because I'm going to get one of those Ring cameras and put it in here so I get an alert anytime somebody comes in."

Ballard nodded.

"That's a good idea," she said.

"So take your little black bag and go call West Bureau and

arrange to hand off the case," Robinson-Reynolds said. "Then call Bosch and tell him his services on the case are no longer needed. That West Bureau will take it from here."

"Yes, sir."

"And then I want you to get together with the Sex team to figure out next moves on the Midnight Men. I want to be briefed before you split."

"Yes, sir."

"You can go now, Ballard."

Ballard stood up, took the lockpicks off the corner of the desk, and headed for the door. Before leaving, she turned back to the lieutenant.

"By the way, I'm off the next three nights," she said. "Did you put somebody on call yet?"

"Not yet," Robinson-Reynolds said. "I'll figure it out."

"How did you know about Lisa and Santa Barbara?"

"Because I was in Santa Barbara. I'm walking on the beach and hear this voice and I look, and there is Moore in a cabana in front of the Miramar."

"Did you say something?"

"Nope. I'm going to bring her in here like I did with you. See if she tells me a story or tells me the truth. And don't you warn her, Ballard."

"I won't."

"If she tells me the truth, we'll be fine. If she lies to me … well, I can't have that."

"I understand."

Ballard left the office and took an immediate right turn, away from the squad room and toward the station's front hallway. She went to the break room to brew a cup of coffee. She knew it was going to be a few hours before she would get to sleep. She also didn't want to be in the detective bureau when Lisa Moore showed up for work and the lieutenant summoned her to his office. She didn't need to have Moore blaming her for not giving her a warning.

As the coffee dripped, Ballard considered firing a text to Moore telling her not to lie to the L-T.

But she didn't. Moore could make her own way and deal with the consequences.

27

Ballard walked into the squad room through the back hallway and saw Matt Neumayer and Ronin Clarke at their
workstations in the Crimes Against Persons pod. Lisa Moore's
station was empty. Ballard walked over, put her coffee down on
one of the half walls that separated the workstations. It was a six-
person pod; one half was the Sexual Assault Unit and the other
was the actual CAPs Unit, which handled all assaults that were
not sexually motivated.

"Lisa coming in?" Ballard asked.

"She's here," Clarke said. "L-T called her in for a powwow."

Ballard glanced toward the lieutenant's office and through the
glass could see Lisa sitting in front of Robinson-Reynolds's desk.

"You know, Ronin, you're not supposed to use words like that
anymore," Neumayer said.

Ballard looked at Neumayer. It did not look like he was serious.

"Powwow?" Clarke said. "My bad—I'll add it to my list. I
guess I'm just not woke enough."

Clarke then turned to Ballard.

"So, Ballard, are you Indian?" Clarke said. "You look like
there's something going on there."

He made a gesture as if circling her face.

"You mean Native American?" Ballard asked. "No, I'm not."

"Then what?" Clarke persisted.

Neumayer cut in before Clarke could put both feet across the line.

"Renée, sit down," he said. "Tell me about the weekend."

She sat in Moore's station and had to adjust the seat up so she could see both Neumayer and Clarke over the dividers, though she was going to talk mostly to Neumayer.

"You know about the new Midnight Men case, right?" she asked.

"Lisa told us before she got called in," Neumayer said.

"Well, I think we need to change the focus a little bit," Ballard said.

"Why?" Clarke asked.

"The new case is up in the hills," Ballard said. "The Dell. And it's not the kind of neighborhood you walk into to peep in windows and find a victim. She was targeted and followed there. At least that's my take. So that changes how we should look at victim acquisition. The first two, the thinking was that the suspects picked the neighborhood because of access and then found their victims. That doesn't work with victim three. So there's something about these victims that connects them, and whatever that is—a place or an event either real or virtual— that's what put them on the suspects' radar."

"Makes sense," Neumayer said. "Any idea where that…point is?"

"The nexus?" Ballard said. "No, not yet. But victim three runs a coffee shop in Los Feliz. That means she has many interactions with strangers on a daily basis. Anyway, that's what I stuck around for. To talk it out with Lisa and you guys."

"Well, here she comes now," Neumayer said. "Let's all go into the task force room. Nobody's using it."

Moore walked up to the pod. She had either gotten a

sunburn over the weekend or was colored with embarrassment or anger.

Ballard started to get up from her chair.

"No, that's okay, Renée," Moore said. "Take it. You earned it."

"What are you talking about?" Ballard asked.

"You got my job," Moore said. "Might as well start today."

Now she had the attention of Clarke and Neumayer, who was already gathering files to take to the task force room.

"I don't know what you're talking about," Ballard said.

"Sure you do," Moore said. "Next deployment I'm on the late show and you're on Sex. And don't play stupid. You set me up."

"I didn't set anybody up," Ballard said. "And this is news to me."

"Me too," Clarke said.

"Shut up, Clarke," Moore said. "This is between me and this backstabbing bitch."

Ballard tried to remain calm.

"Lisa, wait a minute," Ballard said. "Let's go back into L-T's office and—"

"Fuck you, Ballard," Moore said. "You know I'm a single mother. I've got kids—how the hell am I going to work midnights? And all because you got pissed that you had to cover for me."

"Lisa, I did cover for you," Ballard said. "I did not tell the lieutenant one thing about you or this—"

"He already knew, Lisa," Neumayer said. "He knew about the Miramar."

Moore jerked her laser focus off Ballard and onto Neumayer.

"*What?*" she asked.

"He knew," Neumayer said. "The Miramar, right? Santa Barbara? Dash told me Thursday he was going up there for the weekend. If that's where you were when you should have been working with Ballard, then he probably saw you. Did he just ask you how the weekend was?"

Moore didn't answer but didn't have to. Her face betrayed her. She was realizing that the trap she had just walked into in the lieutenant's office had been set by herself.

"Bang, the penny drops," Clarke said. "You fucked up, Moore."

"Shut up, Clarke," Moore said.

"Okay, can we put this little dustup aside for now?" Neumayer said. "Let's all go to the TFR. We've got a pair of rapists to catch."

There was a lull before Moore made a sweep of her hand toward the hallway that led to the task force room.

"Lead the way," she said.

The men got up from their stations and Neumayer did lead the way, a white binder tucked under his arm. Clarke quickly caught up to him, perhaps sensing that the tension between the two women was not something he wanted to get in the middle of.

Ballard followed at a ten-yard distance and Moore took fourth position in the parade. She spoke to Ballard's back as they walked.

"I suppose you want an apology," she said.

"I don't want anything from you, Lisa," Ballard said.

Ballard suddenly stopped short and turned to Moore. They were standing in the back hallway where only the shoeshine guy could hear them.

"You know, you may have fucked yourself but you also fucked me," Ballard said. "I like my job. I like the dark hours and now I'm going to be dayside thanks to you."

Ballard turned and continued down the hall, passing by the shoeshine station.

Once all four of them were settled in the TFR, Neumayer asked Ballard to summarize the weekend's occurrences, since it was now apparent that Moore had played hooky. Ballard gave a concise update and told them about her reaching out to the three victims.

"I have victim three's Lambkin survey here," she said. "The other two should be completed by now. You just have to call them today to collect. When you compare them, see if we get any triple matches. Or even double matches."

Clarke groaned at the idea of desk work.

"Thanks, Ballard," he said. "Why don't you stick around to help?"

"Because I'm going to be sleeping, Clarke," Ballard said. "I worked all night and I've been working this case all weekend. I'm out of here as soon as we're done with this meeting."

"You're cool, Renée," Neumayer said. "We'll handle it from here."

"Good, because I'm supposed to have the next three days off," Ballard said.

"All right," Neumayer said. "Why don't you give us victim three's survey and we'll take it from there. You can go home."

"We also may have caught a break," Ballard said. "These scumbags cut the power to the streetlights near each victim's house. They wanted it dark."

"Holy shit," Clarke said.

"How'd you get that?" Neumayer asked.

"A resident up in the Dell told me the light outside the victim's house was out the night before the attack. This morning I went to the BSL to check work orders and—"

"BSL?" Moore asked.

"Bureau of Street Lighting," Ballard said. "On Santa Monica near Virgil. I checked work orders, and lights on the other victims' streets were cut around the same time as the attacks. Exact times are not known, because they work off complaints.

But the complaint records are in line. I think these guys cut the lights to darken the streets for when they came back to do their evil shit. I asked Forensics to print the posts and access plates on the lights, but my guess is that's a long shot."

"That's good, Renée," Neumayer said.

"But what's it get us?" Clarke asked.

"Dipshit, MLK weekend is in, like, two weeks," Moore said. "We need to wire the BSL, and maybe we get up on them for their next hit."

Ballard nodded.

"Exactly," she said. "And they're already wired. I'll get a call every time a light is reported out between now and then."

Clarke looked hurt that he had not put the obvious together.

"Sounds excellent," Neumayer said. "Maybe we're getting the upper hand on these guys. But we still have to run with the surveys. Ronin and Lisa, pick a vic. Go get the surveys and then let's meet back here and start cross-referencing. Renée, good work. You go home and get some sleep now."

Ballard nodded. She didn't mention that she had an autopsy to go to.

"Call me if you come up with something," she said.

"Oh, one thing before we grab and go," Neumayer said. "I wanted to talk about the media. We've been lucky that they haven't picked up on this. But now, a third case, it's going to get out. Somehow it always does. Now that we have this streetlight lead, I'm still inclined to try to keep the investigation under wraps. But it's dangerous."

It was always a no-win situation. Going public alerted your suspects and allowed them to change the MO being used to track them. Not going public left the department wide open to criticism for not warning people of the menace that was out there. In typically cynical fashion, the decision of whether to go public would be made purely along political lines for the department and with no consideration of the victims who might have been saved from trauma.

"I'll talk to the L-T about it," Neumayer said. "But if this leaks, we are not going to look good. They'll scream that we should have warned the public."

"Maybe we should," Ballard said. "These two are already looking at life for multiple rapes. As soon as they figure that out, they'll probably escalate. They'll stop leaving live victims."

"And that's the risk we take," Neumayer said. "Let me talk to the lieutenant, and he may want to talk to media relations. I'll let you know what is decided."

As they returned to the squad room, Moore said nothing to Ballard. The friendly and professional relationship they once shared seemed completely and permanently gone.

Ballard crossed the room and knocked on Robinson-Reynolds's open door. He signaled her in.

"Ballard, I thought you'd left."

"I stayed around to brief the Sex team. And now I have the autopsy to go to."

"Then you probably heard about the next deployment. You're off midnights, Ballard. I was going to tell you myself."

"Yeah, I heard. And L-T, I gotta ask, Why am I getting punished for Lisa's sins?"

"What are you talking about? You're not being punished."

"She said I'm off the late show and she's on."

"That's exactly right. You go to the Sex table, where I'm sure we'll see vast improvements. You and Neumayer will make a great team. Clarke is a deadweight but generally harmless."

"That's the point. I like the late show. By punishing Lisa, you're punishing me. I wasn't looking to leave midnights."

Robinson-Reynolds paused. Ballard saw his mind churning.

He had started with the assumption that no detective liked working the midnight shift. But that was his view of it, not Ballard's.

"I see where I may have fucked up," he said. "You don't want to move."

Ballard shook her head.

"The only move I'd want is back to Homicide downtown, and we know that isn't going to happen. So, I like midnights. Good variety of cases, no deadweight partner to carry, out of sight and out of mind. It's perfect for me."

"Okay, I'll rescind the order. When the next deployment comes out, you'll still be third watch."

"What about Lisa?"

"I don't know about her. Probably she'll stay where she is and I'll ding her personnel jacket. But Ballard, don't tell her I rescinded. I want her to stew about it for a week till the new DP is posted. That'll be her punishment."

Ballard shook her head.

"L-T, she's got kids and she's going to start making arrangements to get cover on the nights. I think you should tell her. Write her up, put it on her record, like you said, but don't leave her swinging like that."

"This needs to be a learning experience, Ballard. And don't you tell her. Not a word. That's an order."

"Roger that."

Ballard left the station, dejected.

It sometimes seemed to her as though the biggest barricades in the so-called justice system were on the inside, before you even got out the door.

28

The autopsy was routine, except that seeing Javier Raffa's naked body on the exam table showed Ballard the lengths to which he had gone to escape the gang life and set an example for his son, Gabriel. In addition to what she had already seen on the neck, there were laser scars all over the chest, stomach, and arms, a painful map of tattoo removal. She guessed it had taken years to get rid of all the ink. It reminded Ballard of the monks who practiced self-flagellation with whips and other instruments to repent for their sins. Whatever Javier Raffa's sins were, he had paid a painful price.

There was only one tattoo left on the body. It was a rising sun over water on the left shoulder blade. It showed no symbols or words of gang affiliation.

"Well, he got to keep one," said Dr. Zvader, the deputy medical examiner handling the autopsy. "A setting sun."

Ballard realized there was no telling whether it was a rising or setting sun, even though they might have significant differences in meaning.

"Funny," she said. "I was thinking it was a rising sun."

"It's California," Zvader said. "Has to be going down."

Ballard nodded. He was probably right but it made her feel bad. A setting sun meant the end of day. A rising sun was a start. It was promise. She wondered if Raffa knew that his time was short.

Ballard stayed in the autopsy suite until Zvader found the bullet that had killed Raffa embedded in the cartilage of the nose. It had traversed the brain after entering near the top of the skull, killing Raffa instantly and lodging behind the nose.

"I think he was looking up at the fireworks when he died," Zvader said.

"That's so sad," Ballard said.

"Well, it's better than knowing it's coming and being afraid," Zvader replied.

Ballard nodded. Maybe.

The slug was heavily damaged, first by the impact on the skull and then by the cartilage. Zvader bagged the projectile and put his name and coroner's case number on the package before handing it to Ballard.

Ballard headed to the Ballistics Unit to drop off the slug for comparison analysis in the NIBIN database. It was an even longer shot than the shell casing comparison because of the damage to the slug. The database was essentially for casing comparison. So much so that projectile comparison was back-burnered, and Ballard knew she would not be waiting around for a tech to conduct the analysis. She would be lucky to hear anything within a week.

Along the way, she took a call from Carl Schaeffer, the BSL yard supervisor.

"We got one. A new one."

"A streetlight out?"

"Yeah, call just came in. On Outpost."

"First of all, Mr. Schaeffer, thank you for remembering to call."

"Not a problem. I got your card right here on the desk."

"Do you have any details yet?"

"No, she just said that the light outside her house is burned out. I was going to send a truck but thought I'd check with you first."

"Thank you. Don't send a truck. Let me make a call and see if I can get the print car out there first. I or one of my colleagues will call you when it's clear to repair."

"You got it, Detective."

"And Carl, I don't want you to forget to call me when these come in, but I'm not sure I want my card on your desk. Remember, I want this low profile, and I noticed you have the time clock in your office. Everybody punches out there, right?"

"Right, I got you. It goes in the drawer now."

"Thank you, Carl. Can you give me the exact address or location of the streetlight we're talking about and the name of the person who called it in?"

Schaeffer gave her the information. The streetlight in question was on lower Outpost Drive, a winding hillside road that went north from Franklin Avenue all the way up to Mulholland Drive. Ballard considered dismissing the call from Schaeffer because it was still eleven days from the next holiday weekend and in the previous cases the streetlight had been tampered with just a day or so before the Midnight Men attacked. But Outpost was just across the Cahuenga Pass from the Dell. The first two assaults had occurred in generally the same area—the same patrol zone, at least. The Dell case could be the start of a second cluster.

She also had to consider that a fourth attack had already occurred over the past holiday weekend and had not yet been reported. The bottom line was that she couldn't dismiss the tip from Schaeffer.

After dropping off the bullet that killed Javier Raffa at the Ballistics Unit, Ballard drove to Outpost and located the streetlight in question. She stopped the car at the curb to get out and take a closer look. It was an acorn-style light like those in the Dell. She saw no obvious signs of tampering on the access plate at the bottom of the post. The light was located directly across the street from the house from which the complaint had come. The woman who lived there and had called in the complaint was named Abigail Cena. The house was what Ballard always called a Spanish rambler. It was one level and spread wide, with a red barrel-tile roof and a white stucco facade. There were bushes and other vegetation lining the front, going beneath every window. There was also an attached garage that reminded Ballard of Cindy Carpenter's house and the suspected access route of the men who assaulted her.

Ballard first called the Forensics Unit to request that the print car come out and process the streetlight's access plate. She then called Matt Neumayer and told him about the call from Carl Schaeffer at the BSL yard.

"What do you think?" Neumayer asked. "Are they changing things up? This MO doesn't fit."

"I can't tell," Ballard said. "But we also have to consider that if this is them, it may have already happened over this past weekend. That they hit two women, and the streetlight's just been reported now."

"Oh, shit, you're right. It could be a nonreported case."

"I can come out and sit on the neighborhood tonight—not being obvious about it—but I have to get some downtime now. I'm running on fumes. I was thinking your crew could run down who lives in the neighborhood, maybe determine if this Abigail Cena lives alone or if any other women do in this immediate quad of homes."

"Yeah, we'll do it. You go get some sleep. And don't worry about tonight. I know you're off. If we want to stake the place, we'll set it up. Maybe I should get Lisa used to working nights."

That told Ballard that Robinson-Reynolds had not told Neumayer that he was rescinding Moore's reassignment to the late show. She felt bad about holding it as a secret from a good guy like Neumayer, but she was bound by the order from the lieutenant. And she wanted no part in the command games he was playing.

"Roger that," Ballard said. "Shoot me an email if you set it up. I'd just like to know what's happening."

"You got it, Renée. Pleasant dreams."

"Yeah, we'll see about— Oh, wait, did Lisa and Ronin pick up the other Lambkin surveys?"

"They're out now getting them. They went together rather than split up."

"Got it. Well, let me know about that too. It would be nice if we found a triple cross with all three of them."

"Would make our job easier."

"Roger that."

Ballard disconnected and decided she had to stop using "Roger that" as a sign-off. It was getting old. As she was leaning forward to turn the key in the ignition, she saw movement to her left and turned to see the garage door at Abigail Cena's house going up.

There was a silver Mercedes G-wagon in the bay and soon she saw its brake lights flare, followed by its reverse lights. The Mercedes backed out of the garage and then the big door rolled back down. Ballard could only see a silhouette of the driver because of the tinting of the windows, but she thought the hair profile indicated a woman. The Mercedes backed into the street and then headed down to the traffic signal at Franklin two blocks away.

Ballard was dead tired but her investigator's curiosity—both a blessing and a curse—got the better of her. She made a

U-turn and followed the G-wagon. She wanted to get a look at Abigail Cena—if it was her—and see if she fit the victim profile established with the first three victims of the Midnight Men.

She trailed the Mercedes east on Franklin toward Los Feliz. Ballard thought that at least she would be near home when this little exercise ended.

A call came in on her cell from an unknown number. She answered with a simple hello since she was technically off duty.

"Detective Ballard, Ross Bettany, West Bureau Homicide. We need to get together so I can pick up that gangbanger case and see what you've got."

Ballard paused to compose an answer.

"I just left the autopsy and it's not a gangbanger case."

"I was told the guy was Las Palmas."

"Was. He got out of the gang a long time ago. This wasn't a gang thing."

"Well, my last two were, so this will be a welcome change. When can we get together? My partner, Denise Kirkwood, is out today—added a vacay day to the weekend—but back tomorrow. Maybe we could come see you then?"

Ballard was relieved. She needed to get some sleep. She saw the Mercedes she was following turn off Franklin into the parking lot of the Gelson's supermarket at Canyon Drive. A little charge of adrenaline sparked in her exhaustion because she knew from Cindy Carpenter's Lambkin survey that she shopped at this Gelson's as did one of the other victims.

"Tomorrow would be good," Ballard said. "I'm heading home to sleep for the first time in about twenty-four hours. What time? Where?"

"We'll come see you at Hollywood," Bettany said. "Then we can go scope things out, pick up where you left off. How is nine at Hollywood Division? Will you have gotten enough sleep?"

He asked the last question good-naturedly but Ballard was stuck on "where you left off." Those words bothered her, and once again she hesitated in handing the case off. Her good work. Bosch's good work. She wanted to be there when they hooked up the four dentists and Christopher Bonner. *If* Bettany and Kirkwood managed to hook them up.

"You still there, Ballard?" Bettany prompted.

"Yeah, nine at the station is fine," Ballard said. "If you want to do something today, you could write up a search warrant for the victim's business records. I haven't had the time to go through his office at the shop."

"Gotcha. I'll probably wait till tomorrow. Denise does the writing."

Ballard knew that routine. The male detective assumes the alpha role, makes the female do the housekeeping and paperwork.

"So, Hollywood Division—where?" Bettany asked.

"We can meet in the task force room," Ballard said. "It's not being used."

"What's a task force, right?" Bettany said.

The question was rhetorical. He was referring to the drought of proactive police work going on these days. Ballard decided not to engage with that.

"I'll see you then," she said.

She put her cell away and watched as the Mercedes G-wagon she was tailing parked in a blue-painted disabled parking slot in front of the store. Ballard just stopped in the parking lot aisle to watch. She checked her mirror and saw another car pull into the lane behind her, but he had room to go around. After a few seconds, the door opened on the G-wagon and a woman used the side step on the vehicle to get down to the ground.

She looked like she was in her sixties, with white hair pulled into a ponytail. She wore a black mask with big red lips printed on the front. It was garish but Ballard figured the woman probably thought it was funny. She carried her reusable shopping bags toward the automatic door to the store. She did not appear to have a physical handicap.

The woman was far outside the age range of the three known victims. Ballard guessed that if the streetlight across from her house was put out by the Midnight Men, then their intended victim was someone else on Outpost. She decided she would check with Neumayer on their follow-up on Outpost after she had slept.

From Gelson's it was only ten minutes to her building. After entering her apartment, she went directly to the bedroom, put her gun, badge, and cuffs on the bed table, dropped her clothes right there on the floor, and changed into the sweats she had left on the bed from the last time she'd slept. She set a six-hour alarm on her phone, then crawled under the covers of her unmade bed, too tired even to brush her teeth.

She put in foam earplugs from the bed table to help blunt the normal daytime sounds of the city and pulled on a sleep mask to keep out the light.

And she was gone from the world in ten minutes, plunging face-first into a deep sleep, where the water that swirled around her was black and there were garish red lips floating in the emptiness.

PART TWO

USE OF FORCE

29

Ballard felt the weight on her ribs and arms before anything else. She opened her eyes to darkness and realized she had been blindfolded. No, it was the sleep mask. A hand covered her mouth and gripped her jaw. Her first thought was the Midnight Men—*How did they find me? Did they see me on Outpost?* Her memory flashed on the car she had seen in her rearview mirror pulling into the lane behind her at Gelson's.

She tried to struggle but the weight on her was too much. She violently turned her head to the side to loosen the grip of the hand on her jaw so that she could scream, but just as quickly the grip tightened, she was pulled back faceup, and pressure was applied to her chin, pulling her mouth open.

She heard the distinctive metal click of a gun cocking and that threw thoughts of the Midnight Men askew. None of the victims had mentioned a gun. It was two against one—they didn't need a gun.

Ballard realized all the weight was on the top half of her body. Her attacker was straddling her ribs, his legs pinning her arms to the bed. She couldn't move her upper body but her hips and legs were unrestrained. That was the flaw in the attack.

With all of the panicked, adrenaline-charged effort she could muster, she brought her knees up, planted her feet in the mattress and thrust her hips up, tipping her attacker forward into the headboard.

The move was unexpected and the attacker hit the hard wooden headboard with a clunk. The barrel of the gun scraped down Ballard's chin but the weapon didn't fire. Ballard's right arm broke free and she used it to shove the attacker to her left and off the bed. She heard him hit the floor. She yanked off the sleep mask and saw a man she immediately recognized on the floor.

It was Bonner.

He was struggling to get up. His left arm was swinging up and toward her with the gun—her gun—in his grasp. Ballard drew her right elbow back and then pistoned a strike forward into his throat.

Bonner fell back to the floor, dropped the gun, and brought both hands up to his neck. His face flushed red and his eyes widened as he realized he could not take in air. Ballard realized she had crushed his throat with the fist strike. She untangled herself from the blanket and sheet and rolled onto the floor. She now straddled him, swept her gun across the floor behind her, and reached up to her phone to call 911.

"This is Detective Ballard, LAPD, I need an ambulance to four-three-four-three Finley right away. Have a man here who can't breathe."

Bonner started making gagging sounds and his face was now more purple than red.

"Hold while I put it out," the emergency dispatcher said.

Ballard was put on hold. She reached down and tried to put her hand under Bonner's chin to see if she could feel where the blockage was. He pushed her hand away instinctively.

"Stop fighting," she said. "I'm trying to help."

As if responding to her but more likely due to the lack of oxygen going to his brain, Bonner's hands fell away from his neck and dropped to the floor. There was a dry scraping sound coming from his open mouth. His eyes were open, staring up at her, and he was dying.

The dispatcher came back on the phone.

"Okay, we are en route."

"What's the ETA?"

"Four minutes."

"He's not going to make that. He's coding right now."

"Can you open his passageway?"

"It's crushed."

Ballard blurted out her apartment number and the code to the main entrance gate, then disconnected. She quickly pulled up her contact list and called Garrett Single. He answered immediately.

"Renée, how's the noggin?"

"Garrett, listen to me. I need you to talk me through a field trach."

"Wait, what are you—"

"Listen, there's no time. I have a man here, he can't breathe. His upper throat is blocked. I have EMTs coming but he won't make it that long. Talk me through a field tracheotomy. Now."

"This is a gag, right?"

"Goddammit, no! I need you to tell me what to do. Now!"

"Okay, okay, uh, where exactly is the block?"

"Upper throat. He's over a minute without air. He's circling."

"Above or below the Adam's apple?"

"Above."

"Okay, good. Put something under his neck so it's clear and arched, jaw pointing up."

Ballard put the phone on speaker, then placed it on the floor.

She reached under the bed and blindly grabbed a shoe—a running shoe. She reached down with one hand to raise Bonner's neck, then shoved the shoe in like a wedge.

"Okay, got it. What's next?"

"Okay, this is important—you have to find the spot."

"What spot?"

"Use your finger and trace along the front of the neck. You are looking for a spot between the rings. The Adam's apple is the big ring. Go below it and find the next ring."

Ballard did as instructed and found the second ring.

"Got it, got it."

"Okay, you want the soft spot between the rings—do you have a knife? You need a scalpel or a knife to make a small incision."

Ballard reached up to the bed table and pulled the drawer out completely. It dropped to the floor over Bonner's head. She scrambled her hand through the junk she had thrown in there after moving in—all stuff she'd planned to find a spot for later. She found the small Blackie Collins folding knife she had carried when she was in uniform. She depressed the lock and opened the blade.

"Okay, got it. Where do I cut?"

"Okay, the soft spot you found between the rings. The soft tissue. You need to make an incision there. But first, you're sure he's not breathing? You don't want to do this if—"

"He's purple, Garrett. Just tell me what to do."

"Okay, a small incision—like a quarter of an inch wide in the soft tissue between the cartilage. Horizontal and not too deep. You don't want to go through the windpipe. No more than half an inch."

Ballard carefully positioned the point of the blade and pushed it into the skin. Immediately blood came out and ran down both sides of Bonner's neck to the wood floor. But it wasn't much and Ballard took that as a sign that Bonner's heart was shutting down.

"Okay, I'm there."

"Okay, you need to put in the tube so that air—"

"Shit, what tube? I didn't think—"

Ballard reached over and swiped her free hand through the junk drawer while carefully holding the knife in place in Bonner's neck. She saw nothing that would work.

"Do you have a plastic straw or a pen or anything that you could—"

"No! I don't have shit! God—"

She remembered something and yanked open the bottom drawer of the bed table. After she had separated her shoulder surfing a few years before, she had bought a recirculating pump that pushed cold water into a rubber wrap that she could lay over her shoulder to ease the pain and swelling. A clear plastic tube connected the pump to the wrap. She yanked it out of the drawer and put it down on the floor.

"Okay, I found something. Can I take the knife out of his neck to cut the tube?"

"Do it."

"How long do you want the tube?"

"No more than six inches needed."

Ballard pulled the knife back and quickly cut a six-inch length of the tube with the razor-sharp blade.

"Okay, got it. What next?"

"Put one end of the tube through the incision and into the airway. Don't go more than an inch in. Just push it through."

Ballard did as instructed and felt the tube break through and into the windpipe.

"Okay, I'm in. Does he just start breathing, or what?"

"No, you have to get him started. Breathe into the tube. Check his chest, make sure it's rising. Not too hard. Be gentle."

Ballard jumped off Bonner and moved to his side. She gently blew into the tube and saw his chest rise.

"Okay," she said.

"All right, watch his chest," Single said. "You want to see if he breathes on his own."

"It went down, that's it."

"Try it again, try it again."

Ballard repeated the procedure, with no result.

"Nothing. Trying again."

"You may have to breathe for him until the rescue gets there."

Ballard tried again and then crouched low so she could watch the profile of Bonner's chest. She saw it go down as air escaped through the tube. But then it rose again on its own.

"I think…he's breathing. Yes, he's breathing."

"Well done, Detective. How's his color?"

Ballard looked at Bonner's face. The purple was leaching out of it. Fresh blood was circulating.

"It's good. It's getting there."

"Okay, what I want you to do is call me back on FaceTime so I can look at him. Can you do that?"

Ballard disconnected the call without replying and then called back on FaceTime. While she waited for the call to go through, she reached up to the top of the bed table to grab her handcuffs. She snapped one cuff around Bonner's right wrist and clamped the other around the metal bed frame half a foot away.

She looked down at Bonner. His eyes were slits and he showed no sign of being conscious, but there was no doubt that he was breathing. There was a low whistling sound coming from the tube she had inserted into his neck.

Single answered the call and Ballard saw his face. It looked like he was outside, and she could see the yellow brick of the fire station behind him.

"You're hurt," he said. "Are you okay?"

For the first time, Ballard remembered the barrel of the gun being dragged down her chin. She brought her hand up to touch the wound and felt blood.

"I'm okay," she said. "Take a look at him."

She flipped the camera so Single could see Bonner on the floor. She could now hear sirens but was unsure whether they were on her end of the call or Single's.

"You see him?"

"Yes. Uh, it looks good. Actually, it looks perfect. He's breathing and his color is good. You got rescue on the way?"

"Yeah, I think I hear them now."

"Yeah, that's them. They're coming. Who is this guy? You handcuffed him?"

"I just did that in case he woke up. I was sleeping and he broke in. He was going to kill me with my own gun—I think to make it look like suicide."

"Jesus, why?"

"He's a murder suspect. Somehow he found out I was onto him and where I live."

"Holy shit!"

"Yeah."

Ballard tried to think of how Bonner could have known about her and the investigation. The easy answer was Dennis Hoyle. She had spooked Hoyle, and he in turn sent Bonner after her. That reminded her—Bosch had been there as well.

"Listen, Garrett, I need to make another call," she said. "Thank you so much for helping me."

"I don't know if I should have, if this guy was trying to kill you," he said.

Ballard smiled.

"That might be the sweetest thing anybody's ever said to me. I'll call you later."

"I'm here. And Renée, I'm glad you're okay."

After hanging up, Ballard immediately called Bosch. He picked up, and there was no indication of stress in his voice.

"Harry, you're okay?"

"Why shouldn't I be?"

"Because Bonner just tried to take me out. He's on the floor of my apartment."

"Give me the address. I'm on my way."

"No, it's handled. But you're okay? I thought maybe he went to you first."

"All good. You sure you're safe?"

"Yeah. I almost killed him. But I've got people coming. You stay back but be ready. After I clear this, I want to pay a visit to Dr. Hoyle."

"I want to be there for that."

Ballard disconnected. She heard the sirens cut off in front of the building. She knew she had to work quickly. She crouched down and started going through the pockets of Bonner's pants. She found a phone that looked like a cheap convenience-store burner in one pocket and a small leather wallet holding a set of lockpicks—Bonner's way into the apartment—in another. There was no vehicle key or anything else.

She put the pick set back in the pocket where she found it but buried the phone under the junk in the bed table drawer. The rattle of jewelry and other belongings made Bonner stir. There was a louder sound of rushing air from the breathing tube and he opened his eyes as Ballard pulled back from the drawer. He made a move to raise his upper body but then quickly stopped as he sensed something was wrong. He tried to move his right hand but it was cuffed to the bed frame. He brought his left hand up to his throat and found the protruding tube.

"You pull that out, you die," Ballard said.

He looked at her.

"I crushed your windpipe," she said. "That tube is what you're breathing through."

His eyes moved about as he took in the room and the circumstances. Without moving his head, he cast his eyes down and saw the handcuff. He then looked at Ballard and she saw something register in his eyes. It was like he understood where he was and what was going to happen to him.

In one swift move he reached up and yanked the breathing tube out. He threw it over the bed and across the room. He stared at Ballard as his face began to get red. It was then that she heard the rescue team coming through the door to her apartment.

30

Ballard was hours into her FID interview before she knew for sure that Bonner was dead. Her two interviewers had keyed in on what had happened after he had supposedly—their word, not hers—pulled the tube from his neck.

"Look, why would I put the tube into his throat and try to save the guy's life and then pull the tube out again?" she asked.

"That's what we're trying to figure out," Sanderson replied.

Captain Gerald "Sandy" Sanderson was the lead interviewer. He was also the officer in charge of the Force Investigation Division—the man who for years had been tasked with sweeping out the bad cops who got involved in questionable shootings, choke holds, and other unauthorized uses of force. Under the present pressures and politics of the department and the public, it was wholly believed across the ranks that any officer who got into a scrape of any kind was out. The details of the incident didn't matter. Sanderson was there to sand down the sharp edges of the department and make everything smooth. That meant washing out anybody whose actions might be seen as controversial from any angle.

Ballard had felt it two minutes into her interview, not two hours. A murder suspect had obviously followed her and used lockpicks to break into her home while she slept. She had defended herself, and the man had died, whether by his own hand or not, and she was getting hammered by the very people who should have her back. The world had gone sideways, and for the first time in a long time Ballard thought she might lose her job. And for the first time in a long time she thought that might not be so bad.

The interview was taking place in the detective bureau of the Northeast Division, which encompassed Los Feliz. This was routine, but still Ballard felt cut off from her division and the people she worked with. At one point, when Sanderson's second, Detective Duane Hammel, stepped out to get fresh batteries for his recorder, Ballard saw Lieutenant Robinson-Reynolds standing out in the bullpen. That gave her a moment of relief because she knew he would be able to confirm what he knew of her investigation. She had never told him about Bonner but he knew from her last briefing that she was closing in on something.

Ballard had not looked at the time since being woken by Bonner's attack. She didn't know how long she had slept and therefore couldn't fix the hour. Her phone had been taken from her. It was daylight when Bonner attacked and when she was treated at the rescue wagon for the cut on her chin. But now she had been in a windowless interview room for what she estimated was two hours.

"So let's connect the dots one more time," Sanderson said. "You're saying you did not know and had no previous interaction with Christopher Bonner, correct?"

"Yes, correct," Ballard said. "The first time I met him—if you want to call it meeting him—was when I woke up and he was on top of me, trying to stick my gun into my mouth."

"So, how is it that he knew where you lived, apparently knew your schedule, and knew you would be asleep at three o'clock in the afternoon?"

Ballard was thankful that Sanderson had slipped a time marker into his question. She could now extrapolate that it was somewhere between 6 and 7 p.m. But what was more important was Sanderson's asking how Bonner would know her sleep schedule. There was no way Hoyle could know what her assignment or work schedule was from her business card or their brief interaction. She decided not to mention that in her answer to Sanderson.

"As I have said repeatedly in this interview," she said, "I attempted to question Dennis Hoyle at the memorial yesterday for Javier Raffa. He was clearly spooked. In a homicide investigation, one of the first questions is, who benefits? The answer in this case is Dennis Hoyle. My attempt to interview him led to him jumping in his car and driving away. He didn't want to talk to me. I now have to assume he called Bonner, and Bonner came after me. Those are the dots and that is the connection."

"It will bear further investigation," Sanderson said.

"I hope so, because I don't want Hoyle to get away with this or with Raffa."

"I understand, Detective. A moment please."

Sanderson leaned back in his chair and looked down to his legs. Ballard knew he had his phone on his thigh and was probably getting texts from his other FID investigators. Ballard, when she had worked with a partner, had followed the same practice. It allowed for real-time information and questions.

Sanderson looked up at her after reading the latest text.

"Detective, why is Harry Bosch calling your cell phone every thirty minutes?"

Ballard had completely kept Bosch out of her story while being questioned. She now had to answer carefully so as not to step on any land mine. Having now been sequestered for over two hours, for all she knew, Sanderson's team had already interviewed Bosch, and Sanderson already had the answer. She had to make sure their stories matched even though she didn't know what Bosch had said or would say.

"Well, as you probably know, Harry is retired LAPD," she began. "I have had cases in the past that involved some of his old investigations, and so I have known him for four or five years and he's sort of taken on a mentor's role with me. But specifically in this case, I told you that I linked the Raffa murder to another case through ballistics. That case—the victim's name was Albert Lee—was investigated by Harry Bosch nine years ago. When I made that connection, I reached out to Bosch to pick his brain about the case and get any sort of angle on this thing that I could."

"And did you?"

"Yes, it was information from Bosch that allowed me to further find out who benefits. In the Albert Lee case, his business and insurance policy went to a dentist who had loaned him the money to keep his business afloat. That dentist was partners with Hoyle in another business. Bosch helped me make those connections. Bonner became the suspected killer in both cases. But I believe he was sent after these victims, the same way he was sent after me."

"By the dentists."

"Roger that."

Ballard immediately shook her head. She had to stop that.

"So, when we speak to Bosch, he will tell the same story?" Sanderson asked.

"If he speaks to you," Ballard said. "He did not leave the department on good terms. So good luck with that."

"And there is nothing romantic there between you and Bosch?"

"If I was a man and I had reached out to a retired detective with a connection to my case, would you ask me if there was a romance between us?"

"I take that as a no."

"You can take it however you want, but I am not answering questions like that. But I am glad this is recorded."

Sanderson tried to stare Ballard down but she didn't blink.

"Now can I ask you something?" Ballard said.

"You can always ask," Sanderson said. "I can't promise I will answer."

"Have you found Bonner's car?"

"Why would you ask that?"

"Because I assume that if he drove, he parked in my neighborhood, and since he had nothing in his pockets but lockpicks, I assume there will be a phone, wallet, maybe notes and other things, in his car. Maybe the gun that killed my two victims. If I were you, I'd be looking for his car right now."

"I can assure you that the investigation is continuing outside this room, Detective. You don't have to worry about that."

"Good. What about the media? Are they onto this yet?"

"Detective, in this room, I am asking the questions. You have another repeat caller to your cell that I would like to ask you about. Garrett Single, the paramedic you told us coached you through the field tracheotomy. He has called you more times than Bosch. Why is that?"

"Well, I won't really know until I can talk to him and find out, but my guess is that he wants to know if I'm all right."

"He cares about you."

"I think he does."

Ballard braced for the romance question but Sanderson surprised her.

"Thank you, Detective," he said. "And for now I think we

have enough information from you. We are placing you on desk duty until we complete our investigation. In the meantime, I am ordering you not to contact or talk to the media about this incident. If you are contacted by a person in the media, you are to refer them to—"

"Wait a minute," Ballard said. "Who's going to work the case? We're not going to drop it while you and your people decide whether I did anything wrong."

"My understanding is that the case has already been transferred to West Bureau Homicide. They will take it from here. By your own testimony, we are talking about a suicide. I'm sure they will close it quickly and you will be back to work."

"I'm not talking about Bonner killing himself. I'm talking about the Javier Raffa case and the Albert Lee case."

"Again, West Bureau will handle it."

What was in play here only then hit Ballard. Christopher Bonner was ex-LAPD and that was an image problem. Not only was it a huge issue that an ex-LAPD officer was likely a hit man before and after he left the job, but whether he still had connections in the department was unknown. Thanks to Sanderson's questions, Ballard already had one idea about the ties Bonner still had. Add to that the missing murder books, and this was a high-octane scandal waiting to explode in the media. It was best to keep everything compartmentalized. And tying together the murders of Albert Lee and Javier Raffa and solving them would only work against the department.

"I know what you're going to do," Ballard blurted out.

"Really?" Sanderson said. "What am I going to do, Detective?"

"You're going to sand and sweep. Like you always do. This department is so fucked up. It's like we don't even care about victims anymore. It's protect and serve the image instead of the citizens."

"Are you finished, Detective?"

"Oh, yeah, I'm finished. Where's my phone? Where's my gun? I want them back."

Sanderson turned to look at Hammel, who had returned and was standing with his back to the door.

"Her lieutenant has her phone," the sidekick said.

Sanderson turned back to Ballard.

"Check with your lieutenant about the phone," he said. "Your weapon is being processed. You will get that back when appropriate. In the meantime, you can ask your lieutenant about a temporary replacement from the armory. It may not be necessary, as for the moment you are assigned to desk duty."

He waited a moment for Ballard to respond. She didn't.

"Then I think we're finished here," Sanderson said.

Everyone stood up. The men from FID were closest to the door, and Ballard let them leave first. When she was last out of the interview room, she found Robinson-Reynolds waiting for her in an empty bullpen. Through the casement windows Ballard could see that it was full dark outside.

The lieutenant stood up from the desk he had been leaning on with folded arms.

"Renée, you okay?"

"I'm fine."

"I'll take you back to your place."

"Do you have my phone?"

"Yes. They gave it to me."

Robinson-Reynolds reached into his suit coat pocket and produced Ballard's phone. She checked the screen to see what calls had come in. Five minutes earlier Bosch had once again tried to call her.

She decided not to call him back until she was alone, but while her lieutenant watched, she quickly fired off a text telling Bosch she was fine and would call him in a half hour.

Ten minutes later she was in the front passenger seat of Robinson-Reynolds's car, telling him to get to Commonwealth Avenue and head south.

"You're probably going to want to pack some things and stay somewhere else for a while," Robinson-Reynolds said. "A friend's place, or if you want a hotel, I'll find a way to make the department cough up a chit for it."

"No, I'll be fine," Ballard said.

"You sure? Your room is probably a mess—courtesy of Forensics."

"I've got a big couch."

"Okay, Renée."

"So, what about West Bureau?"

"What about it?"

"Ross Bettany called me to take over the case. I'm supposed to meet him tomorrow."

"Then meet him. He's still taking it."

"I want to know if they're going to work it. Bonner was LAPD. It felt in there with Sanderson that this wasn't going anywhere, because solving it means putting that out there: veteran LAPD officer turned hit man."

"You really think they would cover it up—a murder?"

"It's two murders—at least. And yes, I do, because Bonner, the shooter, is dead. As far as Sanderson goes, it's case closed. Taking it the next step and going after the people who ordered the hits, that's dangerous, because all of the Bonner stuff will tumble out and the department gets its ass kicked once again."

"Don't overthink it, Ballard."

Ballard noticed he was back to addressing her by her last name.

"It's not overthinking," she said. "It's the reality we live in."

"Maybe," he said. "But it's going to be West Bureau's reality, not ours. So just follow protocol, Ballard. Turn the case over to the guy and go back to work on the Midnight Men."

"Roger that."

She said it in a tone of resignation that signaled that she would never say those two words again.

31

Ballard crossed the center courtyard to use the stairs, because the building's elevator was so slow. But before she got to the first step, she heard her name called. She turned and saw a man stepping out the door of his first-floor apartment. He came toward her. It was the bicyclist she had met over the weekend, but already she couldn't remember his name.

"Hi," she said.

"Some crazy stuff here today," he said. "Is everything all right?"

"Everything's fine now."

"I mean, I was told a guy broke in and tried to kill you."

"He did. But it's complicated and the police are investigating."

"But you are the police."

"Yes, but I'm not investigating this, so I can't really talk about it."

She started to move back toward the stairs.

"We aren't used to this sort of thing here," the neighbor said.

Ballard turned back.

"That's a good thing, then," she said. "Neither am I."

"Well, I know you're new," the neighbor said. "And I hope that this sort of thing isn't going to be normal. I feel as HOA president that I need to say that."

"I'm sorry, what is your name again?"

"It's Nate. We met in the—"

"The garage, I remember. Well, Nate, I don't consider it normal when somebody tries to kill me in my bed. But you should know that he was a stranger and that it was a break-in, and I was thinking that the next time you have a homeowners' meeting, you might want to review the security around here. He got in here somehow, and I'd hate to see the HOA be held responsible for anything. That could be expensive."

Nate blanched.

"Uh, totally," he said. "I, uh, I'm going to call a special meeting to review building security."

"Good," Ballard said. "I'd like to hear how that goes."

This time she turned and Nate had nothing further to say. She took the steps two at a time and found her front door had been left unlocked by the investigators. Typical LAPD incompetence. She locked it after entering and quickly moved through the apartment to her bedroom. The junk drawer she had pulled out of the bed table that afternoon during the struggle with Bonner was still on the floor. She could see fingerprint dust on its handle. Rooting through the drawer, she found the burner phone she had buried in the junk. She snapped it open and saw that it had either been powered off or its battery had died.

She fumbled with it, looking for the on/off button and found none. She held her thumb down on the 0 button but nothing happened. She then tried the 1, and the phone's screen finally came to life. Once it was fully booted, she went to work checking for stored numbers and recent calls. There were none but the texting app had a single message, timed at 4:30 p.m. that day from an 818 area code. It was just one word: Report.

"Got you," she whispered.

She stared at the phone for a few moments, considering her next move. She knew she had to be careful and conservative.

If she answered the text wrong, the lead could disappear like cigarette smoke in the wind. If she used the phone in any way—to text or call—she could be tampering with evidence. She decided to wait and closed the phone. She went into the kitchen and put it in a Ziploc bag and sealed it. Pulling her own phone, she called Bosch.

"You up for a ride?" she asked.

"Sure," he said. "When?"

"Now."

"Come get me."

"On my way. And, uh, I'll need a gun. They're processing mine and my backup's in my locker."

"Not a problem."

Ballard liked how he answered without any question or hesitation.

"Okay, see you soon," she said.

32

After pulling out of the garage, Ballard drove around the block and found a SID team working under portable lights on Hoover, a block behind her building. There was a flatbed from the OPG moving into position in front of a black Chrysler 300. A table had been set up under one of the crime scene lights, and Ballard recognized the face of the man with a clipboard, writing on what she assumed was an evidence log. She pulled to the curb, got out, and approached the lights.

"Reno," she said.

Reno looked up and clearly remembered Ballard from the callout to Cindy Carpenter's house.

"Detective Ballard," he said. "You okay? Sounded like a close call for you."

"It was," Ballard said. "Did you work my apartment too?"

"I did."

"Cool. And this is the dirtbag's car?"

"Yeah, we're going to take it to the print shed."

"Where'd you find the key?"

"On the front left tire."

Ballard looked down at the table. There were three brown paper evidence bags with red tape sealing them. One had a sticker that warned anyone handling it that the bag contained a firearm. She tried to hide her excitement and act as though she was already in the know.

She pointed at the bag.

"Is that the P-twenty-two?"

"Yup. Also found up in the wheel well. Not a good place to hide a weapon. We always look there first or second. And supposedly he used to be a cop—from what I hear."

"What about ammo?"

"Just what was in the weapon."

"Remington?"

"Yep."

"Okay, well, have a good night."

"You too."

Ballard returned to her car. She was confident that the gun found in the wheel well of Bonner's car had been used in the two homicides she had connected.

She headed off toward Bosch's house, checking the time on the dashboard. She figured that she could pick up Bosch and get to Hoyle's house by eleven. The late hour would work in her favor. Nobody likes a cop to knock on their door that late at night.

Her phone buzzed and she saw that it was Garrett Single calling.

"Hey, Garrett."

"Renée, hi. Are you okay?"

"I'm fine."

"I'm so glad to hear it."

"Thanks for your help. Sorry if it sounded like I was yelling at you."

"Not at all. But, hey, I thought you should know, some detectives from SID were just here talking to me about it."

"You mean FID?"

"Uh, I don't know, maybe. You guys on the other side of the wall have too many acronyms. It's alphabet soup over there."

"What did you tell them?"

"Just that I helped you try to save the guy and then I FaceTimed it with you."

Ballard realized that she had completely forgotten about Face-Timing Single so he could visually check the insertion point of the field trach in Bonner's neck. After the stress and adrenaline flood of the life-and-death struggle had subsided, the moments had lost clarity and she had forgotten details. She hadn't even mentioned the FaceTime call during her own FID interview. She found this lapse understandable—it was the reason she liked to interview a victim of violence multiple times over multiple days. Now she had experienced for herself the way details came back over time.

"Man, too bad you didn't record that," Ballard said.

"Uh, actually, I did," Single said. "I have an app. I thought I should record it in case we needed to look at it again."

"Did you tell them that?"

"Yeah, they wanted it."

"You let them take your— Wait, you're on your phone."

"I just sent them the video. I wasn't going to give up my phone."

"Great, can you send it to me? I just want to look."

"Sure. Is everything else okay? I mean, the guys that came here were asking a lot of questions about you."

"As far as I know, everything's good. It was clean. But I'm still working. I mean, I'm supposed to be riding a desk until the report comes out."

"Then I should let you go."

"Let's talk tomorrow, okay? I think things will slow down then."

"Sure. Be safe."

"You too."

Ballard disconnected. She was relieved to learn there was a video record of at least part of the event that was under investigation. She knew that whatever Single had captured would support the story she had told FID. More than that, she was happy that Single had called.

A smile played on her face in the darkness of the car as she drove.

33

Ballard was delayed in getting to Bosch's house because she went by the station to check out one of the drug unit's undercover cars, grab a rover, and dummy up a couple of prop files. After grabbing the keys to a Mustang labeled as a buy car with audio/video capture, she headed into the back lot to look for the vehicle. She encountered Lieutenant Rivera standing at the open trunk of his personal car. It looked like he was just coming in to work. Guessing that Sanderson and the FID team would not be throwing a wide net in their investigation of Bonner, Ballard decided to go at Rivera herself.

She walked directly to him as he was getting his gun out of lockbox.

"Ballard, thought you were off tonight," he said.

"I am but I'm working a case for dayside," she said. "I need to ask you something, L-T."

"Shoot."

"Last night I asked you about Christopher Bonner. You called him after that, didn't you?"

Rivera bought time by making a show of holstering his weapon and then closing the trunk.

"Uh, I might have," he said. "Why?"

Ballard guessed that Rivera had probably slept through the day and didn't know what had happened.

"Because he broke into my apartment and tried to kill me today," she said.

"*What!*" Rivera exclaimed.

"Somehow he knew I was onto him. So, thanks, L-T. I hope it wasn't you who gave him my address."

"Wait a minute, Ballard. I did no such thing. All I did was pass on that somebody asked about him—like anybody would with a friend. You didn't tell me you were investigating him. You said his name came up in your case. That's it and that's all I told him. He broke in? Jesus, I had no—"

"He's dead."

"Dead?"

"Yeah, and you should expect a visit from FID."

Ballard walked away and left him there. It felt good to make the link, but she knew it didn't fill in all the blanks. She also believed her throwing FID at Rivera would be an empty threat. She did not expect Sanderson to take his investigation much further than he had already.

It took her five minutes to find the UC car in the vast parking lot. She then had to gas it up at the department pump across the street from the station on Wilcox. Finally, she was off and headed toward the hills and Harry Bosch's house.

It was another hour before she pulled to a stop in front of Dennis Hoyle's home, with Bosch sitting next to her and fully briefed on her plan.

"Here we go," Ballard said.

They got out and approached the house. There was a light on over the front door but most of the windows were dark. Ballard pushed a doorbell and knocked. She looked around for a home security camera but did not see one.

After another round of knocking and doorbell ringing, Hoyle finally answered. He was wearing gym pants and a long-sleeved T-shirt with the silhouette of a surfer on it. He held a cell phone in his hand.

"You two," he said. "What the hell is this? It's almost midnight."

There was a surprised look on his face but Ballard had no way of discerning whether it was surprised by the late night visit or the fact that Ballard was alive.

"We know it's late, Dr. Hoyle," Ballard said. "But we thought you wouldn't want this to happen in the middle of the day with the neighbors watching."

"What? You're arresting me? For what? I was asleep!"

Working the late show, Ballard had more than once heard an incongruous protest about sleep being some sort of safeguard against arrest or police questioning. She reached behind her back and under her jacket to take the handcuffs off her belt. She then dropped her arm so Hoyle could see them in her hand. It was an old trick that would reinforce his assumption that he was about to be arrested.

"We need to talk to you," Ballard said. "We can do it here or at Hollywood Station. Your choice."

"Okay, here," Hoyle said. "I want to talk here."

He turned and looked back into his house.

"But my family is—"

"Let's talk in the car."

He hesitated again.

"In the front seat," Ballard said. "As long as we're talking, we're not going anywhere."

As if to reassure him she hooked her cuffs back onto her belt.

"My partner will stay outside the car, okay?" she added. "Not much room in the back. So it will be just you and me talking. Very private."

"I guess," Hoyle said. "It still feels weird."

"Then let's go inside and we'll try not to wake anybody up."

"No, no, your car is fine. Just as long as we're not going anywhere."

"You can get out anytime you want."

"Okay, then."

Bosch led the procession down the stone walkway across the manicured lawn to the UC car.

"Is this your own car?"

"Yeah, so I apologize ahead of time. It's kind of dirty inside."

Bosch opened the passenger-side door for Hoyle, who got in. Bosch closed the door and looked at Ballard as she circled behind the car to the driver's side. He nodded. The plan was a go.

"Stay toward the front," she whispered.

She opened the driver's door and got in. Through the windshield, she saw Bosch take a position leaning against the front fender on the passenger side.

"He looks really old to be a detective," Hoyle said.

"He's the oldest living detective in L.A.," Ballard said. "But don't tell him I said that. He'll get mad."

"No worries. I'm not saying anything. Why don't you two have a detective car?"

"The one we were assigned, the heat doesn't work. So we took mine. You cold? You must be cold."

She put the key in the ignition and turned it to the accessory setting. The dashboard lights came on and she reached for the heat control.

"Let me know if you want more heat."

"I'm fine. Let's get this over with. I have an early start tomorrow."

Ballard checked Bosch again through the windshield. He had his arms crossed and his head down, adopting the posture

of a guy who was tired of these routine interviews. Hoyle
turned and looked out the window at his front door, as though
reminding himself that he had to get back through it before
this was over. Ballard used the moment to lean forward and
reach under the dashboard to turn on the car's audio/video
system. The car was equipped with three hidden cameras and
microphones for recording undercover drug buys. It would now
capture everything that was said or done in the car from that
moment on, putting it all on a chip in a recorder located in
the trunk.

"Okay, I have to start by giving you the standard rights warning," she said. "The department requires it of every interview,
even if someone is not a suspect, because of adverse court rulings
that—"

"Look, I don't know," Hoyle said. "You said you just wanted
to talk, now you're giving me my rights? That's not—"

"Okay, listen, I'm just going to give you the rights warning
and ask if you understand them. At that point, you have a choice:
talk to me, don't talk to me, and we go from there."

Hoyle shook his head and put his hand on the door handle.
Ballard knew she was about to lose him.

She hit the button that lowered her window. She called to
Bosch, who came around the car. She grabbed the rover from the
center console and held it out to him.

"We may need a car for a custody transport," she said. "Can
you deal with that?"

"Got it," Bosch said.

He reached for the radio.

"Wait, wait," Hoyle said. "Jesus Christ, okay, read me my
rights. I'll talk, let's just get this over with."

Ballard withdrew the radio and Bosch nodded. It was going
about how they thought it would.

She put the window up and turned to Hoyle. From memory she gave him the Miranda warning and he acknowledged that he understood his rights and was agreeing to talk to her.

"Okay," she said. "Let's talk."

"Ask your questions," Hoyle said.

"After you saw us at the memorial service yesterday, who did you call?"

"Call? I didn't call anyone. I drove home."

"I gave you my card. I need to know who you told about me."

"I'm telling you, I didn't tell anyone."

Hoyle had raised his voice enough for Bosch to hear it. He looked over his shoulder at Ballard through the windshield. She nodded slightly. Bosch pulled his phone and started making a call. He pushed off the front fender and walked to the front of the car while waiting for a connection.

"Who's he calling?" Hoyle asked.

"I don't know," Ballard said. "But you need to think carefully here, Dr. Hoyle."

Ballard paused and watched Bosch. He held his phone to his ear for a few moments, then took it down and ended the call. Ballard glanced over at the phone still in Hoyle's hand. Its screen was dark. Hoyle had not sent the "Report" text to Bonner— at least not on the phone he was holding. Ballard now had to wonder who had sent it.

"Think carefully about what?" Hoyle said.

"This is one of the moments when the decision you make will affect the rest of your life," Ballard said.

Hoyle turned toward the door and again reached for the handle.

"Now you're scaring me. I'm getting out."

"You get out, and the next time you see me will be when I kick down your door with a warrant and drag you out of there in front of your neighbors."

Hoyle turned back to her.

"What do you want?"

"You know what I want. Who did you call after we met at the memorial?"

"Nobody!"

Ballard started reaching into the backseat of the car.

"I want you to look at something, Doctor."

She pulled two thick files off the backseat floor and onto her lap.

"I want you to know we've been onto you since Albert Lee and John William James."

"Onto what?"

"Onto everything. The factoring, the insurance fraud, the company you and your friends made, the murders…"

"Oh my god, this can't be happening."

"It is. And that's why you have to make a choice here. Help or hinder. Because if you can't help me, I'm going to the next partner. If he doesn't help, I go to the next. Somebody's going to be smart or get smart. And then it will be too late for the others. I only need to put one insider in front of the grand jury. I thought it was going to be you, but it doesn't matter."

Hoyle leaned forward and for a moment Ballard thought he was going to vomit onto the floor in front of his seat. But then he pulled back, eyes closed, misery all over his face.

"This is all Jason's fault," he said. "I should have never…"

"Jason Abbott?" Ballard asked.

"No, I'm not saying another word until you promise to protect me. He'll send his guy after me!"

"We can protect you. But right now you need to give me what I need. Who did you tell about me after the memorial? That is question one."

"All right, all right. I told Jason. I said the cops had cornered me, and he yelled at me for even going to that thing in the first place."

"Do you know who Christopher Bonner is?"

"No, I don't."

"Who found the people you and the others would loan money to?"

"Jason had somebody. I never got involved."

"You didn't know he was going to have them—"

"No! Never. I didn't know any of that until he did it. And then it was too late. I looked guilty. We all did."

"So you just went along with it."

"I didn't have a choice. Don't you see? I didn't want to get killed. Look what happened to J.W."

"John William James."

"Yes. He said 'no more' to Jason, and look what happened to him."

"What about his wife? Was she part of this?"

"No, no, no—she doesn't know anything."

"How many were there?"

"How many what?"

"You know what I'm asking. How many times did the factoring lead to somebody dying?"

Hoyle bowed his head in shame and closed his eyes.

"If you lie to me one time, I will no longer help you," Ballard said.

"There were six," Hoyle said. "No, seven. Javier Raffa was number seven."

"Including James?"

"Yes. Yes."

Ballard looked through the windshield at Bosch. He had been watching them, seeing but not hearing Hoyle talk. They locked eyes and Ballard nodded. She had gotten what she needed. Hoyle was on video.

"Go back inside now, Doctor," she said. "Don't tell anyone about this. If you do, I'll know and I'll bury you."

"Okay," Hoyle said. "But what do I do now?"

"You just wait. You'll hear from a detective named Bettany. Ross Bettany. He'll tell you what to do."

"Okay."

"You can get out now."

34

Bosch had brought a thermos of coffee with him. When Ballard had picked him up, he came out with the thermos and two to-go cups. Ballard had told him they weren't going to a stakeout, but he'd said, you never know.

Bosch had always been a sort of homicide guru to Ballard. Ever since the night she caught him going through files in the D-bureau—long after he'd retired. She wasn't sure whether it was wisdom or experience, or if experience brought the wisdom, but she knew he was never just backup. He was her go-to guy and she trusted him.

They didn't get to Jason Abbott's house until after one. The house was dark, and there was no answer to repeated knocks on his door. They debated whether he knew what was closing in around him and had fled. But that didn't fit with the known facts. He may have learned that Bonner was dead, but even that was a stretch, as the man who had killed himself in Ballard's apartment had no ID on his person. Ballard knew it was Bonner because she recognized him. But his identity would not have been released by the coroner's office until it had been confirmed through fingerprints and other means.

Ballard believed that, at best, Abbott would know only that

Bonner was missing in action. The hit man had not responded to the text or reported back to him in any other way. Abbott may have cruised Ballard's neighborhood and seen the police activity, but again, it didn't seem likely that he had enough information to cause him to flee. Ballard was the only one who had the whole picture, and she had shared it with no one but Bosch.

They decided to stay awhile and watch for Abbott's return. And that was where the coffee in the thermos came in.

"How did you know we would end up out here—maybe all night?" Ballard asked.

"I didn't," Bosch said. "I just came prepared."

"You're like that guy in the Wambaugh books. The Original. No, the Oracle. They called him the Oracle 'cause he's already seen everything twice."

"I like the Original."

"Harry Bosch, the Original. Nice."

He reached to the back for the thermos.

"You ever see yourself stopping?" Ballard asked.

"I guess when I stop, it all stops, you know?" he said.

He put the two cups on the dashboard and got ready to pour.

"You want some?"

"Sure, but you can sleep if you want. These are my normal hours, so I'll be fine."

"The dark hours belong to you."

"You got it."

He handed her a cup of black coffee.

"It's hot," he warned.

"Thanks," Ballard said, accepting it. "But really. I got good sleep until Bonner woke me up. One cup and I'll be good to go all night. You can sleep."

"We'll see. I'll keep you company for at least a while. What about the car? Aren't the narcs going to need it back in the morning?"

"If you'd asked me that a year ago, the answer would've been…well, I wouldn't have gotten the car in the first place. But now, post George Floyd and knee-deep in Covid and defunding the department and everything else? Nobody's doing shit. I didn't even ask for this car. I just took it because it's not going to be missed."

"I didn't know it was that bad."

"A lot of people are mailing it in. Crime is up but arrests are down. And a lot of people are quitting. I gotta be honest, I'm even thinking of quitting, Harry. Think you could use a partner?"

She said it with a laugh, but in many ways she was serious.

"Anytime—as long as you don't need a regular paycheck. You're pretty short of a pension, aren't you?"

"Yeah, but at least I'd get back the money I've put in the fund so far. I guess I could also go back to sleeping on the beach."

"You'd need to get another dog."

Ballard smiled and then thought of Pinto, the dog she was supposed to meet soon. He wouldn't make much of a guard dog, though.

"Still," Bosch said. "It's always easier to change an organization from within. Street protests won't do it."

"You think I'm command staff material?" Ballard asked. "You gotta be on the tenth floor if you're going to change anything."

"Not necessarily. I always thought if you fight the good fight, it gets noticed. And then maybe the next guy does the same thing. The right thing."

"I don't think it's that kind of department anymore."

She sipped her hot coffee and thought she recognized the blend right away. She held the cup up like a toast.

"Where do you get this stuff?" she asked.

"My daughter," Bosch said. "She's always trying different things, then passes them on to me. This stuck. I like it."

"Me too. Maddie's got great taste. You said she has a boyfriend?"

"Yeah, they moved in together. In your neighborhood, in fact. I haven't been there yet. Haven't been invited."

"Whereabouts?"

"You go down Franklin and take the first left after the Shakespeare Bridge at St. George. Up there by the reservoir."

"But you said you've never been there."

"Well, you know, I had to check it out. I haven't been inside—put it that way."

"You're such a dad. Who's the guy? Are you worried?"

"No, he's a good kid. Works in the industry as a set builder."

"That's a union gig, right?"

"Yep. IATSE, Local thirty-three. He does pretty well, and that's all they have coming in with her in the academy. It was slow for him last year but now stuff is picking up. I gave them a little bit to get through."

"You rented that place for them, didn't you?"

"Well, I got 'em started, yeah."

"You're such a dad."

"You said that. Feel more like a grandfather these days."

"Come on. You've got a lot of cases still to work, Harry."

"Especially if I take on a partner."

Ballard smiled and they lapsed into an easy silence. But then she felt bad about castigating the department his daughter was in training to join.

"Sorry about what I said before about the department," she said. "It's just a cycle, and when Maddie gets out of the academy, she'll be part of the new LAPD."

"Hope so," Bosch said.

They dropped back into silence and after a while she heard Bosch's measured breathing. She looked over. He had just dropped his chin and gone to sleep. He still held his empty cup. That was a real skill.

She took out her phone and checked messages and texts. Garrett Single had emailed her the recording of their FaceTime call when he had checked to see whether Bonner was properly intubated during the field trach. Ballard cut the volume on her phone and started to watch it, but then stopped the playback when she realized she didn't want to see Bonner.

Instead, she flipped over to her phone's browser and went to the Wags and Walks website. She navigated to the page for Pinto, the dog she would soon meet. There were several photos of him taken at the shelter.

One short video showed the dog interacting with his foster caretakers. He seemed attentive and wanting to please but he also seemed wary and maybe scarred by past experience. Still, Ballard had a good feeling about Pinto. She couldn't wait to meet him and take him home.

She closed the video when she heard a ping. At first she thought it was on Bosch's phone. But then it sounded again and she realized it was coming from Bonner's burner in the Ziploc, which was in her coat pocket. She pulled the bag out and managed to open the phone without taking it out of the plastic.

The text was just three letters: WTF?

Ballard looked at Bosch. He was still head down and asleep. She wanted to answer the text and attempt to draw the person texting Bonner to a meeting. She could use Bosch's advice here—there were legal considerations to answering the text—but she didn't want to wake him up.

Looking at the burner phone, she saw that the battery was running low and its charging port didn't look like it would fit an iPhone charger. Soon the phone would become useless until charged.

On impulse she started typing a return text on the burner:

Complications. Meet at the lab.

She waited and within a minute the phone started to buzz with a call from the number she had sent the text to. She declined the call and sent a new text.

Can't talk. On the move.

She got an immediate text return:

What complications?

She immediately typed a response.

Tell you at crown. Y or N?

More than a minute went by, then:

When?

Without delay, she typed:

Now. Leave gate open.

She waited for a response but none came. She had to assume the meeting was on. She turned the key on the Mustang and then looked at Bosch. The thrum of the engine was bringing him up out of sleep. He opened his eyes.

"We're on the move," Ballard said. "I set up a meeting at Crown Labs."

"With who?" Bosch said.

"I don't know yet."

35

The security gate at Crown Labs had been left open as instructed. There was a single car in the lot when Ballard and Bosch arrived. It was a Tesla Model S with a vanity plate that said 2TH DOC. Ballard parked close behind it so it could not leave.

"Let's see if Hoyle was telling us the truth," Ballard said.

She pulled the rover out of its charger and ran the plate through the com center. It came back as a corporate registration. The car was owned by a company called 2th-Doc LLC.

"That was one of the companies I traced ownership of the lab through," Bosch said. "Jason Abbott is CEO."

"There you go," Ballard said.

They got out and approached the door with the cartoon tooth on it. Ballard could tell they were under a flight path to the Burbank Airport. There were no flights operating at this hour but the slight scent of jet fuel still hung in the air.

Ballard checked the roofline and noted the cameras at the front corners of the building and over the door. They would not be surprising anybody inside with their arrival.

The door was unlocked. Ballard opened it and went through first, Bosch close behind her. They stepped into a small empty reception area that appeared to be a place for receiving deliveries of lab supplies, not people. It was totally silent.

Ballard looked at Bosch. He nodded toward a darkened hallway behind the reception counter. Ballard pulled the gun she had borrowed from Bosch out of her belt holster and held it down at her side as she moved around the counter.

The overhead lights of the hallway were off but Ballard saw no switch on the wall for turning them on. There were several open doors that led to darkened spaces and one lighted entranceway on the left near the end of the hallway. Ballard moved slowly past the first doorway. She reached in and ran her hand up the interior wall where she thought a light switch might be. She found it, and overhead lights came on, revealing the room to be a large lab with several workstations and assorted equipment and supplies for building dental implants and crowns.

She moved along the hallway, becoming increasingly aware of their precarious position and exposure there.

"LAPD," she called out. "Jason Abbott, show yourself."

There was a long silence followed by what sounded like a muffled scream from the end of the hallway. Ballard started moving swiftly toward the lighted door, raising the gun up in a two-handed grip.

"LAPD!" she yelled. *"Coming in!"*

She crouched low as she went through the door. She could hear Bosch's steps right behind her.

They entered a large office that had a sitting area to the left and a desk to the right. In between was a man sitting in a chair. He was partially gagged with a piece of white cloth stuffed into his mouth and held in place by plastic zip ties wrapped around his head and across his mouth. Zip ties also secured his wrists to the arms of the chair and still more held his ankles to the legs.

Ballard swept her aim across the room to make sure there

was no one else present. She also checked through the open door to a small bathroom that was to the right behind the desk. She then holstered her weapon as she returned to the center of the room.

"Harry? You—"

"Got it."

Bosch moved in, unfolding a knife he had withdrawn from a pocket. He first worked on the gag, pulling the zip tie loop away from the man's jaw to cut it. He then pulled loose the cloth from the man's mouth and dropped it on the floor. Ballard noted that it was a washcloth, likely grabbed from the bathroom.

"Oh, thank god," the man said. "I thought he would come back first."

Bosch moved on to the bindings on the man's wrists and ankles.

"Who are you?" Ballard asked. "What happened here?"

"I'm Jason Abbott," the man said. "Dr. Jason Abbott. You saved me."

He was wearing blue jeans and a light blue button-down shirt with the tails out. The zip ties had left marks on his cheeks. He had a ruddy complexion and blue eyes under a full head of dark, curly hair.

When his wrists were released, he immediately started rubbing them to get circulation going.

"What happened?" Ballard repeated. "Who did this to you?"

"A man," Abbott said. "His name is Christopher Bonner. He's an ex-cop. He tied me up."

After crouching down to cut the ties on Abbott's ankles, Bosch stood up and backed away. Abbott reached down and rubbed his ankles, exaggerating the action, and then unsteadily stood up and tried to take a few steps. He quickly reached his hands out and leaned down on the front of the desk.

"I can't feel my feet," he said. "I've been tied to that chair for hours."

"Dr. Abbott, sit down over here on the couch," Ballard said. "You need to tell us exactly what happened."

Ballard held Abbott by the arm and helped him move unsteadily from the desk to the couch, where he sat down.

"Bonner came here and tied me up," he said.

"When was this?" Ballard asked.

"About two. He came in, he had a gun, and I had to let him tie me up with those plastic things. I had no choice."

"Two a.m. or p.m.?"

"Two p.m. Like twelve hours ago. What time is it anyway?"

"It's after four."

"Jesus. I've been in that chair fourteen hours."

"Why did he tie you up?"

"Because he was going to kill me, I think. He said he had to go do something and I think he wanted me alive and with no alibi when he did it. Then he was going to come back and make it look like I did it. He'd kill me, make it look like a suicide or something and I'd get the blame."

"He told you all of this?"

"I know it sounds fantastic, but it's true. He didn't tell me everything. But I've been sitting here for fourteen fucking hours and I put it together. I mean, why else would he tie me up and keep me here?"

Ballard knew that the more she kept Abbott talking, the more his story would become implausible and the flaws in it would show.

"What was it he had to go and do?" she asked.

"I don't know," Abbott said. "But I think he was going to kill somebody. That's what he does."

"How do you know that?"

"He told me. He flat out told me. This guy, he's had his hooks into me for years. He's been blackmailing me, threatening me, making me do things. And not just me. All of us."

"Who is 'all of us,' Dr. Abbott?"

"My partners. I have partners in the lab, and Bonner bullied his way in and took control. I mean, he was a cop. We were scared. We did what we were told."

Ballard had to assume that Abbott did not know that Bonner was dead. But trying to throw the blame on him was probably the best ploy he could come up with when he saw Ballard and Bosch on the lab's exterior cameras and deduced that it hadn't been Bonner texting him about "complications."

"So you think this was some sort of master plan on Bonner's part?" she asked.

"I don't know," Abbott said. "Ask him. If you can find him."

"Or was it a spur-of-the-moment sort of thing, you think?"

"I already said I don't know."

"Because I noticed those zip ties you were bound to the chair with came from the lab down the hall. I saw a few of them on the floor in there."

"Yeah, then he must have just grabbed them on his way back here to me."

"Who let him into the building?"

"I did. We were closed today—tacked the day on to the holiday weekend. I was here alone, catching up on work and he buzzed the gate. I had no idea what he was going to do. I let him in."

Ballard stepped closer to the couch.

"Let me see your wrists," she said.

"What?" Abbott exclaimed. "You're arresting me? For what?"

"I want to see your wrists," Ballard said calmly.

"Oh," Abbott replied.

He held out his hands, exposing his wrists below the cuffs of his shirt. Ballard saw no sign of injury or any mark that would have been left if Abbott had been bound for as long as he claimed. Ballard had had that experience herself once and knew what his wrists should look like.

"How come you haven't asked me my name?" Ballard asked.

"Uh, I don't know," Abbott said. "I guess I just thought you would tell me at some point."

"I'm Ballard. The one you sent Bonner to kill."

For a moment everything paused and was silent as Abbott registered her words.

"Wait," he then said. "What are you talking about? I didn't send anybody anywhere."

"Come on, Dr. Abbott, this whole thing here, the washcloth and the zip ties, you did that," Ballard said. "Not a bad try for the time you had, but you're not fooling any—"

"Are you crazy? Bonner tied me up. If he tried to kill you, then he did that on his own. And he was going to frame me for it. We're both victims here."

Ballard could picture how Abbott did it. The gag first, leaving it loose enough for him to be able to clench his teeth. Ballard had noted how loose it was when Bosch moved in to cut it.

Binding the feet to the chair's legs would come next. Then put a loose loop around one of the arms of the chair, then bind one wrist to the other side before putting his free hand through the loose loop and pulling it tight with his teeth. She glanced at Bosch to see if he was on the same wavelength and he gave her a slight nod. She looked back at Abbott.

"I could sit in that chair and tie myself up like you were in two minutes," she said. "Your story is shit, Dr. Abbott."

"You have this wrong. I am a victim here."

"Where's your phone?"

"My phone?"

"Yes, your cell phone. Where is it?"

Ballard could tell by his eyes and his reaction that Abbott realized he had missed something, that there was a flaw in his story. He had left something out of the plan.

"It's over there on the desk," he said.

Ballard glanced over and saw an iPhone on the desk.

"What about the burner?" she asked.

"What burner?" Abbott said. "There is no burner."

Ballard looked at Bosch and nodded.

"Call it, Harry," she said.

Bosch pulled out his cell and called the number that had sent the texts to Bonner's burner.

"What's he doing?" Abbott said. "Who's he calling?"

There was a buzzing sound in the room.

"He's calling you," Ballard said.

She followed the sound to the desk. The buzzing kept coming in intervals. She started opening drawers, trying to track it. When she pulled the bottom desk drawer out, the buzzing became louder. There, next to a box of envelopes and a stack of Post-it pads, was a black cell phone matching the one Ballard had found on Bonner.

"You forgot about it, didn't you?" she asked.

"That's not mine," Abbott said. "Bonner—he put it there!"

Ballard didn't touch the phone because she assumed only Abbott's prints would be found on it. And if there were no prints, then they would look for DNA. She closed the drawer. It would be a critical piece of evidence and she would alert Ross Bettany to it.

She came back around the desk and walked toward the couch.

"Stand up, Dr. Abbott," she commanded.

"What for?" Abbott exclaimed. "What's going on?"

"You're under arrest for the murder of Javier Raffa," Ballard said. "And that's just a start."

PART THREE

THE INSURRECTION

36

Ballard called for a car from the nearby North Hollywood Division to transport Abbott to the Van Nuys jail, where he was booked on suspicion of murder. After that, she dropped Bosch off at his house and drove to Hollywood Station, where she spent the next three hours working up the paperwork in support of the arrest and putting together the case package for both the District Attorney's Office and Ross Bettany, who would presumably take it to a prosecutor in follow-up of the arrest.

By nine, she was printing it and laying the pages on the three rings of the murder book when Bettany showed up with his partner, Denise Kirkwood.

"This is your lucky day," Ballard said.

"How so?" Bettany asked.

"I got you an insider willing to talk to save his own ass. And I booked your first suspect about four hours ago."

"You did what?"

Ballard snapped together the rings in the binder, closed it, and held it up to him.

"It's all here," she said. "Read through and call me if you have any questions. I've been going all night, so I'm out of here. Good luck, but I don't think you'll need it. It's all there."

Ballard left Bettany with his mouth open and Kirkwood with

a you-go-girl smile on her face. She got back to her car and drove west until she reached an industrial corridor that ran along the 405 freeway. With the sound of the elevated freeway buzzing overhead, she sat on a bench in a fenced dog yard with Pinto, the rescued Chihuahua mix that was hers for the taking. The brown-and-white dog weighed nine pounds and had the long snout of a terrier and a hopeful look in his amber eyes. She was given a half hour to decide but took less than ten minutes.

The dog came with a metal crate for transport, a five-pound bag of dry food pellets, and a leash with an attached dispenser of biodegradable poop bags. Ballard took him to the beach off Channel Road at the mouth of Santa Monica Canyon, where she sat cross-legged on a blanket and let him run off the leash.

Here, the beach was at its deepest point along the county coastline and nearly deserted. The sky was clear, and there was a slight chill coming in off the Pacific on a wind strong enough to kick sand up onto the blanket. Ballard could see all the way to Catalina Island and the outline of the cargo tankers coming out of the port behind Palos Verde.

The dog had been in a kennel for five weeks. Ballard loved watching him dart back and forth in front of her on the sand. He instinctively knew not to stray far from her. He checked on her every few seconds and seemed to realize she had saved him from a bleak future.

When the dog finally grew tired, he crawled into Ballard's lap to sleep. She petted him and told him everything was going to be all right now.

He was there when Ballard took the call she had been expecting since leaving Bettany and Kirkwood with the murder book. It was Lieutenant Robinson-Reynolds calling to inform her she had been suspended for insubordination until further notice. The lieutenant was formal and used a monotone in the delivery of the notice, but then he went off the record and expressed his disappointment in her in terms of what her actions meant to him.

"You made me look bad, Ballard," he said. "You embarrassed me, running through the night on this—and I have to hear it first from West Bureau command? I hope they roll you out of the department for this. And I'll be right here, waiting to help."

He disconnected before hearing Ballard's response.

"They tried to kill me," she said into the dead phone.

She put the phone down on the blanket and gazed out to the blue-black sea. Insubordination was a firing offense. Suspended until further notice meant that the department had twenty days to reinstate her or take her to a Board of Rights hearing, which was essentially a trial, in which a guilty verdict could result in termination.

Ballard was not troubled by all of this. She had expected things to lead to this from the moment she had hidden Bonner's burner phone in her junk drawer. That was when she had left the confines of acceptable police work.

She picked up the phone and called the one person she believed cared about any of this.

"Harry," she said. "I'm out. Suspended."

"Shit," he said. "I guess we knew that was coming. How bad? CUBO?"

Conduct Unbecoming of an Officer was a lesser crime than insubordination. It was hopeful thinking on Bosch's part.

"No. Insubordination. My lieutenant says they're going to try to fire me. And he's going to help."

"Fuck him."

"Yeah."

"What are you going to do?"

"I don't know. Probably just spend a couple days on the beach. Surf, play with my dog, think things through."

"You have a new dog?"

"Just got him. We're getting along real nice."

"You want a new job to go with your new dog?"

"You mean with you? Sure."

"Not much of a fallback but you would easily pass the background check."

Ballard smiled.

"Thanks, Harry. Let's see how things play out."

"I'm here if you need me."

"I know it."

Ballard disconnected and put the phone down. She looked out at the sea, where the wind was kicking up whitecaps on the waves bringing in the tide.

37

Ballard turned off her phone Tuesday night, got into her sweats, and slept for ten hours on her living room couch, still not ready to return to the bedroom, where she had almost died. She woke up Wednesday in pain, her body sore from the struggle with Bonner as well as the uneven support provided by the couch. Pinto was curled up asleep at her feet.

She turned on her phone. Though suspended, she had not been removed from the department-wide alert system. She saw that she had gotten a text announcing that all divisions and units in the department were going on tactical alert again following civil disturbances in Washington, D.C., and expected protests locally. It meant the entire department would mobilize into twelve-hour shifts in order to put more officers out on the streets. By prior designation Ballard was on B shift, working 6 p.m. to 6 a.m. under the response plan.

She reached for the TV remote and put on CNN. Her screen immediately filled with the images of people, hordes of them, storming the U.S. Capitol. She flipped channels and it was on every network and cable news channel. The commentators were calling it an insurrection, an attempt to stop the certification of the presidential election two months before. Ballard watched in stunned silence for an hour without moving from the couch, before finally sending a text to Lieutenant Robinson-Reynolds.

I assume I am still on the bench?

She did not have to wait long for a response.

Stay on the bench, Ballard. Do not come here.

She then thought of responding with a snarky comment about being accused of insurrection within the department but let it pass. She got up, slipped on shoes, and took Pinto out for his first walk in the neighborhood. She went up to Los Feliz Boulevard and back, the streets almost deserted. Pinto stayed close, never pulling the slack out of the leash. Lola had always pulled the line tight, charging forward, all seventy pounds of her. Ballard missed that.

After coming home and feeding Pinto some of the food from Wags and Walks, Ballard returned to the couch. For the next two hours, remote in hand, she flipped channels and watched the disturbing images of complete lawlessness, trying to comprehend how divisions in the country had grown so wide that people felt the need to storm the Capitol and try to change the results of an election in which 160 million people had voted.

Tired of watching and thinking about what she was seeing, she packed two energy bars for herself as well as some more food for the dog. In the garage, she put both her paddleboard and the mini onto the roof racks of the Defender. She was about to hop in, when a voice came from behind.

"You're going surfing?"

She whipped around. It was the neighbor. Nate from 13.

"What?" Ballard asked.

"You're going surfing?" Nate said. "The country's falling apart, there are protests all over the place, and you're going surfing. You're a cop—shouldn't you be...I don't know...doing something?"

"The department is on twelve-hour shifts," Ballard said. "If everybody went to work now, there'd be nobody to work at night."

"Oh, okay."

"What are *you* doing?"

"What do you mean?"

"What the fuck are you doing, Nate? You people hate us. You hate the cops until the shit comes down and then you need us. Why don't *you* go out there and do something?"

Ballard immediately regretted saying it. The frustrations of everything in her job and life had just misfired at the wrong person.

"You are paid to protect and serve," Nate said. "I'm not."

"Yeah, okay," Ballard said. "That's fine."

"Is that a dog in there?"

He pointed through the window at Pinto.

"Yeah, that's my dog," Ballard said.

"You need HOA approval for that," Nate said.

"I read the rules. I can have a dog under twenty pounds. He's not even ten."

"You still have to have approval."

"Well, you're the president, right? Are you telling me you don't approve of me having a dog in an apartment where somehow a man was able to get around building security and break in and assault me?"

"No. I'm just saying there are rules. You have to submit a request and then get the approval."

"Sure. I'll do that, Nate."

She left him there and got in the Defender. Pinto immediately jumped in her lap and licked her chin.

"It's okay," Ballard said. "You aren't going anywhere."

An hour later, she was paddling west along the Sunset break, the little dog out on the nose of the board, standing alert but shaking. It was a new experience for him.

The sun and salt air worked deeply on her muscles and eased the tension and pain. It was a good workout. She went ninety minutes — forty-five minutes toward Malibu and forty-five back. She was exhausted when she climbed into the tent she had pitched on the sand and took a nap, with Pinto sleeping on the blanket at her feet.

Ballard did not return home until after dark. She had purposely left her phone behind and found that she had accumulated several messages throughout the day. The first was from Harry Bosch, checking in to see how she was faring and to mention that he thought he had seen everything but never expected to ever see the Capitol stormed by its own citizens.

The second message was a formal notification that a Board of Rights hearing had been scheduled for her to appear at in two weeks at the Police Administration Building. Ballard saved the message. She knew she would need to have a representative from the union with her as a defense rep. She would make that call later. But the very next message was from the union and an officer named Jim Lawson saying that they had also received notice of the Board of Rights hearing and were prepared to defend her. Ballard saved that one too and moved on to the next message, which had come in at 2:15 p.m. from Ross Bettany.

"Yeah, uh, Ballard, Ross Bettany here. Give me a call back. Have something to talk to you about. Thanks."

The last message came in two hours later and was from Bettany again, his voice a little more intense.

"Bettany here. Really need a call back from you. This guy Hoyle and his lawyer, he says he'll only talk to you, only trusts you. So we need to figure something out. We obviously need to start talking to the guy. We need to file on Abbott by tomorrow a.m. or the case goes pumpkins. Call me. Thanks."

After an arrest and booking, the district attorney had forty-eight hours to file charges and arraign the suspect or reject the case. The fact that Hoyle was lawyered up also added a complication. Ballard guessed that Bettany had taken what she had given him to the DA, and the filing deputy had wanted more—as in Hoyle giving a formal, voluntary statement as opposed to the surreptitious recording she had made in the car.

Bettany had left his cell phone number with both messages. Ballard thought that calling him back might violate the orders to engage in no police work during her suspension, but she called anyway.

"You know I'm suspended, right?"

"I know, Ballard, but you left me a shit sandwich here."

"Bullshit, I gave you a full package you just needed to walk down to the DA."

"Yeah, I did that, but they said no go."

"Who was the filing deputy?"

"Some stiff named Donovan. Thinks he's F. Lee Bullshit."

"What's wrong with the package?"

"Your taping Hoyle without his knowledge. Hoyle already has a lawyer—this hotshot guy Dan Daly—and he's screaming entrapment. So Donovan looks at the tape and has a problem with it. First of all, who were you talking to when you put down the window and said you might need to transport Hoyle?"

Ballard froze for a moment. She realized she had lowered the window and talked to Bosch while recording Hoyle. It was part of the play but it had been a mistake.

"Ballard?" Bettany prompted.

"It was Bosch, the guy who worked the original case. The Albert Lee murder."

"Isn't he retired?"

"Yeah, he's retired, but I went to him about the case because the murder book's gone. I needed him to tell me about that investigation and we were together when the Hoyle thing went down."

There was a silence while Bettany digested this incomplete explanation.

"Well, that's not a good look, but that's not the problem here," he finally said. "The problem is you told Bosch you might need a transport, and Donovan says that's a threatening and coercive tactic that could get the whole tape tossed. He told me to walk Hoyle through it again, but Hoyle says he will only talk to you. And that's kind of funky, because you tricked the guy but he only trusts you. That's where we stand."

Now Ballard was silent as she considered this change of fortune. A mistake she had made was now working in her favor.

"They have to reinstate me if they want me to do the interview," she said.

"That's about the size of it, yes," Bettany said. "Meantime, Donovan is working on a qualified immunity deal with Daly."

"Have you told anybody about this?"

"My L-T knows, and he's been talking to yours, I guess. Somebody at Hollywood."

Ballard almost smiled, thinking about the jam Robinson-Reynolds was in, having doubled down on her suspension that morning with his terse reply to her text and now needing her back on the job to salvage a multiple-murder case.

"Where is Hoyle?" she asked.

"He's home, I guess," Bettany said. "Or wherever Daly has him stashed."

"Okay, I'll call my L-T and get back to you."

"Make it quick, Ballard, okay? We don't want to kick this guy Abbott loose. He has the funds and the connections to disappear, if you ask me."

Ballard disconnected and immediately called Robinson-Reynolds on his cell. He didn't bother with any sort of greeting and Ballard wasn't expecting one.

"Ballard, you talk to Bettany?"

"Just did."

"Well, it looks like you fell into the shit with your antics the other night and are coming out smelling like a rose."

"Whatever. Am I reinstated or what? We have to get to Hoyle tonight. Our forty-eight on Jason Abbott is up in the morning."

"I'm working on it. Set up the interview tonight. You'll be reinstated by the time you get in the room."

"Is that permanent reinstatement or temporary."

"We'll see, Ballard. It won't be my call."

"Thanks, L-T."

She said it with cheery sarcasm. She disconnected and then called Bettany back.

"It's a go," she said. "Set it up for tonight and then call me."

"Roger that," Bettany said.

38

The reinterview of Dennis Hoyle took place at 8 p.m. at the Van Nuys Division detective bureau. Bettany, Kirkwood, and Donovan were on hand and prepped Ballard on key points that she needed to get on the record. Hoyle was accompanied by his attorney, Daniel Daly, who vetted the immunity deal his client signed. Hoyle was getting off easy, agreeing to plead guilty to conspiracy to commit fraud in exchange for his testimony against Abbott and possibly others. He would take his chances in front of a judge as far as sentencing went. The deal was predicated on his honesty and his claim that he had never engaged in the planning of or had foreknowledge of the murders of people who had accepted loans from the consortium. It was the sweetheart of all sweetheart deals on paper, but Donovan and his superiors had made the call. The unspoken plan most likely included an effort to break the agreement by catching him in a lie. And barring that, the sentencing judge could always be informed of the extent of the crimes Hoyle had engaged in with his cohorts and max out the sentence for the conspiracy plea.

Ballard told Bettany and the others to stay outside the interrogation room and watch the interview on a screen. Since Hoyle claimed he would talk only to her, she didn't want him to think she and Bettany were a team. She entered the small gray room and sat across from Hoyle and his attorney. She put her phone on her thigh, a concession to Donovan that would allow him to message her if he didn't like what he saw on the screen.

"First off, I have to make the legal boundaries of this interview clear," Ballard said. "You need to acknowledge that if you lie directly to me or lie in any way by omission, then the deal is off and you will be prosecuted for conspiracy to commit murder."

Hoyle opened his mouth to answer but Daly reached his arm out like a father stopping a child from walking blindly into the street.

"He understands," Daly said. "That's in the deal."

"I still want to hear it from him," Ballard said.

"I understand," Hoyle said. "Let's get this over with."

"I know it's not in the deal but I also want something else," Ballard said.

"What?" Daly said.

"I want him to give up any and all ownership rights in the property that was owned by Javier Raffa," Ballard said.

"Forget it," Daly said.

"Then you can forget this deal," Ballard said. "I'm not going to let him walk away from this and then take that place away from the family of the man he and his asshole buddies had killed."

Immediately her phone buzzed and Ballard looked down at the message from Donovan.

What the fuck are you doing?

She looked back up and directly at Hoyle, hoping her righteous glare would make him submit.

This time Hoyle put his arm out to stop his attorney.

"It's okay," he said. "I'll agree to that."

"You don't have to," Daly said. "We already negotiated the deal, and that's not—"

"I said it's okay," Hoyle said. "I want to do it."

Ballard nodded.

"The deputy district attorney will prepare an amendment to the deal," she said.

She paused for a moment to see if Daly had more to say. He didn't.

"Okay, let's start," Ballard said.

And so it went. Hoyle's story did not change much from the first time he told it to Ballard. This time, though, she asked questions designed to elicit more about the origins of the factoring consortium and whether the plan from the start was to eventually murder those who borrowed its money. Ballard knew that eventually lawyers for Abbott and anybody else taken down in the investigation would study the transcript of the interview for any crack through which reasonable doubt might slip into the case.

The interview wrapped near midnight and then Hoyle was taken by Bettany and Kirkwood to be booked and released on the conspiracy charge. Meanwhile, Donovan filed formal charges against Abbott with a no-bail hold until his arraignment. Bail would assuredly be argued then.

Soon after concluding the interview and watching them take Hoyle away, Ballard got a text from Robinson-Reynolds. He didn't waste words.

You're back on the bench.

She didn't bother to reply. She went home without a thank-you from anybody. She had turned what was supposed to look like a random New Year's Eve accident into a credible multiple-murder case, but because she had stepped at least one foot over the line, she needed to be pushed to the side and even hidden if possible from the lawyers for the defense.

She had left Pinto in his travel crate and had to wake him up when she got home. She snapped his leash to his collar and took him for a walk. It was a clear and crisp night. The lights of the houses in Franklin Hills sparkled and she walked that way, passing no one on the streets. Even the Shakespeare Bridge was deserted and the houses down below it were dark. After the dog did his business, she bagged it and turned around.

The late-night cable news was all a rehash of the day's staggering events in Washington. There was now word that a police officer had succumbed to injuries sustained while defending the Capitol. All cops go to work each day, thinking it could be their last. But Ballard doubted that officer ever imagined that he would give his life in the line of duty in the way he did. She went to sleep with dark thoughts about the country, her city, and the future.

By virtue of her job, Ballard was used to sleeping during the day and did not change her schedule on her days off. Consequently, she slept lightly and stirred every time any noise penetrated her dozing. Pinto, still getting used to his new home and surroundings, also slept fitfully, moving about in his crate every hour or so.

A text woke Ballard up for good at 6:20 a.m.—not because she heard it come in but because it lit the screen of her phone. It came from Cindy Carpenter.

> How dare you. You are supposed to
> protect and serve. You do neither.
> How do you sleep at night?

Ballard had no idea what she was talking about, but no matter what it was, the words shook her.

She wanted to call immediately but held back because she doubted her call would even be answered. Ballard wondered if the text had something to do with Cindy's residual upset over Ballard's contacting her ex-husband.

But then another, even more disturbing text came in. This one was from Bosch.

> You need to check the paper. You've
> got a leak somewhere.

Ballard quickly got her laptop and went to the *Los Angeles Times* website. Bosch was old-school—he got the actual newspaper delivered. Ballard was an online subscriber. She found the story Bosch was referencing prominently displayed on the home page.

LAPD GAMBLED ON SERIAL RAPE INVESTIGATION: MORE VICTIMS ENDED UP ASSAULTED

by Alexis Stanishewski
Times Staff Writer

After two men broke into a Hollywood home and raped a woman, the Los Angeles Police Department launched a full-scale investigation.

But the supervisor of the investigation elected to keep it quiet in hopes of identifying and capturing the rare team of rapists. No warning was put out to the public and at least two more women were attacked over the next five weeks.

The case, according to sources, is an example of the choices investigators face in pursuing serial offenders. A suspect's routine can lead to capture, but drawing public attention to a crime spree can result in identifiable patterns changing, making the culprits more difficult to apprehend.

In this case, three women were sexually assaulted and tortured by men who broke into their homes in the middle of the night, prompting investigators to label them the "Midnight Men." On Wednesday, officers in the Media Relations Unit remained mute on the case, while Lieutenant Derek Robinson-Reynolds, supervisor of Hollywood Division detectives, refused to explain or defend his decision to keep the investigation quiet. The *Times* has filed a formal request for police reports related to the crimes.

One of the victims said she was upset and angry to learn that the police knew of the rapists before she was assaulted on Christmas Eve. Her name is not being used because of the *Times*'s policy not to identify victims of sex crimes.

"I feel like maybe if I knew these guys were out there, I could have taken precautions and not been a victim," the woman said tearfully. "I feel like first I got raped by these men and then again by the police department."

The victim described a harrowing four hours that began after she was awakened in her bed by two men wearing masks, who blindfolded her and took turns assaulting her. The victim said she believed that the two men were going to kill her when the brutal attack was over.

"It was horrible," she said. "I keep reliving it. It is the worst thing that has ever happened to me."

Now she wonders if her ordeal could have been prevented if the police department had informed the public of the Midnight Men.

"Maybe they would have stopped or maybe they would

have just moved on if they knew the police were onto them," the victim said.

USC crime sociologist Todd Pennington told the *Times* that the Midnight Men case underlines the difficult choices faced by law enforcement.

"There is no good answer here," he said. "If you keep the investigation under wraps, you stand a much better chance of making an arrest. But if you keep quiet and don't make that arrest quickly, the public remains in danger. You are damned if you do and damned if you don't. In this case, the decision backfired and there were additional victims."

Pennington said serial offenders rarely stop committing crimes unless stopped by police.

"You have to realize that even if the police had gone public with their investigation, it is unlikely that these two men would have stopped their crimes," he said. "Instead, they would have changed their patterns. But most likely there would still have been additional victims. And that's the dilemma we face in deciding whether to go public. It's a no-win situation for the police."

Ballard's face had grown hot while she read the article. Two paragraphs in, she knew that the department would likely peg her as the anonymous source for the story, since the only named villain was the man who had sought her suspension. She also knew this would not be the end of it. The *Times* was the paper of record and, as such, set the example for most of the other media in the city. There was no doubt that every local news broadcast would jump on this story, and the department would be under the magnifying glass once again.

She read the article one more time and this time took heart in what it didn't reveal. It made no mention of the attacks all occurring on holidays, and it did not reveal the pattern of street-light tampering. The source of the story had been careful about what information about the case got out to the public.

Ballard was confident that she knew who the source was. She picked up her phone and called Lisa Moore. With each ring she grew angrier, so that when the call finally went to voice mail, she was ready to fire with both barrels.

"Lisa, I know it was you. I'll probably get blamed but I know it was you. You jeopardized an entire investigation just to spite Robinson-Reynolds for putting you on nights. And I know you calculated that I would get the blame for this. So fuck you, Lisa."

She disconnected, almost immediately regretting the message she had left.

39

The story played for two days on the TV, radio, and Internet news, largely fueled by a hastily called press conference at the PAB in which an official department spokesman downplayed the *Times* report, saying that evidentiary connections between the crimes were tenuous, but the fact that each case involved two perpetrators seemed to connect the cases. Luckily for the department, the Capitol insurrection clogged airtime and newspaper space, and the story disappeared in the undertow of the larger story. Ballard never heard from Robinson-Reynolds, though his silence seemed to confirm his belief that she was the initial leak. Ballard also never heard back from Lisa Moore, even to deny the accusation she had left in her message.

Another story that didn't get any traction was the arrest of a well-respected dentist in a murder conspiracy. Ballard was now an outsider on the case but she gathered from a call to Ross Bettany that the investigation was moving slowly. While the arrest of Jason Abbott was put out to the media, the involvement of Dennis Hoyle as a cooperating witness and ex-cop Christopher Bonner as a hit man had been successfully kept quiet. Ballard knew it wouldn't stay quiet forever, especially when court hearings started, but the department had always operated according to the unspoken policy of spreading out the hits to its reputation whenever it possibly could.

On Saturday Ballard took a call from Garrett Single, who asked if she and her new dog wanted to come for a hike. Ballard had texted him a photo of Pinto earlier. He suggested Elysian Park because there was so much shade along the way. Ballard had not hiked Elysian since she was a cadet at the nearby police academy. She thought Pinto might enjoy it and, as Single had pointed out, the trail was dog-friendly and likely to be less crowded than other popular hiking spots. Ballard agreed to meet there, as Single was coming in from his home in Acton, which was far on the other side of the San Gabriel Mountains. Ballard knew of the community as a place where many firefighters lived because they only went to and from work once a week, working three days on and sleeping in the firehouse, then getting four days off. A couple two-hour drives a week were not a big deal.

Monday morning Ballard woke up in Acton, having spent the last thirty-six hours with Single. His home was wedged into a rugged mountainside in the Antelope Valley, where, he had warned her, coyotes and bobcats roamed freely. She made coffee while Garrett showered, and stepped out onto a back deck that overlooked a garden that he told her he had been working on for months. She had a blanket from the couch wrapped around her shoulders. The time with Single had been good but Ballard had felt uneasy and frustrated the whole time. She had been pushed out of everything. The Raffa case had moved into the prosecutorial phase, so that didn't bother her as much as being completely out of the Midnight Men investigation. What doubled the frustration was the fact that she had been vilified by Cindy Carpenter and had heard nothing from Lisa Moore on how the case was being pursued. It left her with little confidence that anyone was getting closer to identifying and apprehending the tag team rapists.

She was pacing in the brush and running the facts of the case through her mind when she heard Single come up behind her. He put one arm around and used the other to pull her hair back from the nape of her neck. He kissed her there.

"What do you think?" he asked.

"About what?" she asked.

"The view. I mean, look at this place."

Ballard hadn't even noticed. She hadn't been looking past her thoughts on the case.

"It's pretty," she said. "Stark."

"It is," Single said. "It's why I like it."

"No, you like it for the real-estate value and the wide-open space. Cops and firefighters always want space."

"True. But I gotta be honest. I like the sharp ridges out here."

"Then I gotta be honest. It's too far away from the water."

"What do you mean? We got the Santa Clara River right over that ridge."

"Yeah, I'm talking about an ocean. The Pacific Ocean. Last I heard, you can't surf the Santa Clara River—even when there is water in it."

"But it's a good counterpoint, mountains and oceans, isn't it? The desert and beach have got at least one thing in common."

"Sand?"

"You guessed it."

Single laughed, and when he stopped, Ballard could hear her phone buzzing on the kitchen counter inside. It was the first time in thirty-six hours, and she had thought she was outside the limit of her cell service, but here it was: a call.

"Let me try to grab that," she said.

"Come on," Single said. "We're talking about the future here."

She hurried in through the door but the phone's buzz died before she reached it. She saw the number was a city exchange but didn't recognize it. She hesitated calling back blindly. It could be about her Board of Rights hearing. She still didn't know if it would take place as scheduled after she had been taken off suspension and then placed back on. She waited and soon a voice-mail message notice appeared on the screen. She reluctantly played it back.

"Detective Ballard, Carl Schaeffer here from the Bureau of Street Lighting. I saw all the fuss on the news about the so-called Midnight Men and I'm guessing that's your case and the cat is sort of out of the bag. But just in case it still matters, I wanted to let you know we got a maintenance call today on a light over in Hancock Park and I'm here if you want to know the details."

Ballard immediately called Schaeffer back.

"Detective, how are you?"

"I'm fine, Mr. Schaeffer. I got your message. Did you send anyone out to repair the light?"

"No, not yet. I thought I'd check with you first."

"Who called it in?"

"A guy we know over there—we sort of call him the mayor of Windsor Square. It's not on his street but people there just sort of know he's the go-to guy on streetlights and other neighborhood stuff. He called it in this morning. Just now, in fact. Right before I called you."

"Can I get his name?"

"John Welborne."

Schaeffer also gave Ballard the phone number Welborne had called from to initiate the maintenance request.

"Was I right about the Midnight Men—them being why you came here about the lights?"

"What makes you say that? Was there something in the paper about streetlights?"

"Not that I saw. I just kinda put two and two together. The paper said three different women were attacked, and you had asked about three different streetlights."

"Mr. Schaeffer—Carl—I think you could've been a smart detective, but please don't talk to anyone about this. That is not fully confirmed and it could hurt the investigation if it becomes public knowledge."

"Completely understood, Detective. I have not told a soul and I certainly won't. But thanks for the compliment. I thought about being a cop way back in the day."

Single came in from outside and saw the serious look on Ballard's face. He held his hands wide as if to ask if there was anything he could do. Ballard shook her head and continued with Schaeffer.

"Can you give me the address of the streetlight we're talking about, Mr. Schaeffer?" she asked.

"Sure can," Schaeffer said. "Let me look it up here."

He read off an address on North Citrus Avenue.

"Between Melrose and Beverly," he added helpfully.

Ballard thanked him and disconnected. She looked at Single.

"I've gotta go," she said.

"You sure?" he said. "I don't go back in till tomorrow. I thought maybe we'd take the dog and—"

"I have to. This is my case."

"I thought you didn't have any cases anymore."

Ballard didn't answer. She went back to his bedroom to gather her things and get Pinto out of his travel crate, where he was sleeping. She had been using clothes out of the surf bag she kept in the car, while Pinto had been treated to canned food from a mini-market in what passed for the town center of Acton. Her stay with Single had started as just a home-cooked meal from Single's backyard barbecue—he had revealed in Elysian Park that he prided himself on good barbecue and she had put him to the test.

After walking Pinto in the scrub area surrounding Single's home, she loaded her things and the dog into the Defender and was ready to go.

At the open door, he kissed her goodbye.

"You know, this could work," Single said. "You keep your place in town and surf when I'm on shift. Three days on the water, four in the mountains."

"So you think because you make a great pulled chicken sandwich that a girl's just gonna swoon and fall into your arms, huh?" she said.

"Well, I also make a great brisket if you'd go back on the red meat."

"Maybe next time I'll break down."

"So there will be a next time?"

"A lot's going to ride on that brisket."

She gently pushed him away and got in the Defender.

"You be careful," he said.

"You too," she replied.

On the way south to the city she waited until she cleared the Santa Clarita Valley and had solid phone service before calling the number she had been given for John Welborne. The call went to the *Larchmont Chronicle,* the community newspaper that served Hancock Park and its surrounding neighborhoods, for which, she learned, he was the publisher, editor, and reporter. That he was a member of the media made the call a bit tricky. Ballard needed information from him but didn't want it to end up in his paper.

"Mr. Welborne, this is Detective Ballard with the LAPD. Can I talk to you for a few minutes?"

"Yes, of course. Is this about the article?"

"Which article?"

"We published a story Thursday about the fundraiser for the Wilshire Division officer who lost his wife to Covid."

"Oh, no, not that. I'm with Hollywood Division. I need to talk to you off the record about something unrelated to the newspaper. I don't want it in your paper—not yet, at least. This is an off-the-record conversation. Okay?"

"Not a problem, Detective Ballard. We're a monthly, and it's a couple weeks till deadline anyway."

"Good. Thank you. I want to ask you about your call this morning to the Bureau of Street Lighting. You left a message reporting that there's a streetlight out on North Citrus Avenue."

"Uh, yes, I did leave a message, but Detective, I didn't suggest that any crime had been committed."

"Of course not. But it may have some connection to a case we're investigating. That's why we were alerted and that's also the part I want to keep quiet."

"I understand."

"Can you tell me who told you about the light being out?"

"It was a good friend of my wife, Martha's. Her name is Hannah Stovall. She knew she could call me and I'd alert the appropriate authorities. Most people don't even know we have a Bureau of Street Lighting. But they know that I know people who know people. They come to me."

"And she called you?"

"Actually, no, she sent an email to my wife, asking for advice. I took it from there."

"I understand. Can you tell me what you know about Hannah Stovall? For example, how old do you think she is?"

"Oh, I would say early thirties. She's young."

"Is she married, lives alone, has roommates—what?"

"She's not married and I'm pretty sure she lives by herself."

"And do you know what she does for a living?"

"Yes, she's an engineer. She works for the Department of Transportation. I'm not sure what she does but I could ask Martha. This sounds like you are seeing if she fits into some sort of profile."

"Mr. Welborne, I can't really share with you what the investigation is about at this time."

"I understand, but of course I'm dying to know what is going on with our friend. Is she in danger? Can you tell me that?"

"I—"

"Wait—is this about the Midnight Men? It's in the same general area of at least two of the attacks."

"Mr. Welborne, I need you to stop asking me questions. I just want to assure you that your friend is not in danger and we will take all safeguards possible to keep it that way."

Ballard tried to change the subject.

"Now, do you know where the streetlight is in relation to her home? How close is it?"

"From what I understand, it is right in front of her house. That's why she noticed it was on one night, out the next."

"Okay, and can you give me a phone number for Hannah Stovall?"

"Not offhand, but I can get it. Can I call you back at this number in a few minutes? I just need to call my wife."

"Yes, I'm at this line. But Mr. Welborne, please don't tell your wife what this is about, and please don't you or your wife call Hannah about this. I need to keep her line clear so I can call her myself."

"Of course, I'll just tell her that the number's needed for the streetlight maintenance order."

"Thank you."

"Stand by, Detective. I'll get right back to you."

40

Ballard held off on calling Hannah Stovall until she had a plan that she could confidently share with her. Strategizing the moves she would make, she drove the rest of the way into the city in silence, with the exception of a short call to Harry Bosch. She knew if there was no one else to back her play, there would always be Bosch. She asked him to stand by without telling him what he would be standing by for, and he didn't object. He simply said he would be ready and waiting for anything, that he had her back.

She got into Hollywood shortly after 1 p.m., took Melrose to North Citrus Avenue, and turned south to cruise by the streetlight in front of the address Carl Schaeffer had given. She did not slow as she passed. She just surveyed and kept moving. Citrus was on the outer edges of what could be considered Hancock Park. It was on the west side of Highland, and the houses here were smaller postwar family homes with single-car garages. Slowly the neighborhood was being infiltrated by redevelopment, which came in the form of two-story cubes being built to the limits of the lot and then walled and gated. Next to the single-level Spanish-style homes that originally populated the neighborhood, the redevelopment looked sterile, soulless.

As she drove, Ballard checked the vehicles parked curbside for any signs of surveillance but saw nothing that indicated that the Midnight Men might be watching their next victim. At Beverly, she turned right, made a U-turn when she could, and then came back to Citrus. She headed back up the street the way she had come. This time when she passed the streetlight in question, she glanced at the plate at the bottom of the post to check for any sign of tampering. She saw nothing, but she had not expected to.

Back on Melrose she turned right and immediately parked at the curb in front of Osteria Mozza. The popular restaurant was closed due to Covid, and parking at the moment was plentiful. She pulled up her mask, got out, and opened the hatch. She got Pinto out of his crate and snapped on his leash. She then walked the dog back toward Citrus, taking a return call from John Welborne while on the way. He supplied Hannah Stovall's phone number and the additional intel that she was most likely home at the moment because she was working from home during the pandemic.

Ballard turned south on Citrus and started down the street on the west side—which would take her by the streetlight. She took it slow, allowing the dog to set the pace while sniffing and marking his way down the street. The only tell she might have given—if the Midnight Men were watching—was to pull Pinto away from the streetlight in question so that he would not mark it and possibly destroy evidence.

Ballard surreptitiously checked the house where Hannah Stovall lived. There was no car in the driveway, and the garage was closed. Ballard noted that it was an attached garage that surely had internal access to the house, just as with the home of Cindy Carpenter.

Ballard kept walking and at Oakwood crossed Citrus and turned back north, walking the other side of the street like a pet owner wanting to give her dog new lawns to sniff and mark.

She checked the dashboard clock after she got back to the Defender. It was two-thirty and possibly a little early to start her plan. She also had Pinto to consider.

There was an overnight dog kennel on Santa Monica Boulevard near the Hollywood Station. She had used it on occasion for Lola and knew it to be clean and welcoming and not too crowded. Best of all, she would be able to use her phone to access the camera in the so-called playroom to check on Pinto.

It took an hour to get to Dog House, start a new account, and put Pinto up for the night. Ballard's heart hurt as she realized the dog might think he was being rejected and turned back in to a shelter. She hugged him and promised to come back the next day, assuring herself more than the dog.

Her parking place in front of Mozza had gone unclaimed and she pulled back in shortly before four, adjusting her mirrors so she could pick up any vehicles coming out of North Citrus Avenue behind her. She then made the initial call to Hannah Stovall and the strategy she had formulated kicked into gear.

Her call was picked up right away.

"Hello, I'm looking for Hannah Stovall."

"That's me. Who's this?"

"I'm calling about the report of a streetlight that is out on your street?"

"Oh, yes. Right in front of my house."

"And how long would you estimate that it has been out?"

"Just since yesterday. I know it was working Saturday because it shines over the top of my shades in my bedroom. It's like a night-light for me. I noticed it was gone last night and I emailed Martha Welborne this morning. This seems to be a lot of attention for one little streetlight. What's going on?"

"My name is Renée Ballard. I'm a detective with the Los Angeles Police Department. I don't want to scare you, Ms.

Stovall, but I believe someone may be planning to break into your home."

Ballard knew no gentler way to put it, but as she expected, Stovall reacted with extreme alarm.

"Oh my god—who?"

"I don't know that but—"

"Then how do you know? You just call people up and scare the shit out of them? This doesn't make sense. How do I know you're even a cop? A detective or whatever you say you are."

Ballard had anticipated having to prove who she was to this woman.

"Is this number a cell phone?" she asked.

"Yes," Stovall said. "Why do you want to know that?"

"Because I'm going to hang up and text you photos of my police ID and my badge. Then I'll call you back and explain what's going on in fuller detail. Okay, Ms. Stovall?"

"Yes, send the text. Whatever this is, I want it to be over."

"So do I, Ms. Stovall. I'm disconnecting now and will call you back."

Ballard ended the call, pulled up photos of her badge and police ID, and texted them to Stovall. She waited a few minutes for them to land and be viewed, then called back.

"Hello."

"Hannah—can I call you Hannah?"

"Sure, fine, just tell me what's going on."

"Okay, but I'm not going to sugarcoat this, because I need your help. There are two men out there targeting women in the Hollywood area. They invade their homes in the middle of the night and assault them. We believe they knock out the streetlights near the victim's home a night or two before the attack."

There was a long silence only punctuated by the repeated intake of breath.

"Hannah, are you all right?"

Nothing.

"Hannah?"

Finally she came back with words.

"Are they the Midnight Men?"

"Yes, Hannah."

"Then why aren't you here right now? Why am I alone?"

"Because they might be watching you. If we make a show, we lose the chance to capture them and end this."

"You're using me as bait? Oh my fucking god!"

"No, Hannah. You're not bait. We have a plan to keep you safe. Again, that's why I'm calling you instead of showing up. There's a plan. I want to tell it to you but I need you to be calm. There is no reason to panic. They don't come during the day. They—"

"You said they could be watching."

"But they are not going to break in during daylight hours. It's too dangerous for them, and the fact that your light is out proves they're coming at night. Do you understand?"

No answer.

"Hannah, do you understand?"

"Yes. What do you want me to do?"

"Good, Hannah. Stay calm. In an hour this will be over for you and you'll be safe."

"Do you promise?"

"Yes, I promise. Now, this is what I want you to do. You keep your car in your garage, right?"

"Yes."

"What kind of car is it? What color?"

"It's an Audi A-six. Silver."

"Okay, and where do you do your grocery shopping?"

"I don't understand, why are you asking me this?"

"Just bear with me, Hannah. Where do you shop?"

"Usually at the Pavilions on Vine. Melrose and Vine."

Ballard was not familiar with the store but immediately computed that this was a different location from the markets frequented by the other three victims of the Midnight Men.

"Is there a coffee shop inside?"

"There's a Starbucks."

"Okay, what I want you to do is get in your car and go to Pavilions. If you have reusable bags, carry one of them in like you're going to do some light shopping. But first go to the Starbucks. I will meet you there."

"I have to leave here?"

"It's going to be safest if you are not there tonight, Hannah. I want to get you out without anything looking unusual. You are just going to the store to pick up a coffee and some dinner. Okay?"

"I guess. Then what?"

"I'll meet you there, we'll talk some more, and then I'll put you in the hands of another detective, who will make sure you are guarded and safe until this is over."

"When should I leave?"

"As soon as you can. You drive up to Melrose and go right and head to the store. You'll pass me and I'll be able to tell if you are followed. Then I'll meet you at the Starbucks. Can you do this, Hannah?"

"Yes. I told you I could."

"Good. Put a toothbrush and anything you might need for an overnight stay in the reusable bag. But don't take a lot. You don't want it to stand out."

"Well, I'll need my computer. I have to work tomorrow."

"Okay, your computer is fine. Make it look like you are carrying more bags inside the one you're carrying."

"Got it."

"And what about a mask? What color do you have?"

"Black."

"Black is good. Wear that."

Ballard knew she would have to wear her LAPD mask inside out.

"Okay, one other thing, Hannah."

Ballard looked down at what she was wearing. Because she had come straight from Acton, she was casually dressed, in jeans and a white oxford borrowed from Single.

"Do you have a pair of jeans and white blouse you can wear?" she asked.

"Uh, I have jeans," Stovall said. "I know everybody has a white blouse. But not me."

Ballard looked over her shoulder to the back seat, where she had various jackets and other clothing.

"How about a hoodie?" she asked. "You have a red or gray hoodie?"

"Yeah, gray," Stovall said. "I have it right here. Why are you asking about my clothes?"

"Because I'm going to take your place. Wear the gray hoodie when you come to Starbucks."

"Okay."

"What's the length and color of your hair?"

"Jesus. I have short brown hair."

"Do you have any hats you can wear?"

"I've got a Dodgers cap."

"Perfect. Wear that, and text or call me on this number before you leave. That way I'll be ready."

"I'll text."

They disconnected. Ballard was concerned that Hannah might do something that would stand out to anyone who had her under surveillance. But it was too late to worry about it now.

It was now time to call in backup. Ballard felt too alienated from her own department to go inside for help. She was already working without a net and probably providing more fodder for the upcoming Board of Rights hearing. Taking stock of her situation, she noted that her boss was the one trying to fire her, while her partner on the Midnight Men case had been anything but a partner. Lisa Moore had proven herself to be unreliable, lazy, and vindictive.

There was no doubt in Ballard's mind who she needed to call. He answered immediately.

"Okay, Harry," Ballard said. "Now's when I need you."

41

The text from Hannah Stovall came in twenty minutes later. Ballard sent her back a thumbs-up and then waited with her eyes on the sideview mirror. A few minutes went by before she saw the silver Audi emerge from North Citrus Avenue and turn right on Melrose. Ballard checked the car as it went by and caught a glimpse of the driver wearing a blue Dodgers cap.

Ballard's eyes went back to the sideview and she waited and watched. She let two minutes go by. No follow car emerged from Citrus. Ballard pulled out and gunned it down Melrose in an effort to catch up to the Audi, but a traffic signal at Cahuenga undid her. When she finally pulled into the parking lot at Pavilions she had to cruise down two aisles before spotting the Audi. She then caught a glimpse of a woman wearing a Dodgers cap entering the supermarket with a reusable shopping bag that looked weighted with belongings.

Ballard parked and quickly moved to the store's entrance. Covid protocols dictated that one door was an entrance, and the exit was on the other side of the front facade. Ballard entered and found the Starbucks concession immediately inside the entrance. There was a line of four people, with the woman with the weighted shopping bag in last position. Ballard checked the others in line, saw nothing suspicious and joined.

"Hannah," she whispered. "I'm Renée."

Stovall turned to look at her, and Ballard discreetly flashed her badge and put it away.

"Okay, so now what?" Stovall said.

"Let's get coffee," Ballard said. "And talk."

"What is there to talk about? You've scared the hell out of me."

"I'm sorry. But you will be completely safe now. Let's wait till we're sitting down to talk about the plan."

Soon they were at a table off the side of the Starbucks counter.

"Okay, I have another investigator on his way," Ballard said. "He's going to take you to a hotel where you can check in and spend the night. He'll be on guard the whole time. And hopefully this will all be over by morning."

"Why did these men pick me? I've never hurt anyone."

"We've tracked them through their patterns, but we don't know all the answers yet. That just means we'll find all of that out when we catch them. And thanks to you being vigilant in your neighborhood and noticing the streetlight, we are in our best position to do that now."

"It was hard to miss. Like I said, it shines in my window at night."

"Well, we got very lucky that you noticed it. So, while we're waiting for my colleague, can I ask you about some of your routines?"

Ballard started going through the questions that were contained in the survey given to the other victims of the Midnight Men. She knew most of these by heart and didn't need an actual copy of the questionnaire. Soon it became clear that Stovall was even more of an outlier than Cindy Carpenter up in the Dell. Though Stovall lived reasonably close to the first two victims, their worlds didn't seem to intersect anywhere, other than favoring some of the same local restaurants. During the pandemic Stovall was working from home and rarely left the house except to shop for food. She didn't even pick up food to go from restaurants, choosing instead to get home delivery. Home delivery had been a subject of interest early in the investigation because the first two victims used it from time to time. But the investigators learned they used different services, and a review of their transactions determined that they had never been served by the same driver.

It was when it came to her personal life that Ballard scored a connection between Stovall and the other victims. Stovall had never been married but she had been in a long-term relationship that had ended badly. Her partner had been furloughed from his job, and tensions rose when Stovall had to work from home like most of the rest of the world.

"I was on Zooms and calls all day and it sort of reminded him of what he had lost," Stovall said. "He started to resent me for not losing my job and for being the one who brought in the money. We argued all the time and soon the house wasn't big enough for the two of us. I own the house so I asked him to leave. It was awful. And talking about it is awful too."

"I'm sorry," Ballard said.

"I just wish this was over."

"You're going to get through it. I promise."

Ballard looked around for Bosch but didn't see him. She also looked for any man who might be watching them. She saw no one who drew her attention.

"What is your ex's name?" she asked.

"Really?" Stovall said. "Why do you need to know that?"

"I need all the information I can get. It doesn't mean it all fits or is important."

"Well, I don't feel comfortable giving out my ex-boyfriend's name. I'm finally in a place where we can text each other without-out resorting to calling each other names. And this would totally fuck that up if you went knocking on his door to make sure he wasn't one of the Midnight Men. I can assure you he's not. He's not even in town right now."

"Where is he?"

"Cancún, I think. Somewhere in Mexico."

"How do you know that?"

"He texted me, saying he was going to Mexico. I assume Cancún, because we went there once and he loved it."

"So he wasn't worried about Covid and going to a foreign country?"

"I asked him that. I didn't even know you could fly in and out of Mexico at the moment. I told him he better not bring Covid back to the company."

"You mean you work together?"

"Well, we did till the pandemic came. Then he got furloughed and I was kept on. That led to some real brawls."

"He got physical?"

"No, no, I didn't mean it that way. Just some knock-down-drag-out *verbal* fights. We never got physical."

"But he's now back in the workplace with you?"

"The department hired him back, yeah. We work at the same place technically, but I'm a designer so I'm working from home. Gilbert is a field engineer and he goes in. That's why I said you better not bring Covid back with you."

"Was he trying to make you jealous, telling you he was going to Mexico?"

"No, I don't think so. He couldn't find his bathing suit and he was just asking if he had left it at the house."

"Was it weird that he was taking a vacation after coming back from being furloughed?"

"Yeah, a little. I was surprised. But he told me it was just a long weekend. An impromptu kind of thing because some guys were going and somebody had a place down there. I didn't really ask questions. I looked for his bathing suit, then texted him that I didn't have it, and that was it."

Ballard looked around again, wondering what was taking Bosch so long. But he was there, standing near the pickup counter, waiting to be called into the conversation. Ballard waved him over and introduced him. Bosch pulled a chair away from another table and sat down.

"Okay, so we're all here," Ballard said. "Hannah, this is what we want to do. I'm going to be you for the night, and you get to stay at a nice hotel with Harry watching over you. I'm going to borrow your hat and borrow your car and go back to your house. If they're watching, they'll think it's you coming home. Then I'll be inside waiting and ready if they make a move. I'll be able to call in backup anytime I need it."

"Do I have any say in it?" Stovall asked.

"Of course. I need your permission to do this. Is there something wrong?"

"Well, for starters there are two of them, right? And only one of you."

Bosch nodded. He had voiced the same concern when they had talked on the phone.

"Well, like I said, I can call backup if I need it," Ballard said. "And we know from the other cases that one always comes in on his own, secures the victim, then lets the other in. So I just have to worry about them one at a time, and I like my chances with those odds."

"Okay, I guess. You're the police."

"I'm going to grab a few things so it will look like I was shopping and then I'm going to leave. I just need the keys to your car and house. You and Harry will wait ten minutes just to be sure and then you two can go as well."

"Okay."

"Do you have any night routines I should know about?"

"Not really, I don't think."

"What about showering? Do you prefer mornings or nights?"

"Definitely mornings."

"Okay. Anything else?"

"I can't think of anything."

"Do you usually have the TV on?"

"I'll watch the news. CNN, Trevor Noah, that's about it."

"Okay. I'm going to grab a few things to put in the bag and then I'll go."

Ballard went to the door, grabbed a handbasket from a stack, and walked into the produce section, where she started selecting apples and oranges in case she needed sustenance while on the vigil ahead. Soon Bosch was standing next to her.

"For the record, I'm not happy about this," he said.

Ballard looked past him to make sure Stovall was still in place at the table by the Starbucks concession.

"You're worrying too much, Harry," she said. "I'm calling backup the moment I hear something. They'll be there in two minutes."

"If they come. You're doing this completely off the books, and coms won't know what the hell you're doing if you call for help."

"I have to work it this way because I *am* off the books. And I'm not about to hand this off to somebody who deep down doesn't even care about the case or its victims. Somebody who would rather use the case to get even than solve it."

"She's not the only one you can bring in and you know it. You just want to do this on your own, no matter the level of danger it puts you in."

"I think that's an exaggeration, Harry."

"It's not, but I know you're not going to change your mind. So I want you calling me every hour on the hour, you copy that?"

"I got it."

"Good."

Ballard put a sweet potato in the basket and decided she had enough to make it through the night if necessary.

"I'm going to check out and head over to her house."

"Okay. Remember, every hour on the hour."

"Got it. And if you spend any time with her, ask about her ex-boyfriend."

"What about him?"

"I don't know—something feels off. I got the same feeling with Carpenter's ex. Hannah's ex took a long weekend in Mexico after being laid off for most of last year. Feels kind of convenient to me."

"Yeah, it does."

"Anyway, I gotta get going."

She turned toward the checkout counters, took a few steps, and then turned back.

"Hey, Harry, you remember the other night when we joked about me going private and working with you?"

"Yeah, sure."

"What if it wasn't a joke?"

"Uh…well, that would be good with me."

Ballard nodded.

"Okay," she said.

42

On her drive back to the house on North Citrus Avenue, Ballard had to call Hannah Stovall with more questions. She knew that this risked undercutting Stovall's confidence in her, but Ballard had to acknowledge, at least to herself, that the plan was evolving from minute to minute as various questions and decisions came to her.

Stovall was with Bosch in his car when she took the call.

"Hannah, how do I open the garage? I don't see any clicker."

"It's programmed into the car. There's a button on the bottom of the rearview mirror. There are actually three buttons but you want the first one."

"Okay, got it. And I forgot to ask, is there an alarm?"

"There is but I never use it. Too many false alarms. And there isn't one on the door from the garage to the kitchen anyway, since that is sort of indoors already."

"And would it be unusual for you to take a walk at night? Like if I want to just get the lay of the land?"

"I should have mentioned that. I usually take a walk when I finish work. To sort of clear my head. I just go a couple blocks around the neighborhood."

"Okay."

Ballard dropped into thought about how she would handle this. The walk time was right now.

"Detective?"

"Yes, uh, this is all good. What do you wear when you walk?"

"Well, I don't change or anything, so whatever I have on."

"Okay, good. What about a hat?"

"Every now and then I wear a hat."

"Okay, good."

"You'll let me know if anything happens, right?"

"Of course. You'll be the first to know."

Three minutes later Ballard pulled the Audi into the driveway of Stovall's house and pushed the button to open the garage. She held her phone to her left ear, posing as though she were on a call so her face would be partially obscured to anyone watching. It was now almost six and the sun had dropped from the sky. The day was slipping toward the dark hours.

She pulled into the garage, hit the button again, and waited for the garage door to close before she got out of the car.

She used a key on the ring Stovall had given her to open the door from the garage to the kitchen. Ballard entered, hit the wall switch to turn on the lights, and then stood still in the kitchen, listening to the house. She heard only the low hum of the refrigerator. She put the bag of produce from Pavilions on the counter, took out the apples and oranges and placed them on a shelf in the refrigerator, and put the sweet potato on the counter. She then bent down to the cuff of her jeans and pulled Bosch's gun out of an ankle holster.

Ballard slowly moved through the house, checking each room. The kitchen had one arched entrance to a dining room and a second one that led to a hallway that ran to the back of the house. She walked through the dining room into a living room. There was a fireplace with a flat-screen TV mounted above it. Ballard checked the front door and it was locked.

She next moved down the hallway, checking out a guest bedroom, another bedroom, which had been converted to an office during or before the pandemic, and a bathroom. Her last stop was the master bedroom, which included a walk-in closet and a large bathroom. The master suite took up the whole back of the house, and there was a back door in the bathroom. It was double-locked but Ballard opened it to check the yard before it got too dark. Stovall had created a sitting area on a wooden deck off the bathroom door. There was an ashtray on a table that needed to be emptied.

The rest of the yard was surrounded by a plank fence that included an enclosure for the city garbage and recycling containers. The enclosure had a locked wooden gate that led to a rear service alley.

Ballard tucked the gun into her pants at the small of her back and flapped her hoodie out over it. She stepped into the alley and looked north and south but saw no vehicles or anything else that raised suspicion or concern. Her phone buzzed and she saw that it was Bosch calling.

"We're in place at the W, two rooms next to each other. We're staying in and ordering room service."

"Good. I'm at the house."

"I still don't like this, you being there by yourself. I should be there, not here."

"I'm going to be fine. I'm about to call Hollywood and put them on standby."

"You know they're not going to like this."

"But they're not going to have a choice."

There was a pause while Bosch thought before replying.

"Why are you doing this, Renée? It's kind of crazy. It didn't sound like you had a solid plan. Why don't you just give it to them to run with?"

"Harry, you don't know what the department's like now. I couldn't trust them not to screw it up."

"Well, remember to check in with me too."

"I know, every hour on the hour. You'll hear from me."

Ballard disconnected and stood in the alley for a few moments considering a plan. Stovall's house was just two homes from the cross street at Oakwood. She realized she could walk out the front door, proceed on her walk posing as Stovall, and come back around to the house through the alley very quickly—and then be inside waiting and ready if the Midnight Men made a move.

She went back into the yard, leaving the door to the trash enclosure unlocked. She entered the house through the door off the smoking deck and left that unlocked as well.

In the walk-in closet she found a small collection of hats. She wanted something that would hide her face better than the Dodgers cap. She found a cloth hat with a wide, floppy brim probably used for gardening or other chores outside. Her hair was a bit darker and longer than Stovall's so she twisted it into a ponytail before putting on the hat. She was also thinner than Stovall. She looked through the hangers until she found a windbreaker that was bulky but acceptable for a walk on a winter evening. She took off her hoodie and put on the windbreaker and she was good to go.

When she turned to leave, Ballard saw a slide bolt on the inside of the closet door. She closed the door, slid the bolt, and then tested the security of the door. The door locked tight and she realized Stovall had made the closet a safe room. It was a smart move.

She looked around inside the closet and found a Wi-Fi router on a shelf as well as a backpack survival kit. Stovall had prepared well and it was good to know there was this space to retreat to if necessary.

Before leaving, Ballard walked through the house once more to decide what lights to turn on. She would not be able to turn anything on once she snuck back inside, since that might alert anyone watching that she was in the house. She left the master closet light on as well as the lights in the kitchen, and one in the living room.

At the front door, she pulled her mask up over her nose to further her disguise, put in earbuds, and then stepped out of the house. She locked the door behind her and put the key ring she had taken from Stovall into the pocket of the windbreaker.

Ballard walked down a path of garden stones to the sidewalk. She looked both ways as if deciding which way to go. Her eyes scanned the cars on the street but it was now too dark to see into any of them. The Midnight Men could be watching and waiting and she would not know. She pulled her phone and angled her face down to the screen as if picking music to listen to, but she continued to scan the street, her eyes just under the line of the hat's brim. She then put the phone away, glanced up at the street-light that was out, as if noticing it for the first time, then turned south toward Oakwood.

Ballard walked briskly to the intersection and turned right. As soon as she got to the alley she turned right again and picked up her pace. Going through the trash enclosure and into the yard took less than three minutes from her closing of the front door. She doubted there had been time for an intrusion but she pulled the gun out from below the back of the windbreaker and entered the house through the door off the deck. Holding the gun at the ready position, she moved through the rooms, careful to stay away from windows that might reveal she had already returned to the house.

She checked the garage last, moving completely around the Audi and looking in and under it. She found no sign of a break-in.

Back inside, she surveyed the house once more, looking for the best place to wait and be ready. She decided on the home office because it was the most centrally located room and it also offered two options for hiding should an intrusion occur. There was a closet with a sliding door that had a large unused space. And along the wall to the left of the doorway, there was a standing four-drawer file cabinet that provided a blind from the entrance.

Ballard took the desk chair and sat down. She put the gun down on the desk and pulled her phone. She called Lisa Moore, though she did not expect her to take the call—not after the message Ballard had left the Thursday before. The call went to voice mail and Ballard disconnected. She then wrote a text.

> Lisa, call me back if you want to
> have a part in taking down the MM.
> I'm sitting on the next victim's house.
> Are you working tonight?

She sent off the message, satisfied that she had at least given Moore the chance to be involved in her own case. She next called Neumayer's desk phone because she didn't have his cell. And the first flaw in her hasty plan emerged. The call went to voice mail and she heard Neumayer's voice: "This is Detective Neumayer. I am going to be out of town until January nineteenth and will respond to your call then. If this is an emergency, dial nine-one-one. If this is about an ongoing case, please call the direct line to the detective bureau and ask for Detective Moore or Detective Clarke. Thank you."

Ballard knew she should now call Robinson-Reynolds or at the very least Ronin Clarke, but she did neither. She decided to wait and see if she got a call back from Lisa Moore.

Her rash and incomplete planning was now beginning to weigh on Ballard. She thought about calling Bosch and taking him up on his offer to be there as backup. But she knew she couldn't leave Hannah Stovall unguarded, no matter how un-likely it was that the Midnight Men knew her current location. She tried to examine her motives in moving so quickly with a plan that was so incomplete. She knew it was all wound up in her growing disillusion with the job, the department, the people that surrounded her. But not with Bosch. Bosch was the constant. He was more steadfast than the whole department.

She tried to push the grim thoughts away by pulling up the video from the playroom at Dog House to check on Pinto. The image on the screen was grainy and small but she managed to see Pinto lying low under a bench, watching the action of the other dogs, possibly too timid to join in. She had quickly reached a point where she loved the little dog, and she wondered why someone had mistreated and abandoned him.

Somehow, in the crosscurrents of thought, she came to a decision. Maybe it was all in the moment, but she knew the moment had been a long time coming.

She clicked off the video feed and composed a short email to Lieutenant Robinson-Reynolds. She reread it twice before hitting the send button.

Immediately, she was flooded with a feeling of relief and certainty. She had made the right decision. There was no look-ing back.

Her thoughts were interrupted by a call back from Lisa Moore's cell number.

"What the fuck are you doing, Renée?"

"What am I doing? Let's see. I got a solid lead and I'm following it. I know that may sound like out-of-the-box thinking but—"

"You're suspended. You're on the bench."

"You think the Midnight Men are on the bench? You think you scared them away? Your little move last week to take the lieutenant down a notch just made them change things up, Lisa. They're still out there, and I know where they're going. They're coming to me."

"Where are you?"

"I'll tell you what, stand by. I'll call you when I need you."

"Renée, listen to me. Something's wrong. Your judgment is off. Wherever you are, you need backup and you need a plan. You're giving the department all they need to get rid of you with a stunt like this. Don't you see that?"

"It's too late. I got rid of them."

"What are you talking about?"

"I just quit. I sent the lieutenant my resignation."

"You can't do that, Renée. You're too good a cop."

"I already did."

"Then, what are you doing right now? Get out of there and call in backup. You're putting yourself in harm's way. You—"

"I've always been in harm's way. But I'm not a cop anymore. That means no rules. I'll call you when I need you. If I need you."

"I don't get it. What are you—"

Ballard disconnected. And immediately she felt the euphoria and assuredness of her decision start to slip away.

"Shit," she said.

She stood up and slid her phone into her back pocket. Picking up the gun, she held it down by her side. She walked to the door, having decided to take another sweep of the house so she would know the layout by heart should she need to maneuver in the dark.

She had just entered the hallway when the house started shaking. Not an earthquake, just a low vibration. A tremor. She realized that someone was opening the garage door.

43

Ballard quickly backed into the darkened office. She stood at the doorway at first and waited. The hallway offered a straight-shot view to the living room and the front door. Through an arched entry on the left was the kitchen and through that she could see the edge of the door to the garage. She fixed on that point, her gun still held down at her side.

Soon the tremor in the floor began again and she knew the garage door was closing. A few moments later, she saw the doorknob start to turn on the kitchen door. The door opened inward, at first blocking Ballard's view of who was coming in.

Then the door closed and a man in dark blue coveralls stood there as she had, listening to the house. Ballard ducked further back into the shadows of the home office but kept one eye on the man. She didn't breathe.

The man wore black synthetic gloves and a green ski mask that had been rolled up off his face because he did not expect anyone to be in the house. He would pull it down when Hannah Stovall came back from her walk. He had a fanny pack strapped around the coveralls, with the pouch in front. His eyebrows and sideburns revealed that he had red hair.

"Okay, I'm in," he said. "Any sign of her?"

Ballard froze. He was talking to someone. She then saw the

white earbud in his right ear. There was no cord. It was a Bluetooth connection to a phone held in a runner's armband on his upper right arm.

Ballard hadn't planned for that—that they would be in constant communication. Another flaw in a very flawed plan.

"Okay," the man said. "I'll take a look around. Let me know when you see her."

The man moved out of the sliver of view Ballard had of the kitchen. She heard the refrigerator open and then close. She then heard footsteps on the wood flooring and could tell he had moved into the living room. She also heard a sound she could not identify. It was a slapping sound that was spaced at various intervals. She heard his voice again but it was farther away this time.

"Bitch has almost no food in the fucking fridge."

He crossed in front of the hallway in the living room and she saw that he was tossing up and down one of the apples she had put in the refrigerator, making the slapping sound as he caught it. She had to think. If the redhead was in constant communication with his partner, she had to figure out a way to take him down without the partner realizing and possibly fleeing.

She wanted them both.

The footsteps grew louder and she knew he was heading to the hallway. She quickly and quietly moved to the blind side of the file cabinet and slid down the wall to a crouching position. She held the gun in a two-handed grip between her knees.

The steps paused and the overhead lights flicked on. Then the man spoke again.

"We've got a home office. Double monitors. Man, she doin' some bidness up in here, y'all...Might need to take one of these for my own setup."

The lights went out and the steps continued down the hallway.

Ballard heard the man report what he saw in the hall bathroom, the guest room, and then the master suite. Their MO had obviously changed, possibly because of the exposure in the media, or dictated by Stovall's stay-at-home schedule. Either way, the break-in came much earlier than in the three prior cases. She knew that this most likely meant they would not wait several hours in hiding, until Stovall went to sleep. Ballard believed the plan was now to move quickly, incapacitate and control Stovall, and then bring in the second man. The master suite was probably out as a hiding place, because that would be where Stovall went after her walk. That left the spare bedroom, the office, and the hall bathroom. Ballard believed the office was the best bet. The desk was set against one wall and the closet was directly opposite, meaning that if Stovall sat at her desk, her back would be to the closet door. The redhead would be able to surprise her from behind—if she went back to work after returning to the house.

Ballard waited, rehearsing in her mind the moves she would make when he returned to the office. One move if he saw her, and one move if he walked by without noticing her on his way to check out the closet.

"Hey, dude, she's got a safe room in her damn closet. The guy didn't tell us about that."

There was silence while Ballard considered what that second sentence meant.

"Okay, okay, I'm looking. You said there was no sign of her yet."

Silence.

"All right, then."

The words almost made Ballard flinch. They were closer. The redhead was coming back to the office.

"I'm thinking the office is going to be the spot."

As he said it, he entered the room, and the ceiling lights came back on. He passed by the file cabinet without noticing Ballard and moved directly to the closet. Ballard didn't hesitate. She sprang from her crouch and moved toward his back. He was opening the closet door as she reached up to his right ear and grabbed the earbud out. At the same time she brought the gun up with her left and held the muzzle against the base of his skull. Holding the earbud cupped tightly in her palm, she whispered, "You want to live, don't say a fucking word."

Ballard put the earbud in her pocket, grabbed the man by the back of the collar, and jerked him backward, holding the gun against him the whole time and continuing to whisper.

"Down, get on your knees."

He did so and now was holding his hands up shoulder height to show his compliance. Ballard pulled the phone out of the man's armband. The screen showed a call connection to someone only identified as Stewart. Ballard put the phone on speaker.

"...happened? Hey, you there?"

She hit the mute button, then held the phone to the man's face.

"Now, I'm going to take this off mute and you're going to tell him that everything's fine and that you just tripped over a box in the closet. You got that? You say anything else and it will be the last thing you ever say."

"What are you, a cop?"

Ballard thumbed back the hammer on the gun. Its distinctive click sent the message.

"Okay, okay. I'll tell him, I'll tell him."

"Go."

She took the phone off mute and held it to the man's mouth.

"Sorry, dude, I tripped. There's boxes and shit in here."

"You okay, Bri?"

"Yeah, just fucked up my knee a little bit. Everything's copacetic."

"You sure?"

Ballard hit mute.

"Tell him you're sure," she said. "And tell him to keep watching for the woman. Go."

She took it off mute.

"I'm sure. Just tell me when you see her."

"All right, man."

Ballard hit mute again and put the phone down on the desk.

"Okay, hold still."

With one hand holding the gun to his head, Ballard reached around to the fanny pack and felt for a buckle but came up empty.

"Okay, one hand, reach down and take off the pack."

The man reached with his right hand. Ballard heard a snap and then his hand came back up holding the pack by its strap.

"Just drop it on the floor."

The man complied. Ballard then used her free hand to frisk him and check the pockets of the coveralls. She found nothing.

"Okay, I want you to get facedown on the floor. Now."

Again he complied but under protest.

"Who the fuck are you?" he said as he went down.

"Lie flat and don't talk unless I ask you to. You understand?"

He said nothing. Ballard pushed the muzzle further into the back of his neck.

"Hey, do you understand?"

"Yeah, take it easy, I understand."

He lowered himself to the floor and she held the gun on his neck all the way down, then put one knee on his back.

She realized that her handcuffs were in her equipment kit in her car, where she had put them while off duty and heading out to see Garrett. Add one more flaw to her plan.

She reached over to the fanny pack the redhead had just dropped to the floor.

"Let's see what you've got in here," she said.

She put the pack down on his back and unzipped it. It contained a roll of duct tape, a folding knife, and a premade, duct-tape blindfold on a peel-off backing that had been intended for Hannah Stovall. There was a strip of condoms and a garage remote.

"Looks like you have a full rape kit here, huh, Bri?" she said. "Can I call you Bri like your partner did?"

The man on the floor didn't respond.

"Okay if I use some of your tape?" Ballard asked.

Again there was no answer.

"I'll take that as a yes," Ballard said.

After putting the gun down on the man's back, she pulled his hands together and wrapped the duct tape around his wrists, unspooling it from the roll as she went. She could feel him trying to keep his wrists parted.

"Stop fighting it," she commanded.

"I'm not fighting it," he yelled into the floor. "I can't get them together."

Ballard thumbed open the knife's blade and cut the tape. She then grabbed the gun and stood up. She put the tape and the knife on the desk and then reached down and roughly yanked the ski mask off the top of his head, bouncing his face on the floor and releasing a torrent of red hair.

"Goddammit! That cut my lip."

"That's the least of your problems."

Ballard reached down and picked up the garage opener. She recognized it as a programmable remote like the one she had been given by her apartment landlord. He had told her that once a year the HOA changed the code as a security measure and he would provide her with the new combination to install. She now understood how the Midnight Men got into each victim's home.

"Who gave you the garage code?" she asked.

She got no answer.

"That's okay. We'll find out."

She stepped back from him, moving to the side.

"Turn your head, show me your face."

He did. She saw a small amount of blood on his lips. He looked young, no more than twenty-five.

"What's your full name?"

"I'm not telling you my name. You want to arrest me, arrest me. I broke in, big deal. Book me, and we'll see what happens."

"Bad news, kid. I'm not a cop and I'm not here to book you."

"Bullshit. I can tell you're a cop."

Ballard bent down and held the revolver out so he could see it.

"Cops have handcuffs, and cops don't carry little revolvers like this. But when we're through with you and your partner, you're going to wish we were going to book you."

"Yeah, who's 'we'? I'm not seeing anybody else here."

"You'll find out soon enough."

She wanted to wrap his ankles with tape to prevent him from getting up but she also wanted to keep him talking. He wasn't giving her anything yet but she felt that the more he talked, the better the chance he might slip up and provide something useful or important.

"Tell me about the photos."

"What photos?"

"And videos. We know you and your pal documented the rapes. For what? For yourselves or somebody else?"

"I don't know what the fuck you're talking about. What rapes? I broke in to steal shit, that's it."

"And who was on the phone with you?"

"Getaway driver."

The man shifted on the floor so that his right cheek was down and he could look up at Ballard. She responded by pulling out her phone and leaning down to take a photo of him. He immediately turned his head so he was facedown again.

"This'll go out all over the Internet. Everyone in the world will know who you are and what you did."

"Fuck off."

"How did you pick them? The women."

"I want a lawyer."

"You don't seem to understand, Brian, that you are not in the hands of the police or, shall we say, the traditional justice system. You were half right. I was a cop, but I'm not anymore. I quit because the system doesn't work. It doesn't do what it's supposed to do to protect the innocent from monsters like you. You're now in the custody of a different justice system. You're going to tell us everything we want to know, and you're going to answer for what you've done."

"You know what, you're fucking crazy."

"What did you mean when you said 'the guy' didn't tell you about the safe room?"

"I don't know what you're talking about. I didn't say that."

"Who told you about Hannah Stovall?"

"Who's that?"

"Who gave you the garage code?"

"Nobody. I want a lawyer. Now."

"No lawyer can help you here. There are no laws here."

Her phone started to buzz. She pulled it and checked the screen. It was Harry Bosch. The time on the screen told her that she was ten minutes late with her hourly check in. She accepted the call and spoke first.

"I've got one of them," she said.

"What do you mean, you've got one of them?" Bosch asked.

"Like I said. As soon as we get the other, I'll call you for pickup."

Bosch paused as he came to realize what was going on.

"I'm questioning him now," Ballard said. "Trying to. If he doesn't want to talk, we can do it your way."

"I'm on my way."

"That's fine. We can do it that way, too."

"I know you're playing to him. Do you want me to call in the troops?"

"No, not yet. Everything's good."

"Well, I'm on my way. For real."

Ballard disconnected and put the phone down on the desk. She picked up the intruder's phone and found it passcode protected. But it had been set to allow previews of texts, and there was a partial message on the screen.

> talked to the guy; safe room added
> after he

The message was cut off there.

"You got a message here, Bri," she said.

"You need a warrant to look in my phone," Brian said.

Ballard fake-laughed.

"You are correct...if I were the police. Anyway, the message is from your partner. It says he checked with the guy, and the safe room in the closet was added after. After what? After Hannah kicked him to the curb? Told him to get the fuck out of her life?"

"Who the fuck are you people?" Brian said.

The tenor of his voice had changed. It had lost the tone of confidence and superiority. Ballard looked down at him.

"You're going to find out very soon," Ballard said. "And it will go a lot easier on you if you answer my questions. Who told you about Hannah Stovall?"

"Look, just take me to the police, okay?" he said. "Turn me in."

"I don't think that's—"

There was a sudden crashing sound from the front of the house.

Ballard startled, then moved back into the hallway, raising her gun. Looking down the hall, she saw the front door of the house standing wide open, the jamb splintered where the lock had been. But there was no sign of anyone in her view. It was in that moment that she realized the man on the floor had given his partner a code. *Copacetic*—she had thought it an odd word when he said it, but it had not clicked in her brain that it was a code.

"Back here!" Brian yelled. "Back here!"

Ballard glanced behind her into the office and saw that the redhead was moving his wrists up and down, counter to each other, and trying to stretch the tape she had bound him with.

"Don't fucking move!" she yelled.

He ignored her and kept churning his wrists like two pistons in an engine.

"Freeze!"

She raised her gun and pointed it at him. Face on the floor, he looked up at her and just smiled.

In her peripheral vision she saw movement to her left. She turned to see another man in blue coveralls and ski mask coming through the doorway from the kitchen into the hall. He closed on her without hesitation. She swung her aim to the left but he was on her too quickly, dropping his shoulder into her just as she fired the gun.

The report was muffled between their bodies as they crashed to the hallway floor. The masked man rolled off her, crossing his arms in front of his chest and groaning. Ballard saw a burn mark and entrance wound from the bullet she had fired into his chest.

"Stewart!"

The shout came from the office. Ballard felt the floor against her back shake as the red-haired man came running into the hallway. Ballard saw that he had grabbed the knife off the desk and held it in a hand still cuffed in duct tape. He saw his partner writhing on the floor and then turned his hateful stare at Ballard.

"You—"

Ballard fired one shot from the floor. It hit him under the jaw, its trajectory going up into the brain. He dropped like a puppet, dead before he even hit the floor.

44

The interrogation room was crowded. There was a lot of coffee breath and at least one of the men in front of Ballard was a smoker. It was one of the few times in the last year that she was only too happy to wear a face mask. She sat at a small steel table with her back to the wall. Next to her was Linda Boswell, her attorney from the Police Protective League. The three men in front of her sat with their backs to the door. It was as if Ballard had to somehow get past them to get out. And sitting shoulder to shoulder they took up the space from one side wall to the other. There was no getting around them. She had to go straight through.

Two of the men were from the Force Investigation Division. Captain Sanderson, head of the unit, was sitting front and center, and to his left was David Dupree. Dupree was thin, and Ballard pegged him as the smoker. She expected that if he were not wearing a mask, she would see a mouthful of yellow teeth.

The third man was Ronin Clarke, representing the Midnight Men task force since Neumayer was on vacation and Lisa Moore was on the outs with Lieutenant Robinson-Reynolds. The investigation had been designated a task force following the media frenzy that exploded after the story had been leaked to the *Times*.

The three detectives normally assigned to the CAPs squad had also been assigned to the task force.

There were three different digital recorders on the table ready to capture the interview. Ballard had been given a Lybarger admonishment by Sanderson. This court-approved warning compelled her to answer questions about the shooting on Citrus Avenue for administrative investigative purposes only. If a criminal prosecution should arise from Ballard's actions, then nothing she said in the interview could be used against her in a court of law. Ballard had thoroughly briefed her attorney on what had happened in Hannah Stovall's house and what had led to the double shooting.

Boswell was now going to try to head things off at the pass.

"Let me just start by saying Ms. Ballard is not going to answer any questions from Force Investigation," she said. "She—"

"She's taking the Fifth?" Sanderson asked. "She does that and she loses her job."

"That's what I was about to tell you if you didn't interrupt. Ms. Ballard—you notice I didn't say Detective Ballard—does not work for the LAPD and therefore FID has no standing in the matter on Citrus Avenue."

"What the hell are you talking about?" Sanderson said.

"Earlier today, before the incident on Citrus Avenue, Ms. Ballard sent her resignation in an email to her immediate supervisor," Boswell said. "If you check with Lieutenant Robinson-Reynolds, you will be able to confirm the email and the time it was sent. This means that Ballard was no longer a police officer at the time of the shooting of the two intruders to the house on Citrus. She was a private citizen and acted in defense of her life when two armed men broke into the home where she was lawfully permitted to be."

"This is bullshit," Sanderson said.

He looked at Dupree and nodded toward the door. Dupree got up and left the room, most likely to find Robinson-Reynolds, whom Ballard had seen in his office when she was brought to the Hollywood detective bureau for questioning.

"No, these are the facts, Captain," Boswell said. "Ms. Ballard can show you her side of the email if you wish. Meantime, she is more than willing to tell Detective Clarke what happened and where a follow-up investigation might be warranted."

"This is some kind of trick and we're not going to play games," Sanderson said. "She answers the questions or we go to the D.A. with it."

Boswell scoffed.

"You can do that, of course," she said. "But what will you go to the D.A. with? It is easily established through the home's owner that she gave Ballard permission to be inside her home. She voluntarily gave her the keys to both her home and car. The physical evidence at the scene clearly shows a break-in and that Ballard, fearing for her safety, fired on two intruders who will soon be officially identified as the serial rapists known as the Midnight Men. So, let's see, you are going to ask the elected district attorney to prosecute, for whatever reason, the woman who killed these two rapists after they broke into the house where she was alone? Well, all I can say is good luck with that, Captain."

Clarke's eyes betrayed that he was trying to repress a smile beneath his mask. The door to the room then opened and Dupree stepped back in. He closed the door but stayed standing. Sanderson looked at him and Dupree nodded. He had confirmed the resignation email to Robinson-Reynolds.

Sanderson stood up.

"This interview is now over," he said.

He grabbed his recorder, turned it off, and followed Dupree

out of the room. Clarke didn't move and looked like he was still working on keeping a straight face.

"That leaves you, Detective Clarke," Boswell said.

"I'd like to talk to Renée," he said. "But I need to—"

The door was flung open, cutting Clarke off. Lieutenant Robinson-Reynolds stepped in. He stared at Ballard while talking to Clarke.

"Was she advised?" he asked.

"She got the Lybarger but not Miranda, if that's what you mean," Clarke said. "But she's willing to talk and says there is a follow-up we—"

"No, we're not talking," Robinson-Reynolds said. "This is over. For now. Step out."

Clarke stood up, grabbed his recorder, and left the room.

Robinson-Reynolds continued to stare at Ballard.

"Turn that off," he said.

Ballard started to reach for the last recorder.

"No," Boswell said. "I don't think that's a—"

"Turn it off," Robinson-Reynold said. "And you can go. I have something to say to Ballard that doesn't leave this room."

Boswell turned to Ballard.

"You want me to stay, I'll stay," she said.

"That's okay, I'll listen," Ballard said.

"I'll be right outside."

"Thanks."

Boswell got up and left the room. Ballard turned off the recorder.

"Ballard," Robinson-Reynolds said. "I find it hard to believe that you set this up to kill those two assholes. But if I find out you did, I'm coming after you."

Ballard held his gaze for a long moment before replying.

"And you'd be wrong—just like you're wrong about me

leaking to the *Times*," she said. "And men like those two? They got off easy. I'd rather they rotted in prison the rest of their lives than get off the way they did."

"Well, we'll see about them," he said. "And I already know who the leak to the *Times* was."

"Who?"

Robinson-Reynolds didn't answer. He left the door open as he left.

"Nice working with you, too," Ballard said to the empty room.

She pocketed her recorder and stepped out herself. Boswell was waiting for her in the squad room. Ballard saw Lisa Moore and Ronin Clarke at the CAPs pod along with the others assigned to the task force. The whole team had been called in to handle the investigation of the two men Ballard had shot. If Robinson-Reynolds had unmasked Moore as the leak to the *Times*, he had apparently not done anything about it yet.

"He say anything I should know about?" Boswell asked.

"Nothing worth repeating," Ballard said. "Thanks for what you did in there. You kicked ass."

"I've been going head-to-head with Sanderson for four years. He's all bluster. The only thing intimidating about him is his breath, and thank god he had to wear a mask."

Ballard couldn't hold back her smile, even if it was hidden by her own mask.

"So he was the smoker," Ballard said. "I thought it was Dupree."

"Nope, Sanderson," Boswell said. "So, now, the bad news. I can no longer represent you since you are no longer an officer."

"Right. I understand."

"I can recommend a good lawyer on the outside should you need one."

"Thanks."

"I don't think you will, because I don't think there's any question about your actions. They were the definition of self-defense. And taking off my lawyer hat for a moment here, it was you who kicked ass today, Renée."

"Things didn't turn out the way I'd planned."

"Do you need a ride somewhere?"

"No, I think I have somebody waiting out there."

"Okay. Pleasure doing business with you."

They bumped fists and Boswell headed to the front exit. Ballard walked over to the Sex Assault pod. Lisa Moore did not look up, though Ballard knew she had seen her approach. Clarke now had his mask off. He used his thumb and forefinger to pantomime shooting a gun, blowing into the barrel, then holstering the weapon like an Old West shooter.

"You guys get IDs on those two yet?" Ballard asked.

"Working on it," Clarke said. "But L-T gave us orders. We can't talk to you now."

Ballard nodded.

"Yeah, I get it," she said.

She left the squad room for what she assumed would be the last time, heading toward the front exit, which took her by the lieutenant's office. Robinson-Reynolds was behind his desk, mask off, talking on his landline. She held his eyes as she walked by. She said nothing.

Bosch was waiting in front of the station, leaning against the side of his old Cherokee.

"All good?" he asked.

"For now," Ballard said. "But this isn't over."

45

On Wednesday morning Ballard and Bosch were at the international terminal at LAX, awaiting the arrival of AeroMexico flight 3598 from Cancún. Bosch was in a suit and was holding a piece of paper Ballard had printed with the name GILBERT DENNING on it. They were standing outside the baggage and U.S. Customs exit, where professional drivers waited for their clients. The flight had landed thirty-five minutes earlier but there had been no sign of Denning yet. Ballard had a photo of him on her phone that she had gotten from Hannah Stovall. But with the mask requirement, it was hard to match a half face to the photo.

The airport was nearly empty. What few travelers there were came through the automatic doors in waves—a clot of people pulling their suitcases or pushing luggage carts followed by minutes of zero traffic. The drivers and families waiting for loved ones continued staring at the six doors.

Ballard was beginning to wonder whether they had somehow missed Denning, if he had walked by them or had taken a shuttle to another terminal. But then a man wearing a Dodgers hat and sunglasses and carrying only a backpack slung over his shoulder stepped in front of Bosch and pointed at the sign he held.

"Hey, that's me, but I didn't arrange for a driver. My car's in the garage."

Ballard quickly stepped over and spoke.

"Mr. Denning? We need to speak to you about your former girlfriend."

"What?"

"Hannah Stovall. We need to talk to you about her. Would you come with us, please?"

"No, I'm not going anywhere until you tell me what's going on. Is Hannah okay?"

"We're here to help you, sir. Would you please—"

"What are you talking about? I don't need any help. Are you police? Show me your badge, show me some ID."

"We're not police. We're trying to keep this from getting to the police. I don't think you would want that, Mr. Denning."

"Keep what from getting to the police?"

"Your involvement in sending two men to Hannah's house to have her beaten and sexually assaulted."

"What? That's insane. You two stay away from me."

He stepped back so he could take an angle to Bosch's left. Bosch shifted to block.

"This is your one and only chance to settle this," he said. "You walk away and it's a police matter. Guaranteed."

Denning brushed past Bosch and headed toward the terminal's exit door. Bosch turned to watch him. Ballard started to take off after him, but Bosch grabbed her arm.

"Wait," he said.

They watched Denning go through the glass doors and step to the crosswalk that led to the parking garage. There were several people waiting for the light to change so they could cross.

"He's going to look back," Bosch said.

Sure enough, Denning looked back to see if they were still

there. He quickly turned forward again and the traffic stopped as the crossing sign started flashing. People started moving toward the parking garage. Denning entered the crosswalk, took three steps, and then turned around. He walked with purpose through the doors, back into the terminal, and right up to Ballard and Bosch.

"What do you want?" he asked.

"For you to come with us," Ballard said. "So we can talk."

"I don't have money. And the health people at the gate said I'm supposed to quarantine for ten days now."

"You can quarantine for as long as you want after we talk. If not, I'm sure they'll find a single cell for you at the county jail."

The blood was draining from Denning's face. He relented.

"Okay, okay, let's go."

Now they walked out of the terminal together.

In the garage Denning was ushered into the back seat of Ballard's Defender. Ten minutes later, they cleared the airport and were moving down Century Boulevard.

"Where are we going?" Denning demanded. "My car's back there."

"Not far," Ballard said. "We'll take you back."

A few blocks later, Ballard made a left into the Marriott Hotel parking lot.

"I don't know about this anymore," Denning said. "Take me back. I want to talk to a lawyer."

Ballard pulled into a parking space in the lot in front of the hotel.

"You want to go back now, you can walk," she said. "But everything changes if you walk. Your job, your home, your life."

She looked at him in the rearview mirror.

"Either way, it's time to get out," she said.

Denning opened the door, got out, and slung his backpack over his shoulder.

Bosch and Ballard looked at him from the car, as if awaiting his decision. Denning threw his arms out wide.

"I'm still here," Denning said. "Can we just go to wherever we're going?"

Ballard and Bosch got out and started walking toward the entrance to the hotel. Denning followed them.

They had booked a room on the sixth floor. They didn't know how long it would take for Denning to spill, and Bosch liked that there would only be one way out, which he could easily block. It was called an executive suite, with a wall partitioning the bedroom area from a small sitting area consisting of a couch, a padded chair, and a desk.

"Sit on the couch," Ballard said.

Denning did as he was told. Ballard took the chair, and Bosch pulled the desk seat out and turned it so he would be facing Denning but also blocking his way to the door.

"I can give you six thousand—that's all I have saved," Denning said.

"And what would you want from us in return?" Ballard asked.

"I don't know," Denning said. "Why am I here? You said it would be a police matter if we didn't talk. I don't know what this is about but I don't want to involve the police."

Ballard waited to see if he would further incriminate himself. But he stopped talking.

"We don't want money," Ballard said. "We want information."

"What information?"

"Do you know what happened at Hannah Stovall's house two nights ago?"

"Yeah, I saw it online in Mexico. The two guys that broke in, she shot 'em."

Ballard nodded as if confirming the fact. It was easy to understand how Denning had arrived at the wrong conclusion. In the news that came out after the Monday-night incident, the LAPD did not name the woman who had killed the Midnight Men, citing a policy of not identifying victims or intended victims of sexual assault. It was clear that had Ballard not prevailed in those moments in the hallway, she would have become the latest victim of the Midnight Men. The department had withheld her identity to avoid the entanglements and questions that would arise should her name and former affiliation be known.

Ballard was not interested in disabusing Denning of his belief. She wanted him thinking that any connection to him might have died with the Midnight Men.

"We know you gave them the layout of the house and the combination to plug into a garage opener," Ballard said.

"You can't prove that," Denning said.

"We don't have to," Ballard said. "We aren't the police. But we know that's what happened and we're willing to keep what we know to ourselves in exchange for the information we need."

"What information?" Denning said. "And if you're not the cops, why do you want this?"

"We want to know how you contacted the Midnight Men," Ballard said. "Because there are others like you out there and we want to contact them."

"Look, that's not what they even called themselves," Denning said. "The media did that. The whole thing blew up in the news last week and I wanted to stop them but it was too late. They went silent. But that's one thing I can prove. I tried to stop it. And if there are others, I don't know them. Can I go now?"

He stood up.

"No," Bosch said. "Sit back down."

Denning stayed standing and looked at Bosch, likely taking

the measure of a man who was twice his age. Still, something about Bosch's piercing stare chilled him and he sat down.

"You need to back up," Ballard said. "Before you tried to stop them, how did you contact them?"

Denning shook his head as though he wished he could redo the past.

"They were just two guys on the Internet," he said. "We started talking and one thing led to another. Hannah, she really fucked me over…and I…never mind. Fuck it."

"These two guys, where on the Internet did you meet them?" Ballard asked.

"I don't know. I was floating around…there's a bunch of sites. Forums. You're anonymous, you know? So you can say what you feel. Just put it out there, and some people respond and tell you things. Tell you about other places to go. Give you passwords. It just sort of happens. There's a lot if you're looking for it. You know, a place where everybody's been there like you. Gotten fucked over by a woman. You sort of go down the rabbit hole."

"This rabbit hole…are you talking about Dark Web stuff?"

"Yes, definitely. Everybody, everything anonymous. These guys, the so-called Midnight Men, they had a site and I got this password. And then…that was it."

"How did you access the Dark Web?"

"Easy. Got a VPN first, then went through Tor."

Ballard knew Bosch was probably at sea when it came to the Dark Web, but through cases and FBI bulletins, she had rudimentary knowledge of how virtual private networks and Dark Web browsers like Tor worked.

"So, how did you specifically find the Midnight Men?"

"They posted on a forum that said, you know, they were in the L.A. area and were, uh, were willing to…do things…to even the score, I guess you'd call it."

Denning looked off to the side, too humiliated by his actions to hold Ballard's eyes.

"Look at me," Ballard said. "Is that what they called it? 'Evening the score'?"

Denning turned his face back toward Ballard but kept his eyes down.

"No, they…I think the heading was 'Teach a Bitch a Lesson,'" he said. "Yeah, and I…made a post about my situation and then they gave me a site and password to check out and things sort of went from there."

"What was the site called?"

"It didn't have a name. A lot of stuff doesn't have names. It was a number."

"Do you have a laptop in that bag?"

"Um, yeah."

"I want you to show us. Take us to that site."

"Uh, no, we're not going to do that. It's really bad stuff and I—"

He stopped when Bosch stood up and came toward the couch. Ballard could see that something about Bosch's demeanor unnerved Denning. Harry's hands were balled into fists, the scars on his knuckles white. Denning leaned back into the couch while Bosch roughly grabbed his backpack and started unzipping compartments until he found the laptop. He stepped over to the desk, put the computer down, and brought the desk chair back over.

"Show us the fucking site," Bosch said.

"All right," Denning said. "Take it easy."

He moved to the desk and sat down. He opened the laptop. Ballard got up and stood behind him so she could see the screen. She watched while Denning signed into the hotel's Internet.

"Some places have blocks on the Dark Web," he said. "They don't let you use Tor."

"We'll see," Ballard said. "Keep going."

There were no blocks, and Denning was able to go into his private network and use the Tor browser to access the site put together by the Midnight Men. The number he typed in was 2-0-8-1-1-2 and Ballard committed it to memory. He then added a numeric password which Ballard memorized as well.

"What's the significance of the numbers?" she asked.

"Numbers assigned to letters," Denning said. "A-1, B-2, and so on. Translates to T-H-A-L—'Teach Her a Lesson.' But I didn't find that out till later."

He said it in a tone that suggested he would never have ventured onto the site if he'd known that's what the numbers meant. He might have been able to convince himself of that but Ballard doubted anybody else would believe it.

"And I think the password is—"

"'Bitch.' Yeah, I figured that one out."

The site was a horror show. It contained dozens of photos and videos of women being raped and humiliated. The men committing the atrocities were never seen, though it was apparent it was the Midnight Men, because the actions matched the reports of the victims in the cases known to Ballard. But there were more than three victims on the site. Cases had apparently not been connected or victims had not reported them, probably out of fear of their attackers or the system they would be sucked into.

Each of the digital files was labeled with a name. When Ballard spotted a file named Cindy1, she told Denning to open it. She immediately recognized Cindy Carpenter, though blindfolded with tape, in a horrific still shot from her assault.

"All right, enough," she said.

When Denning was slow to kill the screen, Bosch reached over and slammed the computer shut, Denning yanking his fingers away at the last moment.

"Jesus Christ!" he shrieked.

"Get back on the couch," Bosch ordered.

Denning complied, holding his hands up like he wanted no trouble.

Ballard had to compose herself for a moment. She wanted to get away from this room and this man, but she managed to get her last questions out.

"What did they want?" she asked.

"What do you mean?" Denning asked.

"Did they want money to do this? Did you pay them?"

"No, they didn't want anything. They liked doing it, I guess. You know, they hated all women. There are people like that."

He said it in a way designed to convey that he was different from them. He hated a woman to the point that he would sic two rapists on her. But he didn't hate all women, like they did.

It made Ballard feel all the more repulsed. She needed to go. She looked at Bosch and nodded. They now knew all they needed to know.

"Let's go," Bosch said.

He and Ballard stood up. Denning looked up at them from the couch.

"That's it?" he asked.

"That's it," Ballard said.

Bosch picked the laptop up off the desk and tossed it, more at Denning than to him.

"Easy," Denning protested.

He carefully slid it back into the cushioned compartment of his backpack and stood up.

"We're going to get my car now, right?"

"You can walk," Ballard said. "I don't want to be anywhere near you."

"Wait, you—"

Bosch stepped into a punch that hit Denning in the gut with a force that belied his years. Denning dropped the backpack to the floor with a hard thud and fell back on the couch, gasping for air.

Ballard headed for the door while Bosch delayed a moment to see if Denning would get up. But it became clear he would not be getting up for a while.

Bosch followed Ballard out of the room into the hallway. He caught up halfway to the elevators.

"That last part was unscripted," she said.

"Yeah," Bosch said. "Sorry about that."

"Don't be," she said. "I'm not sorry about that at all."

46

Bosch drove because Ballard asked him to. As dark as her thoughts were, she didn't want any distractions from them. Bosch handed back her mini-recorder. He'd had it in the breast pocket of his suit jacket. Ballard tested the sound of the recording and it was good. They had Denning on tape. She then started a new recording and repeated the site and password numbers Denning had provided. She then leaned against the passenger door and thought about what she had seen on his computer. After a while, she took out her phone. She had dropped Pinto off at the Dog House that morning. She pulled up the kennel camera and saw him in the familiar spot under the bench. Alert and watching the others. She put the phone away and was better braced for her dark thoughts.

"So...," Bosch finally said. "What are you thinking?"

"That we have front-row seats on a pretty fucked-up world," she said.

"The abyss. But you can't let it get you down, partner. Being in the front row means you get to try to do something about it."

"Even without a badge?"

"Even without a badge."

They were on the 405 freeway going north and coming up on the 10 interchange. Bosch took his left hand off the wheel and rotated his wrist.

"What?" Ballard asked.

"Came in at a bad angle on that punch," he said.

"Well," Ballard said. "I hope you Houdinied him."

She had read somewhere that Houdini had died from a punch to the gut.

Bosch put his hand back on the wheel.

"What are we going to do with this?" he asked.

"I'm still thinking the FBI is the best bet," Ballard said. "They have the skills to deal with all the encryption and masking. Much better than the LAPD."

"I didn't really get any of that Dark Web stuff," Bosch said. "Tell you the truth, I don't even know how it works."

Ballard smiled and looked over at him.

"You don't have to know," she said. "You've got me for that now."

Bosch nodded.

"Well, how about the shorthand, then?" he asked.

"In the Dark Web, nothing is indexed," Ballard began. "There's no Google or anything like that. You sort of have to know your destination, and then one thing can lead to another. That's what happened with Denning. He found like-minded and totally warped people, and that brought him eventually to the Midnight Men."

"Okay."

"The problem is that the Dark Web offers anonymity. He said he has a VPN. That's a virtual private network that masks his computer ID when he's prowling around on websites. Then he also uses Tor as a browser. It's like the dot-com of the Dark Web and it encrypts his moves and bounces them all over the world to further defy tracing them. So he's anonymous in the Dark Web, can't be traced. Supposedly."

"Supposedly?"

"The FBI is plugged in with the NSA and the whole federal alphabet soup of agencies. They're cutting-edge when it comes to this. They're doing things the public has no idea about. So I say we go to them, I give them the site where all that horrible stuff is and the password that'll get them in. That's all they need. They take it from there. They'll be able to identify the three known victims on there. That last one we saw was my case, Cindy Carpenter. And I got the mojo on her ex as soon as I talked to him. He's gotta go down for this. They'll squeeze Denning and make him a witness, but he won't walk. I'll make sure of that. They let him walk, and I know the name of the *Times* reporter that would love that story."

Bosch nodded.

"All of them have to go down," he said.

"They will," Ballard said. "The bureau will go silent but then the hammer will come down on all of them at once. A great reckoning of assholes. And if it doesn't happen that way, then we make a call, and that'll get some action going."

Bosch nodded again.

"When should we go to the bureau?" he asked.

"How about right now?" Ballard said.

Bosch put on the blinker and started negotiating his way to the transition lanes to the eastbound 10. They were headed downtown.

EPILOGUE

Ballard was walking up Finley with Pinto when she saw the black SUV double-parked in front of her building. She had been on a pre-drive walk with the dog so he could take care of business before she headed out to surf Trancas Point. It would take over an hour to get out there. The surf report had a west swell and winds out of the north, perfect conditions for Trancas. She hadn't been to the Point since before the pandemic and was looking forward to being on the ocean up there and riding a few waves. She would go alone, except for the dog. Garrett Single was on duty.

As she got closer she could hear the SUV idling and could tell by the license plate that it was a city car, not a vehicle from a limo service waiting on an airport run. A large man in a suit waited by the passenger-side door for the return of his passenger. She pulled out her earbuds and killed the music on her phone. Marvin Gaye was singing "What's Going On."

When she got to the security gate, she saw a man with gray hair and in a full police uniform, four stars on the collar. It was the chief of police. He heard the dog's collar jingle and turned to see Ballard approach.

"Detective Ballard?" he asked.

"Well, I'm Ballard," she said. "It's not 'Detective' anymore."

"That's what I wanted to talk to you about. Have we met previously?"

"No, not in person. But I know who you are, Chief."

"Is there a place we can talk privately?"

"I don't think anyone can hear us here."

The point was clear. She wasn't inviting him in.

"Then here is good," he said.

"What can I do for you?" Ballard said.

"Well, I've been apprised of your work on some of the cases that have made recent headlines. Your uncredited work, I should say. Both before and after you turned in your badge."

"And?"

He reached into his pocket and pulled out a badge. Ballard recognized the number. It was the one she had worn until two weeks earlier.

"I want you to take it back," he said.

"You want me to come back?" she asked.

"I do. The department needs to change. To do that, it has to change from within. How can we accomplish that if the good people who can make change choose to leave?"

"I don't think the department wants someone like me. And I don't think the department wants to change."

"It doesn't matter what the department wants, Detective Ballard. If an organization doesn't change, it dies. And that's why I want you back. I need you to help bring the change."

"What would my job be?"

"Whatever you want it to be."

Ballard nodded. She thought about Bosch and how he had told her that change had to come from within. A million people protesting in the street wasn't enough. And she thought about the partnership she and Bosch had planned.

"Can I think about it, Chief?" she said.

"Sure, think about it," he said. "Just don't take too long. We've got a lot of work to do."

He held up the badge.

"I'll keep this until I hear from you," he said.

"Yes, sir," Ballard said.

The chief headed back to the car, and the driver held the door for him. The black SUV took off down Finley, and Ballard watched it go.

Then she went surfing.

ACKNOWLEDGMENTS

Many thanks to Team Ballard and Bosch, an all-star lineup of editors, readers, advisers, and investigators who helped the author with this novel in immeasurable ways. They include Asya Muchnick, Bill Massey, Emad Akhtar, Pamela Marshall, Betsy Uhrig, Jane Davis, Heather Rizzo, Dennis Wojciechowski, Henrik Bastin, John Houghton, Terrill Lee Lankford, and Linda Connelly. The detectives roundtable includes Mitzi Roberts, the inspiration for Ballard, as well as Rick Jackson, David Lambkin, and Tim Marcia, inspirations all. Many thanks to all who lent a hand to the author.

ABOUT THE AUTHOR

MICHAEL CONNELLY is the author of thirty-five previous novels, including the *New York Times* bestsellers *The Law of Innocence, Fair Warning, The Night Fire,* and *Dark Sacred Night.* His books, which include the Harry Bosch series, the Lincoln Lawyer series, and the Renée Ballard series, have sold more than eighty million copies worldwide. Connelly is a former newspaper reporter who has won numerous awards for his journalism and his novels. He is the executive producer of *Bosch,* starring Titus Welliver, and the creator and host of the podcasts *Murder Book* and *The Wonderland Murders and the Secret History of Hollywood.* He spends his time in California and Florida.